IMPRESSIONIST

IMPRESSIONIST

A Novel of
Mary Cassatt

JOAN KING

BEAUFORT BOOKS, INC.

New York / Toronto

Copyright © 1983 by Joan King

Library of Congress Cataloging in Publication Data

*King, Joan.
Impressionist: a novel of Mary Cassatt.*

*1. Cassatt, Mary, 1844-1926—Fiction. I. Title.
PS3561.I4785I4   1983   813'.54   82-24371
ISBN 0-8253-0125-4*

*Published in the United States by Beaufort Books, Inc.,
New York. Published simultaneously in Canada by
General Publishing Co. Limited*

*Designer: Ellen LoGiudice
Printed in the U.S.A.   First Edition*

IMPRESSIONIST

Introduction

MARY CASSATT (1844–1926) firmly made up her mind to become an artist even though in 1860 a Pennsylvania woman with such an idea could expect to be crushed by disillusionment.

Today, however, her delicate and powerful paintings remain as convincing evidence that she was not only a successful artist, but a perceptive and tender human being.

Historians have abundantly documented the major events of her life and the colorful world she chose to live in, but we must go beyond history, into imagination, to see that world through the keen eyes of this exceptionally determined woman as she painted her way to fame with the French Impressionists.

This is a story of fantasy as well as fact, born of a need to know her better.

1

NEAR PHILADELPHIA June 1861: In the afternoon Mary and her father started their ride off with a brisk canter over the meadow, an easy walk up the rise and onto the riding path by the woods. It was the usual routine, but today she could hardly contain her excitement. To have finally decided the future was intoxicating. For months she had thought about it. Her mind wouldn't rest until she was absolutely sure it was the right thing for her to do, but now she was. All those weeks of feeling in a fog, grasping her way to the decision, were behind her. There would be no more waking up in the night and going to the window to look at the stars. No more brooding at all. She didn't have any more time to waste. She had already squandered the first seventeen years of her life. But now— that would all change. It was delectable to have it decided, she thought, slowing the horse as she approached a hill.

The sky had been bright blue with only a few spotty clouds when Mary had changed into her riding clothes, but it had since grown dark and overcast. The breeze became a wind and all at once a jagged line of lightning flashed on the horizon. The horses whinnied and Robert Cassatt shouted to his daughter to hurry back to the stables.

As they turned the steeds around, Mary wanted to stop her senses for an instant, to hold in memory this strange light, the earthy smell of the first raindrops, the regal way her father sat on his mare, his head sharp against the heaviness of the sky and set off by the odd green of the hills and meadow. She wished she could keep that picture forever, somewhere in her mind. She urged her horse to hurry, snapping the reins. "Run," she said. "No restraints, run free with all your power." The rushing hoofbeats, the cool wind in the swishing trees filled her with the momentum of blossoming joy. She raced ahead of her father, gaining the primitive freedom of speed, holding onto it, even as the rain wet her cheeks.

When she stopped her horse in front of the stable, she paused astride it, too exhilarated by the ride to want to end it. "How very lovely," she murmured before jumping down and leading the sweating horse to his stall.

A moment later when her father reined up, he stood in the stirrups and looked at her sternly. "Was all of Philadelphia threatened by the plague?"

"It was wonderful. I couldn't help it."

"You were reckless. You know how to ride properly. Why do you press your luck?"

"I'm sorry, Father."

"Don't let it happen again, *ever*, or I will forbid you to ride at all."

She looked at his face then, wanting her expression to show a fitting remorse so that the creases around his eyes would soften and disappear. But it was hard to feel remorseful when she was still tingling with the excitement of the ride. She couldn't keep the smile from her face. How could she look penitent when her whole being wanted to laugh? Her father turned away with a muffled grunt, giving all his attention to removing the saddle from his horse.

Silently they helped the groom care for the horses and when at last they were ready to walk back to the house, her father looked at the rain as though it amused him. "We'll have to make a dash for it," he said. Mary nodded and, without pausing, put her head down and lunged forward into the rain, running blindly toward the house, arriving breathless a few seconds after her father. They stood on the porch and shook away the water before going in.

Lydia and the maid brought warm towels to the vestibule. Lydia frowned at her father. "You're soaked. Let's dry you off before you catch cold."

"Liddy, please don't fuss so. It's nothing. I've been caught in the rain before and survived." He took the towel from her and wiped his face. "Go back to the parlor and tell your mother I'll join you all there in ten minutes."

The pale and slender Lydia retreated almost at once, but paused a moment and smiled at Mary. "Would you like me to help brush the snarls out of your hair?"

Mary turned and looked at Lydia in her white dress that could not conceal the fullness of her breasts or the tiny nipped-in waist. How wonderfully graceful she looked framed by the archway that led back to the parlor. Her copper-colored hair was brushed smooth, and even in the gray light from the window she looked exquisite. For the thousandth time Mary wished she could be like that. And she wished Lydia could always be the way she was today.

"No thank you, Liddy," she said and hurried up the stairs, eager now to change out of her damp clothes and come down and tell them all what she had planned. Lydia would understand, and surely her mother would have no serious objections. Gardner was still too young to have an opinion, and Aleck was such a dear brother—yes, she was very glad his school term was over and he'd be there when she announced it. And she couldn't put it off one day longer. Tomorrow there would be guests for dinner so this was the time.

She waited until Cook served the rum custard and her father had savored a few bites before she said anything. Then she took a deep breath. "Father," she said loud enough to get everyone's attention.

Her father winced. "Lower your voice, Mary. We are not out in the fields in a windstorm."

Gard laughed and Aleck smiled. "I'm sorry, Father," Mary said, "but I have something important to say."

"Say it then—in a soft, well-modulated voice. We're listening."

"All right," she said quietly. "I have thought it over and decided I would very much like to study painting and drawing."

Her father looked up blankly for a few seconds, then he smiled at her. "You always enjoyed the museums and galleries when you were a little girl, especially when we lived abroad."

"Yes, that's because I could always understand pictures even when I couldn't tell what people were saying."

"I'm glad you're so enthusiastic about art. The Bennett School has excellent instructors. In the short time Lydia was there, she did quite a few watercolors, as I recall, didn't you, Lydia?"

"Not many. Most of those I brought home were keepsakes from the other girls. They were very kind to me."

"Such lovely girls," her mother said.

"Bennett's is undoubtedly the finest school for hundreds of miles in every direction," her father said.

Her mother beamed, and Lydia smiled wistfully. Aleck went on eating his custard, but Mary couldn't remain quiet. "I know what a good school Bennett's is, but I don't want to go there. I want to study art at the Pennsylvania Academy of Art. I want to learn how to draw and paint well enough to—"

"To *what?*" Aleck asked, looking at her now with interest.

"Why, to hang my pictures on gallery walls."

Aleck laughed, and her father smiled and cleared his throat. Lydia bit her lip and her mother looked down. Gard was the only one smiling with total approval.

"I can learn to be an artist. I'm sure I'd do well. I'll work very hard."

Aleck winked at Mary. His voice was sympathetic. "And the Pennsylvania Academy is right here in Philadelphia," he said. "That's good luck."

Her father put down his spoon and patted his lips quickly with his napkin. "The academy is adequate to train a person in drawing, and that is all. They teach nothing but art; no music classes or literature or French. It's not for you, Mary. I want my daughters well educated in all the arts, like your mother. And at Bennett's you'll make valuable social contacts. You'll be with the right kind of people. I know what is best for my girls."

"Of course, Father. But I have never neglected literature or languages. My German may be a bit creaky, but my French is nearly as good as yours already, and to tell the truth, I don't care about contacts. We have enough friends already. I don't care about anything they have at Bennett's. I only want to learn how to draw and paint excellent pictures."

She was smiling as best she could, but her father's face looked pinched and there was irritation in his voice. "My dear girl, I will decide what is best for you. I've already given my full consideration to your education and have enrolled you in the institution I determined to be the best. So we'll hear no more discussion."

Mary's cheeks burned. Anger took hold of her as she rose from her chair. "I have given it my full consideration, too, and I still mean to study art."

"Sit down, Mary," her father said calmly, "and finish your dessert. I don't like to see a young lady in this house losing control like a common street urchin."

Mary sat down, but she did not eat her dessert. She searched the faces of her family. Her mother's eyes looked almost sympathetic. Lydia's head was bent as though she was too embarrassed to meet Mary's gaze. It probably seemed unforgivable to Lydia that she wouldn't be delighted to be at Bennett's. Lydia had wanted so badly to go on with her studies there. Well, Lydia was different. Their needs and wants would always be different. Mary's glance moved on to Aleck, who showed his usual good humor. His look seemed to say none of this really matters, let's not be unpleasant. Even thirteen-year-old Gard lowered his blond head and sighed. Mary felt she couldn't sit there for one moment more with all that silence, feeling her father's angry resistance and her mother's helpless sympathy.

But she did. She sat until she was excused and then she went quietly to her room.

Once inside, she threw herself down on the bed. How could she have thought it would be easy? Her father was determined. But not any more than she was, not really. Still, what could she do? She could never bear Bennett's when her heart would be at the academy. What was wrong with the academy? Lots of fine people went there. Society! What did she care of society? It was just full of men who wanted to marry to improve their positions and women who thought of nothing but making the best match. She didn't want to be like that. She wanted to learn to paint.

She paced, glared out the window, brushed her hair, and tried not to keep hearing her father's voice saying he'll hear no more discussion. It made her angry all over again. How did Rosa Bonheur ever do it? She couldn't have learned to paint giant canvases full of horses and riders and trees and sky just as though you were there—couldn't have—at Bennett's. Her father must have been an artist like Elizabeth Vigee-Lebrun's. He couldn't have been like Robert Cassatt. Oh, why must men always be right, even when they're wrong? She wanted to fall down on the bed again, but she didn't. She was through with stupid gestures.

She went to the closet where she kept some of her drawings hidden away in a hatbox. She brought them out, spread them on the bed, and looked quickly at each one. A tree, a barn, her own hands, her feet, a church, quite lopsided, too, a mountain—imagined, not even real. She sighed and put them all back in the hat box. They were not very good. She just knew she had to try to be an artist. It was in her like a fever.

She put a sheet of paper on her desk, picked up her pen, and began to draw the vase of flowers on her dresser. Soon there was a soft knock on the door. She felt a sudden prickling of her skin. She didn't want to be lectured to, but forced herself to say, "Come in." She heard the door open and shut before she looked around to see who was there.

"Lydia," Mary sighed and tried to smile. "Well, it was

13

awful, wasn't it? Here, sit down. Oh, not in front of the flowers."

Lydia smiled and sat on the bed. "I was afraid I'd find you in tears."

Mary shook her head. "If I were going to do that, it would be a waste not to do it in the parlor and have Father see how miserable he was making me."

"You would do no such thing. You have more stubborn pride than any of us."

"I am not a bit stubborn."

"You are. What I meant was if you're really serious about studying art, I know you'll find a way to change his mind, and not with tears."

"I am serious. But how could I change Father's mind?"

"Just by being you."

"Oh, that's no help. I said what I thought and it only made him angry and determined."

"Mother and I will do anything we can."

"Thank you." Mary did appreciate Lydia's words. Lydia always cared; but what could anyone do?

Lydia plucked at the sleeve of her dress. "Do you remember when you learned to ride?"

Mary sighed again and nodded.

"I mean when you first asked to learn to ride? You were only about seven. And Father said no, you couldn't, because you might get hurt."

Mary had forgotten. She remembered learning to ride, but not that he had ever refused to let her. "I thought he wanted me to learn."

"He did, finally, but not until you followed him around like a shadow for a full week demanding to know why Aleck could learn and you couldn't. And you wouldn't accept any answer he gave until he agreed to let you try. I remember the day he came in and announced to us all that he had decided it would be a good idea if you learned to ride."

"Really? I don't remember all that."

"You should."

Lydia smoothed Mary's unruly auburn hair away from her forehead and smiled. "I want one of your pictures to hang on my wall. I like trees reflected in still water. They're so nice."

Mary smiled up at Lydia. She couldn't speak, but she nodded a silent promise.

ON SUNDAY MORNING over tea in the garden, Mary coaxed her father to admit that in the best Philadelphia society a fine portrait was a source of great pride. And the following day after lunch he lit up his pipe and Mary asked if he had ever been deeply affected by a painting.

"I suppose so," he said.

"When? What sort of painting?"

He smiled and admitted that he often appreciated a harmonious scene or a picture of people doing things. He even remembered a battle scene by Delacroix.

Mary had planned to let a comfortable span of time pass with only an occasional nudge until he was ready for serious talk, but his mood that afternoon was conciliatory. She couldn't resist reminding him of the pictures by Rosa Bonheur he had taken her to see in Paris when she was ten. Robert inhaled the smoke from his pipe and shook his head. "That was a long time ago. We saw so many galleries and so many pictures, I can't remember one from the other."

"But you couldn't forget *The Horse Fair*. It was almost alive. You said so yourself. And I remember it was so big I felt like I could walk right in there and mount one of those horses."

He laughed. "I'm sure it was quite remarkable. But my dear, the Cassatt women do *not* do that sort of thing."

"What don't they do, Father?"

"They don't compete in a trade. It's all right to dabble with watercolors for your own amusement. But artists are paid for their work, the same as carpenters and silversmiths."

"Really, Father, how can a banker pretend to disdain money? It is merely to be used well. You've said so yourself, and besides, painting isn't a trade, it's a calling."

"A calling from the devil. I'm sure a girl like you could have no idea how some of those artists live."

"What do you mean?"

Her father shook his head and didn't answer. "Do you mean because they're poor? Well, if more people would buy paintings they wouldn't be. Besides, painting them is important, not selling them."

"Mary, for the love of God, when are you going to realize you will be required to take your place in society and you must be prepared to be a great lady one day?"

"A great lady artist, I hope."

"That is quite enough."

"But Father, you let Aleck study anything he wanted. He said he wanted to be an engineer and it was all settled. We all went to Germany so he could go to the best school. He didn't have to beg or run away from home."

"Enough, I said. I have tried to be patient because I am a just man. And to please your mother I promised to listen and be kind. But you try me sorely, young lady."

Mary was afraid she had gone too far. She had practically accused him of favoring Aleck and she hadn't meant to do that.

"I'm sorry," she said, tears welling quickly without warning. She managed to hold them back only as long as it took to walk out the front door. Still fighting for control, she wandered toward the stables, feeling the hopelessness of being a girl.

But her tears lasted only a few seconds. The fresh air and freedom of the outdoors revived her. One thing was certain; she didn't like angry words with her father. She should have listened to her intellect instead of her emotional impulses. Well, she would have to make it right with him, somehow.

Approaching the stables she felt the heat of the sun, but as she stepped inside the air was cooler and the straw smelled sweet. A soft, comforting noise came from the horses. She patted Dory's neck, looking at the outlines of the animal's head. Hadn't she read once that every form could be reduced to lines and shadings? If she could only draw the mare—if she could get the lines of her neck close to right—maybe her father would look at it and not be too angry with her anymore; maybe it would help.

She ran back to the house, slipped in the servant's entrance, and went up the back stairs to her room. In a few minutes she came back down with a stack of paper and two sticks of charcoal.

She sat on the rail across from Dory's stall and started drawing with a sweeping line that should have resembled Dory's upper neck. "Oh, dear no." Mary started again, touching the paper lightly. This time it was better, but the horse moved, and the pose was gone. Frustrated and fighting that hopeless feeling, she shouted for the groom. "Get over here, Bucky, and hold that mare's head for me."

The boy tumbled toward her, looking astonished. He reached for the horse, but she moved again.

"Get on the other side of her. Go ahead. It's all right if you pat her. Keep her head just like that."

Mary started again, working faster, her hair and neck damp with the heat. She could not think of anything but that horse, the shape of the shadow under the eye, the dark around the ear, the neck line in relation to the lines of the head. Oh, it was too much to see all at once. The mane, the light striking a twitching muscle. Oh, how did Rosa Bonheur ever do it so perfectly? It wasn't right at all. She began again. Sweat dripped onto the paper. This time it was a bit better. Hours passed. The groom moaned and said he had to go and do his chores. Mary waved him on and continued to sketch. When the charcoal and the paper were all used up and Mary's hand felt cramped and her back ached, she put the last paper on top of the rest and stood, patting the charcoal dust from her hands. She was smudged and tired, but she felt better. The hopelessness was re-placed by an excitement; as difficult and frustrating as the drawing had been, it brought her some contentment, too. It was as though she knew deep inside that she would make art her life no matter what. Somehow she would learn what she needed to know.

The next morning Mary didn't go riding with her father. She woke up with more determination than ever to make a good drawing of Dory. She borrowed Lydia's stationery and some of the brown paper Cook used in the kitchen and with a pocketful of broken bits of charcoal, she went back to the stables. Although her father and Dory were gone, Caesar, the other horse, was there. Mary led him to the open doorway where sunshine illuminated his coat. "Bucky, hold Caesar's head, will you?"

Bucky did as he was told and Mary sketched. "Watch the riding path and tell me when you see Father coming."

Bucky nodded.

This time the drawing went a little better. On the fifth sketch she developed the drawing to include the details, but too late she realized she had placed the ear a bit too far back and the drawing was ruined. She started again. When her father was seen riding up the path, Mary hid the drawings in a milk can that was only used to haul water in the winter. She went back to the house and looked at pictures of horses in picture books, measuring the length of the legs, the space from the shoulders to the tail, the head in relation to the whole.

The next day she sketched Caesar again. After more than two hours, she was ready to quit when something happened and she felt the roundness of the form, a foundation of flesh and muscles underlaying her lines. This time it was different. She saw and she put down, and there was a rightness about what was happening on the paper. When Bucky waved she told him to be still. She drew furiously, relentlessly. Caesar was coming out of the end of the charcoal and her heart ws aflame with excitment.

Twenty minutes later, as she skipped along the path toward the house, she saw her mother and Lydia walking toward her. Before her mother could comment about her appearance she blurted out, "Don't worry, Mother, it can be soaked and washed. It's only charcoal."

"When you are presentable, your father and I want to talk to you in the parlor, dear."

Mary sighed and nodded. "Yes, Mother. I shan't be long."

She hurried up the hill to the house, glad that neither Lydia nor her mother noticed the sheaf of papers she was carrying. She wanted to look at them in a proper light after she had rested and had regained some sort of perspective.

Even as she bathed, Mary's mind still explored ways of seeing and recording on paper what she saw. It would have been better if there had been more light in the stable and more shadows. Or maybe if she had tried several angles, she would have found a better arrangement. She would need more time.

She chose a dress her father especially liked. It was the color of grass in the springtime, and although she would not be cool in it, she liked the feel of the white lace ruffles around her wrists and neck. And Mother said it made her look stately. But before she went down to join the family, she had to have one more look at the last drawing now that her eyes were refreshed.

She went to her desk where she had put the drawings. The picture she had worked on so long and ardently was smudged and her joy dissolved when she saw it wasn't right. How could she have been so sure it would be good? Suddenly a hot feeling of frustration overwhelemed her. Maybe she could never learn. She tossed the drawing into the wastebasket, smearing her hand with charcoal dust as she did. Vigorously she wiped the traces of charcoal on a towel and walked downstairs full of anger and impatience. The afternoon's practice was wasted. Her father was probably right after all. How could she even dream of such miracles as she had desperately wanted while she sketched the mare? She couldn't make excuses about the light and the angles. The truth was she didn't draw very well. She had to practice much more and maybe even then—

Lydia must have heard her on the stairs, for she stood at the banister smiling up. "Hurry, Mary, we're all waiting for you."

"I'm coming."

"Don't be dismal now. Please. Not today. I couldn't bear it if you weren't as glad as I am, and I'm fairly bursting."

"I can't be glad, but I'll be decent. Why in heaven's name are you bursting?"

"Just because. Come on."

Mary sighed and let Lydia lead her by the hand to the parlor where their mother was seated at the piano, playing softly. Aleck and his father looked up from the chess board and Gard, who had been watching the game, stood up straight and smiled.

"Here they are," her father said, beaming directly at Mary.

She had the feeling she was going to be told that someone was coming for a nice long visit. Who could it be to so delight Lydia? The Wattlesons? Cousin Eugenia? Albert Bailey? Father's business friends were always charming to Lydia. That must be it. Mary sat on the sofa with her face poised in a pleasant smile.

"A small glass of sherry?" her mother asked.

Mary was puzzled. "It isn't anyone's birthday, is it?"

"No," her father laughed, "but it could be an occasion for a toast."

Mary looked questioningly at Lydia as she took her small glass of sherry. Robert Cassatt held his glass up in the gesture of a toast. "To the enrichment of the lives of the Cassatt family and all Philadelphians and citizens of the world through the art of drawing and painting, and to Mary Stevenson Cassatt in her new undertaking."

Did that really mean—? "Father, do you mean . . . are you saying that I might be permitted to study art after all?"

"That's exactly what I'm saying. Tomorrow I will make all the arrangements."

Mary looked at her father's beaming face and felt unworthy, yet grateful. She rushed to put her arms around his neck and as she did, she spilled her sherry down the front of his shirt. "Oh, dear."

But her mother stepped in with her handkerchief and wiped the front of her husband's shirt, smiling and shaking her head. Mary found she couldn't say much of anything, not even a simple thank you. She couldn't seem to talk or think clearly enough to ask why he had changed his mind.

"When I saw you in the stables this afternoon," her father was saying, "I was sure this was what had to be done."

"And it was strange," Lydia interrupted. "We were having iced mint tea and talking about Mr. Lincoln's aims when all of a sudden Father said he had to go to the stables to see about Dory's knee. He saw you drawing again and it struck him that . . . "

"Liddy, Liddy," her father gently scolded. "Don't carry on so. I had been reconsidering the whole thing and this happened to be the time the decision was finally made."

"But Father," Lydia said, "you just put your tea down in the middle of a sentence and wandered straight to the stables." Lydia took a deep breath. "You didn't even know he was watching you, did you, Mary?"

"No."

"You were concentrating. It was all meant to happen just like this."

Mary smiled at Lydia, then at her father. "Thank you," she said. "I'll try to learn. I truly will."

They all laughed and hugged Mary. Their faces were full of faith and hope, but she had a cold feeling in her stomach. She really didn't draw very well. Could she ever learn?

2

THE CARRIAGE STOPPED in front of the Pennsylvania Academy of Art on Chestnut Street. Mary stepped out, walked up the broad marble steps that led to a portico and two Doric columns, paused inside the circular room under the high dome, and sighed. At last.

Later, as she was led down a corridor by the registrar's assistant, the smell of turpentine and chalk and old walls tickled her nostrils, and there was something else in the air. Perhaps it was the essence of a concentrated struggle to learn what she longed to master. On that first day there was a twinge of excitement she couldn't deny.

But by the end of the week it was gone, swallowed up by the sharp need she discovered within herself to make progress. By then she had separated herself from the women who seemed to enjoy showing the others how inferior their own work was. They would talk lightly of it and say they would probably never get it right. Mary could have joined their chorus, for her work quite honestly wasn't any better than theirs, but the fact that her drawings did not measure up to what she had envisioned at the beginning was not something she took lightly.

Eliza Haldeman seemed to feel like she did, so Mary chose her as a friend, the one she preferred to sit beside while they struggled to draw acceptably from plaster casts of ancient statues. She worked happily, though she was often unsatisfied with her skills and frustrated that she had not achieved more; yet she was not in sympathy with the others in the class when they complained and actually groaned over the boredom of plaster casts. Mary, strangely enough, was not bored. She was glad they didn't move and she could draw until she got it right.

The drawing instructor, Mr. Carroll, shuffled through the classroom, his hands clasped behind his back, saying "mm" or "unn" as he looked over a student's shoulder at the drawing. One day he cautioned them to measure their proportions, and he showed how to do this by squinting at a piece of charcoal held at arm's length across the subject. "Estimate what portions of the charcoal approximate the width, and what proportion approximates the length. Oh, yes, and pay attention to the value gradation in the shadows." Mary was glad he actually said something useful. It seemed that when Mr. Carroll talked about shadows, she was drawing the basic shape; when he mentioned proportions she was working in shadows. He seldom criticized or praised any of the students' work, though once or twice she saw him smile and say, "That's better."

After drawing class one afternoon when the weather was fine, Mary walked to the courtyard and was struck by the way the light streamed over the statue of Ceres in the corner. She sat down on a bench in the shade of a huge hawthorn tree and began to sketch. After a while Eliza and Imogene, another student, came to walk in the courtyard. When they saw Mary, they laughed. "Don't tell me you're actually sketching another statue when you don't have to," Imogene said.

"Aren't your hands just rigid?" Eliza said, imitating Imogene's tone.

Mary shook her head and tried not to look too unpleasant, though she didn't remove her gaze from the statue.

"There's nothing worth copying in Philadelphia," Imogene said. "One has to go to the Continent."

Mary had heard that sentiment many times before, and of course, she knew there were many more art treasures abroad.

"There's going to be a party at my aunt's tomorrow," Eliza said. "She asked me to bring a few friends. Please come, Mary."

"All the best people go to the Haldemans," Imogene said.

"There will be people you know," Eliza offered.

Imogene laughed. "Unless you'd rather stay here and draw silly statues. As for me, I'd rather put on a party dress and flirt with a few cultivated men. Who knows what might happen?" Imogene's tone of voice irritated Mary and she answered too quickly.

"I'm tired of cultivated sneering. The last society party I went to will hold me for quite a while."

"Aren't we touchy?" Imogene said, looking over Mary's shoulder at her drawing. She snickered. "It's out of proportion. It looks like Sampson on the left and a wing from the Christmas goose on the right." She giggled as she raised her eyes heavenward. "Don't worry, Michelangelo," she said, and both girls laughed.

Mary dropped her pencil in the dried leaves at her feet. "Don't sketch too hard," Imogene said as they walked on, her piercing laughter carried on the air. Mary didn't see Eliza glance back with a half-apologetic, half-pleading look. Mary understood only one thing at that moment—that some day she would excel. She would show them all.

After that she worked even harder. She sat in the front during anatomy lectures so she wouldn't be distracted from her purpose by gazing at the other students. She studied the charts showing the muscles in the male and female bodies. The first time the doctor discussed the pelvic area, Mary burned with embarrassment. And when he actually touched his pointing stick to the female pelvis on the chart, she felt as though she couldn't breathe. It was unbearably degrading to actually be forced to look and think of such things. Through the icy droning of the doctor's voice she wondered if her father could have known there would be this. No, he would never have permitted her to be horrified in this way. No one could have expected such gross disregard of human propriety. Yet, she sat still in the front of the lecture room day after day, listening to the anatomy lessons.

She drew from plaster casts a whole year before she was allowed in a life class. During that first summer vacation she drew flowers in vases, still life studies of kitchen utensils, and every one of Lydia's hats. Then, when the new term began, there was more drawing and sketching. Mary itched to paint with color. She grew more and more impatient with each passing week. Drawing was important, she knew, but color was life itself. "When?" she asked the instructor.

"When the class is ready and not until then."

Mary wanted to kick and scream and tell them all to get ready, but she waited patiently and drew. Sometimes she would draw her face in the mirror. She liked to draw faces. There could be nothing else so interesting. The droop of an eye could change the whole mood, and the mouth—oh, what miracles could be done with that mouth line, and a shadow at the edges of the mouth could turn a calm face to melancholy. Faces in color would be even more exciting, but even without color a face could be drawn to tell its story. Her own face was not easy to draw. She looked in the mirror and usually hesitated. Hers was undistinguished, thin with a pointy chin. Her nose was absolutely ordinary, not quite straight, certainly not classic. The gray eyes were small—nothing wrong with them either, but at least her brow and forehead were pleasing. That was something. She knew the face in the mirror well enough to change a line here and there, just to see what would happen. A fraction of a fraction, a mere heaviness of line could make it lovely or ugly or funny or strange. Drawing was important, even more than color—and she could prove it. She could take watercolors and paint the drawings she had done of her face and even if she colored it blue, the face would not look so different as if she changed a single line. That discovery about drawing excited Mary and she wanted to talk to someone about it. She carried the thought around for half a day before she had to express it. Fellow student Tom Eakins was standing near her as they both drew from a model. He listened, nodding, smiling a little, and after a bit she realized he had already made the very same discovery. "Drawing," she said, "is everything." Her voice carried across the quiet room and some of the students snickered.

"Observation," Tom said, "has to be without prejudice and accurately rendered—then the drawing can count for something."

"Color is important too," the instructor announced in a loud voice, "and tomorrow we will draw with a two-color palette."

Mary drew in her breath. *And now—color.*

The days at class passed too quickly. Mary dreaded her second summer vacation. She would actually miss all this discipline, and she was just getting comfortable with oils. Of course, she wanted to be with the family, to ride and have time to read, but she didn't want to forget anything she had learned or seen or was beginning to understand. There was so much more to learn about color.

After the first excitement of seeing everyone at home, Mary became restless. The conversations after dinner between her father and Aleck failed to excite her as they had. She used to interrupt with questions and arguments but now the things they talked about saddened and frightened her. She wanted to believe in Mr. Lincoln, but how could there be so much disagreement among people? Wrong was wrong, but apparently each saw right on his side, even the South.

When she had been home for a week she excused herself after the evening meal and went directly to her room. She had become depressed with the thought of war. She could bear no more when even Aleck talked about joining up and going off to kill. Gard too, listened with ferver and wanted to fight—why, he was too young to realize what war was. How could men accept killing so easily? She could never accept it. Never. The only war she would enter was the battle to be in the front line of art. She could no longer maintain a serious interest in anything else. The only challenge worth the trouble was putting her visions on paper or canvas. She must draw something serene and simple. She sighed, searched her room, and finally took out her hat with the satin bow and the egret feathers.

After a moment of observing the subject, she slashed lines onto the paper with furious energy. She would create beauty, not ugliness. She forced herself to work with calm concentration.

Presently there was a knock at the door. She knew it was Lydia and shouted for her to come in. Lydia entered slowly. Mary noticed that she seemed tired. Her eyes were puffy and she pressed her hands together. "Sit down, Lydia."

"I came to see if you might like to play whist with me, but I see you're busy."

"Not too busy. I'll finish this in a few minutes and play whist if you like. I was trying to paint away the damned war."

"Oh, it should be damned. Father talks about it every day. At night I dream of being in the middle of a battle sometimes. The noise is deafening. There are gunbursts and men moaning in pain. Father says we can't stop it. Mr. Lincoln is doing the best he can."

"He could order the army to quit fighting," Mary said.

"But slavery would go on."

"Can the South force us to take slaves if we don't want to?"

"It's more complicated than that. But even if it weren't, can people turn their backs on injustice?"

"Isn't anything preferable to killing?"

Lydia sighed and looked ill. Mary put down her work. "We'll play whist."

"Yes, we'll play, but we won't forget. Oh, Mary, I hate it too. But we are only helpless women."

Mary stared at Lydia. "Helpless? Why are we that?"

"Men run the world, don't they? And they take care of women, don't they? Doesn't that make women rather helpless?"

"It doesn't have to be that way. I want to run my own life."

Lydia smiled. "You can until you marry, since Father is liberal with us, but then someone will marry you and give you babies."

Mary frowned. "I have other, more important things to do first. But what about you? Are you going to marry Jeremiah Williams?"

Lydia looked down at her hands and spoke softly. "No."

"No? You were fond of him, and he couldn't take his eyes from you."

27

"I was more than fond of him. I wanted to marry him—but—the doctor says I am not to have babies. My health has never been just right. I couldn't bear to be a burden to him when with someone else he could have those things every man wants."

"So you stopped seeing him?"

"Yes, and then he joined Mr. Lincoln's army."

"You miss him, don't you?"

Lydia's yes was so soft, Mary couldn't hear it, but the anguish in her eyes and her sad smile brought Mary to her knees at her sister's feet. "If he would leave you to go off to war—and kill people—he isn't worth your tears. I shall never marry either. I shall become an artist and live independently. When I am successful, we can be together. You will be my model, won't you? And we'll have hundreds of beautiful hats and good horses and a grand house to entertain our friends in. And we'll have men too, by the droves. Handsome, rich men will fall at our feet. It will be fun. Marriage could get to be dull as ditchwater, but freedom can never be dull. We'll travel wherever we want. We'll be free."

Lydia's smile became laughter. "Mary, you are sweet. You are remarkable in so many ways, but you dream too much."

"No, I don't. You wait and see. I shall live like a man and be free. And I shall have a house grander than this without owing a penny or a promise to anyone. I swear it."

Lydia shook her head. "And stop swearing, please."

Mary went back to working on the egret feathers with small quick strokes. Lydia watched her, fascinated. "It's very good. Really. Tell me, what is it like at school? Are people as Bohemian as they say?"

"Bohemian?"

"You know. Do they live like gypsies?"

Mary sighed. Her eyes flashed an instant, then she looked off. "Oh, no. I'm learning nothing Bohemian. I am only learning how to draw and that's the main thing, but the way it's done isn't right. I know you're going to tell me I shouldn't expect too much. Everyone always tells me that. But I will continue to expect fair treatment and I hope I go on expecting it all my life."

"My goodness. What's so unfair?"

"It's just that—well, maybe I'm being silly, but it's true and it isn't fair."

"What? Tell me. I won't think you're silly. I promise."

"All right. It isn't fair to assign all the very best instructors to the men and give the women the doddering old professors who can hardly see anymore or some spiritless little lambs who don't bother even to lecture."

"They don't do that, do they?"

"Of course they do. I've talked to Tom about it and he tells me of the lively discussions the men have. Sometimes I think they just don't take women seriously at the academy. Maybe we don't take ourselves seriously enough."

"It's possible that some women don't," Lydia said, "but not you. You're determined."

Mary sighed. "I hope that's enough."

"Don't ever doubt yourself, Mary. You shouldn't." Lydia's face was set with faith in her.

Mary didn't doubt that faith. "But . . . I don't have a gift, Lydia," she whispered.

"I don't understand," Lydia said.

"I don't either," Mary admitted. "Tom says that talent is just the willingness to work harder than other people; it's discipline on top of more discipline. But he draws better than the instructors already. He does it almost effortlessly."

"And you think he has a special gift?"

"He drew cows on his slate in the first grade. He drew backgrounds for the Christmas plays. He always loved to draw."

"He told you all this?"

"I asked, Lydia. I wanted to know why he was so good. He's modest. I had to ask a lot of questions, but it looks to me like he has something special—a gift. I've watched him."

"You have a different kind of gift," Lydia said.

"I pray you're right because my mind is made up. Gift or no gift, I have to do what I'm doing."

MARY RETURNED from her summer vacation eager to get on with her studies. However, right from the start of the term she found she had to work even harder than before; there were so many elements to grasp. While she worked to become skilled in applying oil paints with broad and narrow brushes, she also had to think of achieving a good sense of color harmony and a strong design. There were more lectures discussing composition, more talk about the masters and their principles and techniques. Study became more intense than it was during the first years at the academy. However, strangely enough, there was not as much satisfaction as there had been at first. The fun and excitement had turned to toil and pain. She worked in a frenzy week in and week out, month after month.

Toward the end of her third year the advanced students were invited to participate in a competition. All the works entered would be graded by the dean and the best displayed in the annual spring show.

This seemed like Mary's chance. It was important to her to excel, to take her place as a leading art student. She wanted so much to see her work labeled number one that she thought of nothing else day and night. She had been assigned to the still life category, although she would have preferred to do a portrait or a seated figure. However, still life had the advantage of always being available. She accepted her assignment with only a small burst of objection uttered as an initial reaction before she had time to consider it. That very afternoon, though, she had her subjects selected: a wicker sewing basket, a doll, and a toy soldier. It would be like painting Mother, Lydia, and Aleck, or Gard through things they had possessed.

Mary made not dozens of sketches to work out the composition, but hundreds of them. She felt great excitement as she sketched her composition onto the canvas, expecting to make it the very best still life possible, deserving of recognition and honor. She could see it in her mind's eye, the golden browns of the wicker basket, the pale and faded doll, worn with a child's care, and a staunch toy soldier in the dark blue-gray uniform with gold braid. The dress of the doll would drape over the edge of the basket to unite those elements, and the soldier would face them, drawing the whole picture together with its gaze. The background would be simple, just tones of greens.

When everything was ready she began the underpainting with a wash of umber, never for a second losing sight of her goal of excellence. She had worked hard to get to this. She had suffered many frustrations, ruining canvas after canvas with false starts that had to be scraped off and begun again. She had seen her instructors shake their heads and cry, no, no, no. And the worst of it was that her work seemed even to herself unbelievably bad. Her drawing had fallen off when color and composition occupied her efforts, and a poorly executed detail would often stand out and ruin the whole effect. But it wasn't impossible. She knew she was getting close to being able to do it. And now there was time to devote to a single painting. Now was the chance to put together everything she had learned, and show the instructors and other students and her family —everyone—that she was becoming an artist. The doll, the soldier, and the sewing basket. It was so simple and honest it was beautiful. The light was arranged precisely right. She vowed she would not work on her entry when she felt tired. She would use fairly small brushes and work for fine detail. She painted every morning from ten until noon, attending regular classes during the rest of the day.

One day when the painting was well along, perhaps a day or two away from being complete, a particularly stern instructor stood beside her easel and frowned. He didn't say anything. He simply stood for a long time frowning. Mary stopped. She looked critically at the painting, but saw nothing objectionable. "What's wrong?" she said at last.

"The basket. Take a good look at the basket."

Mary did, but still didn't understand what he meant.

"Don't you see—the value is too light. Darken it." Then he passed to the next student's easel.

Mary looked again at the painting and especially at the basket. If it were brown instead of straw-colored, the doll would stand out more because of the added contrast. Perhaps that would strengthen the composition. She had worked long hours on that wicker basket, but if she could make her painting better, she would. The morning session was almost over. However, she skipped lunch and stayed on to work, getting a rich brown. She painted out the detail she had struggled so long to put in. Yes, it did do something for the doll, but now the wicker basket was the darkest element and not the soldier. She lightened the shadow of the soldier's uniform. The balance was still off somewhat. The massive dark basket gave too much weight to the left side of the canvas. Well, the background could be changed enough to compensate for it. She rapidly darkened the right corner, working her way to the middle area behind the doll's head. She was late for the next lecture, but the soldier was getting lost and she didn't know what to do about that. Something was needed. Perhaps a line of yellowish light around the shoulder decoration. She hastily brushed a bit of pale yellow on the shoulder and a patch of the uniform became a most ghastly green. Mary felt nausea, then as though she might cry. She scraped the wet paint off the soldier, cleaned her brushes and left it like that, not because she wanted to, but because the room was going to be used by others. She felt sick. If she didn't finish it by tomorrow or the next day, it would not be dry enough to hang in the spring show. She kept asking herself what she could do to save it. It was slipping away, turning into a beastly mess. Why did she ever darken that basket?

When the studio room was unlocked in the morning Mary was waiting to get in. One look at the painting filled her with despair. "What happened, Mary?" a voice asked.

She turned and saw Tom looking at her darkened canvas. It was hard to keep the tears back at that moment.

"Yesterday it was nearly perfect," Tom said. "I thought you were finished, and now it's gotten so confused and muddy. What are you going to do?"

Mary couldn't reply. She looked sorrowfully at Tom and turned back to the canvas. She picked up her palette knife and scraped the paint off. When it was as smooth as she could get it, she wiped the surface with a rag dampened with turpentine. There was nothing to do but begin all over again. She laid the elements in with a wash of umber, and as she worked she hated her instructor with a sinful intensity and herself for listening to him. There was so much angry energy to use up, she had the composition sketched in again in half an hour. Working rapidly, she did the underpainting in a very thin wash and stayed in the studio until she was long past tired. But it was coming back. The next day she avoided using those colors she knew would take a long time to dry. It meant more mixing of colors. She couldn't use any buttery thick paint for the highlights either or it would never dry in time. The surface was smooth and thin. She wished she could have made the colors thicker and richer, especially on the soldier's brass buttons and braid, but it was too late.

When she was finished, the painting looked surprisingly good, especially the work she had done on the doll. The thin layer of the paint enhanced the poetry she had recognized there. Yes, she was pleased with it in spite of all the problems. She had to rush to get it framed in time, and was totally relieved when the painting was finally submitted to the committee.

After that, there would be a week before the show was hung, and no one would know how the paintings were rated until the show opened. Mary crossed her fingers and hoped.

During that long week she began copying one of the paintings at the academy. Her choice was *Deliverance of Leyden* by Willkamp. Copying presented a new way to learn. At least it was new to Mary. She must see and puzzle out how to achieve the effect the master accomplished. After a while Mary imagined she was Willkamp, tried to think like Willkamp and use her brushes and apply the paint like he had done. Her own ways were abandoned and she was amazed at how much she could learn by doing this. Eliza and Tom were each copying from a portrait by Charles Willson Peale. Mary looked over Eliza's easel to view her work. "Isn't it wonderful what you can learn from copying?"

"True," Eliza said, "but how did he ever get such red flesh tones without making the face ridiculous?"

"That's another interesting problem," Mary said. "Maybe if the rest of it were darker . . . " But she cringed at her own words. "Oh, please forget I said that."

Tom smiled and looked at Eliza's painting. "He probably built it up with layers of transparent glazes."

Eliza examined the surface of the painting more closely and nodded.

"I think you could learn all you needed to know from copying the great painters," Tom said.

"That what *they* did," Eliza said. "That's how it's always been passed down."

"And that's what I am going to do," Mary said.

"You're going to run out of masters unless you go abroad."

"I suppose that's true," Mary said. "When I think of all the great paintings I saw when my family and I lived in Europe, it makes me ache."

"Italy especially," Tom said.

"But Paris has the Louvre," Eliza said. She sighed and went back to her easel. Tom looked thoughtful. "I'm going to try to get a year or so of copying after I finish at the academy."

"Wouldn't it be splendid to copy Rembrandt, Frans Hals, Velazquez, or El Greco?" Mary said. "We have nothing like that in America."

"I know," Tom said. "The academy has so few treasures. As students we've made a good start here, but I mean to make art my life."

"So do I," Mary said.

Tom smiled. "With the Cassatt money and your marriage possibilities, surely you'll never have to worry about your livelihood."

"Nevertheless, I want to paint exactly as though my life and livelihood depended on it."

"It's a lot of work for a woman."

"But no more than for a man."

Tom shrugged and picked up his brush, dipped it into the blue mixture on his palette. Mary went back to her own easel. After a while she was thinking of Velazquez and the thousands of museums in Europe crammed full of masterworks. It would take decades and decades for America to catch up. It probably never would. America was building a nation; it couldn't take time out for art yet.

After Mary cleaned her brushes and put her work away for the day, she paused before she turned to go. "See you at the show tomorrow," she said to Tom and Eliza.

Tom looked up grinning. "I'll be there when they open the doors, same as you."

"Not me," Eliza said. "I want someone to come back and tell me all about it before I go."

Mary was up early the next morning. Since it was Saturday, the carriage would be by shortly after noon to take her home for the weekend. Only today Father would surely come himself since she had told him about the spring show. It was scheduled to open at eleven sharp. Mary was frantic to see how her painting had done.

She put on a plum traveling dress that fit so tightly around the shoulders and bodice she could not move as freely as she liked. But the skirt flowed gracefully around her ankles so that when she wore it, she felt elegant, especially when she put on the matching hat. As she stuck a pearl hatpin through the crown of the hat she thought she at least looked like a woman who could manage almost anything, even painting a prize picture.

She would go to the office first and get the envelope containing her grade and the instructor's comment and proceed directly to the hall to see the show. At ten forty-five she could stand it no longer. She walked slowly to the office, hoping to arrive just on time. She was early. No one was there and she had to stand in front of the door and wait. Finally, Tom came sauntering along looking very calm. He probably didn't care so much, she thought. Besides, it would be impossible to care as much as she did. Her stomach fluttered when she thought of going into that auditorium.

She received her envelope with a handshake and good wishes from the clerk at the desk. Since they were already opening the auditorium doors, she put the envelope into her pocketbook to read later. "Come on, Tom, let's hurry."

The auditorium was totally transformed. Mary couldn't help

being impressed. She paused a moment near the door to look around and spotted Tom's entry even before he did, a log house in a clearing with a small figure chopping wood. He could really draw. He was probably the best draftsman in the academy. She would be glad if his picture was first, but when they came closer to it, it was marked with a number two. He was smiling, and she remembered to congratulate him and tell him how very excellent it was. "If I had been the judge it would have been first."

They walked slowly to the place of honor, and there was hung there a dark painting of a man on horseback. Mary numbly studied it for a moment, and when she turned away she didn't know if it was good or not—it probably was. She didn't seem to think anything. It was first, and that was what mattered. Hers wasn't either first or second. But hers must be here somewhere. She could still hope for third or honorable mention. Her knees felt rubbery as she walked along examining the pictures. Oh, there was third. Eliza's. Mary's vision became temporarily blurred, but only for a moment. They walked on, and then she saw it.

"There it is—in the corner."

Tom touched her elbow and seemed to lead her to the place. "It looks mighty good to me," he said. "What you did was wizardry when you think of what happened."

He spoke sincerely and she wanted to believe everything he said, but it sounded like an excuse. "Thanks, Tom." She mumbled apologies and left him.

Once out of the auditorium, Mary went off down the corridor and out into the courtyard. It was cold enough to see her breath as she sat on the stone bench and unlatched her pocketbook. There was her envelope, waiting to be opened. She ripped it apart and unfolded the small sheet inside.

There was a numerical grade of 82 at the upper left of the note. She read: "The composition would have been stronger and the effect more pleasing if you had seen fit to darken the large basket as I believe I suggested. As it stands your interpretation seems weak and lacking power. There is no quality of color due to the thin consistency of the paint applied. Work harder on surface techniques and the placement of dark masses to create a mood of power. The delicacy of the painting might appeal to a woman, but lacks general appeal."

Was it because she didn't take his advice? He was *wrong*. And the doll should have been handled delicately. She was sure the second version was more honest than the first. "General appeal indeed," she mumbled as she crumpled up the paper and put it back into her pocketbook. She sat staring at Ceres for a moment. Then she went back to the sitting room to wait.

Over the next months Mary copied from paintings and worked from the model in life classes. But she no longer cared what any instructor at the academy thought of her work. Their opinions didn't matter because they were controlled by a narrow set of rules that allowed no exploration. They demanded darkness and a certain mellowness of tone. They wanted formal arrangement and perhaps a likeness, but Mary sensed it was not the essence of art they appreciated, but only the stultifying established standards with no allowance for change or individuality. Mary imagined how an artist like El Greco would have survived at the academy. She needed more than this if she were going to make art her life.

Mary brooded over what to do, and finally decided there were no alternatives. She needed more study. She needed to soak herself in the art of the ages.

She had certainly mentioned to her mother and father and, of course, to Lydia that her interest in becoming an artist was strong. They seemed to approve and to be proud of her achievement, but when she told them what she really wanted to do next, she had never seen her father's face so angry.

"I can't believe you're serious. Well-bred women don't go off to study abroad *alone*. It's outrageous."

"Serious artists must do it, Father. It's the only way they can master their art."

"Nonsense, you've had excellent instruction and you've worked hard and done well. But enough is enough."

"I haven't learned nearly enough."

He shook his head and looked truly exasperated. "Why couldn't you learn to play the harp or paint on china like a proper lady? Why this impossible obsession?"

"It's not impossible."

"Well, I could *never* permit you to do such a thing."

3

WHEN MARY GRADUATED from the academy, her family re-joiced and gave her presents. Her father's gift was a lovely riding horse. "Remember Mary, you're twenty-one now and it's time to get out in the world, ride, enjoy yourself at dances and parties. You've worked hard enough for your art."

Certainly her father meant well, but Mary was not interested in parties or in meeting eligible men, which was what her father want-ed. She was set on continuing her studies in European museums. She had to believe that given time and the proper urging, her father would not continue to withhold his blessings from her. But she could not wait idly for it to happen. Her strategy was to keep the question alive, to force him to continue to examine his stand. Artist friends were invited for tea to meet the family and discuss the advantages of study abroad. An art instructor who had recently returned from the

Continent was willing to tell what great experiences Europe offered. Thomas and Eliza, who were both from respectable families, came and talked about their plans to study abroad. Robert Cassatt was always polite, but his no was still unwavering.

Lydia declared almost daily that Mary would win out. Mary could always count on Lydia to suffer along with her and make the situation look sunny and hopeful. Still, Mary knew instinctively her greatest ally was her mother. There was never any spoken support between them; nothing more than an occasional look passed across a room, but it was enough.

Then one rainy afternoon before supper Robert asked them to assemble in the library. "I received an important letter in the mail today," he said. "I'm sure you'll all be interested in its contents."

Aleck was already seated and merely glanced up from his book when Mary and Lydia came into the room. Gard was happily cracking chestnuts by the mantel and throwing the shells into the fireplace. While her father unfolded his letter, Mary lit the lamp on the desk. She did not expect this business to take long, and as she sat down next to Lydia and studied her mother's passive face, she thought what a picture her mother would make. Then Gard sat down beside her and the composition became more dynamic, full of contrasts, her mother's serenity and grace against Gard's careless, pink-cheeked vigor.

The letter is from Granger Barrie," her father said. "He worked in the same brokerage firm with me ten years ago. We were good friends and he is a man I would trust with my life."

All eyes were on Robert, but he turned his gaze to Mary. It was then she wondered if it could have something to do with her campaign.

"Granger Barrie is established in Paris with his wife and daughter, so I inquired after the possibility of receiving his protection and guidance for you, Mary. With a man like Granger Barrie looking out for your welfare, I would allow you to study in Paris."

Mary felt a tingling start at the base of her neck and sweep across her back and envelop her. "Oh, Father," she whispered. She clutched Lydia's hand. "And what did he say?"

"He said he and Clara would be honored to have you stay with them in Paris. Those are his words. You may read it," he said hoarsely, handing the letter to Mary.

She couldn't have been more delighted. "Oh, Father—how can I thank you?" Before she read the letter she hugged everyone, her father, her mother, Lydia, Aleck, and Gard, and by then her eyes were too blurry to read the words and Lydia had to read it.

Robert smiled but his eyes were serious. "Your mother will travel with you and see that everything is arranged with the Barries. We must find a worthy artist to guide your studies and when it is all arranged, you can go."

Mary did not want guidance from anyone, worthy or not; all she needed was access to the museums. But she did not protest. It was a time to be grateful, not argumentative. She would agree to anything as long as she had this chance.

BEFORE THEY SAILED in that summer of 1866, Mary had several serious talks with her father about how she should conduct herself, being mindful that she would perhaps meet people leading lives entirely unacceptable to proper American and particularly Cassatt standards. "Remember you are an American and you are *my* daughter."

The intensity of his words made Mary look closely at him. Suddenly she understood. He was worried about men! French men. Were they supposed to have extraordinary appeal? Well, he needn't worry. She would dance with them at parties and joke with them. But she surely wasn't going to let anything else happen. "I won't forget," she said. "I'll be the same person I am now."

He looked at her thoughtfully and smiled. "You and Aleck are both strong-minded, and you have your mother's thirst for culture." He shook his head. "You will write once a week without fail?"

"Yes, Father, and don't worry about me. Please. I won't be swayed by all that hand kissing. I'll become a saint if it would help. I'll wear a sackcloth and chant or wear garlic around my neck to scare off all the male temptors in France. I'll—"

"That's quite enough," Robert said sternly, and Mary smiled. He really had earned some peace.

On a bright morning in September all the writing back and forth and the waiting were over. Lydia, Aleck, Gard, and her father saw them off. There were hugs and tears and last minute reminders, but finally Mary and Katherine were on board, waving their handkerchiefs from the rail when the ship eased away from the dock.

After the crowd on the dock was out of sight, Mary did not want to think about the unfirm sea beneath them. She strolled with her mother on deck. This was the day she had waited for. It was a lovely cool day and she looked her best in her gray wool dress trimmed with dark red piping, bought especially for the crossing. Her mother was undoubtedly the grandest lady on board. How lucky she was, Mary thought, as they walked briskly along, smiling at the other passengers. But it was not long before Mary's legs felt rubbery and her head a mite dizzy. "I believe we should go below deck," she said.

In spite of her determination not to let the mere movement of water rule her, Mary seemed to lose strength and her queasy stomach sent misery bounding through her. She remembered being sick as a child when they sailed but she had never experienced such a complete turning inside out.

After a few days she could not even get out of bed unassisted. The steamy beef smell of broth was nauseating, but she attempted to swallow it for her mother's sake. She did whatever she was told, or tried to. She couldn't think for herself anymore. When she closed her eyes, her visions were of death, destruction of cities, pestilence and horrors of all kinds. When she did not close her eyes she remembered the time at home when Lydia was so sick and wanted Mary to talk to her, but Mary had only stayed a moment and had gone off riding with her father.

The days went by slowly and Mary hardly ever left the cabin. On calm days she tried to read, but it was better if her mother read to her.

WEEKS LATER, when they arrived in France, Mary had to be helped off the ship and taken to a hotel to recuperate a few days before going on. She was unspeakably weak, but glad to be on land again. On the first evening that Mary could function normally, she asked if they could take the train to Paris early the next morning. Receiving no argument, she begged her mother for a day or so to look at Paris by themselves before they called on their friends.

"I supposed we could walk in the parks and visit the Louvre first."

The prospect of such a day made Mary feel doubly alive, incredibly lucky, and so excited about being there at last that she hardly slept.

Paris was clutched in an orangey mist. The view from the hotel room was bewitchingly veiled so only hints of buildings could be seen through the haze. Mary could hardly wait to rush out and become lost in the fog, too. However, Katherine insisted they have a proper breakfast first.

Mary impatiently agreed, and then found the breakfast bread so delicious she was sure she had never tasted anything so wonderful before. And the plums were unbelieveably succulent. She had to be cautioned not to overdo. But it had been so long since she'd enjoyed a meal she didn't care if she overdid or not.

After breakfast they walked through the city, striding through the dissolving mist into the heart of Paris. Leaves fell at their feet and ghost-like statues appeared now and again. A hint of the river and a sweet earthy smell were in the air. Mary gazed at ancient buildings that had crumbled and been rebuilt before Philadelphia even existed. The wide boulevards were lined with small trees and alive with people and carriages. Fountains spewed a glistening spray, and pastry shops smelled sweet and yeasty. After walking a few hours, they took tea at the Maison d'Or, and were still exhilarated from the sights of the morning when they arrived at the Louvre.

Mary's enthusiasm for the paintings spread to her mother, who had always enjoyed picture galleries, but never gave stress to the importance of a single work or significance of any particular artist. Giovanni Boltraffio's portrait of a young man thrilled Mary with its perfection and subtlety. It was hard to stop looking at it long enough to see the others, but when Mary heard her mother sigh and shift her weight restlessly from one foot to the other, she realized that they should view more than this one painting. Mary promised to walk more quickly from one to the next, but she hadn't progressed more than a few feet when a madonna by Tiepolo completely enthralled her. It was a character study with downcast eyes describing the acceptance and humility of her role, while the delicate shadows somehow told of the nobility of being the mother of God. The eyes of the cherub she held in her arms revealed the babe's inherent greatness. Mary could not turn away from this luminous portrait. "I would like to copy this one some day," she said softly.

"But there's so much to see," her mother said. "At this rate it will take us a year to rush through the later Italian period."

"Oh, but look at that Titian," Mary said, moving toward a painting that had caused her to tremble the instant she saw it. "Such power. Don't you see? There's no other way to find it. It's all here. The masters have given it to all who care to study them. If Father were here, he would understand, too, wouldn't he? If he could only see these again—"

Her mother nodded. "I think I understand now why this is so important to you, and I will talk to him about it."

Mary drew a deep breath, trying to collect her wits and come back to earth. There was no need for her to see everything today. She would be back hundreds of times. It was her mother who must make the day count, and she had mentioned earlier that she wanted to see some Watteaus and Gérômes. In French, Mary asked an attendant where they were to be found. She was told crisply, and she took her mother's arm and led her along the corridor.

It was surprising to her to walk outside again, hours later, into the fading sunset. Her mother sighed. "I believe we shall have to hurry or we'll keep the Barries waiting tea." Mary nodded and they found a carriage to take them to their destination, which would be Mary's new home.

"Tomorrow we will call on Monsieur Chaplin."

Those words pricked Mary's exalted mood. She had promised her parents that she would continue a formal supervised training under a successful practicing artist. M. Chaplin had been chosen, and of course Mary would respect her parent's wishes, although she had wanted the freedom to copy the masters unimpeded by studio exercises. And yet, formal study would offer companionship of other artists, and criticism. She did want criticism if it was the right kind. However, narrow-minded prejudice only angered her. And sometimes it was hard to tell which was which. But that was tomorrow, and as for now, she just wanted to sit back in the carriage and rest. She sighed. "Do your feet hurt, Mother?"

"They do. How did you know?"

"Mine do too. Could we slip off the shoes for a minute or two?"

"And never squeeze back into them? It's the worst thing you can do. And a lady would never do such a thing."

"Oh, I know. I meant just while we were in the privacy of the carriage."

"Never, unless you're in the privacy of your own boudoir."

"Poor mother, you've let me quite wear you out."

"Only my feet and legs. I'm sure I shall rally easily enough with a cup of tea."

"I would like a cup, too. Perhaps three cups and a little French tart."

Katherine smiled. "And on the boat I wondered if you would ever eat again."

"I don't want to think of that swaying monster. I pity you having to go back. You'll need a good rest before you step onto those decks again, too."

"A short rest will do. A few weeks, then I must return to your father."

CLARA WITT BARRIE and Granger Barrie greeted Mary and Katherine in the drawing room. The last time Mary had talked to them she had been quite a bit younger and they had treated her like a child. Now they both seemed warm and interested in her as a person. Their older daughter Louisa had married an Englishman and only visited them occasionally. The youngest daughter, Angela, however, still lived at home.

The tea was bracing and so was Clara's smile. Here was a woman who was capable and secure and busy with her own life. Mary liked her immensely.

"I want you to meet some of our friends," she said, "both American and French. I have invited a few intimates for Thursday evening."

"How kind you are," Mary said.

They spent a pleasant evening, although much of the conversation concerned reminiscences that Mary could only listen to with some boredom, but all in all she was quite pleased with how her life was moving.

Angela appeared the next morning at breakfast, a tall boyish girl of fifteen. She usually rode her horse early in the morning, but since it rained she said she thought she would stay and meet Mary. Angela attended a private finishing school. Angela and Clara both talked about the school as though it were a privilege to go there. However, Angela did not pursue any subject beyond a quickly gotten-to point. When she was tired of a thing she simply bowed her head and came up in the middle of something entirely different. While Mary was still forming a picture of the school in her mind, Angela asked if she had seen any of Edgar Degas's pictures.

"Who?" Mary asked.

"Edgar Degas. He paints gorgeous horses and jockeys at the Longchamp."

"I don't believe I've seen his work. Is it good?"

"My art professor thinks so. If you want to see some of his pictures I'll show you one in the window of the Durand-Ruel Gallery."

Out of politeness and appreciation of Angela's gesture, Mary agreed at once, saying she would love to go and see this artist's work.

Clara smiled and put her hand on Angela's shoulder. "The artist Mary is most interested in is Monsieur Chaplin, who will be her teacher. We have quite a few friends who own his work." She looked at Granger.

"Yes, five Chaplin portraits hang in our firm's lobby. He's done some portraits of the founders. Not the sort of picture to display his appeal to society, but quite adequate in every way."

Mary tried to appear enthusiastic. "That's nice."

"I rather like this fellow Degas's things, too," Granger continued. "He's from an old banking family. I knew his father slightly —not a good businessman at all, gracious old fellow, though—good blood there."

"All right," Clara said. "I have a plan. Angela, you and Mary go in the carriage with Granger, step inside a few minutes so Mary can see the Chaplins hanging there, then take the carriage on to the gallery. Katherine and I will have a long morning together. After the gallery you will go to your classes, Angela, and Mary can come back here in the carriage, lunch with us, and afterward Katherine and Mary can call at Chaplin's studio. How's that?"

"Fine," Mary said, a little surprised at having her day planned so thoroughly for her. While she had to admit it sounded like a good idea and everyone seemed pleased with it, Mary silently declared she would not allow her days to be so planned in the future.

The Chaplin paintings hanging on the walls of Granger Barrie's firm were indeed adequate. Actually they were larger than life, as fitting a formal, rather opulent lobby. Chaplin had painted the portrait of one of the partner's wives last spring and Mary was assured that everyone who saw it loved it. Mary however, was still lukewarm about working in his studio. She envied Thomas, who was coming over and would go straight to the Louvre and set up his easel.

After leaving Granger, Mary and Angela deviated from the plan long enough to stop for one of Angela's school friends, Louisine Elder, and the three of them took the carriage on to the Durand-Ruel Gallery.

When they arrived they stopped to view the Degas painting in the window. "What do you think of it?" Angela asked.

Mary looked and nodded her head. "But how did you know?"

"Know what?"

"Why, that this would appeal so strongly to me."

"I knew you liked to ride and you liked to paint pictures."

Mary laughed and pressed her face close to the windowpane. The painting was a dazzling scene with sleek horses mounted by jockeys in bright silk shirts. There was enough movement and sunshine to take her breath away. "This is exactly what I wanted to find in Paris, an art alive and singing, and based on learning from the past. This is it. Edgar Degas. I shall remember that name."

"Let's go inside," Louisine said. "There may be more to see there."

Mary blinked and turned away from the window. Inside there were indeed more Degas paintings and also two pastels. Mary examined them with growing interest. "I wonder how he achieves such brilliance with pastel."

Just then M. Durand-Ruel approached politely. "You admire this work?"

"Very much."

"We feel lucky to be able to display Degas's work. He rarely exhibits publicly and only a few dealers interest him."

"What does he do with his paintings if he doesn't exhibit them?" Mary asked.

M. Durand-Ruel frowned and smiled at the same time. "Many remain in his possession in case he should want to work on them again."

Mary thought it sounded strange for such a fine artist, but she shrugged and looked around at some of the other paintings, studying a Courbet she particularly reacted to.

When they left the gallery, Mary itched to get her hands on a brush. She felt she must get back to work. Up until then she had rather dreaded being a student again. She had wanted to study independently, but perhaps her parents were right about this. She would learn whatever she could from Chaplin.

4

THE DAY AFTER her mother sailed, Mary began her studies at M. Chaplin's studio. It was a place so unexpectedly roomy and full of light, it seemed blessed and prosperous, as though everyone and anyone would approve of whatever happened there. The walls and cupboards were painted white. The students dressed smartly and wore white muslin frock coats to cover their clothes. The maestro, as he was fondly called by the students, wore a black frock coat. He was a tall but fragile man with thinning hair and brown eyes. His smile formed slowly. Mary set up her easel in a spot between the cupboard and the end window where she could see the entire room.

There was an invisible line beyond which the seven students did not venture unless invited. That was M. Chaplin's own territory. Here he had set up his own massive easel in a position so his work would be seen by the students as he painted. His end of the room contained all the classic props; palettes hanging on the wall by their thumbholes, framed paintings, unframed canvases on smaller easels. There were busts and draperies to use in backgrounds as well as books and prints. Yet it was neat and uncluttered. There were a few comfortable chairs and a divan. Tea was brought in the afternoon, and personal talk was then allowed. Mary found it a friendly place and didn't mind being teased by the others about her quaint American accent.

M. Chaplin was working on a family portrait. "Groups are the most difficult assignments an artist can tackle," he said. "They can't be avoided, nor should they be. One must be careful not to have one individual more important than the others. A sitter feels slighted if he is put in profile and would challenge you to a duel should you show the back of his head. We have here five front views of equal importance, which must be shown in some plausible but not monotonous manner. Once the picture is well-composed, half the work is done."

A model for one of Chaplin's family group arrived to pose, and the students set up their canvases and easels to make their studies of him. Chaplin painted on a separate canvas to be copied onto his larger canvas later. The model stood with one knee bent in the composition, not an easy pose to hold, so the length of time he could pose before he needed a rest was limited.

Mary liked the angle from which she was seeing him. His stout stomach was in profile and his face a three-quarters view. She sketched quickly and began to lay in an underpainting, putting down the tonal values. There were many pauses during the session. M. Chaplin worked efficiently in the academic manner. His palette was subdued, and his flesh tended to orange, while Mary saw brilliant contrasts and painted exactly what she saw. Chaplin painted the figure as though it was standing in a smoky yellow shaft of light. It gave a finished, faraway look to the subject. Most of the students paid more attention to M. Chaplin's techniques than they did to their own small canvases. But Mary hadn't painted in so long she reveled in the act of painting, and she wanted to do this subject. Her attention was directed to her canvas rather than to watching what the maestro was doing. During tea M. Chaplin asked if she was having some trouble seeing his canvas.

"No, I see it perfectly," she said.

He frowned, looking at her canvas on the easel. "Perhaps you should watch more carefully." He smiled. It was not an angry reproof, but she understood she was expected to copy his technique and not simply to observe the model.

The next time a model came, she copied Chaplin's technique, his colors, and, as much as possible from her vantage point, his placement of the figure on the canvas. The result was a rather alien peach body. How could she make flesh look like flesh when the dungeon yellow light had to pervade everything? Maybe something was wrong with his vision. But what he did was thought to be lovely by his patrons and his students as well. Courbet wouldn't have done it. She wished she could have studied with him. The flesh he painted looked as though it would bleed if it were pricked with a pin. That was the kind of humanity she wanted to paint. Real flesh, real people.

THE PEOPLE she had met in Paris advised her to listen to Chaplin and to enjoy the gay life, too. After all, she was in Paris now, which was no place to be too serious. Perhaps they were right, Mary thought.

Paris was not all M. Chaplin or even the Louvre or the Paris Salon. Paris was also parties, music, and dancing, and as a prerequisite, there was fashion. Mary was drawn to it like a child to chocolates. Her taste was for elegance, and in Paris elegance was available without ostentatiousness. Clara Barrie had taken Mary to the best houses, and Mary had shopped also with Clara's friend Madame Savoi, a strikingly beautiful Spanish woman who taught arts and poetry at the finishing school Angela and Louisine attended. Mary learned a great deal about making the most of fashion. Her allowance was adequate, but did not accommodate extravagances. She spent only what she could afford, demanding quality and style.

Whenever she entered a café, heads tended to turn. The Barries had introduced Mary to people outside the pale of both art and finance. It was all distractingly stimulating. And it wasn't long before the right kind of gentlemen expressed an interest in her, but Mary, though flattered, valued her independence above everything and did not devote much of her precious time to them. At twenty-two, she was confident there would be plenty of time later.

Each Monday and Saturday mornings were devoted to copying, usually at the Louvre. But that wasn't enough. She also wanted to learn what was being painted and accepted today. It seemed that many of the most appealing new works were subjects painted out-doors. Mary wanted to try that, but again there seemed never to be enough time.

One Saturday while copying a Correggio at the Louvre, Mary was extraordinarily stimulated by what she was doing and lost awareness of the time and of the fact that the carriage would be waiting for her and that she was to have lunch with Angela and Louisine. She was lifted out of Paris altogether and became the sixteenth-century Italian artist in Parma, designing decoration for a magnificent cathedral. The angel she rendered became her own and through this small study she could easily project a vision of the cathedral's whole architecture, such was the power in Correggio's drawing of the angel.

She was jerked back to the present when she heard an impatient voice calling her name. Angela was standing at her elbow looking angry. "Don't you know what time it is? We've been waiting in the carriage for an eternity and a half."

"I didn't realize. I'm sorry." She took one last look at the Correggio angel and began hurriedly to put her things together.

Angela examined Mary's copy and the original, comparing the two. Mary's wet colors were brighter. "Somehow I like yours better, but I know I shouldn't when he is the master and you're only a stupid girl who can't tell what time it is."

Mary laughed, knowing she was forgiven.

In the carriage Angela said, "I'm as hungry as a tiger."

"Let's try that café near the Gallerie Durand-Ruel. It looked inviting."

"What do you want to see at the gallery this time?"

"Angela, really! You're too cheeky, and it doesn't matter to me. Any café you like is fine."

"I'd love to go to that one," Louisine said. "Can't we go there, Angela, please."

"I heard that some of the artists who exhibit at Durand-Ruel's have lunch there," Mary said.

"Well, well," Angela smirked.

"Courbet has eaten there," Mary added. "If it's good enough for him—"

"Tell me, though, would we know any of these artists if we saw them?" Angela asked. "Or could we tell by the paint under their fingernails?"

"Mary would know," Louisine said. "I only wish I knew half as much about art as Mary does."

Angela shook her head good-humoredly at her two friends. "I'm outnumbered, I see. You're two of a kind—art and artists; doesn't anyone care about horses anymore?"

They all laughed. Then Mary turned to Louisine. "You're interested in art seriously, are you?"

"Oh, yes. It would be impossible not to be with all the art talk I hear at school and at home and all the pictures I go to look at. I guess I can't help caring and wanting to know more. And since I've met you it has seemed even more important."

"And you have good instincts. I realized it the first day I met you."

"I can't paint or draw well at all, but I care about beautiful art, yet there's so much I don't know."

"That's because there's a magic to it. When all the skills and elements work together something is created that goes beyond what is physical, and it goes beyond one lifetime into others. It can cross nationalities and language barriers and it can speak out and reach us. I think it's just as important to be able to be reached as it is to reach out. People like you who bother to look and understand make the artist's struggle worthwhile. Without you, it would be a sterile and empty exercise."

53

"I never thought of it like that," Louisine said. "But a lot of people don't ever get a chance to look at good paintings."

"I know. In America especially."

"That's true," Angela said. "I never saw a picture gallery when we lived in Virginia."

"I hope that will change some day," Louisine said. "I think Americans will some day buy art like Europeans do."

"America will have its own artists," Mary said.

"Like you," Angela said.

AFTER LUNCH they strolled across the street and looked in the window of the gallery. "We might as well go inside," Angela said. Mary and Louisine didn't argue. A painting by Manet caught Mary's eye immediately. It was of a woman in a garden in brilliant sunlight. Louisine found a pastel by Degas. She called Mary over to look at it. "What do you think?"

Mary looked and admired. "The magic is there, isn't it?"

"That's what I thought," Louisine said, "but I wanted to know if you did, too."

"It's unmistakable. I think he's one of the finest artists in Paris. And this is an exquisite example of his work. Look at the subtle gradations in the flesh tones, the perfect modeling. Look at the fleeting expression he captured. Remarkable."

"I like his horse pictures better," Angela said.

"Yes, they're fine," Mary said. "But this little pastel is extraordinary."

Louisine's eyes shone. "I'm going to buy it," she said.

"You're what?" Angela said.

"I have some money left from my last allowance and I just got this month's. I can just about cover it. I'll be poor in money for the next month and rich in art forever. That's a bargain, isn't it?"

"Yes, it is," Mary said. "You won't regret buying this."

"I want it. I'll take it to America one day and for now I'll hang it in some lovely corner of the house. Oh, it's going to be exciting to own it."

Mary's admiration for Louisine soared. Her courage and conviction set her apart. She acted—did what she wanted to do. And Mary realized with a pang that she wasn't doing what she wanted. She was spending most of her time in M. Chaplin's atelier going through exercises that meant nothing to her when her time would have been better spent at her easel in the Louvre or maybe sketching outdoors. At least she wanted to try that. It seemed refreshing and lifelike.

Perhaps courage is infectious, for as Mary sat in the carriage next to Louisine, with the wrapped picture on Louisine's lap, Mary made up her mind to quit going to Chaplin's and to pursue her real studies at the museums. She made her announcement right then and there to Angela and Louisine. "And if either of you would pose for me, I'd like to paint in the garden some time."

Angela shrugged. "I hate to be still—but there are lots of girls at school who wouldn't mind."

"I will, of course," Louisine said.

On Monday morning Mary went to Chaplin's studio a little later than usual. She felt free, though she hadn't done anything about quitting. There was just that one nasty task left. She would simply tell him and pick up her things and leave. Halfway through the morning she began to dread the scene she was rehearsing in her mind. Chaplin wasn't going to like it and neither was her father. But it must be. It was already decided. Still, she was hot and nervous thinking about it—so much so that she hadn't realized that she had painted the model in a manner decidedly unlike Chaplin's until he looked at her canvas and exclaimed, "What happened here?"

Mary looked at her canvas. The flesh was pale Correggio, the modeling strong and the brushstrokes showing. It must have been her nervousness or the look on his face that caused her to lose control for a few seconds. She giggled at herself and her indiscretion.

"Explain this, will you please," he said, bristling with irritation.

"It's just that I am not attuned to your methods, I'm afraid."

"Really?" he sputtered and drew himself up to his full impressive height. "If you refuse the discipline, you are wasting your time here."

"I suspect I am."

"You appear to be one of those spoiled American children who will persist in going along in your uncultured way. If you do not want to listen and improve, I cannot help you."

"Then I shall be forced to help myself. You have been very kind, I'm sure, but I shan't be back."

He made himself taller still and looked down at her. "Poor child, you will end up drawing designs to embroider on pillowcases for your friends. But, if that is what you want, I wish you luck."

There was no need to stay for the rest of the session. Mary packed up her things and left. She didn't like the way it had gone. She wanted to say good-bye to the other students, but out of politeness or embarrassment, they avoided her eyes.

Out on the street, though, it felt wonderful. Here she was free to haunt the museums. Free, that is, as soon as she wrote to her father and explained. She sighed, thinking at least it would be much easier to do in a letter than face to face. In a letter she could present it in a way that would make him glad she had had the prudence to discontinue her association with such a place.

MARY'S DECISION to take her own direction seemed to give her new strength and energy. Her copies from the masters became firmer. She sketched Louisine in the garden, seated reading a book and standing leaning on a railing, but when she set up her easel to paint outdoors, she discovered there were many problems she had never encountered while painting indoors in a studio with a north window. Outdoors the sun moved across the sky so fast that the shadows that pinned the composition together simply moved all over the place. And sunlight was so bright it seemed impossible to record—it glared into her eyes—and effects she observed and yearned to put down, like the shimmering quality of leaves, were so fleeting she could not study them long enough to capture anything she saw.

Mary remembered some Manet canvases. He had gone after the effect, ignoring small details. But there was much more in his work. Then Mary remembered that Eva Gonzales, one of Chaplin's students, had mentioned studying under Manet for a time and modeling for him. Mary went to the address of Chaplin's studio, waited in a glove shop next door, and when she saw Eva, she rushed up to her.

"Hello again. I'd like to talk to you; can we have tea?"

Eva was surprised, but agreed. They walked to a café nearby on the Avenue de Clichy and on the way Mary explained her reasons for leaving Chaplin's studio.

When they had seated themselves at a quiet table in the corner of the café, Eva raised her eyebrows. "And so you're going to try plein air painting. Well I don't blame you. It's something I had to try, too, but there are so many problems with working outside, you have to be able to paint fast. I felt I needed more training."

"But you must have learned some things you could tell me. What does Monsieur Manet do when the wind blows the canvas over onto the wet grass?"

Eva laughed as though it had happened to her. "You could take pastels."

"But that is not what Manet does."

Eva tilted her head. "First, are you quite sure you're talking about Manet?"

Mary looked puzzled.

"Some people, especially foreigners, get Manet and Monet mixed up. They're good friends and both are interested in working outdoors, but Claude Monet gets some bold sparkling effects by using a brilliant palette with no black at all. Manet often finishes his outdoor sketches in the studio. Monet doesn't. Monet is intent on preserving the freshness of the moment."

"Maybe I did see some of Monet's work and attributed it to Manet. But they both paint in outdoor light, don't they?"

"Oh, yes."

"What I want to know is *how?*"

Eva smiled and took a deep breath. "They work fast. They paint directly without doing an underpainting. They often use thick paint right from the start and they arrange the canvas so the sun doesn't shine on it. I will introduce you to some friends who paint outdoors regularly. They are doing some remarkable things. You might like to join them on one of their painting treks."

57

"I would like to, of course, but—"

"Well, they come here for refreshment. I daresay I'd like to go on such a holiday myself away from that dreary studio when the weather is so fine." Eva glanced up as the door opened and someone came in. "Marcel," she called, and a young Frenchman joined them at their table. Mary smiled brightly when Eva explained Mary's interest in painting outdoors, but she was uncomfortable at the idea of pushing herself on this young man, who was obviously not like the men she usually saw. This Marcel was coarse and uneducated. He had no polish whatsoever. Look at the way he drinks his beer and wipes his mouth with the back of his hand, she thought.

"Hallo," Eva called again, and two more men joined their table. Mary smiled again and realized she was the only one having tea. The two men ordered absinthe, which was what Eva herself was drinking. They were a jolly group and seemed genuinely interested in the problems of painting outdoors.

"So you quit Chaplin's to be on your own?" one of the latecomers said. "He wouldn't accept me. I was mad with jealousy when Eva was accepted."

His friend Paul, who looked older than the others, smiled. "To be able to say you were one of Chaplin's students could get you a few portrait commissions."

"And then I would be expected to paint that yellow-orange flesh. No thank you."

"Do I hear principles?" Marcel asked.

"Then you don't care for portrait painting?" Paul asked.

"Oh no," Mary said. "I certainly do want to paint people, but I want to paint truthfully. I don't want to paste an artificial style on an accurate rendering of features and call it a portrait."

"Bravo. You must join us on our next outdoor painting trip. Truth is what we are after, too."

Mary smiled and nodded. She did want to join them. They obviously knew what they were about and had admired much of the same works she did. They were doing what she wanted to do. But to accompany these men was unthinkable for a woman like herself. "Perhaps Eva would like to come," Mary heard herself say.

Eva was not free, of course, and Mary hesitated. She couldn't go off with these men she had just met, but Paul was older and surely a gentlemen. Even though he was poor, good breeding showed. She hated the constraint of being a woman, with virtue to protect at all costs. Men didn't have to worry about virtue. They were free. She envied them. Could she suggest that she invite a companion, perhaps Angela, or anyone? She did so want to join them and learn from them what she could.

"I shall bring my wife along so you'll have another woman to talk to," Paul said. "She sometimes consents to model for us."

Mary beamed. There was no longer a reason to hesitate. "What should I bring?" she asked.

"Only what you can carry easily. A small canvas."

"Walking shoes," Paul said, "and a hat to shade your eyes."

"What time?"

"We'll meet here at nine o'clock."

Mary was exhilarated. Her father wouldn't approve. Well, it couldn't be helped. She had to learn a few elements of this new way to see and paint.

5

SHE SHOULD HAVE KNOWN it was too perfect to last. Just because she stopped reading the newspaper, the news didn't go away. In 1870 Paris was threatened. Mary heard the talk everywhere she turned. The Prussians were coming out of the north. There was talk of bloodshed. As the ranks of the French army swelled, the Barries whispered about being ready to return to America. Clara Barrie packed boxes of valuables to be shipped to her parents' home in Virginia for safekeeping. The Prussians were still advancing, but surely they would be repulsed any day. Paris was ablaze with sunshine and excitement and Mary, for the first time, was directing her own life and doing it in a most delightful way.

However, that ended the afternoon Clara Barrie called her into the parlor. Mary entered smiling, with Angela on her heels. They stopped short when they saw the telegraph messenger. He handed Mary an envelope.

"Thank you," she muttered, and he tipped his hat and left.

Clara stood wringing her handkerchief. "Well, read it, dear. It's from America."

Mary's stomach fluttered as she ripped open the envelope and unfolded the paper. It was from her father. RETURN TO PHILADELPHIA IMMEDIATELY. When she read the first line aloud, she sat down on the divan, and with a sinking feeling spreading over her, she read the rest. PASSAGE HAS BEEN BOOKED AND PAID FOR STOP YOU SAIL ON THE 23RD STOP CONFIRM BOOKING STOP LETTER POSTED TO GRANGER BARRIE SETTLING YOUR AFFAIRS STOP WE FEAR FOR YOUR SAFETY AND COUNT THE DAYS UNTIL YOUR RETURN STOP.

Mary stuffed the message back into the envelope, but knew there was no way to change this decision. She would have to go away and leave the life she loved. Angela pressed her hand. Mary swallowed, and blinking back a tear, told Clara she could never thank her enough for everything.

"We will be going, too," Clara said, her own voice unsteady. "Granger hoped, as we all did, that the Prussians would be stopped at the border. When that didn't happen and they kept advancing, there was nothing any of us could do."

"Of course. I see." Mary, feeling control ebbing away, excused herself to begin her packing.

SHE FELT ILL even before the ship sailed. The sickness washed away all her other concerns, even her regret at leaving Paris. It took away all thought, all sense of time and continuity. It was all consuming, and the only relief would be home and the faces of her family. Day and night the rolling sea erased her passion for art as it seemed to erase her will altogether. She longed for the comfort of her mother, and remembering her mother's advice, she forced herself to walk as much as she could, and to take the air once a day. But at night in her delirium she imagined a burning, devastated Paris. She tried to draw, but her hands shook so she could hardly hold the pencil. She tried to read. She thought of dear Lydia, and Aleck, married now to Lois Buchanan and the father of a son, of Gard away at school, and of riding with her father the way they used to. She was going home, putting all those torturous miles of ocean between her and the Paris she loved.

She had enjoyed the Barries; they were good to her. But when she saw her mother and father, Lydia and Gard, and Aleck, Lois, and baby Eddie waiting on the dock, she wept with deep joy. They all wept. But soon enough their faces were all smiles again. She was home and happy to be there.

On the second night after her arrival, when she felt quite well again, she wanted to show her mother, father, and Lydia the paintings she brought home. The boxes containing her work were carried into the parlor and her large easel was fetched. Then one by one she put the pictures on the easel for them to view, explaining how she had happened to paint each one. There were paintings copied at the Louvre and studies done at Chaplin's studio and the rest were entirely her own works.

"These last three probably seem unfinished, but they were done outdoors, painting directly on the canvas while in the field. Some artists do this exclusively and I did enjoy the times I went with them."

Her father seemed particularly pleased with Mary's progress. "You are a professional artist now," he said with pride.

"You've worked hard," her mother said, "and we're proud of you."

"I love the girl leaning on the railing," Lydia said, picking it up and looking at it closer.

"It's one of my first outdoor paintings. Louisine Elder posed for it. Would you like to have it?"

"Oh, I couldn't. It's so charming, you'll want to display it."

Mary laughed. "I hadn't thought of that."

"Why haven't you thought of it?" her father asked rather sternly. "You trained yourself to paint well enough to have your pictures in the best galleries. You're an artist and you must do what artists do; display your work."

"Yes, I suppose so," Mary said, remembering with revulsion the stories she had heard from her friends in Paris about the humiliation of taking their paintings to a dealer only to have him shake his head and send them away. Mary had been grateful she didn't have to do that. Her art was her passion and it didn't have to serve as a means of putting bread on the table.

"I don't suppose it's right to display the copies made at the Louvre," her father said thoughtfully.

"Oh no, they're studies."

"I think we should show the others to a dealer in Philadelphia."

"No, Father," she said, "they're not good enough yet."

"We'll see."

"I think they're good," Lydia said.

Katherine interrupted. "The sensible thing is to get an opinion from a dealer."

Mary looked once again at the canvases strewn around the parlor. They no longer were her own treasured belongings. They were objects for commerce. It was a shock somehow, though she knew it shouldn't have been. She intended some day to display her work, but these—it was hard to think of offering any of them for sale. It was like she herself would be on display. They were so personal. Didn't they understand?

Her family had accepted her professional status before she had. And here was her father showing her the room he had redone as a studio so she could continue her work. He said he had hoped she would want to do a portrait of her nephew.

"Yes, of course." She was stunned by all this, not at all prepared for it. She was a student, not a master. Did they really believe she could paint a professional portrait? Her head was spinning and yet she wanted to try.

Later that same week, Mary and her father took a few paintings to a respected dealer in Philadelphia. He was a fastidious-looking man of about fifty who did not smile as he accepted the paintings with cool dignity and had them taken to a back room to examine them. "Pardon me," he said, leaving Mary and Robert to wait in the salon. She passed the time by looking at the paintings hung in the room. They were mostly English and academic with a few picturesque landscapes. She thought a work by Winslow Homer had unique appeal. When the door to the back room opened, the dealer looked directly at her father, avoiding Mary's gaze altogether.

"We will take two of the paintings on consignment because of the family's position and influence. However, you must realize there is really no market here for—ahem—*ladies' paintings*."

Mary thought he spoke the last words with such disdain it was as though they had asked him to handle week-old fish. Mary burned with humiliation and anger. She felt the urge to curse him the way she had heard the stableman curse, or worse. Why was *he* so haughty? Ladies' paintings indeed! She would show that snobby jackass one of these days.

Robert's face was stony as they took *all* the paintings back to the carriage and started home. Only a few words were spoken on the way. Mary guessed her father was as angry as she. They rode home in silence.

The next day, when her humiliation had faded somewhat, Mary wanted to put the incident out of her mind. She sketched the maid and her father and mother, then settled down to doing a study of Lydia in oils. The sun streamed through the window and illuminated Lydia's face from the left, causing her hair to glisten and her skin to take on a transluscent quality. They were alone and after a while Mary asked, "Have you been well?"

"Mostly, yes."

"Your eyes look puffy."

"I know, and my ankles are swollen today. It's not been bad though, not since July. I had a bad spell then. Did Mother write you?"

"She did, but she's always careful not to worry me."

Lydia smiled wanly, and squinted.

"Is it tiring you to pose?"

"No, I find it relaxing. It makes me feel useful and I so seldom am."

"That's not true and you know it." As Mary spoke she saw something in Lydia's face she had never seen before, a straight-out gaze of helpless acceptance, but it lasted only a moment and was replaced by the usual smile. Still, it seared itself in Mary's consciousness and made her think that Lydia in her quiet life had experienced enough to make her bitter, but she would not be so. She had the same store of determination that Aleck and Mary had, and all of it had to be used to keep going happily on with her life. It hurt Mary that her lovely sister hadn't yet been cured of her kidney ailment. She always did exactly what the doctors advised.

Lydia chattered now about people they knew, and who had called and what had happened in their lives. Mary thought it strange Lydia said practically nothing about their sister-in-law. Lois was a proud girl, President Buchanan's niece. She was pretty and Aleck adored her. But Lydia had not mentioned her once. When brought to the subject of Aleck's family, Lydia talked at length and with pleasure about her nephew Eddie.

"It would be such fun having him here, but she keeps him so tightly in tow it's impossible to play with him. Oh, but it will be different when you begin your portrait of him. He'll stay the whole afternoon each day."

"I hope so. I'll need quite a lot of time to do a good job."

"Insist on it right from the start," Lydia said. "Tell Aleck."

"Yes, I will."

"Aleck will some day be a millionaire, you know."

"Aleck?"

"He's doing very well with the railroad."

"That's nice."

"Yes, I'm glad for him." Lydia's smile was constant. Mary wondered how she could ever paint the courage of that smile. She looked carefully and drew, and when it was done, it was a satisfying study, but there was so much more she didn't know how to show.

The next day Lois brought her son to pose. Mary had not expected the costume Eddie wore: a red velvet suit with white lace collar and cuffs, ruffles at the knees, and a wide sash. His long golden curls were brushed to a sheen under his velvet hat. He stood reluctantly by his mother's side as Mary glanced at him and smiled.

"We'd like a formal portrait," Lois said. "I shall have the carriage here for him at five each evening. You'll be through by then, won't you?"

Mary nodded. She said she would prepare some sketches first and together they could choose the best pose. Lois agreed to look at sketches the next day, kissed Eddie, and was off to attend a luncheon, leaving Eddie's nana to care for him. Mary was surprised but somewhat relieved that Lois didn't want to stay for the sitting. Lydia fairly trembled with pleasure at having Eddie to themselves. She did not waste a moment after his mother was gone to ply him with surprises she had been planning.

Mary sketched him seated, holding a sailboat. She sketched him standing, which was more difficult for both of them. She hesitated doing him as he sat on the floor laughing and playing with the dog; hardly a formal portrait. Nevertheless she sketched it. Maybe Lois would change her mind and ask for something less traditional.

As it turned out Lois was definitely set on the standing pose even after Mary recommended having him seated. "Eddie will stand as straight as a solider, won't you, son?" she said. Eddie nodded.

"A graceful drapery with a little shimmer in the background should do nicely," she added.

Mary nodded; although she would have chosen a simple costume, a comfortable pose, and a natural background. She shook her head after Lois had taken Eddie away. So this is what it's like, she mused. It's no wonder some artists dislike doing portraits.

Between Lydia bringing him cookies, Nana washing his hands, and Eddie asking constantly if it was time to rest yet, the sessions went slowly. It was only natural for a child to fidget, especially while trying to stand in one place. But the more she worked, the more determined she grew to complete the picture to the satisfaction of all. She had to prove to her family all over again that she could paint, especially after what that dealer had said. Even though no one spoke of it, she could not forget those words or the haughty way in which they were delivered. Her portrait of Eddie must be absolutely professional; none of her own fancy would be allowed to show.

When the portrait was almost finished, Mary's father came into the studio after dinner to look at it. "Lois wanted a formal pose," Mary offered. Robert nodded abstractly. It was not the portrait he came to discuss.

"I have made some inquiries of art dealers in Chicago."

"You what?"

He sat in his upright manner, crossing his legs. "Philadelphia is hobbled by its own narcissistic self-importance. In Philadelphia you can never be counted if you were born in Pittsburgh. What I'm saying is that society here tends not to look at merit. It looks at birth. You'll have to show your paintings in a more democratic city and I have it from a knowing source that Chicago is indeed that kind of a city."

"You think I should send my work to Chicago?"

"Send it or take it. I truly think your work deserves a better reception than it could get here."

"Father—I—you really think—" Mary found herself unable to speak.

"I think you are a professional and now you must think and act like a professional. That means you're going to have to face these dealers. Be proud of what you've achieved; approach these business-men like a man would approach them."

Mary still didn't know what to say. Being a professional was complicated. "But I don't know anything about business."

"You know what you want a dealer to do. You want him to take your paintings and sell them for you. So you go up to him and you smile and you present him with a letter of introduction, if you like, and you tell him you have some paintings you'd like him to handle for you. Then you show him the pictures just as you showed us."

Mary smiled nervously. "It sounds simple."

"It is."

"What do I say if he says there's no market for ladies' paintings?"

Robert raised his eyebrows. "If you choose to argue the point, you would be well justified."

"I suppose that's about the worst thing that could happen."

"Yes, and you've already survived that bit of rudeness."

Mary nodded and looked at her father. Amusement slowly rose within her. "You have thought it all through, haven't you?"

"Indeed I have. It's a father's duty to advise his offspring in business matters."

She gazed into his shrewd eyes. He was looking upon her the

same way he looked upon Aleck, giving her the same credit. He wanted her to succeed as much as she herself did. Only now she wanted it doubly, for his sake as well as her own. And it was important that she herself perform the humiliating task of taking her own wares to market. That was part of being independent. Was it possible that her father understood her and her needs better than she did?

"I'll take your advice," she said smiling. "Will you help me?"

"Naturally. I intend to do what I can."

"Oh, and Father, do you think it would be all right if Lydia went with me?"

"Lydia?"

"Wouldn't she enjoy a trip away? Trains are very comfortable. And her health seems good. Besides, I would take care of her."

His face went blank. "It's a question that will take some thought," he said. "It might help her spirits, but let me think about it."

THE DOCTOR examined Lydia and pronounced her fit enough to travel. However, she was to restrict her diet to eliminate all rich foods and rest at least fourteen hours out of each day. He provided a list of foods that should not be eaten; included was chocolate, which Lydia loved now and then.

Lydia was delighted to be asked to go. She didn't mind the diet at all. As long as she could have tea and toast she would be content.

A few days later while Robert was in the studio overseeing the packing of Mary's paintings, he looked up suddenly from the task to coach her about what she might say to the dealers. "You're not to hang back and let them do all the talking. At times like these, parlor manners are not necessarily what is needed. Do you understand?"

"Yes, Father, I think I do. I am to be a businesswoman."

"Yes, but no flim-flam. Oh, never mind that; I know you wouldn't. You have too much pride."

"Too much?"

"No—no. You'll do just fine. I'm sure you will. You can be very convincing when you put your mind to it." He smiled.

Mary had the feeling it took great restraint for him to stay home and let her do this alone. Yet now that he had brought her to this challenge, she realized how important it was for her to do it herself. What a father he was. She had never loved him more than at this moment.

6

LYDIA AND MARY, accompanied by Lydia's maid, Mrs. Currey, left on a morning train. Lydia looked radiant as they sat gazing out of the window at the fields of corn whizzing by. Mary, however, felt uneasy. She tried to concentrate on the book Aleck had given her. It was an exciting kind of story, just what she needed to take her mind off the swaying of the train. But the words and letters swam crazily across the page as the car swayed. She put the book down and smiled at Lydia, who put her book down, too. "Have you read anything good lately?" Mary asked.

"Mmm," Lydia pursed her lips thoughtfully. "I found Mesmer's theories quite interesting and now there are Darwin's new ideas."

"Darwin?" Mary repeated. "What do Mother and Father think of your reading that?"

"Father is fair. He doesn't expect me to follow him or Mother in everything. But I've never discussed Darwin with them."

"I don't think Father would approve, from what I've heard of Darwin."

"It's not like what you heard. It's logical. He's a scientist. I envy men like Darwin, especially since I've been feeling my world shrinking about me lately. Wouldn't it be lovely to travel like this all the way out to Wyoming territory?"

"Maybe some day you will."

"Maybe. Wouldn't you like to go, too?"

"I don't think so. I don't care for soldiers and Indians warring and all that hardship you hear about."

"Indians have a fascinating culture," Lydia said, her gaze drifting off. She retold tales she had read of Indians and their customs. Mary listened, letting Lydia's enthusiasm and interest spread to herself. Lydia expressed her thoughts in a way she never did at home. And Mary responded, pouring out her own thoughts, her nervousness over this trip, her fear that Chicago art dealers would be just as difficult as Philadelphians. "And I'm afraid my work isn't good enough. I didn't do it expecting to take these pictures to a dealer. They were mostly done as serious practice."

"They're better than many pictures hanging in quite respectable places," Lydia said. "You must believe in yourself."

"I know I must, and I'm not sure I do."

"Your paintings are good. Father and Mother both know art. They looked at yours objectively. Aleck thinks you're good enough to paint a picture of his Eddie. And so does Lois. They can afford the best artist in the country."

"Oh, Lydia, they're all family."

"Don't worry. We'll find an art dealer who will recognize your talent."

Mary sighed. She would be glad when it was over and they were on their way back home.

They looked at hundreds of farms and small towns and when they finally arrived in Chicago, the sight of the tall buildings and busy streets was oddly exciting. "Here we are," Lydia said. "Isn't it wonderful?"

"I hope so," Mary answered.

They took a public carriage to their hotel. Mary decided the first thing she would do in the morning was take her work to the art dealer on the top of the list. There would be no putting off. The very nearness and certainty of the event excited her, made her want to face these dealers with pride. She couldn't sleep because she spent all night imagining conversations that all ended in the dealers flooding her with praise. Not once did she imagine it the other way.

She set off toward the closest art gallery first, taking three small paintings that she could easily carry in a shopping bag. Lydia and Mrs. Currey stayed at the hotel and had breakfast. The gallery was three blocks from the hotel and when she got to it, she thought it looked rather small and dingy. But she swallowed and went inside. There was a woman dressed in blue at the desk. She was tall with a flat face. When Mary came in, the woman looked up and took off her glasses. "Hello," Mary said. "I'd like to speak to the proprietor. Would that be you?"

The woman smiled. "That would be my husband, Mr. Frost. He's gone today. Might I help?"

"I brought some paintings. I thought perhaps your gallery would want to show them for me. I studied at the Pennsylvania Academy of Art and in Paris with Charles Chaplin." Mary drew a deep breath.

The woman looked serious. "Do you have the paintings with you?"

"Yes, in here," Mary said, holding up her bag.

"I could tell you if it's worth coming back," the woman said.

"I suppose you could." She carefully took out one of the pictures. It was wrapped in tissue so the frames wouldn't get marred. The woman took it and unwrapped it and held it out at arm's length. Mary's face burned and her stomach muscles tightened. But the woman smiled.

"It's very pretty."

"Oh," Mary smiled. "Thank you."

"May I see the others?"

Mary nodded and handed her the next one. The woman unwrapped it and Mary brought out the last one and began taking the tissue off it. She stared down at Louisine with a green parasol, hoping Mrs. Frost would like it, or at least that she wouldn't say anything about ladies' paintings.

"They are all very nice," the woman said. "I think my husband would want to take one or two of them and see how it goes. We'd have to take them on consignment, though. That's the way we do business. We charge a thirty percent commission to unestablished artists. Is that agreeable?"

Mary nodded. She had no idea if that was good or bad. What was it her father had told her about commissions? She couldn't remember.

"I wish we had room to take them all. But when we sell the ones we have, you can bring more."

Mary nodded, searching for something to say.

"This one definitely," the woman said, indicating Louisine and the parasol, "and I think this one with the blue hat. Give me your name and address and we'll be in touch with you."

Mary sat down and wrote out her name and address. She thanked Mrs. Frost, took her receipt, and said she thought Chicago was a lovely city.

SHE WAS ANXIOUS to tell Lydia. When she got to the hotel, the urge to hurry was so great, she could not control it any longer. She pulled up her skirt and ran up the stairs. The room door was locked but Mrs. Currey opened it quickly and Mary sailed in. "Frost Galleries took two of them on consignment," she announced.

Lydia hugged her. "I knew it," she said.

Mary put the remaining picture down on the crate that contained her other paintings. "Now I'll have a cup of tea or coffee and we can shop. No more business until tomorrow."

That night after dinner they went out to take some air, but it was cold and windy and they hurried back to the warmth of the hotel, wishing they had brought heavier wraps.

Mrs. Currey had set up the board for a game of parcheesi, when they heard a frantic knock at their door. Mrs. Currey answered it. "A fire!" she said, returning to the rooms with terror on her face. "We must get our coats and pocketbooks and gather in the lobby."

Lydia looked utterly distracted, but in a moment fumbled for her shoes. Mrs. Currey rushed to help her.

"A fire? In *this* hotel?"

"No, I don't think so, Miss Lydia, but somewhere close by. He said we should be in the lobby in five minutes." Even as she spoke, there was a noise in the hall, hurried footsteps, and excited voices.

"What about my paintings?" Mary said. She went to the crate, but found it too heavy to budge.

"We'll get someone to bring them down," Lydia said. Her face was flushed as she hurried with her shoes. Mrs. Currey snatched Lydia's coat and hat from the closet, and grabbed her own. "Let's hurry."

"Wait, Mrs. Currey," Mary pleaded. "I think if you could lift one end of this crate, the two of us can manage it."

There was another knock at the door and a uniformed doorman asked if everyone was ready to leave. Mary told him they needed help with the crate. He shook his head. "I'm afraid you'll have to leave the crate."

"That's not possible. My paintings are in there."

The doorman looked sympathetic, but shrugged. "Only people are being evacuated. There is not enough room for all of *them* in the carriages. And since you cannot carry this, you'll have to leave it."

"Maybe we *can* carry it. Mrs. Currey, see if you can get that end."

Mrs. Currey heaved her shoulder to the crate and it moved a few inches.

"All right," the doorman said. "When all the guests are safe, I'll come back and get your crate." He smiled reassuringly, and laid his hand on Mary's shoulder as he led them to the door.

"Come along, Mary," Mrs. Currey said. "That is the most sensible thing to do. We can't carry a crate and take proper care of Lydia at the same time."

Still Mary hesitated, staring at the crate. Should she take out a couple of paintings and leave the rest until later? Before she could act, she felt herself being pushed by Mrs. Currey and pulled by Lydia.

There was an air of panic in the lobby. The orange glow of the fire casting its bright surges skyward could be seen from the street in front of the hotel. The strong wind, changing directions, spreading flame, created dozens of growing and spreading fires. Lydia's eyes were open wide with fear. They huddled together, listening to announcements barked through a horn to the guests. They were told to remain calm, that carriages would take them to safety. The strongest were asked to walk.

Mary looked at Lydia's strained face and worried. She hadn't had her rest. The trip had undoubtedly tired her. And now what would Lydia have to bear?

After a tense wait they squeezed into a carriage with four other people and were driven away. The streets were filled with people all moving and shouting. The fire still advanced. They could hear it and smell it and they couldn't help looking back at the glowing sky and the blazing tongues that seemed to leap out of the earth.

At first Mary was in a daze. It seemed a nightmare she would soon wake from, and yet it was worse than that. What nightmare was accompanied by such a fiercely blowing cold wind? Lydia was shivering. Mary couldn't think of what to do next, except that they must find a shelter for her sister.

When the carriage stopped, they were at a clearing near the shore of the lake. There were tents silhouetted against the eerie sky, and when they stepped to the ground, a bitter cold wind became the immediate enemy. A baby cried nearby. People stood, hugging their shoulders and gazing at what seemed like the whole city in flame. For an instant Mary thought of a painting by Turner, of London burning in yellows and orange. Then with a pang, Mary thought of her own paintings in the hotel. She didn't want to think of flames dancing maliciously over the heavy wooden crate, consuming fifteen of her best paintings. The icy wind stung her cheeks and made her eyes water. She must get Lydia into the shelter of a tent. That was all that mattered now.

They hurried toward the tents, where hot cider was being

served. Mary, Lydia, and Mrs. Currey each took a cup, hoping to gain some warmth from it. Mary had never seen so many people all in one place, crowded together like chickens in a coop. Had there ever been so many stunned faces assembled before? Even so, a few people tried to make a joke of their predicament. Lydia smiled and helped an old woman to a place where she could sit down. Yes, people do have to help each other, Mary thought. Following Lydia's lead, she took a crying baby from an exhausted-looking mother's tired arms. She rocked it gently until it stopped crying and closed its eyes.

It was a night none of them would forget, full of the sounds and odors of people huddled too closely together, not knowing how long they would be in that place or what had happened to the places they had left. People blew their frosty breath on their cold-stiffened fingers as announcements of the fire's devastation were given. Everything in the block where the hotel had stood was burned. It was unbelievable, but the announcements were repeated every few minutes. There was no doubt it was true. The city was burning like straw.

Just before morning, when the announcements had stopped and people were trying to sleep, Mary closed her eyes and let herself realize the paintings were gone. But what were a few paintings compared to a city?

In the morning Lydia's eyes were swollen and her skin was dull and ashen. After one look at her Mary was determined to find a room, though it seemed to be an impossible task. She talked to the woman who was in charge. No, she shook her head sadly. "The hospitals are full."

"I don't want a hospital," Mary replied but the woman shook her head. Dejectedly, Mary wandered away from the encampment. She saw a boy walking along the road with his dog and she stopped him. "Do you live around here?"

The boy nodded. "Down there," he said.

"I was hoping to find someone like you who would like to earn some money."

"Doing what, ma'am?"

"Finding a room in a nice home where three ladies could stay for a night or two. I would be willing to pay up to twenty-five dollars and I'll give you ten dollars if you find a satisfactory place. My sister is not too well and needs to rest."

"Ten dollars! Did you say ten dollars?"

"That's right. Do you think you could find us something soon?"

"Wow—I think so—but I don't know."

"Just a simple room. I'll be in that brown tent by the two oak trees. My name is Miss Cassatt. Can you remember that?"

"Miss Cassatt." He nodded. "And you'll be in the tent by those two oak trees."

"And I would pay extra for a carriage to take us there."

"I don't know . . . gee . . ."

"Try—please."

"Yes, Miss Cassatt."

Mary wondered if she'd ever see him again. Rooms anywhere around would be very dear. But she had a little hope as she went back. He would try.

Lydia looked miserable and admitted she was tired, but became cheery when Mary told her about the boy. "I'm sure he'll come back," Lydia said. "A bed would be nice; if I could only rest, I'd be all right."

Fear suddenly gripped Mary; what would happen to Lydia if they did not find a room? She would be sick and then they *would* need a hospital. Mary felt helpless. Lydia's eyes were already glassy and her hands trembled. Mrs. Currey looked worried, but when Mary came back, she went off to find out if there would be tea or coffee available. "Poor Mrs. Currey," Lydia said. "We mustn't worry her."

"No."

"There is water in that pitcher on the table," Lydia said.

"Yes. I hear they have plenty of water now. Can I get some for you?"

Lydia sighed and moistened her lips with her tongue. "I'm awfully thirsty, but I shouldn't drink when my body wants to retain fluids. See how my wrists have gotten; touch it."

Mary pressed her thumb and fingers over Lydia's wrist. The flesh seemed puffy and spongy.

"That's fluid. My body isn't taking it off properly."

"But if you're thirsty, maybe your body is telling you to drink to start things functioning."

"If I don't drink, the thirst will go away, and I'll quit being thirsty."

"What does the doctor say?"

"Not to drink—but once I did it anyway. When no one was around I drank four glasses of water all at once. I felt very wicked and I think I expected to die. But when I woke the next morning, I was better."

"Then have a glass of water if you want it. If it might help, why not?"

"Mrs. Currey watches me. But all right, I think I will."

Mary brought the water and watched Lydia drink, hoping it wouldn't hurt her. She believed it wouldn't, but what if it did? She felt her heart quicken as she retrieved the glass from Lydia's hand.

"Just a little more," Lydia said, but Mary hesitated, until she glanced at Lydia's expectant eyes. She went back to the table, filled the glass half full and brought it to Lydia.

"Thank you."

Mary sat down next to Lydia, took her sister's hand, and examined her wrist again.

"Don't worry. I have these ups and downs. It's nothing. I'll be fine. It's you I worry about. Oh, Mary, your beautiful paintings." Lydia's eyes welled with compassion.

"There's nothing we can do about that now," Mary said, trying to sound unaffected. "I will paint more."

"How can you take it like this? It was the most awful thing."

Mary smiled. "No, maybe it wasn't. I thought about it during the night. I went over each one of the paintings in my mind until I realized something I'd only felt hints of before."

"What?"

"That if I had known when I was painting that portrait of

Angela in a blue hat that it would be put up against the best paintings
and offered for sale, there would have been more work in the dress
and hair and the shadows with their delicate shadings. But when I
did Angela and the one of Louisine in green, I didn't challenge my
skills much. I wanted a pretty effect. And when I got it, I quit. Those
paintings were an immature student's work. I must have suspected it
all along, but I was so blinded by the approval of others that it didn't
come clear to me until now. It's best they're gone so at least I can't
cling to my own imperfections, admire a few good effects, and fail to
paint with all of my abilities."

Lydia frowned. "I loved those paintings. I don't understand—"

"What it means is I have to work harder. Like the old masters
worked, and not like a hack who turns out something pretty and
does it over and over."

"But what's wrong with something pretty? I delight in seeing
beauty. Am I wrong to love beauty for its own sake?"

"No, I love it, too, but it's not enough."

"It is for people like me. At least we have the ones you left
behind and the portrait of Eddie."

Mary pursed her lips and looked off. "The portrait of Eddie is
something to be ashamed of."

"Mary! How could you say that? It's perfect. You worked hard
to make it perfect. You did it as a professional."

"The pose is wrong. The costume is wrong. The whole thing is
artificial."

"Oh, no, Mary. It's fine."

"Lois seems to like it well enough, but I can tell you it is despic-
able. I'll be glad to have it as a constant reminder that I must work for
truth. I need more study, more work."

Two hours passed. Lydia shivered and her breathing became
labored. She didn't complain, but Mary was worried, and it was clear
by Mrs. Currey's downcast looks and quiet manner that she was
concerned, too. The *railroad,* Mary thought. If they could only reach
someone from the railroad who knew Aleck, perhaps someone
would put them up until they could arrange to leave. But they were

four miles from the nearest railroad station, and there were no trains running. How could she find someone who knew Aleck? There must be a way to get help—she must think.

Suddenly, she saw a dog from the corner of her eye and stood up just as the boy spotted her.

"My father is waiting with the buggy. I hope it's clean enough. Ten dollars is enough to buy shoes for all us kids and the room has two windows and a big bed. My father and mother usually sleep in it, but they'll sleep upstairs in the attic for a few days."

Mary smiled, and turned to Lydia. "Come along. We don't want to keep them waiting," she said.

7

MARY HAD SENT a telegram home saying they were safe. She hadn't mentioned her paintings in the message, but her father must have guessed. When they got home he avoided Mary's eyes for an hour. She finally told them the paintings had burned, and there was a short silence. Her mother said the consoling things Mary expected to hear. Lydia again lamented the loss and the unfairness of it. Her father looked serious, grunted, and said nothing.

In the days that followed, Mary painted her mother sewing, did two studies of Mrs. Currey, and asked her father if he would sit for her. He agreed, and on one of those quiet afternoons as Mary concentrated on the drawing of her father's eyes, he moved suddenly, thwarting her analysis. She put down her brush and was about to suggest a rest, when he said, "You've been a different person ever since the paintings burned."

"Yes, I suppose you're right. I've been reassessing my work."

"Your paintings seem better. I noticed when I first saw the painting of Mrs. Currey."

Mary nodded.

"But you have not been happy at your work. You don't smile. You drive yourself and your sitters."

"I'm not unhappy," she said, "But I'm not satisfied."

"What doesn't satisfy you?"

"I want to stop being a student and become a working professional artist, and yet I think I need more study. I'm working as earnestly as I can to see how far I have come, and what I need."

"And what have you decided?"

"I need another year in the museums with the Italian and Dutch painters. Oh, Father, I know if I could have that, I could begin my professional career without all this uncertainty."

"A year away?"

"Yes."

"Your mother and I had hoped you'd stay home. I even talked to a real estate broker about renting a studio here in Philadelphia. He showed me a choice piece of property in the most fashionable neighborhood. Since we have adequate connections here, it wouldn't be long before you could build up a good following."

"I think I need another year's work."

"Perhaps what you need is the independence of your own place to work."

Mary didn't want to hurt her father. He had given her so much, but she felt strongly that she was close now to what her whole being cried out for. She couldn't stop. There was something she hungered for. "I appreciate everything you've done, but I'm not ready, and I don't think Philadelphia is ready for me." She smiled and picked up her brush.

"At least let me show you the place," he said. "I could take you there now. The carriage is ready."

THE PROPERTY was truly an artist's dream. It was located on an avenue lined with prosperous shops and tea rooms. There were other successful portrait studios nearby. That meant the comradeship of other artists. Her father had thought of everything. Inside there was as much room as there had been at Chaplin's studio in Paris. "It's lovely," Mary whispered. "I can't imagine how any studio could be nicer."

"This could be the end of your journey."

She was overwhelmed. She thought about that hateful art dealer. In time she could make him sorry he insulted her.

"What do you say?"

Mary nodded and stammered. "It's perfect. Let's think about it, though."

On the way home she conjured dreams of a life she hadn't before contemplated. She would love being close to her family and at the same time free to work undisturbed in such a place.

When they got back, Mary went to her studio room, looking around at the cluttered space. The light there was woefully inadequate, but still she was disturbed. She studied the unfinished painting of her father on the easel. In anguish she examined the other works, and after a while she went to find her father. He was hunched over his desk, his glasses slipped down to the end of his nose. He smiled when he saw her.

"Father, don't think me ungrateful, please, but I need another year of study. I cannot take the studio." She took a long determined breath. "I promise you that after one year I shall be good enough to have paintings hung in the Paris Salon."

Robert Cassatt pushed his glasses back on the bridge of his nose and looked at her squarely. There was a trace of sadness on his face. "All right, all right. You can go for one year."

MARY REMEMBERED particularly the works of Correggio she had copied at the Louvre. His greatest work was in a cathedral in Parma. She searched among her things for the copies she had done of his work, and the next morning after she had worked on her father's portrait she brought them out and showed them to him.

"These were from studies Correggio did for his decoration of a marvelous cathedral. I've heard how beautiful the ceiling is, more beautiful than Michelangelo's work on the Sistine, some say. And I've heard the frescos in the cathedral are going to ruin, just crumbling off the walls."

"Surely there is a restorer at work. Italy wouldn't let great works be lost, would she?"

"I hope you're right. Anyway, Parma is where I'd like to work for a while."

"Who would you be with in Parma?"

Mary sighed. Of course he would want to know that, and she quickly got to work. Since she knew no one there, she started with a letter to friends she had known in Paris who were now living in Rome. She asked them to make inquiries for her. It took three months to make arrangements satisfactory to her father. But when it was done, Mary felt better about it herself. While in Parma she would study drawing and engraving under Carlo Raimondi, who, she had learned, felt the same way Mary did about studying the masters.

It was with a great sense of purpose she embarked for Rome. The days aboard ship were lost to her in spite of Mrs. Currey's and Lydia's medicines. The sea could not be tricked and won the battle over her again. It was the price and she paid it willingly.

Rome was even lovelier than she had imagined. But it was, as she had feared, too full of wonders and distractions, each as lovely as the last, like the endless necklace of pearls she chose as a gift for Lydia. The only copying she was able to manage was contained in one sketchbook. However, she had begun a portrait of her hostess in a black dress and hat. It was an honest painting and as she worked on it, she became excited about the quality of it. It was the sort of thing she had wanted to do but hadn't yet achieved. Mrs. Cortier was as pleased with the portrait as Mary was, and made Mary promise she would finish it in Parma and send it back.

"You haven't flattered me at all, have you? But this makes me like myself the way I am. You must finish it. I shall have it properly framed. If it turns out as well as I think it will, I will personally see that it is sent to the Paris Salon."

Mary promised.

THE TRAIN RIDE to Parma started pleasantly, and the day grew so warm it was impossible not to have the windows open. The fine dust of a parched countryside sifted steadily through the window. By the time Mary arrived at the Parma station, she was choked with dust and covered with it from her hat to her new Roman kid shoes. It was quiet in Parma at that hour in the afternoon. No one met her since she had not known precisely when she would arrive and consequently made no arrangements. She enjoyed the feeling of independence for a few minutes, but then there was the problem of getting her luggage transported to her rooms. When she asked a porter to summon a carriage, he merely shrugged and laughed. She tried again, speaking slowly, but again the porter's response was one of amusement. She tried asking him in French, and he nodded his head, but still did not seem to understand. She turned to go find someone else who might understand either French or English, but the porter tapped her shoulder. When she turned to him, he pointed to a public carriage drawing up to the front of the station. She answered his questioning look with a vigorous nodding of her head. He smiled and took her luggage to the carriage. She did not forget the gratuity her father had cautioned her to have ready.

The heat was oppressive and the dust gathered along her hot neck, but she was excited and happy. She realized she would have a difficult time communicating at first, but she'd manage. After all, here was the isolation she craved. Here there would be nothing to disturb her.

The rooms that were reserved for her were on the third floor of a good house close to the academy. From her window she looked down on pink brick palazzos, and in the distance was the spire of the cathedral. After she had bathed and rested, it was cool enough to stroll along the street. She wanted to locate the academy and the museum, perhaps see the theater built in honor of Verdi, and find an attractive café or two. It was wonderful to be on her own, and she would be able to do what she wanted most. She paused in front of the museum, knowing that inside were Correggio's madonnas. There would be a few Parmagianinos, too. She could hardly wait to get started.

She returned the next morning just as the doors were being opened. Her heart was full with anticipation as she began copying the Madonna and St. Jerome. Even as she struggled with the work, she felt good fortune in her bones. This was her opportunity. The lack of artificiality in these subjects could teach truth as well as structure. She painted until one o'clock, then went outside to find a café. She couldn't help smiling at people she passed. At the café she read from the menu, pronouncing her words carefully. When she had eaten her lunch of fish in a delicious sauce and sipped her tea, she hurried back to the museum and worked until it closed.

She felt tired walking back to her rooms that evening, but she was absolutely satisfied. Her mood bordered on the euphoric. She felt she had done the perfect thing in seeking Correggio. The next day she would have to go to the academy and take her place as a student of Carlo Raimondi.

Carlo was a short cheerful person approaching his fiftieth year. His French was slightly better than Mary's Italian, but it wasn't long before she could understand most of what he said, though being understood herself was still a problem, eased somewhat by Carlo's patient, cheerful disposition.

His disorderly workrooms worried Mary quite a bit. She could not abide slovenly habits. They were an indication of weakness and an undisciplined mind. Yet when she saw Carlo's work all of her convictions about disorder dissolved. There could be nothing undisciplined about this man's mind. Although he also taught painting, he considered himself primarily an engraver. His lines were sure and beautiful beyond expectations. Mary admired his skills and earnestness at once. And Carlo found his new student more than industrious. From that first day on, their arrangement was a satisfying one, even though Mary could not express her thoughts very well in Italian. But words weren't the only means of communicating; their work spoke.

Mary divided her time between her formal training at the academy with Carlo and her informal work in the museum and cathedral. Three days a week were spent with Parma's masters and on the other three she went to the academy. She worked from early in the morning until the sun had set. She could not get her fill of work, and on Sunday she would sketch outdoors.

Her first project at the academy was a portrait of a girl with a mandolin. Carlo watched with interest as her work progressed, praising it and offering a few suggestions. There were other portraits after that, including a dancing girl posed to present a difficult foreshortening problem. Carlo was challenging her and she eagerly accepted it. When the painting was half finished, he nodded and clucked. "It is good to turn a problem into a strength. It would benefit you now to do a group of two or three figures. I think you can do this, and here I may be of some help."

Mary liked the idea, but had to search her mind for some appropriate setting for three people to be pictured together. She recalled a painting she had seen by Manet several years before of people on a balcony bathed in sunlight. They were gazing out at something unseen below. She thought of pictorial arrangements, of a triangular composition with intertwining arms and the line of the subjects' gaze tying the picture together. Two women and a man, the man somewhat in shadow.

Carlo was pleased with her sketches. "You ought to try etching on copper, too," he said. "Your drawing is strong enough and your hand is sure."

"When this trio is finished I will try it," she said.

Setting up the models to make the preliminary drawing was not as simple as using a single model. She started the sketch, blocking in the heads, the angles of the shoulders. Lorenzo, Carlo's apprentice printer, braced himself with one hand on a post, his head tilted. As she worked, she envisioned the final painting with excitement. While the models rested, she called to Lorenzo, "Do you have a hat with a swooping brim?" Carlo heard her question and brought the hat. Mary put it on Lorenzo's head and he assumed the pose and held it. When she finished sketching the hat, her voice was soft, "Thank you, Lorenzo. I have it now."

After her drawing was blocked in on the canvas she painted from the models separately. When she was well into the painting she realized she could have done more with Lorenzo's face. It was a strong, nicely boned face with dramatic possibilities she hadn't seen at first. But as the picture was already carefully planned, Mary kept Lorenzo in the half light behind the figures of the two women. On the afternoon of the last of Lorenzo's sittings, he remained in the studio, admiring the finished painting. When Mary was ready to leave, Lorenzo offered to carry her bag.

"Thank you," she said. "That's kind of you."

"You are going directly home this time?"

"Why, yes."

He smiled. "I only asked because if you did want to go to the cathedral as you sometimes do, I would carry your bag there, also."

"Thank you," she said, not showing her surprise at his knowing that she often went to the cathedral after leaving the academy.

"You are quite a woman," he said.

Mary laughed.

"What I mean is you work very hard. I have been here at the academy two years now. I've met many artists, but none who work as hard as you, not even a man."

Mary nodded, smiled, and walked faster. Compliments and flattery of any kind made her uncomfortable and Lorenzo's words made her more uneasy than ever.

"Sometimes you have tea in my cousin's café."

"Rosa—your cousin?"

"Yes." He smiled. "I hope you will allow me to take you there today. Maybe you would like to speak in French," he continued.

"What? Yes, I would certainly like that. I didn't know you spoke French."

"May we have tea?"

She hesitated only a moment. "All right, if you like."

LORENZO ordered the tea and a spicy teacake, though he admitted he usually had a glass of wine at that time of day. Their conversation had switched to French and Mary found herself wanting to talk. She began by discussing the fresco of the Ascension in San Giovanni Evangelista and the Assumption in the dome of the cathedral. "They are disintegrating," she declared passionately. "These are treasures that can never be replaced."

"Yes, it's sad. I have heard it all my life. People come and look. They say this will be done, that will be done—and nothing happens." His face was very expressive; he was strongly masculine and yet more charming, in some ways, than a woman. He combined that manner with a haughty pride. She could see him as a prince, a general, or as—her mind raced. She gulped her tea. "Would you consider posing for me again?" she asked, "as a bull fighter in costume?"

"And what about the bull?"

She laughed. "Without the bull. Now that the balcony scene is finished I could do a painting with you as the main subject with light streaming over your face and perhaps a girl offering you a rose or something. I would like to do a picture with two figures. Carlo recommends it, and if you would consider posing again, I would be very happy."

"Then I could not refuse," he smiled. "A bull fighter, eh? I went to the bullfights in Seville and they are very exciting."

"I imagine they are."

"Then you have not been there."

"No, I haven't."

He laughed. "It should not be so surprising. But Americans have done so much, it seems. And you are an American."

She smiled.

"What is it like where you come from? Is your home like those of Parma?"

Mary described their home in Philadelphia, the hills and the trees and stables. She talked until she was weary. And Lorenzo talked to her of his life. He was going to be a printer with a shop of his own some day. But first, he was going to be a bullfighter.

8

MARY CAME TO THE STUDIO excited about her new project. "Carlo," she called, "I'm going to paint two figures, a girl in profile and a bullfighter in costume."

"Yes, yes, two figures—good. But before we talk about that, I have something to say about your trio."

Mary, seeing his serious look, walked to the painting, alarmed.

"I'm going to ask you to do something you may think is difficult."

Whatever did he mean? Mary looked at the picture. No, she would not redo it. If he told her to darken something or make some other change, she would absolutely refuse. When Carlo's gaze caught hers, she was prepared to resist almost any suggestion.

"You must send it away."

"What?"

"Enter it in an exhibition."

Mary swallowed. Her defenses melted away.

"Yes, this is the painting you must enter. Take the chance. If you are refused, it is the world's loss, but at least you have done your duty as an artist."

Mary stared at the painting. Exhibit? Like at the Paris Salon? Surely it wasn't good enough? But she could only find out by submitting it, even if the consequence was probable rejection. "I suppose I could have it framed and sent off," she said. "I have a friend in Rome who could take it to a good frame shop there and have it packed and shipped to Paris." As Mary spoke, her body felt numb and heavy while her spirit became as light as the breeze. What if they didn't reject it? Wouldn't she just love to write to her father and say, the Paris Salon will be exhibiting my painting. But they would probably send it back with a condescending note. The judges are so hard to please. You always hear about very fine things being rejected. So how could she expect—

"I know it's difficult, but an artist must enter, and keep working and entering until the work begins to move along. It's one of the hardest parts of an artist's life."

Already tasting the scourge of rejection, Mary nodded. "I will do it as soon as it is dry enough to send." She touched the top of the canvas with her fingertips, feeling the slight tackiness of the background. "I will write my friend today."

"Good, that's settled. Now what is this about the two figures?"

"Lorenzo said he would pose—full face in a matador costume, and I'd like to have Anna, too, offering him a rose or a glass of wine. What do you think?"

"Show me the sketches," he said smiling.

"First we must find a costume and hope it fits."

Carlo smiled. "Don't forget the torreo's hat. Hats can give marvelous lines, as you have discovered."

LORENZO looked magnificent dressed as a matador. In his costume he had gained the grace and poise of a perfect model, and seemed to enjoy posing.

After three or four painting sessions with Lorenzo and Anna, Mary could tell this painting was going to be even better than the balcony scene, which she had sent to Rome for framing. In this new work there was a vitality that seemed to spring from the canvas where the curtain of light revealed Lorenzo. Anna became an attractive prop, a pointer to direct the viewer's attention to him. His costume with all its glittering splendor was unimportant—only his face bathed in light, and his vitality, his mouth with its parted lips, in a half smile, his eyes looking down, mattered. Mary felt a keen excitement as she painted his lips.

She had to be reminded that it was past time to stop. Lorenzo quit the pose and Mary reluctantly put her things away.

"It's late," she said as they stepped outside and noticed how dark it was, "but I'd like to walk a bit."

Lorenzo said nothing as they headed toward the palazzo. Mary was happy because her work was going well. The breeze washed over her, and the night smelled faintly of flowers. They passed the fountain and walked up the hill toward the cathedral.

"I love Parma," she said.

"And Parma loves you," He answered and took hold of her hand. "Be careful of your step here."

Mary looked down, but left her hand in his. He was walking very close to her. They walked silently to the courtyard behind the cathedral. They paused by a hedge. Her gaze was fixed on the lines of his mouth even as it came closer to her face. He whispered her name before his lips touched hers.

"No, you mustn't," she said.

"I must."

His arms were around her. What a wicked and lovely thing it was to kiss a man like that. Why had she avoided it so long—it was so exciting. But she instinctively drew away and took a deep breath. He was magnificent. So this was how it felt. She looked at him and noticed the change in him, too. His eyes were glassy. His lips fuller and pinker. She had but two thoughts, first to kiss again, and second, to turn and run away as fast as she could. She did neither. She turned and began walking slowly as they had before.

In a few minutes she had regained her senses enough to say that she had to hurry home. He said they would go, but he kissed her again before they started and she let it happen, knowing all the while it would have to be the very last time. She was not going to get caught up with what was called blinding passion. She knew how many of her classmates at the academy had been turned away from their art by love. It was inevitable that she would experience this splendid depravity, but this was enough. She did not want it to affect her life as she had planned it. She would tell him how it had to be.

The next day she went to the museum and copied a madonna and child by Correggio. As her brushes raced over the canvas with sureness, her mind went over the day before, and each time she thought of the kiss, a sweet warmth spread through her. Stop, she told herself, and think of Correggio. And, for a while, she did.

That night she wrote her mother and father a long letter. She wrote letters to Lydia and Louisine Elder, who had just returned to Paris. She was addressing an envelope when she heard a soft whistling from the street below and knew at once it was Lorenzo. She did not move, but sat like a monk, wishing herself a thousand miles away. He was out there waiting . . . for what? A chill ran up her back. She turned down the lamp and moved stiffly around the room, afraid to get ready for bed, or to look out of the window because he might still be there and if she saw him. . . . Soon the whistling stopped. Maybe he had gone, or maybe he still waited, silently. It was a long night.

The next day was gloriously bright and as she walked to the academy, she thought mostly of her painting. By midmorning she began to wonder why Lorenzo had not stopped by the studio as he usually did.

In the afternoon she worked with Carlo, engraving on copper plates, and became so engrossed she could not believe it when he said it was time to go. Her designs were simple, but the results were extraordinary. Carlo was pleased, although he seemed particularly quiet. Everything seemed quiet, subdued. She hadn't seen Lorenzo at all and didn't want to ask where he was.

That evening she met Lorenzo on the road. "Wait for me at the café," he said and continued up the street toward the academy. She wanted to call and say she couldn't wait, but it was too late. He was gone. Tea? Well it wouldn't matter if she had tea with him. She did want a cup of tea, and she ought to tell him she had no romantic intentions.

She finished one cup of tea and decided he was not coming and that she should go home. But before she could pick up her things he was there.

"Carlo had me running errands all day," he said. "I was afraid I wouldn't get back in time to see you."

He looked at her across the little table, smiling as he had in the picture, and she knew she would stay a few minutes.

"Hey, this tea is cold. Rosa, a little wine," he said. And he smiled again and asked how the painting was coming.

"Very well." As she explained, he poured her a small glass of wine.

"Here's a toast to your torreador."

She sipped the wine and listened to him explain how he hurried through his errands to get back in time to see her. He seemed suddenly enormously honest to her. He had no reserve. He was completely open about his feelings. She couldn't remember ever meeting anyone quite so undevious. Perhaps that was why she liked painting him. She always wanted to get to the truth of people and so often it had to be done through symbols. She glanced up at him just as he took out a cigarette and lit it. She watched as he drew in the first breath of smoke. The way he looked at that moment sent a shiver through her. The effect of the light on the bones of his face, his skin, his profile, and half-closed eyes: it all said something vital. She wanted to paint that very moment. "Lorenzo," she said. "I would like to paint how you looked just then, lighting your cigarette."

He smiled.

"Will you pose?"

"If you like."

"It would be a very masculine picture."

"Is that good?"

"What I saw was good."

He laughed.

"Would you mind if I just sketched it quickly now while it's fresh in my mind? I have paper and charcoal. Remember how you held your head."

"Like this," he said.

"A little more to the left, head down about a half an inch. There, now the hands—out—yes, like that." She sketched quickly and in a few minutes she had the angles and the main lines established. She knew how the light must fall, and as the picture began to emerge, she felt a rush of excitement.

Walking slowly home later, she tried to remember what exactly she was going to tell him. It had seemed so clear before, but now it was muddled. When they turned the corner near the house where she lived, he took her hand. She pulled back, but he held fast. "Don't do that," he said. He eased her around the side of a wall where they were protected from the street. Before she could stop him he kissed her with such force she could not resist. She had never been so warm or so full of terror and curiosity.

"I want to marry you," he said.

For a moment she could say nothing. She shook her head. "I can't."

"You can."

"No, I am an artist, not a romantic. I've worked hard to be a painter."

"That's why I love you."

He kissed her again softly, lingeringly. "We can be married. You can paint and I will be a printer." He went on, telling her how perfect it would be. They walked and she let herself wonder what it might be like. There was so much she didn't know about love.

When she finally returned home that evening there was an unusual letter from her mother. The first part was all about the engravings she had sent home, but then the tone of the letter changed. It seemed to say her mother wasn't well and needed a rest. She would like to meet Mary in whatever city she wanted to go to next. Mary was bewildered. How could she answer it? She couldn't leave Parma *now*.

A FEW DAYS LATER, as she was finished the torreador and the girl painting, she asked Carlo's opinion. He looked at it a long time and rubbed his chin, frowning.

"What is it, Carlo? Tell me if you see where it needs something. You don't think it's completely impossible, do you?"

"No, no. You have done a fine thing. The conception is good. The execution is good. The girl in profile couldn't be more perfect. It's what you've done with Lorenzo that demands some kind of comment.

"This is difficult." He frowned. "You see, I know what you saw, and I know Lorenzo. Artistically, you have a painting you should exhibit. It has power. But the torreador you painted is not Lorenzo."

"You mean it's not a likeness?"

"No, I don't mean that. You lionized him. He is a good enough Parma lad. But he's not what you think or what he wants you to think."

"Perhaps not."

"Be careful."

"I asked him to pose again. I made a sketch of him lighting a cigarette. I hope you're not angry."

"I would be angry if I thought—you asked about the painting. Yes, it is good, but there is much more in the big world for you to paint."

Mary nodded. His words echoed around her as though her father had spoken them. He was trying to help; surely he was only thinking of her welfare as an artist. She could not resent the things he said, but he didn't know Lorenzo as she did.

ONE BRIGHT MORNING several days later she found herself humming as she finished the background. "I'm finished with the portrait," she said when Carlo arrived at the studio.

He had looked at the painting every day as she worked and now stood staring at it with a hint of a frown. "It's very good."

"You said you'd like to print some of the engravings today," she said.

"Yes, we can use the small press. Lorenzo won't be here to help. He's sick."

"I wonder what's wrong."

Carlo shrugged. "I'm sure it's nothing serious."

"I hope not." But the news depressed her. The day no longer seemed quite so bright.

That afternoon she set out toward the cathedral. It was a shame Lorenzo was sick. She would like to see him, maybe take him something to make him feel better. Tomorrow if he wasn't better she would ask his cousin about him. Her mind was so occupied with Lorenzo that her pace had slowed and she climbed the hill toward the cathedral without being fully aware of her surroundings. She jumped when a shadow seemed to leap out before her.

"Mary, I've been waiting for you."

Lorenzo took her hand and pulled her off to the side of the road. "Lorenzo! What on earth? You should be taking care of yourself."

He laughed. "Don't look so astonished. I'm not a ghost."

"But aren't you sick?"

"Do I look sick?"

"No, you don't look sick at all."

"Of course not. It's too fine a day to waste. I have a lunch in my rucksack. We'll go down by the olive groves. I know a perfect spot. Come on."

"No, I can't."

"What do you mean, you can't?"

"I'm going to the cathedral."

"Nobody cares if you go today or tomorrow. You can do that whenever you like. But we may never find another day like this. It was made for us."

She could not remember ever seeing him look quite so happy. She didn't want to spoil it for him, but her plans were made. "My time at the cathedral is important."

"More important than me? I had hoped our friendship meant something. It's the most special thing in the world to me, Mary.

Please let us have a little time together. Is that asking so much?"

"It's not that, Lorenzo. It's the discipline."

"I know," he said. "But lunch can't hurt, can it?"

She hesitated. "Well, maybe a half an hour."

He led her across a path that went down to a valley behind the cathedral. They walked swiftly down the hill away from the cathedral and away from the city.

"This is beautiful," she said later. She glanced up at the protective tree branches above and nibbled a piece of cheese. He sat across from her on the grass, staring at her with eyes full of love. She sipped her wine and began to talk almost incessantly. Maybe it was the wine or perhaps she was afraid to stop. He wanted to hear more about her home and she told him all about the things she used to do there, the riding—how she missed that. Before she realized it, he had filled her wineglass again and sat down closer to her. She would go soon; but right now he touched her hand as she talked, gently kissed her fingertips. His cool breath tickled her arm. How comfortable it was to have him close. She could see herself in his eyes as she leaned back onto the grass.

Tenderly his kisses covered her face, her throat, her shoulder. He loosened her blouse a little and she could not stop the welling of pleasure within her. And there was a force so strong, so undeniable that even though she feared it, she could not stop it.

"I love you," he whispered, and nothing else mattered.

It was four o'clock in the afternoon when she sat up, looked all around her, and realized how she had given herself to him. It wasn't a dream. She had been on fire. Even now there was a glow that could be fanned to a flame by just seeing him asleep on the grass, watching his even breathing. Without warning, tears welled up and overflowed. She buried her head at her knees and was sobbing uncontrollably when he woke.

"Please don't," he said. "It's all right. We'll be married soon. It's all right. I promise you."

The next day Carlo noticed her drawing was unsteady, her images unclear. "You are not concentrating on your work," he scolded. "Can't you forget about Lorenzo long enough to draw, or is all of this unimportant now?"

Mary was already upset; his criticism was enough to make her slam down her drawing board in anger. "This *is* important," she shouted. "It has always been important. But love is important, too."

Carlo's face softened and regret replaced his irritability. "I was afraid it would happen. You could have been a successful artist— maybe even a great one."

"I'm not going to stop working."

"You *have* stopped. Look there. You cannot divide your life. Art demands all. And a Lorenzo demands all. You cannot have both."

Mary stared at him, battling back the tears.

"Ah, I see you don't believe me. It's hard work to be an artist. Even those people with what they call natural genius have to work hard. Nothing of value is easy. I thought you knew all that. And being a woman lessens your chances of success considerably. You had accomplished so much, I had hoped you would go on and realize your dreams. You're the best student I have had in a long time. To see you throw it all away on a man like Lorenzo tears my heart."

"I wouldn't throw anything away. I would go on working."

"Impossible."

"I don't think it's impossible. Why do you?"

"Because in Parma a wife is just that—a wife. She has babies. There is no time for art." He sighed. "I am just an old man but I grieve for you. Don't think I am heartless. I know what love is. I yielded to it myself. I love my family and I love Parma, but love is not everything."

Mary could not work any more that day. She went home and lay down on her bed. Carlo was wrong. She would not give up her work. Carlo was ruining her happiness. It wasn't true. She wouldn't give up her work. She couldn't. What a terrible thing to say. Lorenzo understood. She closed her eyes, thinking of Correggio's work in the cathedral. Suddenly she was compelled to copy a fresco. Strength seemed to ooze back into her limbs.

She was breathless when she arrived at the top of the cathedral steps, but did not stop. There would be time to catch her breath later as she worked. She felt like she had the first day she came to the cathedral, full of awe, overpowered with Correggio's mastery. She set up her easel and took out her brushes and paints.

She worked until her fingers throbbed, but there was no real weariness. On the contrary, there was exhilaration. People occasionally moved around her, but she never felt they were close.

Lorenzo found her.

"I thought you'd be here," he said. "The harvest festival is beginning. There is dancing in the street. Come along. I feel like celebrating."

"Not now," she said.

"Yes, now," he said. "This is festival time."

"No, I can't. I must finish."

"You've been here all afternoon."

"When I finish, I'll freshen up and join you."

"No, no. This is festival. Everything stops."

"I'll stop when the light is gone."

He laughed, put his hands over her eyes and said, "The light has gone." He pulled her toward himself. "Please," she gasped. "Not here."

"Why not? You're my woman now, aren't you?"

"I'm an artist—remember?" Her voice sounded more angry than she intended. She looked back at her canvas, seeing without consciously thinking that the background blue had gotten too bright. It had to be grayed with a bit of sienna. Just as she dipped her brush to the palette, Lorenzo jerked the palette from her hand. There was a smile on his lips, but his eyes were hard. "If we're going to be married, it's time you started to listen to me."

"Lorenzo, please."

"We're going to the festival now." He pulled her close and kissed her.

"Stop," she whispered. "We're in the *cathedral*."

His arms held her, and he laughed. "There's no one to care if we have a little kiss or what we do."

It was true. The cathedral was empty. "You are my woman," he had said. The light was fading all around them, but Correggio's frescos still glowed. Their outlines shimmered before her eyes even as Lorenzo's palms gently rubbed her back, even as his body pressed close to hers. But her need was for Correggio. She did not struggle with Lorenzo. She smiled and stepped away. He took the canvas down, set it aside, and folded the easel. Mary stood watching him. It was as though he were far away in a dream, and Correggio spoke to her in a voice like Carlo's. "It's impossible."

Silently, Mary followed Lorenzo out of the cathedral, her determination growing with each step. When they reached the palazzo, she turned to him, seeing clearly the danger he represented.

"I'm not joining you for the festival. I'm going home," she said. "I'm very tired."

Lorenzo laughed, insisting that a few minutes at the café table over a glass of wine would take care of everything.

"No," Mary declared. "I'm going home."

"But there will be dancing and singing and laughter. No one can be tired during a festival. It brings life to the body." He took hold of her elbow, pushing her in the direction of a café.

Mary stopped short, jerking herself free. "I'm not going to the café. I'm going home. Good night, Lorenzo."

His eyes seemed dazed for a moment, but then he raised his head in a most lordly manner and shrugged. With that, Mary turned and walked away from him, tightly gripping the handle of her painting satchel.

9

MARY DROPPED THREE LETTERS in the post box and boarded the train to Madrid with a heavy feeling that she was closing a door that could never be opened again, as though an important part of her was being left behind. One year more or less; what difference should that make? She felt older and depressingly lonely. There was a sense of loss, a lassitude similar to the emptiness she had felt when her brother Robbie died. She remembered that day clearly though it had happened when she was only nine years old. She had sat by the window, watching the rain, thinking about poor Robbie's body, and how it would be never to see him alive again. She had watched the rain and was hardly able to move.

That was how she had felt on the train to Madrid. She'd never see Lorenzo again. He'd get her letter tomorrow. And he wouldn't know where she had gone. The letter would be the end of it. Carlo was the only one who would know, and she wrote him only just enough information so he could send letters in case one came from home. She had written her mother to meet her in Amsterdam. And while waiting, she would be working in Spain. She could not stay another day in Parma, even though leaving it numbed her.

Lorenzo's face overlayed everything she viewed from the train. She tried reading the newspaper, but his image persisted, blotting out other thoughts. When she finally arrived in Madrid, she found it different enough from Parma to be stimulating. She liked the architecture and the flavor of the city itself, and when she first entered the Prado and set up her easel near a green-hued El Greco, she felt at home. This was her life, this world in a canvas. There could be no other.

After nearly two weeks in Madrid she thought she had completely accepted the end of her impossible romance. But one day as she walked through a park toward her hotel, enjoying the sight of swooping pigeons, she unexpectedly walked past a couple sitting on a bench. Their heads were close together as they talked. Mary looked the other way, but she heard their laughter, pitched high and full of delight. It stung her ears. She became unbearably restless and lonely. Thoughts of Lorenzo and visions of an idyllic life in Parma plagued her again. She was no longer sure she had done the right thing.

She went to Seville, thinking another change would help. Carlo had a friend there he had spoken of often, Paul Estes. He was an artist who studied under Carlo ten years ago. Mary had seen his work at the academy and felt so attuned to it she had no hesitation about calling on him. It proved to be a good decision. When Paul saw the *Torero and Young Girl*, he urged her to send it to be exhibited.

Mary stared at Lorenzo's beautiful mouth in the picture and felt again a sharp pang of loss. Yes, she wanted to send it off. Maybe she had to.

After a month in Seville she went on to Amsterdam, settled into the hotel, and began at once to copy Rubens. She worked intently for long hours; her loneliness and yearning for Lorenzo too much to bear idly. She was constantly tempted to write him, but remembered her promise to her father as well as Carlo's words, and she resisted the urge.

She next traveled to Haarlem to copy the work of Frans Hals, and when her mother finally arrived in Holland, Mary was so relieved and happy, the tears she had held back streamed down her cheeks. She was not alone.

They talked all day and into the night and early morning. Mary wanted to hear everything about Lydia, Aleck and the children, Gardner, and her father. They planned to shop and sightsee. Mary talked about Seville and Madrid, but not about Parma.

The next few days were consumed with going about Amsterdam, seeing the important buildings, visiting the shops, and going to concerts, opera, and plays. When they settled into a more relaxed pace, Mary wanted to do a half-length portrait of her mother, who by then was more than willing to sit quietly with her daughter.

It was while she painted on the portrait that Mary found herself able to speak of Parma. "It was quite a useful time. I needed both Correggio *and* Carlo Raimondi."

"Yes," her mother said. "Mr. Raimondi sent glowing reports of your progress."

"Really? Carlo wrote you?"

"A few very short letters just to let us know you were progressing satisfactorily."

Mary nodded and painted her mother's brow, thinking that she possessed a most perfect, ageless beauty, full of a serenity and grace that Mary doubted she could ever achieve. Lydia was like their mother, while Mary had inherited a restlessness from her father. Mary concentrated on capturing her mother's beauty.

"We were surprised at how suddenly you left Parma. You were completely intrigued with it. When we got your last letter and you were leaving so suddenly, we wondered if there was something wrong."

"Nothing much," Mary said. "I wanted to see Madrid and Seville." Her mother's face so forcefully revealed her skepticism that Mary stopped talking and met Katherine's gaze. "Did Carlo say anything in his letters to worry you?"

"Your father became worried."

"I see. That's why you wrote that you needed a vacation and wanted to meet me in some other city."

"That's part of it."

Mary sighed. "I don't know whether to be angry or glad."

"Please don't be angry. We all miss you. I wanted to come."

Mary smiled and continued to paint. "I just hope some day I'll look half as well as you do in black." She was not angry at Carlo or her parents or even Lorenzo. She knew she should be glad that it was over and she had not given up her dream. She had her family; she did not need the debilitation of love, did not want a husband making decisions for her.

"What are your plans now?" Katherine asked simply.

Mary's brush stopped and she looked up into her mother's face. "All I can think of is Paris."

Katherine smiled. "I suspected as much."

"I'd like a little time in Antwerp for more Rubens. Not only was he a great classical artist, he painted his own time and his own people. Before Rubens I didn't know so much could be said with human form and gesture.

"Haven't you even considered London?"

"Yes, I've thought of it. But I hate crossing the miserable water. And what they're doing there now isn't worth crossing for. They're too steeped in the classic—it's all Roman noses and Greek costumes. They're not seeing the England of their own time. I want to paint what is real."

"I can't qualify as an expert, but I think your work is stronger than ever."

Mary sighed. "I think I have gained much in the past few weeks. I have a new appreciation of realism and a new sense of costume and props. They have to reflect the person and that person's real life. I would never permit dear Eddie to dress in a velvet suit again."

Katherine laughed along with Mary. "I rather liked Eddie dressed that way, but it's not really like him, that's true. But what about the matador? That's a costume."

"Yes, it's since I painted it that I reconsidered costume—because of the matador." As she talked the image of Lorenzo came back so vividly she felt a shiver race through her. It was not dead yet. It could still sting.

Katherine stood up and came to Mary. "You loved him, didn't you?"

Mary nodded and let her mother's comforting arm go around her.

"Could he have made you happy?"

"He was—the most exciting person. I can't tell you how much— well, I only know I have to paint. And Lorenzo . . . oh, I don't know . . ." Mary sighed and buried her head at her mother's breast and Katherine comforted her, glancing once at the picture of the matador propped against the wall.

THE LETTER came from Carlo the day before they were to leave Amsterdam. Inside the envelope was another envelope addressed to Mary Stevenson. She had used only her given names when she submitted the painting. With a sharp pang she realized it was from the Paris Salon. Her hands shook. They probably rejected it, she thought. It's part of the struggle for an artist. I won't let it matter too much. She drew a deep breath and opened the letter. Her eyes traveled over the words twice before she fully understood. Then her hands began to tremble.

"Mother, oh, Mother. I was accepted. *On the Balcony* will hang in the Paris Salon."

She hugged her mother unmercifully hard and had never felt so happy.

10

MARY WAS BOUYANT when she and her mother finally arrived in Paris. It seemed like coming home. The city was a carnival. People wore beautiful clothes and carefree smiles. Perhaps there were ghosts in the cellars, but it was hard to believe that during the four years she was gone from the city there had ever been a bloody war. Her Paris was the same or perhaps more splendid. She thanked God, Carlo, and her mother that she had come back. Now all she had to do was to make something of herself here and fulfill her promise to her father.

First they called on the Barries, then Louisine Elder. These few years had added poise and assurance to Louisine and she fairly glowed with excitement for her life. She insisted on having a dinner party and a night at the theater that very week.

They went to the opera house for a ballet performance. There was a gala atmosphere, and as Mary sat back and looked over the crowd, she wondered how Lorenzo would have liked life in Paris. He probably wouldn't come to this place, she thought; wouldn't care for any of this. But was he lonely? Even as she wondered, Louisine leaned over and whispered in her ear. "There is Princess Giavona Roberto with Edgar Degas. And I believe that is his sister and her husband with them." Mary took up her opera glasses and looked. "He's of royal blood, I heard," Louisine whispered. "I bought another of his paintings. Did I tell you?"

"No. You must show it to me as soon as we get back. Um, he's nice looking, isn't he?" Mary judged him to be about thirty-eight. "I imagined he would be older." He had a mustache, quick dark eyes, and a pouty sort of mouth. She liked the proud way he held his head and the flair with which he wore his black suit and short cape. Mary watched him sitting with his legs crossed, chatting amiably with his party, until the lights dimmed and the ballet began.

It was all very exciting, but Mary realized that too much of Paris society life would keep her from her work. It could be just too pleasant if she wasn't careful.

The next morning she mentioned her fears to her mother over breakfast. "I want to live like I did in Parma," she said. "I need all my time for work. I can't go to parties and the theater at night, have tea in the afternoon and shop for frills and still get anything important accomplished. I want to live independently."

"Independently? Do you mean to have an apartment where you live *alone*?"

"Yes."

"But your father would never approve of your living in Paris alone and completely unprotected. How would it look?"

"To whom?"

"Mary, please don't take that tone with me."

"But if the neighborhood was right, and I had a few rooms with a studio, I could produce more work than if I had to live under someone's protection and schedules. I am a mature woman. My character is set. I want to devote all my time to my art—as a professional."

"Women who live alone are always rather . . . suspect."

"But certainly we are above that sort of thinking, aren't we, Mother?" Mary paused but her mother didn't answer. "You and Father know there would never be anything to be suspect of, don't you?"

"Of course. Of course, *we* know that."

"Then let me try this," Mary pleaded. "I do so want to be independent. And some day I hope to be able to support myself completely from my work."

"That's what we all want for you, but you must let me think about it."

"And while you're thinking, can we look at a few places, just to see what is available and what the prices are?"

Katherine sighed.

After three days of looking for apartments, Katherine had become used to the idea that Mary could live alone. She made no secret that she did not like it, but admitted that some compromises were necessary for a daughter in such exceptional circumstances. She had framed acceptable explanations for her husband and family, and so offered no more resistance when Mary found the apartment in Montmartre she wanted to rent. It seemed a safe place, close to friends, and the price was reasonable.

Katherine stayed long enough to see Mary settled in her new home. "Your father may not like this," she said when the move was complete, "so you must write to him often and reassure him."

Mary promised. When Katherine herself had seen to the hiring of a suitable housekeeper, and was convinced that Mary could manage well enough, she made plans to return home. Before she sailed for America she wanted to visit London.

Although Mary was becoming restless for work, she was sorry to part with her mother. She missed the family so much sometimes she ached to see them. But she knew she had to live her own way, apart from them, if she were ever to make the jump from serious student to professional. And if she failed to make that step, she would sorely disappoint her family. They put their faith in her. Gard's and Lydia's letters were always filled with expressions of confidence that

Mary was pursuing exactly the right course, and even Aleck took the time away from his duties as vice-president of the railroad to write her letters of encouragement. She did not want to fail any of them, especially her father.

After Katherine sailed, Mary began to paint as though her life depended on it. She produced work that was as perfect as she could make it. She spared no effort. Everything was her best, and yet she continually attempted to surpass her last work. As the weeks passed she amassed a surprising quantity of work. There came a day when she knew what she must do, and selected a few paintings to take to an art dealer. Durand-Ruel was her first choice. She took a portrait of a young woman with foliage in the background and a picture of a waiflike girl of eight sitting under a tree.

Early one morning, with the paintings carefully wrapped in brown paper, she set off. As the carriage made its way along the streets that led to the Gallerie Durand-Ruel, Mary remembered the Philadelphia art dealer. She remembered also the things her father had told her. She would take her chances.

When she entered the gallery she saw a very young man in a brown suit standing with his arms folded across his chest. He came toward her solemnly, his eyes directed at her bonnet.

"Can I be of service?"

"I would like to speak to Monsieur Durand-Ruel."

"Certainly," he said, glancing at her package and then quickly away again. Suddenly she felt very warm. Her scalp itched. She should have written a letter first. It was too late now. She smiled broadly. "Would you tell him please that Mary Cassatt would like a few words with him?"

"I'll see if he's free. Would you like to put your package down?"

"No, thank you. It's not heavy."

The young man walked slowly to the back of the gallery. What would she say if the young man came back and said that M. Durand-Ruel was too busy to see her? She supposed she'd have to smile and say thank you and go home and think of another way to do this wretched business. Did all the artists who painted these have to do this, she wondered as she looked around. Surely the elegant M.

Degas didn't stand around like a frightened butterfly. He would have gone about it much more cleverly if he had to go about it at all. Perhaps Durand-Ruel came to him.

She watched the doorway, wishing the young man in brown would just come back and say whatever he had to say and get it over with. She sighed and put the package down by her feet. Finally, he returned.

"Follow me, if you please." He smiled and Mary followed meekly. At the top of the stairs the young man opened a door marked private and stood aside while Mary entered. Monsieur Durand-Ruel was seated behind a desk. He stood when he saw her. "Good day, Miss Cassatt. Please come in and sit down. Ah, you have brought a painting?"

"Yes, two." She remembered to smile. "I thought perhaps—" Her mind went blank. Thought perhaps what? For an instant her silence seemed unbearable.

"May I see?" he asked, gently taking the package from her.

She nodded and sat down.

When he saw the pictures he smiled at once. "I understand you are the Mary Stevenson whose painting hung in the Salon this spring. It merited a splendid place. These are just as well done. In fact, I find them even more appealing in their simplicity."

She hesitated. "Do you mean you'll take them?"

"Of course. It is a privilege."

Mary let the warmth of his words wash over her, leaving her limp with relief and gratitude.

"Tell me about yourself, won't you? Where did you study? Where do you live?"

Seeing an honest interest in his eyes, Mary responded as fully as she could.

"So you have just come back to Paris. My brother and I are having a dinner party tomorrow night for some of the artists whose work we handle. We would be honored if you would come, too."

"Oh. Thank you. It is I who am honored."

"Berthe Morisot will be there. I think you'll like her. Here, let me show you a piece of her work." He rose and led Mary to a small room in the gallery. He pointed to a picture of a child in a garden holding a sleeping cat. He smiled. "Isn't it lovely? Berthe is young and earnest, the same as you. She's Manet's student. I think you would enjoy knowing her."

"I'm sure I would," Mary said.

As she left the gallery without her paintings, Mary thought of how they would look on the gallery walls, displayed along with the work of the best artists in Paris. She felt exhilarated. Father would be proud. Her head was so light she walked all the way home. When she got there, she penned a letter to Lydia, describing the goodness of M. Durand-Ruel.

The next evening fourteen guests attended the party. M. Durand-Ruel introduced her to Berthe, a pretty, tall, and compulsively cheerful woman who made Mary feel like a dear friend.

The conversation throughout the evening was of artists and their art. M. Pissaro was Mary's dinner partner. He seemed a gentle person, reminding Mary of one of her father's friends. Though she found him completely charming, she noticed how the cuffs of his suitcoat were frayed. These were not easy times for artists, and this seemed to be the general sentiment of the evening. She deduced that most of the artists depended solely on the sale of their work to live.

When dinner was over and they were sipping coffee, Berthe invited Mary to come along with her on a sketching trip. Mary was more than pleased, and they chatted amiably over arrangements.

The sketching trip was the beginning of a strong friendship. Mary felt it from the first when she saw how Berthe carried her paints, how she moved and how boldly she painted. Berthe explained Manet's philosophy about capturing a moment in light. One must train the eye to see quickly and record the visible light in daubs of paint. It wasn't necessary to model in the classical sense, because, if the observation was accurate, a kind of modeling would result of its own.

Mary tried to paint the landscape before her with broad quick brushstrokes, putting on the paint thickly and not brushing it into the surface, but leaving it and turning her eyes to the next area, getting the color and value right, putting it on, leaving it. She worked at fever pitch. At the end of an hour there was her land-scape. It was not half as bad as she had expected.

Mary sketched as often as she could with Berthe. Once Manet came along with them, and it was a wonderfully instructive day. He seemed to relish the opportunity to demonstrate his theories. His convictions, as well as his control over his methods, impressed Mary deeply.

However, Mary was a portrait painter above all else. Landscapes were a useful exercise, but could the principles Manet used in painting a moment in light be used for portrait work? When she adapted it in painting a little girl sitting by the window in her studio, she was struck with the freshness she had been able to seize.

It wasn't long before acquaintances and friends began to bring their children to Mary for a simple study. Some of these were included with the paintings she displayed at the Gallerie Durand-Ruel. Those little portraits were more a pleasure than work, and yet they must have had a certain appeal. Lately she was often nicely surprised when M. Durand-Ruel went over her sales with her at the end of the month.

One afternoon while she was painting on the portrait of Denise, her maid, Louisine Elder appeared in the studio, her voice full of excitement. "I simply had to show you what I bought in London."

Mary hadn't seen Louisine in more than a month. She stopped her work and asked Denise to make tea.

"When did you get back?"

"Today. But I had to show you my incredible bargain."

"Please do. What did you buy?"

"Well, I went to a showing he had in London, and saw his work was quite as good as you said it was. Oh, Mary, some of it gave me goose pimples."

"Whose showing?"

"Why, Whistler's, of course. Remember when you showed me his painting at the Salon. You said it was quite the best thing to come out of England."

"Ah, yes."

"So naturally I wanted to see more when I was in London. After the show I went directly to his studio and told him I had thirty pounds to spend and I wanted to have something of his because Mary Cassatt assured me his work had merit and besides I liked it."

Mary laughed. "That sounds just like the sort of nonsense you would spout off to a perfect stranger."

"He didn't seem like a stranger after I'd seen his work, but he did have a strange look on his face when he asked me in. First off, he asked me if I knew you. And when I said you were my best friend, his manner became very cordial. I told him I had collected your work, owned several by Degas, a Monet, and a Pissarro—and he was impressed. Really, Mary, he was a prince after that. He asked all about you. He knows your work just as you know his."

Mary smiled. She knew Whistler came to Paris and stalked the Salon show the same as she and her friends did. "Where is this bargain?" she asked.

Louisine produced the painting of a tall slender girl standing alone, and Mary admitted she had indeed struck a remarkable bargain. "You are becoming a gifted collector if you got *that* for thirty pounds."

Louisine laughed. "That's what I thought, although I don't know if anyone but you and I appreciate what a bargain it is."

"You should try to get a Renoir when your pocketbook recovers. I have a feeling the value of his work is going to zoom up. If you don't get something in the next few years, you'll pay double."

"Degas's work is shooting up, too. But no wonder."

"Yes, he is a true master."

"That isn't what I mean," Louisine said, lowering her tone. "He's in desperate straits you know."

"Now how did you hear that?"

"Father told me before I left Paris. I'm surprised you haven't heard. What happened was that his father died owing tremendous sums. Degas insisted on paying it off in full and that meant he had to sell everything, including his house and his art collection—everything—and move into a hovel."

"How awful," Mary said. "That sort of sacrifice wouldn't be expected in America, I'm sure."

"Of course not. They were business losses. Father says it was a case of family pride."

"It's hard to imagine a man like that in a hovel," Mary said, remembering the glimpse she had of him at the theater.

"Maybe that's an exaggeration," Louisine said. "I have no idea of what Father's definition of a hovel is. Well, I must be off." Louisine took her Whistler painting, kissed Mary's cheek, and was gone.

ALL THE NEXT DAY it rained hard. The studio was heavy with gloom and the sky seemed to get progressively darker as the day went on. But Mary's day was brightened by the delivery of a letter from home, addressed in her father's hand. She looked forward to reading it over tea.

> *My dear Mary,*
>
> Thanks for your letter of the seventeenth. News from you is always a tonic for your mother, Lydia, and myself.
>
> I must tell you the bad news first—your dear sister has been sick for a month. Your mother took her off to a spa in Virginia. It may have helped somewhat, but she remained in bed for another two weeks after that. She made us promise not to tell you until she was well. She is so much better, it's hard to believe she was ever sick. She sends her love, of course, and is sending you a book by Tolstoy she just finished and thought you would like.
>
> Your mother is worn out from all the worry. She doesn't sleep well at night when Liddy is sick even though a nurse is close at Liddy's side.
>
> Gardner has done quite well in his studies of banking and will become much more successful in the field than I ever was. He has a singular zest for it which I lack. Your brother Aleck is busy and traveling far and near for the company, but he is fit and sends you his regards, too. Eddie and the baby will spend a few weeks with us while Aleck and Lois take a trip to New Orleans. We are looking forward to this very much, as you can imagine, and your mother is busy thinking of all manner of little treats to lay by for them.

Now I come to another matter that has to be examined. This is the subject of finances. Our agreed-upon year has passed by, as you may realize. And now you must take on the responsibility of supporting your studio. You are deriving income from your work in the manner of a professional person, therefore, I expect you to pay for your expenses such as painting supplies, framing, and studio rent. I shall, of course, continue to provide for your living expenses, but even here I shall caution you to manage the monthly stipend carefully.

Mary stopped reading and stared ahead, contemplating what the letter really meant. She had not expected this. How much were her expenses? Her income was not nearly enough to cover costs, including gold-leaf frames and sitters' fees. This would change things. She would have to get more commissions, or perhaps ask more for her work. Maybe she should do more etchings or engravings, as Durand-Ruel sold these more easily than paintings. She walked into the studio with the letter still in her hand. She looked at the work in a different light. This meant she must approach her work differently. She would not make compromises with her principles. She could use simpler frames, and she could spend less time on studies and copying at the museum and more time making pictures that might be sold.

For a time she felt quite anxious about her new situation. For the first time in her life she was expected to produce money. She was well aware that others had to do it to live. Most of her friends would consider her lucky.

After the letter, she worked in a different way, assessing what might become of her paintings and what she could produce. She gave more thought to making prints. She etched or engraved the plates in her studio, took them to a printer, and then stayed to oversee the printing herself to make sure everything was exactly right.

In addition to printmaking, Mary worked on her portrait of Denise with the idea that it should be her entry to the Paris Salon. A good portrait in the Salon show could open many doors. And she was sure she could make this portrait a superb work. She saw in Denise a quiet dignity that could almost stun. She worked painstakingly on the silkiness of the dress and the softness of Denise's hair.

The light concentrated upon the face with an echo of it falling on the sewing. There was no doubt in Mary's mind that it was her best painting. Maybe she was dreaming, she thought, but when she looked at the canvas with the frame propped around it, she felt confident of her future, thinking that if she could have painted this, she could surely earn enough money from her painting to support her studio.

Along with the portrait of Denise, Mary also entered the portrait of Mrs. Cortier. Here she felt she had succeeded in showing the good humor of the woman through an honest, straightforward pose. The frames she had settled for were expensive, but if she saved on groceries and didn't buy anything else, she could pay for them.

One afternoon after the paintings had been sent to the Salon, Mary was puttering in the studio when Berthe came to call. It was such a pleasure to see her, Mary's whole mood brightened. She had quite neglected her friends these last weeks as she worked on the portrait.

"I thought you might like to see our show," Berthe said. "Remember, I told you about it a month ago and you said you would. It opens today. Won't you come with me?"

Mary remembered Berthe telling about it. The group of artists she belonged to were having a special showing. Yes, she did indeed want to go. "I'll change as quickly as I can." Berthe waited in the parlor while Mary shouted from the bedroom. "What works did you submit?"

"Four or five things. Remember that time we sketched the boys picking vegetables?"

"Of course."

"That one. And a full-length picture of my sister standing in the kitchen. The rest are smaller things."

Mary changed her clothes in less than five minutes and they were off together to see this exhibit of independent artists, where there were no juries. All the work was for sale and each person in the group was allowed to show whatever he or she wished.

"Monet has a painting I particularly wanted you to see," Berthe said. "I won't describe it. Wait until you see it."

THE SHOW was like nothing Mary had ever seen. She had seen many of the individuals' work before, a piece or two at a time. She knew they were each devoted to the idea of painting the effect of light, mostly outdoors. But not even her familiarity with their work had prepared her for the sensation of seeing all these paintings together. She was reminded of a many-faceted diamond with light striking off it.

As they walked through the room, Mary felt the sensation of light actually coming from the paintings themselves. The work was new and strong and more real than art had ever been. She hadn't realized what had been happening, perhaps because she was working in the same direction herself. Berthe was apparently not so struck as Mary was, but she too remarked that the total effect was more than she ever expected. When their eyes were numb they went to a nearby café. They talked about the paintings and the people who painted them.

"Is it true Degas had to sell his possessions to pay off his father's debt?" Mary asked.

"Ah, yes, it is true."

"Such pride."

"Yes. I noticed you studied his dancer for quite a while. To tell the truth, your work reminds me of his."

Mary smiled. "What is he really like?"

"He's a snob, and he can tear a person to bits with his criticism."

"Is it unreasonable criticism?"

"Truthful, I suppose, but his standards are undoubtedly higher than anyone else's. He has a very bad temper and enjoys making public and witty insults that leave his enemies devastated."

"Oh, dear."

"I like him," Berthe said, sipping her tea. "He can be charming."

The next morning when Mary opened the pages of the newspaper she saw the headline, "Is Madness the Theme of Art Show?" Her eyes scanned down the column. "The exhibit was characterized by unbalanced views of various subjects, daubed onto canvases with nary a thought for drawing." And further down it said, "People of sensibility are advised to stay away from this clamor of colors which gives the dangerous impression of the interior of a madhouse." As she read she felt a growing outrage. Monet's painting was so ruthlessly attacked she could not bring herself to finish reading. The words were blurred by her memory of the painting of the harbor at Le Havre at sunrise. It was titled *Impression*. This painting in particular and the whole show in general was dismissed as being a mere impression and nothing more. In another paper there was even a cartoon showing a pregnant woman being barred from entering the exhibit hall because of the danger to her unborn child.

These attacks upon the value of her friends' work hurt Mary as deeply as if the attack were directed at her personally. She made a point of seeing those of her acquaintance who had work in the exhibit to add her voice to the few who appreciated what they were doing.

WITH HER OWN WORK, she grew tired of etching and since she had produced enough good work to keep Durand-Ruel stocked for months she experimented with pastels, remembering Degas's wonderful effects with that medium. Her days were quiet and industrious but there was a nagging worry about the money her father now expected her to earn. She wished she had a commission to do a portrait.

While she was working one day, Denise came into the studio and told her there was a delivery man at the door who required *her* signature. Impatient with the interruption, Mary wiped her hands and followed Denise to the hallway.

The delivery man smiled. "Sign here, Mademoiselle Cassatt."

Mary glanced at the package. It was in the shape of a painting. "What's this?" she asked. But the man only shrugged and went off.

"There's a letter with it," Denise said.

"Oh, so there is," Mary said as she removed the envelope. It was from the Salon. She ripped open the envelope with trembling hands.

"We are sorry to inform you your painting, *The Young Bride*, has been rejected. The jury was of the opinion that it did not meet the high artistic standards set by the Paris Salon."

"There must be some mistake," she muttered. "This portrait of Denise is surely better than anything I've sent before."

Mary took the painting into the studio, tore off the wrappings, and looked again. No, she hadn't been wrong. That painting was as perfectly drawn and executed as she could have made it. She wrapped it again, called for a carriage, and went straight to the office of M. Greenchamp, a member of the jury.

He received her at once, kissing her hand and expressing his regret at having to reject such a well-begun portrait.

"But what was wrong with it?" she demanded.

"The color, my dear. There was no decorum, no refinement. If you would tone it down, especially the flesh, it would undoubtedly be accepted next year. We at the Salon do not approve of shocking the sensibilities with raw pigment like these impressionist infidels. There is a refinement expected and demanded of paintings accepted here."

"Refinement. I'm not sure I know what you mean. Are you saying that an artist must conform to strict rules to express his own truth? That there can be no departure from this—refinement? Flesh tones must always look alike?"

"My dear, you have a precious talent. Don't let it become mired in the new madness."

"Are you saying that if I did nothing but tone the flesh, the portrait would be acceptable?"

"Yes, otherwise it was quite fine."

"All I have to do is kill the very effect I struggled so hard to capture."

"It offends, my dear. I'm sorry. I've certainly admired your other work. I have always been instrumental in having your work accepted. Now go home and think about this calmly. We'll chat about it another day." He rose and showed her out, but Mary turned, stared at him with disgust, and left without another word.

She went back to her studio feeling as though she were being crushed in a vise. She needed the Salon, but how could she give up her freedom to paint as she must? She would be nothing more than a hack. Yet what would she do without the Salon? Where could she go?

She looked around the studio at her work, her eyes darting from one painting to another. She saw them as part of the furniture, detached from her inner reality. She was tired, disappointed, depressed. She had no wish to paint at all.

For days she could not work. She walked, and sometimes did nothing at all. The only thing she thought of to do was shop with Louisine. Even shopping seemed pointless after a bit. She could not afford to buy anything else and neither could Louisine. But it was better to be with a friend than to be alone. Finally Louisine asked Mary why she wasn't working, and when Mary tried to explain, Louisine did not seem to understand.

Two days later, before Mary had bothered to get up and get dressed, the maid brought a message to her bedroom that Louisine and a friend were waiting in the studio.

Louisine was extremely cheerful. "There you are at last. I want you to meet my friend, Mary Ellen. She's an American, too, and went to my school. I've told her all about you and how you always need models. Well, Mary Ellen said she thought it would be a privilege to sit for you."

"Oh, yes," Mary Ellen said. "Your work is quite impressive. Louisine has been showing me more of it while we waited for you. Of course, if you don't want me to pose, I'll understand. You must be very busy."

"Nonsense," Louisine said. "We didn't come all the way here for nothing." She laughed and turned to Mary. "Hasn't she an interesting face?"

"Indeed," Mary said. "If you really don't mind posing, we could start with a few sketches." She took up her pastels for the first time in weeks. She could not hurt their feelings by refusing. She posed Mary Ellen and began sketching, halfheartedly at first, but after an hour or so, she thought that perhaps Louisine had understood. There was nothing else she could do with her life but work. Paris Salon or not, she did love to paint.

Still, her sense of depression did not leave her until the next afternoon, when Denise came into the studio and announced that Monsieur Edgar Degas would like to see her.

11

M. Degas's face was exactly as Mary might have expected, dark eyes, even features, a pride showing in the way he held his head. He was dressed fashionably in dark brown with cape and gloves. Yes, she would have recognized him anywhere from the glimpse she had of him at the theater four years ago.

"Our mutual friend Monsieur Tourney promised to introduce me properly today, but we had no sooner set off when he was called back on some family matter, and rather than wait, I took the liberty of coming unescorted."

"I'm very glad you did. I have admired your work. Would you care for tea or coffee?" Mary said.

"No, thank you. I came mainly to congratulate you on the portrait I saw yesterday at the Salon. I can't tell you how enamored I am of it."

The sound of the word Salon brought a reaction of anger. Mary's back stiffened, but she tried not to show her hurt, which had festered rather than healed.

"Is something wrong?"

"Why no," she said. "Thank you. I'm glad if you liked the portrait."

"It isn't simply a matter of liking it. When I saw it I only wished I had done it. I felt that you see things as I do myself. It was as if we were traveling parallel paths."

He smiled, and Mary, overwhelmed by his words, became embarassed and tongue-tied. Feeling her face burning, she looked away from him.

"I hope I didn't come calling at a bad moment. You were working on an important painting?"

"No, no. It's just that I didn't know what to say. Your own work is the finest being done today, and to say we are on parallel paths—well, I should protest, but it's kind of you."

"Nonsense, I never said a kind thing in my life. Your work interests me because you display the same passion I have always clung to. And you do it extraordinarily well. I had hoped you would show me more of your work."

"Oh certainly. Shall we go into my studio? Everything is there."

"That's precisely what I'd like," he said smiling.

His smile reassured her. He must have sincerely liked her painting of Mrs. Cortier. She undoubtedly did have the same ideas about art as he did. Otherwise why would his work hold so much attraction for her?

The first thing he saw was the portrait of Denise beautifully framed and still setting on an easel. He walked straight to it, looked at it seriously, and turned to Mary. "Your maid. Very strikingly done."

Mary sighed and looked at the floor, then glanced back at him. "The Salon rejected it," she said, feeling as though she had laid bare her soul.

"Of course. You have done something exploratory in the way you handled the light. The rest is classical enough."

"That's it exactly. If I were to tone it down, I was assured it would be accepted."

"You're angry."

"Yes. But what good does it do to be angry? If I want my work hung in the Salon, I must abide by aesthetic rules laid down by narrow-minded dictators."

"I agree with you. They are crushing talent with abandon."

"How do you satisfy them? Your work is new and stimulating and yet you exhibit at the Salon."

"I did. But I have decided to ignore them for the same reasons you mention. I have joined the group of artists who call themselves Independents. They submit to no juries and take orders from no one."

"Oh yes, the group of newspapers call impressionists. Pissaro is one, and Berthe. I envy all of you."

Degas smiled. "Then I shall wait no longer to ask you what I came to ask. Will you join us and become an independent?"

Mary inhaled deeply. "Me? You want me?" Visions of the exhibition she had seen with Berthe flooded her memory. How exciting it had been just to see! To be a part of it! With the impressionists, she could be free at last. "Oh, yes," she said. "Emphatically yes."

Degas smiled. "I'm glad I didn't wait for Tourney."

Mary showed him the other work she had in the studio, asking for and receiving criticism. His eye was good; his comments seemed exactly what she needed. Finally Mary asked him to look at her pastels. She brought out her portfolio and opened it for him. "I have seen your work in pastel," she said, "and I've wanted to create the richness you manage to get, but I've never been able to approach it."

Degas looked through her sheaf of pastel drawings with interest. He nodded. "I have experimented a bit, picked up some tips here and there. If you'd be interested I could teach you what I can. It shouldn't take long, judging from these."

"Would you? I would be more than interested."

"Good, come to my studio on Tuesday about ten, and we can begin."

After he left, Mary could hardly believe her good fortune. She sat down in the chair in the studio and went over it in her mind. Degas *here*—and he liked her work. He was charming. Berthe was right. Mary closed her eyes and remembered the way he had looked when he saw Denise's portrait. It was clear he felt the way she did about it. Parallel paths—could it be true?

All at once Mary realized that although they had talked for nearly three hours, she knew nothing more about him than she had before he came. Well, she knew more about his thoughts on art, but nothing more about him as a person, and come to think of it, she had revealed nothing factual of herself either. It was queer how they could pass over those things and get right to the matters that concerned them most. She had been awe-struck at first, so overwhelmed by him and his reputation. While they were in the studio, it was as if they had always known each other. Mary sighed and went back to her painting with new zest, but all the while holding Tuesday in her mind.

WHEN THE TIME came however, she was as nervous as she had ever been. What if he had forgotten? What if she drew clumsily? Would he make one of his caustic remarks and wither her away? Perhaps it wasn't true that he had an acid tongue. Mary couldn't believe it after talking to him.

She dressed carefully but didn't know if she ought to take a frock coat to protect her clothing or not. She decided not to. When she was ready she took one last glance at herself in the mirror, pinched her cheeks, and touched her lips with rose ointment. She took a small box of pastels and a few sheets of rolled paper.

His studio was only a mile away. It couldn't be a hovel, she thought as she walked, though there were disgraceful places for rent in the quarter. No, she couldn't believe Degas would live in anything like that. He dressed so like a gentleman. Everything about him had to be respectable. His manners and appearance were perfect. She hoped she wouldn't be too early, and that he wouldn't forget, or be in one of his ugly moods if it was true that he really did have them.

When she arrived at the address, the place looked quite ordinary; it was modest, but respectable. Taking a deep breath, she knocked on the door. After a moment, Degas himself let her in. "Good morning," he said. "Well, I see you didn't forget, Miss Cassatt."

"No indeed. But do call me Mary."

He nodded. "And I am Edgar."

She thought he seemed different, almost uncomfortable. She smiled as he took her things and led her to the best chair in the studio. She felt uncomfortable, too. Something was wrong.

"Are you sure you want me to stay?" she asked. "If something has come up, I'll understand."

"Nothing has come up. It's this wretched place." He looked at the walls sadly. "I try not to care so much, but when someone like you who's used to fine surroundings comes—well, I was once a first-rate snob. I'm not good at being humbled."

"Really, Edgar. Your studio has quite a bit of flair. Many artists would think it a palace. It's all very well to know fine surroundings, but not being able to do without them is impractical, isn't it? I prefer to be independent of all that, don't you?"

Edgar laughed and nodded. "You are quite right, of course," Again he laughed, and every trace of tension was gone.

"May I look at some of your work before we begin?" she asked, already looking at the paintings on the wall. Her eyes stopped at a group painting of a woman in black, two girls,, one of whom seemed to be moving, and a seated man, his back to the viewer but his head turned in profile.

"It's a private painting," he said.

"Private?"

"If I were to attempt to show it at the Salon, it would be ridiculed because of the arrangement. I could not allow these people to suffer riducule."

"Who are they?"

"My aunt and uncle; the girls are cousins. He has an important position in Italy. I'm keeping it here at the moment."

It was natural, vital, and unposed. But he was right. It was out of the ordinary and would surely be criticized, if not rejected, though it was masterfully conceived and executed.

"Is this the reason you decided to quit the Salon?"

He hesitated a moment. "A serious work of art should not become an object of ridicule. Look what happened to Manet when he showed his lovely *Olympia*. Because it was a departure from the so-called standard, both the artist and the painting were abused. And the more often such a thing is allowed to happen, the more thwarted the artists become until the creative spirit dwindles and art becomes decadent. It has happened too many times in history. The artist who cares must take a stand. I feel it is my solemn duty."

"So do I. But standing apart and opposing the Salon brings ridicule, doesn't it?"

"From the Salon, of course. And newspaper critics will naturally print whatever will boost the newspaper's circulation. Still, there were a few voices raised in our defense, and there will be more."

"I'm sure there will," she said. "With the independents' show at least the public was allowed to see and judge for itself. It wasn't left to a few supercilious judges."

"I shall never submit my work to a jury again," he said.

"If everyone would refuse to submit to juries, they would lose their power."

"Exactly so. If artists are willing to put their lives in the hands of these little tyrants, they're going to get what they deserve."

Mary leaned back and smiled. "I wouldn't have believed it could make so much difference, but since your visit, I have painted with no thought of pleasing a jury, and the freedom I feel has given me such a surge of ideas, there could never be enough time to carry them all out."

Edgar laughed. "Excellent, excellent. That's exactly how it struck me."

Mary took a step forward, glancing about. In a moment she saw a pastel, matted and resting against a wall behind a work table. "How did you do that? That thick, rich, delicious green and pink!"

He glanced where she pointed and laughed. "I cheated some." He stood up. "You see, as I worked I applied steam directly to the paper, changing the particles to a paste which I then worked with brushes. And I blew on a fixative between several layers. I believe there were three or four separate layers in that one, the final layer left without fixative. Come, I'll show you."

Edgar lit the flame under a tea kettle, laid out a sheet of paper, tacked it to a drawing board, and drew from a sketch of a dancer in his sketchbook. He drew quickly, using only a few colors, seldom glancing at the sketchbook. Mary studied the way he held the chalk, the way he stroked it across the paper, sometimes using long sweeping strokes, sometimes short hatchings.

By the time the small drawing was complete, the tea kettle simmered and spewed out steam. Edgar held the drawing board up to the column of steam coming from the spout of the kettle. He held the board at angles, moving it so as to capture the steam in the places he wanted it. With brushes, he worked the liquid pastel. It dried quickly. He then blew a fine mist of fixative gently on the surface. Without waiting for it to dry, he began the process again, going over the dancer's tutu and the areas where he wanted to indicate brilliant light.

"Yes," she murmured. It seemed so simple. Why didn't she think of it?

"Now I'll show you another trick that must be used sparingly. It's less trouble than steam, and it's good for smaller bright spots." He crushed a light blue pastel and added the fixative drop by drop. When the crushed pastel dust was moist enough to form a wad he could pick up, he pressed it onto the light part of the tutu, using a pushing movement. When he removed his hand, the color was rich and splotchy.

"It's beautiful," Mary said.

"Now, you try it for the hair." He handed her a sienna pastel. She took it with some trepidation. She was going to tamper with his beautiful drawing. But he was smiling, trusting her. She crushed the pastel as he had, trying to use the same hand movements. She applied the medium, drop by drop, and pressed it into a wad. She paused, studied the hair area, weighing the effect it would have. "Can we put a highlight over this later?"

"We can do anything that's needed."

She took up the wad and pressed it onto the paper, trying for the effect he had used with the blue in the tutu. When she took her hand away and looked at the hair, she smiled. He handed her a towel to wipe her hands. "Now for the highlights. The flesh color will do."

Mary picked up the pastel he had used for the skin tones and applied it in light scumbling movements to the hair.

"Bravo," he said.

She examined the picture closely and nodded. A smile formed on her lips.

"You may keep that if it would help," he said.

"Oh, may I?" She felt ridiculously inadequate. It was a superb gift, something she would always treasure.

"There are a couple of other things I could show you," he said. "I begin sometimes with a monoprint. I could do a simple gouache of your face, for instance, then print it on paper and finish the print in pastels."

"That sounds quite involved, but I suppose the effect is worth it. I'd like to see it."

"Yes, the effect is hard to explain. I consider it weight without heaviness, but let me show you."

Mary posed while he painted her in gouache, and all the while he worked, he talked about what he wanted to do, the pictures that were only miniature seeds in his head, the hierarchy of art, each new work, becoming a part of something else he was building, a life's work that would fit together and become a whole that could be broken down again into major subjects. "I can never leave a subject until I am satisfied I have really seen it and expressed it."

As he worked on the gouache, Mary said very little. She listened, wondering whether any of what he said applied to her. She had never thought of a hierarchy of work. She thought only of the painting she was working on or the one she was planning, but not of a body of work, not of examining a subject and expressing it completely. Her mind was racing.

"What sort of new subjects interest you?" he asked.

She smiled. "I have wanted to do people in a theater audience. Individuals, not crowds. I have seen so many paintable subjects there, but it's hardly the place to drag one's easel or sketchbook."

"You mustn't be afraid to draw anywhere, anytime."

"At a theater performance?"

"Why not? You're an artist."

Mary could think of no answer so she merely smiled. He continued working in silence a moment. The studio was quiet, and she was startled when there came a knock and a voice called, "Hey, Edgar."

Edgar turned his head. "Come in."

"You're working, I see," a man said as he poked his head in the doorway.

Mary recognized the face of an engraver she had chatted with briefly at the Louvre, where they both had been copying in the same area. She tried to remember his name. "Henri Desboutin," Edgar said as he introduced them.

Mary smiled and nodded. "Hello again. I believe we talked once at the Louvre."

"Yes, you were the girl at the Titian?"

"No, I was doing the Tiepolo next to it."

"That's right, the madonna. Nice to see you again. I never expected to see you modeling for Edgar."

"Miss Cassatt is interested in pastel."

"I see. Then I don't suppose either of you would be interested in going round to the café for a bowl of soup and a glass of wine?"

Edgar put down his brush and reached in his pocket for a glance at his watch. "That sounds like an inspired idea, Henri. How does it sound to you, Mary? Could you do with some nourishment?"

"Fine."

Edgar pressed a smooth paper over the painting and made one print. "Now that will dry while we are gone."

In a few minutes they were off, walking in the midday sunshine, Mary between the two men. The streets of Montmartre were alive with people hurrying or just strolling, and with smells of food from the cafés. There were sounds of pounding hammers, tinkling music, barking dogs. Mary felt as alive as the street. They went to a café she knew was frequented by some of the independents. The waiter greeted Edgar and Henri by their first names.

"Mary has consented to be one of our group," Edgar said when they were seated.

"Yes," Mary said. "I was very happy to be asked. It's given me an wenormous sense of freedom knowing I shall not have to submit to another jury."

"I hope your lovely skin is sufficiently thick," Desboutin said. "You will be looked upon as a madwoman in a den of crazed idiots."

She smiled. "I have read the notices."

"It's no small thing being attacked like that. It hurts, and you seem a fragile and sensitive young lady. I just hope you won't be disappointed."

"I'm not as fragile as I look, and I'll worry about the barbs only when they happen."

"Good," Henri replied, holding his wineglass up. "To the newest independent."

Mary sipped and thanked him. She had seen his prints at Gallerie Durand-Ruel and wished she had paid more attention to them. It was going to be wonderful to be an independent. There will probably be other days like this, she thought, but even if there never was to be another one, she would have no regrets. She had already spent hours with Edgar Degas, learning from him. It was the best thing that ever happened. The sun had never seemed so dazzling. Even the soup was by far the most delicious she had ever tasted.

After lunch Henri lit his pipe, and it struck Mary as she watched him puffing and settling back that it was a natural picture. "I should like to paint you just like that some time."

Edgar and Henri laughed loudly.

"Why is that so funny?"

"It isn't," Egar said. "He is an excellent subject. You were attracted by the way he holds the pipe."

"More the way he looks out over it."

Henri shook his head and laughed again. "I wouldn't miss it," he said, looking at Edgar and chuckling.

"The reason our friend is so amused," Edgar said, "is because he has only just posed for me and was glad to be done with it."

"Edgar insisted I look drugged and dissipated. What a pose."

After a while they left Henri and returned to Edgar's studio. Mary, refreshed from lunch, was anxious to get back to the lesson. She examined the monoprint carefully before he began to work in pastel. Then she stood behind his left shoulder, watching his every move as he worked to finish the portrait.

She watched and contemplated. She had seen a lot today, although she would not know if she had learned anything until she did some new work in the medium herself. She was anxious to begin a serious pastel study of her own and use some of the things she had seen. Tomorrow, she thought. But how could she thank him? She could never express what she felt. And it was time she ought to go. She had spent nearly five hours in the company of this man. Her father would have been scandalized.

When she was ready to leave, Edgar insisted on walking with her and carrying her things. There was no refusing; he simply came along. "I can't thank you enough," she said.

"It was entirely my pleasure. I hope you will like working in pastels. I like it because I love lines. I think in lines and create with them and pile them on top of one another and never get enough."

She pressed her lips together, then smiled. "Would it be outrageous of me to do some studies and ask you to look at them and criticize them?"

"I would be pleased," he said.

He seemed to grow quieter as they approached her apartment. "Thank you again," she said at the door.

He paused. "Another thing," he said. "I wondered if you would be so kind as to attend the theater with me this Friday evening?"

"That would be lovely," she said, trying not to show her amazement, "You won't mind if I carry work things, like pastels?"

12

It HAD BECOME the custom for the independents to meet in a congenial café on Friday evenings, a tradition that had continued from the early days before they had formed a group. In fact, it was at these get-togethers that the idea of standing united against the tide was born and grew. The gatherings continued to be occasions to find solace in each other and to explore new ideas affecting the freedom of art.

Manet was looked on as the father of the movement and was always given a special table. Degas too was accorded a place of honor. The others looked up to them as leaders and spokesmen.

One evening in the spring of 1878 Edgar asked Mary to accompany him to the café, assuring her that she would find it interesting, that Berthe Morisot often joined Manet's party there. Although it wasn't the sort of place a refined young lady from Philadelphia should frequent, especially in the company of so many men and so few ladies, she really wanted to go. After all, she was an artist just as the others, and she needed to share their friendship, their ideas and frustrations. So, in spite of her moral misgivings, she went and they all welcomed her. After one glass of wine, she found herself being drawn into the charged atmosphere of the union, and she was no longer aware of the proportion of the sexes. They were all artists in a mood of rebellion and righteousness for the sake of art. They were all working consciously toward new ways to inject truth in their work. They were reappraising every aspect of art, searching, arguing, groping in half light and listening to one another. Mary's mind was set aflame by the discussion. That was the first of many such evenings for her.

One night, however, the conversation had been more stimulating than usual and Mary had stayed later than was her habit. One of the newer young men whom Mary knew only as Josef was setting forth his ideas about how to improve the image of the group. "It would be stupid to open our arms to anyone who ever put paint to canvas."

"Now wait," Edgar said. "The artistic standards of the group are extraordinarily high. We do not invite immature artists or hacks."

"But we must be careful not to lower our principles and invite those who still paint Salon pictures and are not committed to showing the world as it is in the light of day."

"The light of day," Edgar repeated. "Is that your definition of principle?"

"The painting of light is the kernel of what we are trying to do, isn't it?"

"Not at all," Edgar said. "It is but one element. Truth is the kernel. There is light; there is movement; there is time. Perspective and substance and many important things make up the world as it is and as it seems. If you can't appreciate that, you should pursue the Salon."

"I maintain the principle that painting a subject in the immediacy of sunlight is the basis of our way of seeing life around us."

"Under your principle then," Edgar shot back, "Da Vinci's *Last*

Supper is not worthy to be among our work. Your principle would have it that Manet's *Olympia* was a Salon painting, I take it."

Loud laughter broke out at the tables, but the young Josef did not join in. "I still say we are painters of light first."

"Perhaps that is true in your case, or perhaps you want too badly to be an impressionist. You want to be recognized as one. You are like the gardener who would prune his trees so close to the trunk, no branches could survive, and you would scratch your head and wonder why the tree died. You are a near-sighted hangman who would have us practice the same control over artists as the jury of the Salon."

There was more laughter and bravos for Edgar. When Josef looked as though he would say something more, he was shushed by the others. Edgar smiled, and although Mary agreed with everything Edgar said, she felt a certain compassion for young Josef. But that was the way of it, she supposed. She ought to drink her coffee, smile at the unfortunate boy, and go home.

Edgar must have sensed her readiness to leave the café, for he reached for his hat and passed her a look that said I'm ready. She nodded and stood, wishing everyone a good night.

The gaslights in front of the café glowed brightly in the cool black evening. Mary breathed deeply of the sweet smokeless air. It was refreshing after the closeness of the café. Edgar took her arm and walked so near her that her shoulder touched his arm from time to time. It was pleasant walking home like this. The quiet of the night brought a sense of peace. Edgar was in a rare and exalted mood. He raved about the beautiful nights in Italy when he was a student, traveling about from museum to museum. He even lapsed into Italian. Mary laughed at what seemed like his pretentious airs. It reminded her of Parma and perhaps, because of Edgar's closeness, of Lorenzo. Her feelings about Lorenzo came back in a poignant wave and were accompanied after the first wash, by other feelings; embarrassment, regret that she had behaved so immorally. But here she was with Edgar, feeling something similar to that agony, only this time there would be no foolishness connected with it. She knew where her loyalty and affection and deepest love was centered.

Edgar surely felt the same way. It was evident in everything he said. His thoughts, his observations were for art. It was wonderful luck to have a friend like him.

All of a sudden he was quiet. He laughed when he saw how befuddled she was.

"I'm sorry," she said, "I was thinking of Italy and my mind wandered."

"I asked if you wanted to go to a play next week? It's something new and meaty."

"Next week. Oh, I forgot to ask if you would go to the Barrie's dinner party next Thursday."

He groaned.

"They have been very kind to me and they want so to meet you. They, and their friends, own your work. I thought it would be fun for you to meet them."

He stopped walking and looked at her. "People who buy your pictures expect a great deal of cleverness. I always feel they're disappointed I'm not taller. But never mind all that. I shall be delighted to go to the Barrie's party if it would please you."

"It would. Louisine Elder will be there. She's been such a dear friend and she bought her first Degas when she was fifteen. I was with her. Of course, I never thought I'd know you then."

"Do you?"

"Yes, I do."

He frowned. "You know something of how I work, and how I think about art. You know some of the things I dislike. I have my own standards in art and in life. Some of the others think I am unbearably snobbish. I am."

She laughed. "You? You're not at all snobbish."

"I do look down on many of the things they accept, for instance, a certain coarse Bohemian lack of basic principle."

"My feelings are exactly the same about that."

"I thought so."

"Why do you look so downcast then?" she asked. "A moment ago you were full of Italian good cheer, and now . . . I don't know. What's bothering you?"

"Ah," he said, throwing back his head, "it's simply that, although they say I'm snobbish, sometimes they think we are like them."

Mary sighed. Maybe he really was a snob. But she didn't want to pursue that. "Let's not worry about what someone might think. What was this play you mentioned? I'm sorry—I interrupted you. Forgive me."

"Play? Oh, yes. It's something Duranty mentioned. But that's what I meant. Everytime I think of going out, doing something, I think of asking you. I'm afraid I am monopolizing too much of your time. And if it causes you to be uncomfortable, if you think there is any kind of unwholesome talk, you have only to say no and I will understand."

Mary was beginning to understand. "Have you heard anything unwholesome?"

"No, no. Still, if I should be the cause of creating trouble for you, well, how could I forgive myself?"

"And how could you forgive the unfortunate person who would say anything unwholesome about either of us?" She smiled.

"Quite right," he said. "Some things are unforgivable."

FOR THE BARRIES' party Mary wore a silk dress with wide lavender and red stripes. It was a departure from her usual conservative taste. Wearing it had an effect on how she felt and acted. She was bolder, more sure of herself. She liked to paint models in striped clothes because they gave her lines that defined the body it covered. Edgar once told her he found them confusing and unnecessary. She found them intriguing.

When Edgar arrived to escort her to the party, he did not comment on the dress, but he seemed happy. It was a good omen, she thought, for he had told her that when he brooded about his work and realized that it was not right, he was not fit to be with people.

The guests were a brilliant group. There were so many titles it was hard to keep them straight, but Mary had met some of the people before, and Edgar remembered them quite easily, and was already acquainted with some. He seemed as enchanted by Louisine as she was with him.

Just before they went into the dining room, Clara Barrie, a Belgian countess, and Mary were chatting. The countess said she wanted to ask Edgar if he would do a portrait of her two daughters. "I heard he did not do portraits. You should know, Miss Cassatt. Does he?"

"He certainly does portraits," Mary said, "what he doesn't do is take commissions. He requires complete freedom to pose his models and guarantees to please only himself."

"How entrancing," the countess said. "Do you think he would agree to paint my daughters if I gave him complete freedom?"

"I think it would be best to ask him, Countess. I'll go with you and bring it up if you like."

"Wonderful," the countess said and went with Mary. They found Edgar, and when the question was asked, he looked thoughtful a moment. "Your daughters must be lovely creatures, and I would be honored to paint them when they become of age. The problem is I have no knack with young children. I am too stern and demanding. I am not the one who can do justice to the very young. Fortunately, though, I do know a person who can capture the charm of the little ones."

"My daughters are four and two. I suppose they are a bit young for a proper portrait. Perhaps Monsieur Degas would do me instead."

Edgar looked at her face, turning it gently with his hand on her chin to gain a view of her profile. "I think you would be a perfect subject, but I wonder if it wouldn't be wise to preserve a picture of you with your two baby daughters. This is, after all, the only time in your lives when it can be done." He turned his head to Mary. "Excuse me, but I believe Louisine is trying to get your attention. There, by the mantel. It's quite all right. The countess and I understand."

Mary left them and found that Louisine had not been trying to get her attention at all. Mary thought it strange, but Louisine went on so flatteringly about her gown she quite forgot Edgar and the Countess.

In the dining room Mary smiled across the table at Edgar. He was seated between Louisine and the countess, and the three of them were most animated. Although he claimed to disdain any form of adulation, Mary suspected he liked it well enough in small doses.

After dinner the ladies had their coffees in the drawing room while the men smoked and sipped brandy in the dining room. The countess ambled to the sofa with Mary. "Edgar tells me you are excellent with child models."

"I usually do enjoy painting them. You couldn't find a more beautiful subject, could you?"

"Edgar thought you might be willing to show me some of your portraits. I would love to see them."

"I'd be happy to."

"I'd like to have portraits of my two daughters, and Monsieur Degas has convinced me I would be fortunate indeed if I could engage you to do them."

"Oh," Mary said. "He is very kind. You're welcome to come round and see what I have done."

"Would tomorrow be convenient then?"

"Tomorrow? That would be fine," Mary said. She did want to paint the countess's daughters. A few commissions were all she needed to cover her studio expenses, and children were never tiresome.

On the drive home, Edgar said nothing about the countess or his conversation with her until Mary brought it up. Then he smiled. "You have the patience and the talent for it."

"And you have only the talent?" she asked.

"Exactly."

"She's a lovely woman."

"Then why not put her in the picture with the children? That ought to be something. They'll all be screaming and pulling each other's hair. The mere thought of it agonizes me and makes me wish I had been more charitable toward you." He shook his head and brightened. "Of course you aren't obliged to agree to anything. No thank you is better than turning into a raving madwoman."

"I would very much like to do the countess and her daughters. I'm sure they're sweet little things."

"I admire you," he said.

"I know. The countess told me."

"I admire you for reasons she wouldn't guess. I wish I could tell the world how much I admire you, Mary." His voice turned low. He reached for her hand, and brought it to his lips. Time stopped at the moment of his touching her gloved fingers to his lips. Time was extended and preserved in the warmth of her mind and the memory of her quavering nerve endings. Their eyes met and stayed steadfast in spite of the rolling vibrations of the carriage wheels. "Edgar," she whispered as their faces inched closer until their lips met. The thrill of his kiss flooded her wth a palpitating excitement. She had never experienced anything so overwhelming. But she mustn't lose control. She smiled and moved away. She looked into his eyes but could not talk. However, he spoke softly to her and it was all too soon when the carriage stopped at her home. He walked to the door with her and their voices whispered the parting words they always had in the past, but their eyes penetrated further.

"Tomorrow?" he said, and she nodded and smiled as she went in. Once inside, her spirit detached itself immediately and went flying around the room like a fluttering hummingbird.

By morning she was almost normal, and remembered to act her age. She was a woman past thirty, not a girl of sixteen. Soon the memory of that moment in the carriage was reduced to a piece of pleasure that could be contained. She sighed.

The countess came at two, and after looking at Mary's work, proclaimed that Edgar was right. She wanted Mary to do the painting and, yes, perhaps mother and daughters would be the best. It was to be done at the home of the countess, if Mary didn't mind.

"No, not at all. The children will be more comfortable there. It would be best." It only took a few minutes to make the arrangements. And when the countess had gone, Mary's head was reeling with pleasure. She knew that the countess was a leader in her circle and if the portraits pleased the countess, there would be others.

She thought of Edgar again and would have walked to his studio to see him, but the postman arrived and left a letter from her father. She eagerly sat down to read it.

The news was such a surprise to her, she sat staring off a full minute, absorbing it, before she grabbed her shawl and hurried off to tell Edgar.

13

Edgar was at his easel, working on a painting of a dancer. It was something he had been working on for a month, and Mary had watched it progress with interest, amazed at how much important detail he could draw up from his memory. To him a model was a distraction.

When Mary came in, Edgar put down his brushes and came toward her. "How good to see you."

"Oh, Edgar, I have to talk to you."

"What is it?" he said. "You look agitated. I hope my actions last night didn't upset you, because the last thing I would ever want to do is upset you. Any liberties I may—"

"No, no. I wasn't thinking of last night. I mean, of course, I thought of it. But I'm not agitated over that—I mean I'm not agitated at all. I was thinking of what is going to happen."

"Sit down," he said. "Can I get you tea while you tell me about it?"

"No, thank you," she sighed. "It's wonderful, really. My family is coming over to live with me. My brothers are both settled now, so Mother, Father, and my sister Lydia are coming here. We'll be together again. It's been years since I've been home. I almost die every time I cross the ocean, so they're coming here. And it will be easier to have only one household for Father to support."

"That's quite a surprise, isn't it?"

Mary nodded.

"Coming all of a sudden, are they?"

Mary nodded again. "In a month or so, the letter said. I didn't notice when it was posted. I expect they are on the way or close to it. I must look for a bigger place to live."

"So you must."

"I shall probably not see you so often."

"Why not?" He pulled down his waistcoat impatiently. "You will still be working, won't you? You're not giving up your vocation."

"How could I do that? I'll work, but I can't say where. I can't say anything until we're all settled in an apartment."

"That's fine for your living quarters, but you must rent a studio here in Montmartre. Remember, you will be exhibiting with the independents this year."

"I'm not apt to forget anything as important as that."

"It's quite simple. You will live with your family and you will keep a studio near here. You need it to protect your time to paint."

Mary sighed. "My income from painting must cover my expenses."

"That's good. It will keep you in your studio and out of the millinery shops."

Suddenly Mary laughed. Edgar laughed. They looked at each other and Mary was tempted to rush into his arms, feel his closeness once again. But no, that wouldn't do. She must not act like a schoolgirl. He was her friend; she wanted him to remain so forever. She moved away, sat on a stool, and pulled off her gloves. "Oh, Edgar, I know you're right. I shall rent a studio nearby and continue my work just as though there was no change. Lydia will pose. Wait until you see her. She's beautiful. Hidden away inside her delicacy is a strength you can only see rarely. I don't mean courage. There is more."

"I am anxious to meet her."

"I have missed them all."

"A family is a blessing to—" He stopped speaking and turned away. She suspected he missed his dead parents very much. She had heard that something had come between Edgar and his brother. Although he had many friends, he was a man alone, and she knew he meant it deeply when he said a family is a blessing. She couldn't keep herself from reaching for his hand. He looked up and smiled.

"If you like, I will help you find a place suitable for your family," he said.

"Would you?"

"Desboutin might know of a studio. He remembers these things. We'll ask him when he comes this afternoon."

"Yes, he might know of something. I feel better already. How can I thank you?"

"We'll begin looking tomorrow." He smiled and their eyes met. She felt longing for him build all at once. She took a deep breath and relaxed. "Good," she said. "Today we shall work. I want to finish my portrait of Henri. I see your canvas is almost finished. This will be one you'll want to exhibit in the show of independents or impressionists, whatever name is decided on."

"I shall never vote to call myself an impressionist."

Mary tossed her head back. "It would not seem such a poor name if it wasn't regarded as an insult."

"My work is not a quickly gained impression, and neither is yours. It's a false title and serves no one."

"What we call ourselves isn't important. I despise it when the group wrangles about details like a name. People will call us whatever they like." Though Edgar grunted as though he might be prepared to argue, she went on quickly. "Producing very good work to uphold each other is what we must concentrate on. Quality is all that should matter to us. For myself, I think the studies I have done of women in the loges at the opera are my best."

"Yes, the one I saw is quite strong." He looked thoughtful. "It's the other side of the stage from mine that interests you."

"To me the audience is part of the performance. Because their little dramas are hidden, they become all the more intriguing."

"Little dramas? Is that what you see when a beautiful girl flutters a fan?" he asked.

"It occurs to me, but that is not what I paint, is it? You can't trap me into admitting I paint any less intellectually than I should."

He shook his head and smiled. "How can you know me so well to see through all my schemes to convince artists to put intellect over sentiment at all costs?"

"As long as you say *sentiment* and not emotion or mood, everyone agrees with you. But, the lines are not always clear."

Edgar groaned.

Desboutin arrived, and without a word about it, sat on the model's stool and assumed his pose. "I just saw Pissarro and Gauguin in the café. They said they were coming by."

"Fine," Edgar said. "Then Gauguin accepted our invitation to join the independents?"

"So it would seem."

"Gauguin's work has almost too much force," Mary said. "If anyone combines both intellect and emotion and poises them at sword's point, it's he."

"Not at all," Edgar said. "He's all intellect and style. I would never have sponsored his memberhsip if I didn't believe that."

"He uses intellect and style to convey emotion," Mary said.

"Of course," Edgar said, "but he doesn't *use* emotion."

"If you ask me," Desboutin said, "emotion is implicit in his style. His primitive lines *are* emotional. He uses saturated color in great masses, but nothing is impulsive about his work. It's all intellectual."

"That's what I admire about him," Edgar said.

Mary smiled and concentrated on Desboutin's eyelids, her mind wandering from the talk as she worked. Desboutin rambled on almost incessantly and it was good, for his eyes gathered the distant spark she needed.

She was about finished when Pissarro arrived with Gauguin. Mary was glad to stop work and greet them. She had a special affection for Pissarro. "How is it going for you, Camille?" she asked.

He shrugged. "I could complain, not for myself, but for my poor wife and children. What will happen to us if Monsieur Durand-Ruel goes under?"

"What! Durand-Ruel? He can't."

"Do people buy paintings when carrots are so dear?"

Mary looked at the others, her questioning eyes linked finally to Edgar's.

"I don't know," he said. "I've heard some mutterings. It's probably true."

Desboutin nodded gravely.

"We can't let this happen," Mary said, determined to see that he received the financial help he needed. "Durand-Ruel is the only hope the independents have."

She had been so caught up in her thoughts, she had not realized Gauguin was gazing intently at her painting. "You have captured the force in the eyes," he said.

She turned to him and smiled. If she had pleased Gauguin, she was pleased herself. He had a ruthless eye and would not flatter any more than Edgar would. As she looked at him, she thought he had a terrible intensity hidden in his thin angular face, and yet he looked poor, and so determined. She glanced again at Pissarro. His face was etched in pain. Perhaps he had come in from the country, gone to the Gallerie Durand-Ruel to sell a picture or two to live on, and had learned of the trouble there. So there was nowhere for him to turn, and he must return home empty-handed.

The conversation had turned to the exhibit and they spoke as though it could bring fame and fortune. Mary did not join in the discussion. Desperate men had to have something to pin their hopes on. In the meantime perhaps a good meal, Mary thought, would lighten the day. "Would you care to have dinner at my place?" she asked, looking first at Pissarro, then the others.

Edgar accepted for them all, praising Mary's cook. He was all in favor of the little party, and the others seemed cheered by his mood.

"I'll go now and tell Cook," Mary said.

"All right," Edgar said. "We'll be along in a little while."

Pissarro put on his hat. "I'll see you home."

Mary was glad for his company, and when they had gone a short ways, she confided, "My family is coming to live in Paris. They're settling here with me. I want to find them a lovely apartment, and I was thinking how nice it would be to have a few good paintings already in place. I have one of Edgar's and a small Renoir, but I'd like a landscape. I was hoping to buy one at the exhibit, but they'll be here in a few weeks. I thought if you have one available, you might let me buy it to present as a welcoming gift."

"I certainly have a landscape for you. I have dozens of them. And, you may choose the season," he smiled.

"Autumn, I think. It should be fairly large. My father loves riding horses in the country. He's used to the hilly woods of Pennsylvania, but I know he would like your work."

"I'm very glad for you. Nothing can take the place of family. Not even art."

"That's true."

"I mourn for Degas, Desboutin even Gauguin. A family is what they need."

"Maybe they're different."

"Being alone makes them different. Take Degas, for instance. He was such a social fellow when he had wealth and position and his father was alive. After his father's death, he became depressed. He was quarrelsome and resentful. He has changed, though, since you befriended him, and we all thank you for it."

Mary laughed. "He has been a good friend and teacher, but he still becomes depressed and moody. I do not give in to those moods. If an hour passes without a single cheery word, I simply leave him."

Pissarro laughed. "Perhaps you are teaching him as much as he is teaching you. At least he is not using despair as a theme in his work this season."

When they arrived Mary took his coat and brought him tea.

"Cook is excited about our little party. It's no trouble at all, she says."

Pissarro seemed comfortable there in her living room, a bit less careworn than before. It wasn't long before the others were at the door.

Desboutin and Gauguin were smiling, but Edgar had a strange look on his face. His cape was pulled tight at the throat. Mary looked at Edgar, expecting some form of explanation. Just then a squeal came from under his cloak.

"Whatever was that?" Pissarro said. "Sounded like one of the neighbor's pigs."

Edgar leaned over and placed four tiny feet on the floor. When he stood up, there was a small furry creature shaking itself. Mary laughed. "It's a puppy." She knelt down beside it and gently patted its head.

"It's for you," Edgar said. "I noticed how you stop on the street to smile at little dogs."

Mary looked up at Edgar. She hadn't been so touched in a long while. She picked up the little dog, hugged it, nuzzled it, and when she looked at its face, laughed at the blank look in its eyes. "What is its name?"

"Imperia, I was told," Edgar said. "It seems to fit, but you can call her anything you like."

"Imperia," Mary whispered. She held it, smiling up at Edgar.

14

AFTER A BUSY MONTH of unpacking and getting settled into the apartment, the Cassatt family was finally at home in Paris.

"We are going to be comfortable here," Robert announced to Mary and Katherine at breakfast. "It's a cheerful place with those big fireplaces in all the bedrooms. And the servants' rooms are quite adequate. So often they aren't. I don't know how you found such a handsome place," he said smiling at Mary.

"I looked from morning 'til night. And Monsieur Degas was kind enough to help me."

Katherine poured coffee. "I think we are settled enough now to invite your Monsieur Degas some evening. We must meet him."

"Good, I'll invite him tomorrow if you like." Mary glanced at the clock, and across the table at Lydia's empty place. "Isn't Lydia coming to breakfast?"

"No, dear. I'm afraid we've quite spoiled her lately. She takes breakfast in her room."

"Still? I thought a rest after the crossing would have fixed everything by now."

Robert rattled his paper and looked over his glasses at Mary. "This has been a busy time. A great change in all our lives. Liddy needs more rest than she used to, and mornings are not her best time. As soon as she has had time to move around and have breakfast, she'll be down."

"I see." Mary was beginning to understand. All her life she had expected that Lydia would improve. It seemed odd to her now that she could have clung to that belief for so long. Lydia was not going to get better. The realization of it should not have been a shock, but it was. She felt cold. "Does she prefer not to be disturbed?"

"Yes," Katherine said. "When she's ready, she gets dressed and joins us."

Mary was quiet for a moment. "I asked her if she would pose for me. Do you think that will tire her?"

"Do her good," Robert said.

"I really must get back to work soon," Mary said. "I've promised to exhibit with the group of independent artists I told you about, and I have only one painting finished."

"Of course, you must paint," her mother said.

"Do you think it would be all right to knock on Lydia's door and ask if she would like to come with me and pose?"

Katherine looked at the clock. "Give her another ten minutes." After a pause she poured more coffee in Mary's cup. "I should like to meet your friend, Monsieur Pissarro, too. His landscape with the colors of fall is a constant pleasure."

"I'm glad you like it. He lives quietly in the country, but I'm sure he'll bring the family with him to Paris soon."

Mary got up and went to the window. It seemed a warm day. Imperia got up from her pillow in the corner and wagged her tail. Mary smiled. There was something about the funny little dog with its wiry hair and blank expression that always made her smile. She bent over and patted its head. "Would you like to go for a walk?" she asked. "Very well, we shall go out a moment." She turned to her mother. "Just to the garden."

The air was sweet outside. Mary was restless for work. She wanted to put her hands and eyes to the task of painting. She thought of her studio on the Avenue de Clichy and her heart beat faster. She could not wait another day.

When she returned to the dining room, Lydia was sitting on the chair by the window reading the newspaper. She looked up and smiled at Mary. "Good morning." The sight of Lydia reassured her.

"Would you like to pose for me today?"

Lydia put the paper down in her lap. "That would be fun indeed."

LYDIA LOOKED AROUND the studio as though it were a circus full of delightful surprises. Her enthusiasm did not flag, even after an hour of looking at sketches and watercolors, oils and pastels.

"Will you do me in oils or watercolor?"

"Oil, but first I must do some sketches."

"In pastel?" Lydia urged.

"If you like. What I want to do is a portrait of you in a loge at the opera."

"Is that why you have all those sketches of theater interiors?"

Mary nodded. "And I bought a dress to paint you in. It's pale yellow and just the sort of thing worn to the theater this season." Mary opened the closet and drew out the dress.

"Mmm," Lydia said as she took it. "I don't think Father will approve of the neckline."

"He will after a few months. It's the fashion now. I'll help you get into it."

Lydia shrugged and unfastened her high-necked dress. "I've never worn anything so scanty, though I've heard you French women are all disgraceful." Lydia laughed as she tossed her dress over a chair and wriggled into the shimmering gown.

"Just the way I knew you'd look," Mary said, more than pleased with the effect.

"It fits perfectly, doesn't it?" Lydia twirled around. "I told you this would be fun. How do you want me to pose?"

"On that chair. Here, let me hang up your things. There, sit down and imagine being in the theater."

Mary hung the clothes hurriedly and set out her papers and pastels plus a few bits of charcoal.

"This is grand," Lydia said, leaning forward and smoothing out the folds of the dress. "It's strange to think of being here. I can't believe it some mornings when I open my eyes and instead of cabbage roses I see blue and white stripes on my walls. I rush to the window and it's really Paris out there. Philadelphia is gone forever."

Mary stopped sketching a moment. "Gone forever?"

"For me."

"Is that what you wanted?"

"Oh yes, I had wanted it for ages. But I didn't say it to them. I knew it was impossible. We were established in Philadelphia. Mother sometimes said she wished we could all be together and I'd say I did too. It was Father who finally said it would be nice to live in Paris with you."

"Didn't you hate to leave your friends, and Aleck and Gard and the children?"

"Not as much as I wanted to come and be with you in Paris and see it the way you do. It's so good to be here." Lydia leaned forward and looked most earnestly at Mary. Mary saw the joy in Lydia's face, and all at once understood that her sister's happiness was in the present. The past no longer mattered. The future was not Lydia's concern. Now, with its tiny pleasures, was where she existed.

"That pose," Mary said, seeing exactly what she wanted. "Can you hold it?" She didn't wait for Lydia to answer. She pinned a new sheet onto the drawing board and quickly caught the lines of the pose. She was possessed by what she saw. The bare round shoulders, the light on the hair, the face alive with Lydia's special intelligence. She worked intently until Lydia drew a long breath. "I can't hold this pose another second," she said.

"Stop, by all means. I'm sorry."

Lydia stood up and stretched. "It's just that I was thinking so hard about not moving, it became impossible."

"You don't have to be that still. I should have told you."

"Can I see it?"

"Surely. What do you think?" Mary moved away and Lydia looked at the drawing. She smiled. "So that's what I look like to you. That's nice. I like being your model."

"We could go out for tea and stretch our legs."

"I'd have to change; and you're not finished."

Mary thought. "No, you don't have to change. I keep a large Italian shawl here." She went back to the closet. "Won't this do?"

Lydia raised her eyebrows and put the soft shawl around her shoulders. "I really do want a cup of tea," she said, her eyes sparkling.

"It probably wouldn't do at all in Philadelphia, but it will be stunning on Avenue de Clichy."

"Then tea it is, and back to work for us," Lydia said.

They walked across the Avenue and up a few doors to a tea room Mary liked. Lydia was enchanted with it. "Ladies unaccompanied don't do this in Philadelphia, or have you forgotten?"

"I haven't. It seems to me, though, that there is nothing unseemly about ladies taking tea in a public place."

"As long as we don't tell Father."

"Father will have to realize we are not in America. We're both over thirty and besides the French are freer. You'll notice it in many things now that you live here. The new writing is experimental and stimulating. The music, too. Everything is freer."

Lydia smiled and looked down. "Even love?"

"What?" The question was unexpected. Mary hesitated. "I suppose free love is going too far," she said. "But I have heard the arguments and some people, even women, condone it. Well, they seem to condone it in the abstract. It still seems immoral to me no matter what they call it or how intellectually it is looked upon."

Lydia sighed.

"You didn't think for one moment, I'd—"

"Oh, no, not a moment, but I thought it possible that you could condone it in the abstract too. You are somewhat of a rebel."

"Perhaps, but love is too complicated. It leads to so many other things."

Lydia wrinkled her nose. "Now, why are you being so sensible when I thought you would give me some insights into this progressive thinking the magazines talk about."

"Why would I know anything about that?"

"You're progressive. You do what other people assume women can't do, and you do it better than anyone."

Mary glanced again at her sister's face. If Lydia thought that of her, what difference did it make what anyone else thought? It was the nicest compliment she had ever heard. But along with the pleasure it brought her came that ache that only Lydia's smile could bring.

Afterward they strolled back to the studio by a different route. "I want to stop and invite Edgar for dinner tomorrow," Mary explained.

Edgar was at work on a small but complex canvas of a backstage ballet scene. As soon as she had done the introductions and invited Edgar, and he had accepted, Mary studied the canvas with awe. "It's remarkable. It's ambitious—perfectly balanced, and so cleverly. Only you could do this." She had always been impressed by his work, but this was more. This was genius. It turned her artist's blood to rivers of excitement.

"I've missed seeing you," he said.

Mary shyly met his gaze. "I'm back to work now. We're settled in, and Lydia is posing for a portrait."

He smiled. "You'll stop by from time to time then?"

"Oh yes, I shall."

"I have friends who want you to paint their daughter."

"When I finish Lydia's portrait, I can do it. How old is the child?"

"Four or five, I believe."

"I'll look forward to it."

"And I'll look forward to dinner with the Cassatts tomorrow."

Mary and Lydia smiled and said good-bye. It was odd how formal he seemed, except for that moment when he said he had missed her. Hadn't she been formal, too? His manner bothered her. It wasn't what she expected. She wouldn't have been surprised if he had been moody and quiet to the point of being rude. She couldn't recall his ever being so subdued.

"He didn't seem quite himself," she explained to Lydia as they walked to the studio.

"I don't wonder," Lydia said. "I felt there was some strain. It could have been because of me. I think he's very nice."

"He is, but doesn't always appear to be."

"Is he in love with you?"

"Lydia! Really."

"I suspect he is. And you are not sure, are you?"

"Lydia, we are artists. We have that in common. I have no time for romantic adventure. It's the sort of thing that could ruin me."

"I believe you're afraid of it."

"Suppose I am?"

"You admit it?"

"Why not? I fear what it could do to me. I don't want to be a wife responsible to a husband and children. I can never give up my work. I want to be independent. My work is adventure enough."

"I think neither one of us was meant for love. Still, we're women and it's silly to pretend we don't have womanly longings even if we can't have the ordinary satisfactions. I don't mind most of the time. I have so much. But there are moments." Her voice trailed off and she shook her head.

"I have my work."

Lydia looked up. "And what good does that do when that hollow burning comes?"

"Oh, work can take that feeling and use it. There's an energy that comes out of that need—and if it gets hold of a subject, there can be a great wave of satisfaction when the results build steadily and a painting comes alive."

"How lucky for you," Lydia said. "Do you think it works like that for him, too?"

"How could I know that? Edgar is an artist and that's how I know him. As a man I don't know and try not to wonder."

"So that's it—you try not to wonder. I'll wager he does the same and tries not to wonder about you."

"Maybe it would be best if we all didn't wonder, including you." Mary opened the door to her studio and stood back while Lydia went in first. "Come on now," Mary said, "let's forget Edgar for the moment and get back to work. I will finish the pastel by tomorrow. Then we can begin the painting for the exhibition. If you feel like it, that is."

"I will."

"Good. I talked to the theater director and have permission to come in an hour before the performance to do the drawing. We can start there if you are agreeable."

Lydia was enthusiastic. Mary went back to work on the pastel portrait. It was coming along so well, it exceeded her original vision and almost seemed to have a life of its own. The expression she wanted was there. She told Lydia to rest, and stood back and looked at it. Yes, it was good. She thought of showing it to Edgar. Perhaps he could see something she didn't, some fault or a way to improve it. Well, tomorrow she would look at it again when her vision and judgment were refreshed.

"It's very beautiful," Lydia said.

THE NEXT EVENING they all sat in the drawing room. The lamb was roasting in the kitchen. Mary amused herself by sketching her father as he read. "He's late," Robert said.

"Nonsense," Mary said. "This is not late for Edgar. I didn't specify an exact time for him to arrive."

"It looks as though you should have."

"Father, you're ruining my sketch with those unpleasant lines in your forehead." She laughed. "I think we should have our sherry now."

"Before he arrives?" Katherine said. "I couldn't."

"I could," Robert said.

"He loves music," Lydia said.

"That's true," Mary said. "Did I tell you?"

"No, but I saw his pictures, remember? It was clear from the way he painted musicians. It was as though he really wanted to show the music and make it a part of the painting."

Mary was astonished. Lydia had seen something in her casual viewing of his work that she had entirely missed. She had seen the musicians only as pictorial elements. "I think you're right. We'll ask him tonight."

Finally Edgar arrived, undaunted and charming. Robert talked about horses and Edgar recommended several farms whose animals were of noble stock. Robert was interested, for Edgar did seem to know what he was talking about. When they had examined the subject to the point of repetition, Mary realized she should have invited a few other people. She had thought only of having Edgar know her family. She hadn't thought of what an awkward group it might be for conversation. Katherine, however, changed the subject. "We're all anticipating the exhibit of independent painters. We have nothing at all like it in America."

"Yes," Edgar said, and his expression turned grave.

"My goodness, why do you seem so downcast? Mary is quite looking forward to it."

"I know," he said, gazing off. "but it takes a certain courage to want to participate in this exhibit. I do it because the Salon is squelching living art. It wants to perpetuate an art that has been exhausted. Anything new and vital is crushed, rejected, and called unsuitable. One must not question the Salon. It has always been the taste of France. It has been the only forum an artist could seek. It's entrenched in our society. If you aren't in the Salon, you aren't a *real* artist."

"That sounds bleak," Katherine said. "Mary told us the last show of the independents was not too well received, but perhaps this time it will be better."

"That is what everyone hopes," Edgar said, "but hopes are usually unrealistic, I've found."

"We are all working for excellence," Mary said. "We will show nothing but our best work. I cannot believe that all of Paris will turn its back on us."

"Paris has always appreciated art and enshrined her artists," Robert said.

Edgar shook his head. "The newspapers devoured us last time. It was a spontaneous feast. You see, when the critics discovered what power they had to make themselves talked about, they each tried to outdo the other. All they needed to do was to make monkeys out of these so-called artists, flatter their reader's Salon-bred taste, and they became celebrities. I doubt if any of last year's critics will have a change of heart."

"It's something like war," Mary said. "The critics are both our objectives and the enemy."

Lydia cocked her head. "But critics are not the Salon. I should think there would be some writers who would look at the other side."

"Those who do will have to be very careful if they want to be published," Edgar said.

"I don't know," Katherine said. "This venture seems of doubtful value if all you can expect is derision and censure."

"My dear Mrs. Cassatt," Edgar said. "If we are practical and sensible, that is what we would expect, but most of us are dreamers, always assuming someone will agree with our vision."

Robert glanced at Mary, his expression reflecting Edgar's worry. "I hope this decision to thumb your nose at the Salon will not ruin all your chances of becoming successful," he said.

Mary raised her chin. "I don't want Salon success."

"There was a time when that's precisely what you wanted," he answered. "If you are going to paint, you must have patrons of some kind. That's only ordinary business sense. In finance, for instance, I may have the best securities on the market, but I can't distribute them if I have no one who wants to invest."

"That's right, Father, and that is the chance we must take if we are ever going to have freedom in art."

"It's an interesting war," Lydia said. "And Edgar and Mary are in the front lines. I think they are both brave and adventuresome."

"Hrrumph," Robert commented, and helped himself to another small glass of sherry.

15

THE PORTRAIT OF LYDIA in the loge had progressed quickly and
turned out as well as Mary had envisioned it. Lydia herself was
proud of it, and wanted to pose again. She insisted there was enough
time before the exhibit to do another. Mary needed no more encouragement. She began immediately a painting of Lydia in profile
having tea in the drawing room. This work inspired yet another,
which would reveal the social nature of the five o'clock tea. The new
painting was a more ambitious composition containing two figures
sitting at interesting angles, a tea set, and patterned furnishings.
Mary's purpose was to capture everyday life as she knew it, and she
composed the scene with Lydia's face partially covered as she drank
from her teacup. The other figure was of a friend. Mary worked
relentlessly and one morning when the friend was not there, Mary
asked Lydia to sit in her place. The final woman on the left was a
composite, but the result was quite fine.

She was just finishing the tea painting when Edgar reminded Mary of his friend who wanted a portrait of his daughter. Mary agreed to do it at once. The child was recovering from chicken pox, but was well enough to pose.

She took a public carriage to the Benoit home and was led to a light-filled sitting room. Little Simone was lying on the rug, frowning over the pieces of a puzzle. She was glad enough to leave it and begin posing. Mary liked the girl immensely in spite of her squirming and scratching. She had even been tempted to draw the pock mark on her cheek, but resisted. Simone asked if her favorite toy could be in the picture, too, and Mary agreed. This would give her a chance to express the relationship between a child and her doll.

Again Mary's work went well. She attributed her marked improvement to Edgar's insistence that she practice glancing quickly at the model, memorizing what she saw, and painting from this image instead of expecting sitters to be immobile. The portrait was well advanced the day Simone's aunt and two cousins arrived for a two-day holiday. Mary took the painting and left, promising to be back for one more sitting the following week.

With the painting back in the studio, she examined it in the best light and worked on the background. While she was working, a knock sounded at the studio door, startling her. Before she got up to open it, she heard the latch open and Edgar's voice calling, "I saw your curtain pulled back, and thought you must be here. How did it go with the wicked little darling?"

"Edgar," she greeted. "Simone is a dear child. I've loved painting her. In fact, I was just working on the portrait. Would you like to see it?"

Edgar went to the easel. In a moment his expression became serious. "I suppose they like it," he said.

"Yes, they seemed pleased."

He lowered his head and stood with his hands behind his back.

"But it doesn't please you," she said, bristling in spite of wanting to calmly hear his criticism.

"It's a sentimental mess," he said. "Whatever possessed you to

throw in the doll? It looks like a dress rehearsal for motherhood."
His dark eyes penetrated hers. "That child stamped on her nurse's
feet the last time I saw her, and you have her looking like a cherub."
Suddenly his face brightened. "But I really should congratulate you.
It is an admirable bourgeois painting. It's what the world is crying
for—something sentimental, pretty, and ordinary."

His words and sarcastic tone stung bitterly. Mary looked at the
painting because she could not look at his face. She was too shaken
with anger and did not want to see his accusing eyes. *Was* this work
sentimental? She knew Edgar couldn't lie, but that didn't make her
less angry with him. It was a pretty picture and Simone's mother did
like it. Even then, while he was still standing there despising it, she
knew that she would scrape off the paint and start over fresh.

"I'm sorry," he said, and he went to the door.

She had not managed to say good-bye or even turn to look at
him go. She was devastated, unsure of her ability.

She took the canvas and scraped the paint off with a flat palette
knife. Then she rubbed it smooth with a turpentined rag. When
every trace of the sentimental portrait was gone, she sighed, and
looked again at her portrait of Lydia. Seeing it gave her the will to go
home, rest, and return to do an unsentimental painting of Simone.

She didn't try to explain to Simone's mother. She merely said
the proportions weren't quite right and she wanted to begin again.
Madame Benoit was bewildered, but courteous. Mary did not waste
time discussing it, and began again, sketching furiously. However,
after hours of work, nothing she sketched seemed good enough.
Simone was growing tired. Mary had posed her with her dog, sitting
in three or four different chairs, in front of the window, both
standing and sitting, by the piano, in her hat and without her hat.
She told Simone to rest and looked through her sketches one by one,
wondering what was wrong. Had she lost all judgment? She would
simply have to choose one of the sketches and begin. Perhaps the
one by the window with the little dog. Just then she happened to
glance up and see Simone sprawled out on the chair, slumped backward and half-asleep. The dog was asleep on another chair. Mary

knew at once she would paint Simone exactly like this and include the other chairs and the dog and the light from the window. She felt a surge of excitement as she pushed away her other sketches.

The work absorbed her for days. She had three canvases ready for the exhibit: *Lydia in the Loge Wearing a Pearl Necklace, The Cup of Tea,* and the portrait *Mr. Moyse Dreyfus,* although she had hoped to finish this one, too. Later there was to be a show in New York she had been invited to exhibit in; and perhaps she would exhibit the Simone. First she had to be absolutely sure the painting was as perfect as she could make it. There could be nothing for Edgar to pick at. She could not bear his mocking criticism of her work again. She could almost hear him saying "but why have you muddled that space," or "your perspective is off a bit," or—. She was still angry at him, though she had to admit he had been right, and if he hadn't said what he did and forced her to see the sentimentality, she may have gone right on doing the same thing again and again. But even after admitting that to herself, she was still angry. She hadn't gone near his studio or the café where they had often met. Lydia was always asking if she'd seen Edgar, and she always acted as though she didn't have time for such social nonsense.

At first she would have done anything to avoid him, but lately she had almost hoped he would come round and apologize. She shouldn't expect it, though. He never seemed to apologize for telling the truth as he saw it. Maybe some day she would call on him and ask after his health and put the incident into the forgotten past. It wasn't as important as his friendship, although there was no excuse for the way he said it or the contempt in his eyes. No, she would never go to him and humble herself when he was definitely the one who had slammed the door.

She wrapped the paintings she intended for the exhibit and took them to a frame shop just a short distance from her studio. She needed a walk in the air. She hoped it would clear her head. Perhaps she would stop at the studio of one of her other friends on the way back or have tea in the café where she might see some of them. Since she had Lydia to talk to, she had neglected those things—unless Edgar went along with her. Well, she didn't need Edgar.

Business was brisk at the frame shop. There were dozens of impressionists' works to frame before the 1879 exhibit, but Mary was promised hers would be ready in three days and delivered to her studio. She chose the frame moldings with care and left the shop thinking great progress had been made. Her mind was on the excitement of the exhibit as she walked along the avenue toward the café.

Not many people were there. She was about to take a table by herself when Henri Desboutin appeared. "Hello, Mary. Won't you join me at the table by the garden?"

"Thank you," Mary accepted. She sat down and they began immediately to talk of the exhibit. Henri berated those artists who could not get the necessary information to the committee on time to have proper catalogs printed.

"There are those like Degas who promised thirty pictures to the catalog committee and sent only a half dozen. It makes it impossible to plan hanging space."

Mary searched her brain for a plausible explanation. "He must have intended to borrow some pictures from friends who own his work."

"He's in one of his depressed moods," Henri said. "Surely you have noticed."

"No, I haven't seen him for a while. I've been trying to finish some things for the show."

"Well, I warn you not to cross his path. He is telling us all how there is no compromise with excellence. That's his excuse for having only six or eight things finished, the implication being that those of us who have all our work ready have compromised ourselves."

"He never compromises," Mary said.

Henri shrugged. "Gauguin is worse. We haven't heard anything from him yet. If he does bring any work, it will be too late for the catalog. And Monet is too depressed and broke to care. Caillebotte is going about collecting Monet's work and insisting that he be represented with us."

"Caillebotte cares more about the show than anyone," Mary said.

"Some say he feels guilty about being rich."

"What nonsense," she said. "He might as well feel guilty about being six feet tall."

"Of course it's nonsense. He feels we need Monet's work. With Berthe gone to have her baby, and Renoir and Manet wooing the Salon, and Degas in one of his worst glooms, the rest of us have to do more."

"What has Cezanne decided to do?" she asked.

"He and Sisley are defecting, too. They'll be missed, of course, but we're still strong as long as we have a few like you."

Mary smiled, finished her tea, and said she must get back to work. However, she did not go to her studio. She went straight to Edgar's and knocked and waited. There was no answer. He must be there, she thought. She knocked again, louder than before. When she stopped there came a shout from inside. "Go away. I'm too busy."

She tried the door and found it unlocked. She went in and stood just inside the door. He did not turn from his work, ignoring completely that his door had opened and shut and someone might be standing there. "I'll leave if you are determined to snub me," she said.

He turned quickly then, and on seeing her, dropped his brush and shook his head. "I'm sorry. I thought it must be someone I didn't want to see."

"Do I fall in that category?" she asked.

He laughed nervously. "Never. Come in. It's wonderful to see you. I thought—I was afraid you were still angry."

"I can be civil even if I am angry."

"I apologize."

"Let's forget it happened."

His eyes were dull and sad. "I don't know why I do things like that. It wasn't what I intended at all, you know." He moved from his chair and stood close to her, looking intently into her face. "No, when I was on my way to you that afternoon, I had only the tenderest thoughts. I wanted only to see your smile, the way you looked in your green dress, and I even had a volume of poetry I was bringing to you. Then, when I was there and you showed me your work, I saw you as an artist, not a woman."

"I know. You were right about the portrait. I destroyed it."

"I'm sorry."

"Nothing for you to be sorry for."

His eyes became intently fixed upon her face. "I cannot forget it. I've thought of little else. It's made me look at myself, and what I am, and how I think about you, and our art."

"Edgar, don't make too much over it. It's finished."

"No, it's not. I've been miserable. I came here when I left you, feeling dizzy and confused. I threw the poetry into the fire, and dragged out my own work and examined it as I examined yours, and I judged my canvases like I had never seen them before. I found crushing faults that my pride had let slip. It made me sick. Art is worth nothing if it's only a manifestation of pride. It has to be pure love and excellence. Anything less is unforgivable."

Mary felt waves of tenderness as she looked at him. She reached for his hand.

He looked into her eyes. His cheek muscles twitched and his pupils glowed strangely. "You must know I love you," he whispered. "I have for months. You're the focus of my life." He kissed her hand. "I only hoped you would care for me, but," he shook his head, "you're afraid, and I understand that. You're an artist, and love is a threat to your independence as an artist. Am I right?"

The sound of his voice made her tremble. She could not think clearly. What he was saying had been true until now. Suddenly she could not deny her love, especially to herself.

He put his hands on her shoulders. "Am I right?" When she did not answer, he shook her.

"Yes, Edgar. I am afraid, and yet, if I were not to see you again, I would not care about anything." She turned away from him and took a deep breath. "I know almost nothing about love, except that it can make me vulnerable. It can take away my strength to live for my art, and I know I cannot trade that."

"That's what I sensed. Was I afraid I couldn't seduce the woman and, therefore did I try to seduce the artist? Is that why I said what I did? Was I trying to assert myself over you in that way? Pride phrased the words. What kind of love am I capable of?" His voice trailed off to a whisper. "My dearest Mary. I wish you could forgive me."

"There's nothing to forgive."

"There is. It represented the worst of me."

"You only told the truth."

"If I had met you before, I would have asked you to marry me. Maybe you would have considered it; now I have nothing to offer."

Her flesh became a blanket of emotion, but she was determined not to lose control. "I could not have loved you any more than I do now, but marriage demands so many things." She looked pleadingly for him to understand.

"But I would not ask—"

"It isn't what you would ask—"

"Do you think I would subvert you?"

She sighed. "You are quite opinionated and forceful. I am less so."

He shook his head and smiled. "I think that is why I love you." He laughed. "You are not afraid of any truth."

"Edgar," she said, stepping away from him. "If I hadn't come here, what would you have done?"

"If you hadn't, and if I, out of stubborness and pride, did not go to you, I would be the most miserable man on earth. That's all I know about what could have been."

She smiled and sat on the divan. "I was at the café and saw Henri. I came here on impulse because of talking to him. I might not have. It was an accident almost, and if I hadn't, we would still be enemies."

"Not enemies. We were never that."

"But we'd still be apart."

"It won't happen again," he said.

"If something does separate us, please, don't stay away."

He sat beside her and took her hands. "We shall never be separated."

"And Edgar, don't stop criticising my work. I need it."

"Only if you ask me to."

"All right. Now tell me what you've been working on."

He turned back to his work area. "This one," he said, pointing to his easel on which a framed painting rested. "And those." He pointed to some others propped against the wall and drying, most of the pictures that had been finished months ago.

"Aren't those the paintings you had all ready for the exhibit?"

"Yes. I'm reassessing and reworking. That's what I've been doing."

"Why? There was no need."

"They weren't good enough. They needed work."

"Of course they're good enough," she said. "They're magnificent. It's dangerous to go back over them, judging the brilliance of wet paint against the dull dry parts."

"I know, but people will see, and they will look for weaknesses. They don't understand dramatic distortion."

"But they do understand painting that moves them."

He looked troubled. "I just took what I thought was a last look at them before the show and they didn't seem good enough."

"They will be the finest work hanging in the entire place."

He groaned. "I know I should work on the new things I started. I haven't finished this dress rehearsal at the ballet and I have begun a pastel of a nude having her hair combed." He glanced back at the framed paintings. "These have to be right before I let them go."

Mary had never seen him so nervous and unsure. She guessed he had been alone too much these past days, and had fallen into self-recrimination so deeply he could not judge his own work. It might be best to get him away from the studio for a while. "I think you need some air. You look exhausted. Let's walk up to the top of the butte and look down on Paris. Then I'd like to show you my new painting of Simone. I'm having a bit of trouble with the background." Mary stood up and reached for his hand.

They walked and Mary spoke cheerfully to him, finding things to laugh at as they went. By the time they reached the top of the hill, he was almost cheerful. He held her hand as they walked down, and she felt as though she would burst with happiness. They arrived at her studio, and Edgar walked directly to her easel. "Is that it?" he exclaimed. "My God." He looked at her as though he could not quite believe she had done it.

"It's that floor space between the chairs I stopped on. The light was shining on it, but when I did it that way, it broke up the picture. It separated the elements too much."

"It's a marvelous arrangement. You have absorbed the Japanese print and made it French. How did you ever get a pose like that? She is completely oblivious of an audience. It's the sort of feeling I wanted to get with my nude having her hair combed, a private look at a real person."

"But the floor space between the chairs—it's wrong."

He squinted at it and then nodded. "I think if it were flatter and grayer than the chairs, it would stay down better. May I?"

She nodded, and he picked up a brush and squeezed some color on her palette. He mixed up a flat gray and painted the troublesome area. "The sunlight puddling on the floor was too distracting, that's all," he said. When he finished, he walked to her side and looked admiringly at it. "What splendid style."

"Thank you," she whispered.

"No, my dear Mary, thank *you*. Before I saw you today, I was deep in despair. I could not see any reason for going on with my work. Now, because of you, my dear Mary, I am so happy." His words touched her so deeply she trembled and felt a rush of tears forming. Before she could gain control he drew her near and kissed her. Her tears dissolved in the turbulent wake of that kiss. She did not draw away, but clung to him, forgetting her fears and resolves. Her entire body seemed transformed and made lighter. He kissed her hand and her neck slowly and tenderly, and then her mouth again. It was so exquisite, she could have gone on forever, swimming in pleasure, and yet, something made her step back and take a deep breath. "Wait, let me think."

"You want to remember you are the artist first. I know. I have chosen the same lonely path. Don't think now, let me hold you. Let me love you. We must be a man and a woman, too." He raised her chin gently and kissed her again.

She must have always wanted him like this. Edgar was her only consciousness; his soul was enveloping hers. What else could matter?

"We're going to make love, aren't we?"

"We are."

"Oh, Edgar, I want you." She did trust him. She believed him and she loved him. What was there to fear?

They were together on the divan. His shirt was gone. A fine tuft of hair on his chest closed over her breast. "I've loved you from the start," he whispered as he kissed her shoulder.

There was nothing to fear. He was Edgar, and she wanted him.

16

A PARTY was planned at the Cassatt household the evening before the opening of the 1879 exhibit. It was Lydia's idea. They all needed a party, she said. Edgar thought it was a dreadful plot, considering all the infighting the group had experienced getting the show together. Everybody had taken a stand about everything. Edgar himself had been unreasonably insistent that they drop the name impressionists and adopt independents instead, in spite of many opponents. "Who would have thought of a party?" he said. "But then, of course, I wouldn't miss it."

Although Mary was in favor of the party, she was strangely quiet and offered few ideas. It turned out to be Lydia who really made the festivities. It was she who insisted that flaming drinks should be served, and that the exhibition poster should be displayed. It was she who hired a pianist and harpist. And she insisted on wearing the same yellow dress Mary had painted her in, since the painting would be displayed in the show.

When time for the party arrived, Lydia was pale but beautiful as she stood alongside Mary greeting the guests. She hugged Mme. Pissarro, and took her by the hand to show her how lovely Camille's painting looked over the mantel.

Before long music and gaiety was filling the room. Lydia, in the midst of it, glowed like the morning star. When Gauguin arrived, he stopped short and stared. She came toward him extending her hand. "I am Lydia, Mary's sister."

"How do you do," Gauguin said slowly. After a pause, during which they gazed at each other, Gauguin remembered to introduce himself and once he found his tongue, he stayed at her side, telling her of the beauties of the Brittany coast, even as she smiled and greeted the other guests. When Mary saw he was not going away, she came to greet people herself.

In addition to Mary's artist friends, Lydia had invited a few patrons such as the Barries and Louisine Elder. Louisine unabashedly sought out Edgar, asked all sorts of questions and hung on his every word. It was a sight Mary expected would fill her with contentment and pleasure, but contentment was not what she felt when she looked at Edgar. It was something she didn't understand. Love of course, was there; but it seemed to awaken other conflicting emotions in her. Vile feelings twisted through and around the happiness. She wanted him to smile only on her, to talk wittily to her alone, to always want to please her. He should want to be near her as badly as she wanted to be near him. She ached to be near him. Why was she standing apart watching everyone else? Was she afraid people would guess how it was between them? He was acting exactly as he always did at parties, keeping himself haughtily available to those who sought him out. And she herself went about smiling at the guests, playing hostess, playing the virtuous woman artist, covering up the anxieties, the inexcusable needs that were growing within her.

And there was Lydia; tonight her smile was magnificent. Why was Gauguin trying to impress Lydia with his gentlemanly manners? He was no gentleman. He flaunted his immorality, while Lydia was innocent. He was keeping her to himself. Mary couldn't bear it. She would steer Gauguin to some other corner, but as she approached, it became clear that Lydia was too happy to disturb. Mary was troubled. Why should she be upset because Gauguin could make Lydia look so happy? What was happening to her? Her emotions were irrational. She glanced around the room for a sight of Edgar. There he was, talking to Granger Barrie. She could join them. But why didn't he seek her out? She moved aimlessly among the guests, smiling, and finally gravitated toward Pissarro and Caillebotte.

"It's sad," Pissarro was saying. He paused and smiled when he saw Mary approach. "Oh, we were talking about poor Sisley being rejected by the Salon."

"Yes, it is too bad," Mary said, "but he shouldn't have defected from us."

Pissarro nodded sadly. "But poverty is so hard," he said. "Sisley wasn't used to it, and neither was his wife."

"Cezanne was rejected, too," Caillebotte said. "His wooing of the Salon did nothing but further alienate him from Paris. He has gone back to the country a bitterly disappointed man."

Mary twisted her lips petulantly. "Why must they submit to the Salon when we have banded together to fight this sort of elitism?"

"We all know that not more than a handful of people will buy anything without the Salon's blessing on the artist," Calliebotte answered.

Pissarro nodded. "They need to sell their work."

"But so many defectors," Mary counted them on her fingers, "Renoir, Cezanne, Sisley, even Eva Gonzales. I don't understand it."

"At least Manet was accepted," Pissarro said smiling, "though they hung him poorly. And our friend Renoir is launched. I think he will be quite successful now."

Pissarro was undoubtedly the kindest of men, she thought. He did not condemn the defectors; he wished them well. Pissarro was right; poverty was hard. Edgar had been livid when he heard it. She was glad he was not there as they talked of defection. When she thought of poverty, she thought of Monet and realized he wasn't there. "Have you seen Monet?" she asked.

"The man is depressed," Pissarro said. "His family has cast him out. His wife is ill. He and their boy never leave her side. Why should he, when his beautiful work is treated as a joke. He paints to keep his spirit alive. A party would be unthinkable for him."

Caillebotte smiled. "I collected twenty-six of his works, and they will be the glory of the exhibit. Perhaps some angel will come down from heaven and buy them all and he will never have a worry again."

"Angels are scarce," Pissarro said. "At the last exhibit there was not one to be seen or heard."

"But two years have passed," Mary said, trying to sound cheerful. "Surely there will be some change, a few more people on our side."

Pissarro smiled. "Monsieur Durand-Ruel claims some day it will be different. If he is willing to gamble on us, it gives me hope."

Edgar approached them, smiling, carrying a full glass of champagne. "Who dares speak of hope in the presence of a true cynic?" he said as he joined the group. "It's the most bourgeois star in the firmament."

"What is the least bourgeois?" Pissarro asked, turning to Edgar.

"Absolute realism. One ought to accept reality as a permanent state. If everyone did, there would not be so many dashed hopes and crushing defeats. The truth is life goes on much the same as it always has. The chances are greater that it will get worse rather than better. Who among us was not happier as a child than he or she has been since?"

"We must all work for improvement," Mary said.

"And hope for the best," Pissarro added.

"Improvement is its own reward. There should be no need to hope for the best," Edgar said. "Hope for nothing."

"I'm sure that even you don't believe that," Caillebotte said, "though you do not exude hope."

The others smiled in agreement. Edgar sipped his wine. "Why should anyone exude hope? It's unfounded. One should be especially realistic before an exhibit. Some people will come to look, some will laugh, some will go and have a drink and forget it entirely five minutes later. It's a place to go to be amused on a dull day. Perhaps, if some prosperous young matron wants to teach her husband a lesson or impress her friends with her daring, she will buy a small painting. And then it's over and life goes on as before. We are all stuck with a lot of paintings we don't know what to do with. We take them home since we the artists are the only ones capable of appreciating them properly. Oh, it's true some of us may eventually place a few works and some will fare badly—go into debt, perish— who knows? The situation will remain exactly the same, some hoping, some regretting—"

"Stop, please," Caillebotte said. "I feel myself sinking. I don't wish to drown in your sordid brand of realism this early in the evening."

Pissarro laughed. "You are a pessimist, dear fellow. And you may be right, but leave us a shred of hope, please. It's all an old man has some days."

Edgar swallowed some wine and arched his eyebrows. "If you all wish to delude yourselves, go right ahead, but when it's all over, you will wish you had steeled yourselves with reality."

"If I were so empty of hope," Pissarro said, "I should not be able to paint at all."

"Nor could I," Caillebotte said. "The ordinary fools among us must have our dose of hope now and then. What about you, Mary?"

Mary nodded. "I would never have begun to paint at all if I didn't have the hope—faith—that I would do well. Each time I start a painting, I confess, I have hope for it."

"Ah ha," Caillebotte said, "What do you start a painting with, Edgar?"

"Conviction. A desire to portray an intellectual decision and other things, but never hope."

"You are an enigma, my dear Edgar," Pissarro said.

Mary felt a strong mixture of fear and love when she heard Edgar speak. She loved this hopeless, joyless realist, but his ideas could fill her with despair. She wanted to console him, to prove he was wrong, but he was too convincing. He would prove to her instead that he was right. And if that happened, she would be nothing—annihilated truly. She felt a chill, and her glass trembled in her hand.

ON THE MORNING of the first day of the show, Mary and Lydia went early to Edgar's place to invite him to lunch with the family and then to go to the opening of the exhibition with them. "I hate exhibits," he said. "If I go, I may not be able to stay. Go with your family by all means."

Mary did not wish to abandon him to his wretched agitation. "Come now, there's no need to stay any longer than you like."

"No, I don't care for public parades."

"Public parades!" Lydia said laughing. "It's the exhibition you have all worked for."

"I am not in the mood for public sneering, cozy lunches, or women brimming with laughter."

Mary's anger flared when she saw Lydia blink and her smile disappear. "And we are not in the mood for your insults, well-meant though I am sure they are," Mary said, pulling Lydia along.

However, after they had gone a few blocks, she was sorry she had given in to her temper. Edgar was alone and more full of fears than anyone suspected. She wished she had insisted he come with them. Or at least have offered him comfort of some kind. She was not very good at nurturing. What did she know about these womanly things? "What should I have done, Lydia? Should I have stayed and been more patient with him?"

"Maybe it would have helped, but it could have made him worse. For a second I had the feeling he wanted to cry in your arms. He's not like anyone I've ever known. I think Gauguin might be somewhat like him. Have you noticed how his eyes flare up when he talks?"

"No, I haven't. Did I ever tell you he has a wife? They're separated, but nevertheless he's not the sort you would want to know more personally."

Lydia laughed. "Nevertheless, he is puzzling."

"Not at all. He's talented and completely self-centered. You must understand that."

"Why *must* I?" Lydia demanded.

Mary refused to answer. She was not going to argue with her sister, too.

THE EXHIBIT HALL was crowded. There were so many people, it was hard to see properly. Mary tried to hear the tone of the crowd instead of particular words. There were no angry shouts, only an occasional spurt of laughter here and there. Mary walked with her father directly to a wall on which three of Edgar's paintings hung. Lydia and Katherine followed. Mary couldn't help but admire the pictures again in this setting. She would like to have heard what the other viewers were saying, but the couple who were looking as she approached moved on. Katherine pronounced Degas's work pure genius.

They moved on and in a moment they were standing before several of Monet's landscapes. Mary thought they were breathtakingly beautiful, and Lydia sighed over one she was particularly taken with, of trees reflected in water.

"Looks like he used the canvas to wipe his muddy feet on," a man's voice said. Mary turned sharply to look at the speaker. He was well-dressed and jovial. The woman he was with smiled at the remark and they walked on.

Mary thought of Edgar's words on realism as she walked along with the crowd. He could not bear to hear such slander, she thought. That was why he didn't come. Perhaps it was best. She, though, was going to listen to reality.

When they arrived at the wall where Mary's painting of Lydia hung, they all stopped. Lydia and Mary exchanged a glance. Mary couldn't tell how it looked, not really; it was too familiar, but there it was among all the others. Robert clucked. "Doesn't it look grand, Mother?"

Katherine smiled. "It makes me insufferably proud of both my girls."

A middle-aged woman paused and looked at the painting, too, and turned to her companion. "Now that's what I enjoy." Mary wanted to move on, but Robert and Katherine wanted to linger there.

"We'll meet you later," Lydia said.

Lydia led Mary around the corner. "Is there some quiet place where I can sit down? I'm dizzy. If I can just rest a moment, it will pass."

Mary saw how pale Lydia had become. She took her arm and whisked her away. There was a room with a few chairs that had been used for uncrating pictures and as a work area. Mary hurried, hoping Lydia would not faint. When they reached the room, Mary removed Lydia's hat, and unbuttoned the top buttons of her dress. "Lower your head, dear." She kneaded Lydia's hands. "Any better?"

"I think so, but my ears still ring," Lydia said. "I'm weak. I'll have to sit here a while before I can go."

"It's all right. They won't be looking for us yet." There was a silence. Mary looked at Lydia with her head thrown back now in extreme repose. Such a frail white neck. "I'm sorry about this morning," Mary said, "and what I said about Gauguin. It's none of my business. I don't know why I thought it was."

"Don't think about it. You didn't say anything wrong. It was I who spoke sharply and ought to apologize."

"You have nothing to apologize for, Lydia. I'm not myself—the excitement over the exhibit, I suppose."

"Maybe that, or it could be Edgar. Anyway, let's not ever argue."

"No, we won't." Mary paused. "I'm in love with Edgar. You guessed, didn't you?"

"Yes."

"He talked of our future together. I do love him—but—"

"I understand," Lydia said.

"You do?"

"You don't want to be captured by marriage. I know how you feel about that. We've talked about it enough."

"Yes, but even if I should change my mind about marriage, he has a very bad temper sometimes."

"Yes, I know," Lydia murmured.

"I shouldn't marry him," Mary said.

"Probably not."

"Once he said he wouldn't ask because of his financial reverses."

"Well, then, he won't press you," Lydia said, fanning her face with the program.

"No, but I don't care about wealth. It's not a real reason not to marry, except to his pride."

"Perhaps you should wait," Lydia said. "Mother and Father are going to need you, too. I will never be much help to anyone."

"Don't say that."

"You know it's true," Lydia said. "I know it's true, so why pretend? We all do too much pretending. If you love him, love him. You don't have to sell yourself in matrimony."

"Lydia, you shock me. Really."

"I don't wonder. I've pretended quite well for so long, no one would ever guess I had a contemplative thought in my head."

"I didn't mean *that*. I just thought the idea of free love would be repugnant to you."

"Is it repugnant to you?" Lydia asked.

"I thought so, yes, but now—"

"Exactly. Why shouldn't you take what happiness you can? If I have any regrets at all, it's that I didn't snatch my happiness when I could have. I was too high-minded for that."

"Perhaps it's not too late," Mary said.

"Perhaps it is. I'll rest a bit longer while you find Mother and Father."

LATER THAT SAME AFTERNOON, Edgar came to Mary's home. He was dressed entirely in black, except for a brilliant white shirt. He looked distinguished and proud and not the least fearful or cynical, but there was that look of remorse on his face that she had so recently seen.

"I came to apologize, which I seem always to be doing."

She smiled. "Come in. A glass of sherry goes well with unnecessary apologies."

"Thank you. I hope to make this my last apology. In the future I shall conduct myself so that it won't be necessary."

"I hope that doesn't mean you're going to avoid me."

"That would probably be a good idea, but my resolutions don't go that far."

Mary poured a glass of sherry for both of them. "I'm glad you're here. I understand perfectly about that business earlier, and I don't want to hear another word about it." She smiled and tossed her head. "The exhibit was crowded. It looked fine, however, Lydia became ill so we did not stay."

"Ill? How is she?"

"She is resting comfortably. Mother and Father are with her now."

"I'm sorry."

Mary sipped her sherry and sat down. "Your work could not look better."

He stared at her without answering a moment. "I suppose I must go. I want to get it over with. Would you care to go back with me and take in what you may have missed?"

"That's a good idea."

"Splendid." He sat down across from her on the sofa. "I wanted to say some other things, but—" He looked around the room as though to assure himself that they were alone. "It's hard to know where to begin." He paused and she waited. "I've done a lot of thinking since that day—we—"

"I know," she said.

"I hope you are not torn with regrets over it, because I don't want to ever be the cause of your least distress. I care too much. I know I am not in a position of offer you a life of ease, and yet I want to offer you what I have—my life."

"Are you proposing marriage, Edgar?"

"I am."

Mary felt her body stiffen. There were tears somewhere deep within her, but she did not want to dissolve now when she needed all her wits.

"You know how I feel about you," he said.

She nodded. "And you know I feel the same for you."

He looked as though his heart would melt as he leaned toward her. "Marriage is a cataclysmic step." Mary began, "It changes everything. I have heard it said that you preferred to remain a bachelor, and I confess I have expressed the same disdain for marriage. We have both devoted ourselves to our art."

"But all that was before."

"Before our indiscretion?"

"Before us. Look, if you think that's the only reason I proposed marriage, you're wrong."

"One of the main reasons."

"Not at all. It merely brings the question out."

"Yes, it does."

"Well, will you or won't you?"

She pressed her lips together and looked down at her hand. He sighed, and slapped his knee. "I don't know why I expected you to just say yes and rush into my waiting arms. Of course, you want to think about it."

"Are you very disappointed?"

He looked at her for a long time before he spoke. "Do you think I have lived alone all these years and haven't been lonely? Do you think I've never once ached for someone to share my thoughts, my meals, to have a child perhaps with some *one* person who might understand me. How obsessed with that ideal I could become if it were not for my other obsession. When I see my brothers and friends with their wives, I think that I should be a better husband for wanting it so much longer, if only I could find the person who could understand."

She avoided the intensity in his eyes. Mary thought that if she married him, she would live for him, paint for him, love him, nurse him, endure him, and be swallowed up by him. She did not want to lose him, but she did not want the tameness of marriage, the mutual capture that seemed always to become stale. She wanted to keep her pledge to art. She wanted something else for them. What it would be, she wasn't sure. He stood to go.

He walked to the door. Mary followed, searching her mind for something to say, but just as he touched the doorknob, he turned and smiled. "I had something else to propose to you, but this isn't the time." He put on his hat. "I'll call for you early tomorrow and we can look at the reviews together."

17

EDGAR ARRIVED EARLY the next day with an armload of newspapers. Robert, Katherine, and Mary were having sandwiches and tea in the dining room and Edgar joined them. "Good day," he said. "And how is Lydia?"

"Much better," Katherine answered. "The doctor has seen her and prescribed another day of bed rest."

"I brought a book I thought might amuse her for an hour or so," he said. "It's a comic play my nephew wrote about a modern artist." Edgar handed the package to Katherine. Mary, unable to contain her curiosity one instant longer, took the newspapers from him, laid them on the table, and began leafing through the one on top, swiftly reading the headlines.

"Here," she said, nervously glancing up. " 'Service for Impressionists. You are invited to attend the funeral services, procession, and interment of the impressionists. This painful invitation is tendered to you by the independents. Neither false tears nor false rejoicing. Let there be calm. Only a word has died. In spite of this change of name the painters continue to daub in the same slovenly manner as previously.' "

"Such slander," Katherine said. "Can't you find anything more newsworthy?"

"That's not so bad," Mary said. "It sounds almost like teasing. We can take that if people will be curious and come and look."

Robert agreed. "Publicity can be very useful in matters such as this. When I read such stuff, I may decide I should like to see for myself."

"Here is another headline," Mary said. " 'Exhibition of Independent Artists—A Disappointment.' " Mary raised her eyebrows at Edgar and read on. " 'All the impressionists are poor technicians. As I see it they are pioneers. For a moment Monet inspired great hopes, but he appears exhausted by hasty production; he is satisfied with approximations; he doesn't study nature with the passion of the true creators. All these artists are too easily contented. They woefully neglect the solidity of works meditated upon for a long time. And for this reason it is to be feared that they are merely preparing the path for the great artist of the future expected by the world.' "

"Perhaps next time we should call ourselves John the Baptists," Edgar said, moving closer to the table. He picked up a paper that had been folded and marked. " 'The most garish and jangling of all the unschooled charlatans is perhaps the group's newest member, a man called Gauguin. His work screams mercilessly from the walls in harsh primitive colors, leaving any sensitive soul who wanders in with a headache and palpitations. Next to this, the work of M. Degas is relief. Here is an observer of contemporary life who has known the elements of civilization. Overall the show is without distinction, but a modicum of charm is present in Miss Mary Cassatt's too few canvases. In spite of her personal style, which is not completely free, Miss Cassatt has nevertheless a curiosity, a special grace, for a flutter of feminine nerves passes through her paintings, which are more poised, more calm, and more able than others on view.' "

"Well, well," Robert said, beaming. "That sounded flattering."

Mary was surprised that she would be singled out for praise. "Isn't it strange," she said, "how they didn't recognize the beauty in Gauguin's work, that they couldn't feel the power there, or that they don't know that Monet is changing the art world and that Edgar is a lot more than an observer of contemporary life?"

"It's true they have misjudged many of our friends," Edgar said, "but I don't quarrel with being called an observer of contemporary life. It's exactly what I attempt to do."

"I think these reviewers are without taste and common decency," Katherine said. "What good could come from throwing one insult after another? It's disgusting. What do they mean, her personal style is not completely free? Free of what?"

"You are absolutely right, Mrs. Cassatt," Edgar said as he tossed the newspapers into the wicker waste basket in the corner. "There's no reason to read any more of this twaddle."

WHEN MARY and Edgar arrived to see the show, a carnival atmosphere prevailed in the exhibit rooms. There were many of Edgar's friends there, people whose portraits he had painted, society people he had known. There was a dancer and an actress who had modeled for him. For being as alone as he most often was, he had a great many friends. Mary was glad they took the trouble to come.

She spotted Callebotte's tall lanky frame, waved to him, and pulled Edgar's sleeve. "Let's see what he has to say."

Calillebotte had advanced a large part of the money for the exhibit and had assumed the role of manager. He followed with interest the admissions and sales. He smiled widely as they approached him.

"How is it going?" Edgar asked.

"Well," Caillebotte answered. "Admissions are running twenty percent higher than last exhibit. Sales are not so good, but they are better than last time. Who knows, that could change."

"Are they as hostile as last time?" Mary asked.

"No," Caillebotte said smiling. "They have fun with us. I hear a few grunts, but never at your canvases, or yours, Miss Cassatt."

"What about Monet's and Gauguin's?"

"That's a different matter. Gauguin is met with rancor. He was here when some poor fellow made a degrading remark and he did not take it lightly. I was afraid for a moment we might have a duel right here in the gallery, but as luck would have it, Desboutin took the patron aside and explained in his inimitable manner the error of his way, while I took Gauguin out for a drink and explained how we must enter into the joke as graciously as we can."

"He would never accept that," Mary said.

"True, but he was willing to forego the duel."

Edgar shook his head sadly. "Gauguin works day and night; he's given up every comfort for his art. He has nothing else."

"He doesn't care about pleasing the public," Mary said. "He cares only about the search."

"And so often the best are treated the worst and the worst are given medals," Edgar said.

"Don't go into that, please," Caillebotte said. "If you do, Miss Cassatt and I will become so depressed about the future, we will want to put our brushes away forever."

Mary smiled. "I have felt that way before after such conversations, but I will never quit."

"Some do after years of disappointment. Why not you, Edgar, if the future is so hopelessly grim?"

"I will quit when I die or go blind," he said.

AFTER SEEING THE show, Edgar's mood was improved. He was almost bouyant when they left the gallery and began walking back. After walking a short way, he wanted to stop in a café to get out of the wind.

They ordered coffee and Edgar dabbed his handkerchief at his left eye, which had a tendency to run when the wind irritated it.

"I've been wondering what else you were going to propose yesterday," Mary said.

"Oh, yes, that. Well, I was thinking of starting an art magazine as a vehicle for our art and philosophies."

"A magazine?"

"Precisely."

"A magazine?" Mary repeated. "You have to have a lot of people—a whole organization—to do something like that, don't you?"

"I don't see why if I can enlist you and perhaps Pissarro and Monet and draw on the other independents to contribute. The printing can be done by one of our friends in that field, and *voilà,* we have a magazine. It can be our voice. People have heard of the notorious independents, and they may be curious enough to want to know what we are trying to do."

"It's inspired. A magazine! I would never have thought of it, but it could be the answer. We could attack all this misunderstanding. We could take up the problems of Monet first. All his genius has gotten buried under obsessive criticism. If we could explain his aims and show his absolute control over his medium, we would reach a few people."

Edgar smiled. "I knew I could count on you."

"Of course. I'll do all I can."

"The first issue can contain some prints by about four of us. Next issue four others and so forth. This time perhaps you, myself, Pissarro, and Monet—if he'll agree."

"He might if you ask him."

"I was thinking of having Pissarro do it. They're close and he is good with people, much better than I."

"Yes, but Monet is so depressed, perhaps we should all three go to him."

"Quite right. That's a good idea."

Mary's mind already accepted the magazine as a reality. She could almost see it. "This is really exciting. How did you ever think of it?"

"It wasn't exactly my idea. I was talking to Caillebotte and he was cursing the power of the reviewers to devastate careers when by and large they were ignorant about anything but surface prettiness. 'If we only had our own voice,' he said, 'we would not be so at their mercy.' "

"I see. And you thought it only fair that we should find that voice." She smiled. "It's brilliant. We could take our struggle to those who wanted to enter it. People like the Barries would care."

"I have been examining the question for several days and I've put together a dummy," he said. "Would you like to look and see what you think?"

"Indeed I would."

"Good," he said. "Let's find a carriage and get out of the wind."

They went to Edgar's studio. He had done some sketches for a lithograph. She said she would like to try another loge picture—perhaps in softground—perhaps a full figure. They talked about the excellent discipline of printmaking, but they did not talk of love, or any of their feelings about each other, or of marriage. It was almost as though they had never for a moment thought of those things. Courtesy and kindness, yes, and friendship, but nothing personal. They were too genteel, entirely too proper for such thoughts. It was a natural role to play. She did it as superbly as he, though all the while she wanted to tell him volumes. But how could she begin when they were like this? There would be other times. They would work together on the magazine. They would see each other nearly every day, so why should she burst into an emotional outpouring. He hated cheap emotionalism, and so did she. So it was art they discussed until he saw her home. He said a crisp good night without so much as touching her hand. And she did yearn so much to touch him. Oh, she wanted much much more than that. She wanted him—all of him. "Good night," she said as she opened the door and went inside.

18

MARY AROSE EARLY and went to the studio before the others were awake. She had to work. During the night she had seen Lydia's face a dozen ways. Then, when she had almost drifted to sleep, she was awakened by the image of Edgar's face, the way he looked at her yesterday, and that image persisted in her mind, making sleep impossible.

She had done dozens of drawings of Louisine's friend, Mary Ellen, seated in a theater. Now, using a technique she had learned from Edgar, Mary began a painting from her drawings of Mary Ellen in profile, holding an open fan. The dress must be white, she thought. Mary was intrigued with the problems of painting whites, because nothing was ever pure white. She had learned much from studying Pissarro's snow, and she felt the excitement she always felt when starting a new painting. Work was like a balm. It soothed her. It drove other thoughts from her mind. Time was lost to her.

Around noon she heard two sturdy thumps on the studio door. She knew it was Edgar before he came in. "Come along to the café with me," he invited. "Fresh air and a cup of tea will do you good."

"Wonderful," she said.

They walked to the café and found a table by a window. On it was a single rose in a chipped white vase.

When Mary glanced across at him she thought he looked as though his good cheer was somewhat put on, that perhaps he hadn't slept well. "How is your etching going?" she asked.

"Quite badly. I am going to begin again, but first, I want you to see the plates Pissarro has done."

"Has he finished them?"

"He has, and his work is fine. We ought to have an excellent first issue. Your work is impeccable, and with Gauguin and Monet lined up for the next issue, I don't see what could be better, but Caillebotte still complains that our progress is not fast enough."

Mary looked down. "It's no wonder he's getting impatient; it *has* been months since we promised we'd have it ready for printing."

"But we've never done it before," Edgar said. "How could we be expected to know how long it takes? I'm tired of Caillebotte's ultimatums."

Mary smiled. "I think you're hoping he'll want to redo the piece he wrote."

Edgar sighed. "At least his is written. I'm still throwing away most of what I write."

"You're too critical of your phrasing. When we talked about it, your thoughts were clear, and exactly to the point. I should have written it all down as you said it."

"I should make more notes," he said.

"You should just write it and leave it alone."

He sighed. "It's a monumental task explaining a movement as though it was one great surge when it is actually a collection of dozens of individual struggles, each somewhat different from any other."

"You have to pick out the points most of us agree on: keeping art alive, the right of artists to explore new visions."

"I know, I know. We must make notes. Perhaps today, between the two of us, we could work out a plan."

Mary nodded, anxious to undertake the task. When they had finished their meal, they walked toward Edgar's studio, strolling, enjoying the air, thinking of ideas to be explained in the first issue.

When they arrived at Edgar's studio, he paused in the middle of the room and seemed to be gazing at the top of her head. She walked to the small table where she always put her hat and gloves. Standing there, slowly removing her gloves, she felt his gaze. The silence seemed heavy. "We should use the prints to illustrate the points we wish to make wherever we can."

"Yes, yes," Edgar said, moving suddenly. He produced Pissarro's plates.

Mary examined them carefully. "I hope there's enough focus here on this one," she said. "Color carries a scene on canvas, but an etching must stand on composition."

"I had the same thought when I saw it. But the light on the side of the tree and the horizon should be enough. We shall have to wait till it's printed to know for sure." He spoke slowly and softly and when she glanced at him, he looked away from her.

"This one of the cart on the street is excellent, isn't it?" she said.

"Mmm, and it's not too cluttered, which was the fault with the plate I did this morning. If it had been a canvas I could have simplified it easily, but copper is uncompromising."

"Yes." They were standing close together over Pissarro's plates. She had been leaning over and when she straightened up, she felt his closeness, and recognized the hunger in his eyes. Almost involuntarily she touched his arm lightly. His lips twitched, but he remained still, holding her gaze a moment, then he turned, bending his head down. "I promise I won't touch you," he whispered.

The sound of his words made her want his touch more than anything.

"I know the kind of high moral standards you have," he said. "I'm glad. Such integrity is rare, and I shouldn't keep wanting when we are such good friends. Nothing must happen to that. If you were to quit seeing me, I wouldn't, I couldn't—"

"Edgar, I want you to touch me. I want what you want."

He looked up, stared a moment as though he was not sure. When their eyes met, there could be no mistake. In a moment they were together, arms entwined.

"Edgar, we tried, but we cannot deny this."

He searched her face. "Are you sure?"

"When it comes to this, I am not sure of anything."

They kissed long and tenderly. When he released her, she looked into his eyes. Her voice trembled. "Now I am sure."

"Will you come upstairs to my rooms?"

"If you wish," she said.

He took her hand and led her up the dingy stairs to his living quarters. She had never been there. She should not be there. It was all very bourgeois, sneaking up dark stairways, hoping no one saw, the type of act she had always abhorred. But, if they were married, the same thing would be blessed. She loved him and wanted him; she would not let herself think of being discovered. The idea chilled her nevertheless. How could she bear the shame?

He opened the door and lit the lamp. The room was large, but it was sumptuously draped in heavy blue satin. There were Persian rugs, pictures in gold leaf frames, carved furniture of the kind she had seen in the best French houses. There was a chair and a divan covered in fine blue silk, a small piano with a gold candlestick on it. Everything in the room spoke of a world of wealth. They sat on the divan and Edgar sighed as he took her hand and brought it to his lips.

His bedroom would be through the door to their right. All at once she had a sudden urge to run away.

"Are you worried?" he asked with a hint of a nervous smile on his lips. She looked into his eyes and nodded ever so slightly before their lips met. With the kiss her desire overcame her fears. His body pressed hers close and she wanted nothing but his closeness. She sighed and trembled as his hands lightly traced over her neck and arms. So many clothes. Yet to take them off and stand naked before him again was painful to contemplate. Nakedness was nothing to them, they had painted dozens of nudes. But this was different. This was revealing herself completely, physically and emotionally. As he held her, murmuring in her ear, touching her throat, his hand slipping gently to her breast, she wanted nothing to come between them, and she reached for her buttons eagerly, looking into his eyes with promise and love.

When her dress and shoes were removed, she stood in her petticoat a moment, smiling at him as he unbuttoned his shirt. "I want to paint you like this some day," he said, "and keep the picture by the bed so I can see it just before closing my eyes and again the moment I wake up."

"Don't think of it. Think of this," she kissed him and they went to the bedroom.

It was dim in the room, not quite dark, but she could see that the furnishings were just as rich and ornate as in his other room. Perhaps these two rooms above his studio in Montmartre must seem like a hovel to him after having always lived in an estate that must have been one of the finest in France. This was all that remained of it. She turned and looked at his shadowy chest. Her gaze met his sensual eyes, and passion flowed. She removed her petticoat, tossing it on a chair, and went to his arms. In a wave of pleasure they lay down together. Oh God, how she loved him, wanted him. She found herself caressing his body without shame, her dear perfect god, her genius, for whom she craved hopelessly. This was what life was made of, she thought.

Later, when their passion was spent, Edgar propped himself up on his elbows and gazed at her with affection. "Mary, I wish you would let me paint you like this."

"Would you let *me* paint *you* like this?"

"Of course," he said. "Would you like to?"

She didn't answer. In a way she would like to, but if a painting like that ever got in the wrong hands—she shuddered. And if he painted her and it too got in the wrong hands, she could never show her face in Paris.

"I must go. We are not married, lest you forget."

"We should be."

"Not us," she said, "we love each other too much."

He laughed. "You know me too well."

"I know you are cantankerous and moody. You can devastate me as completely as you can elevate me. What would happen to us?"

"I suppose we would quarrel and be miserable part of the time. I wouldn't mind that so much, but I would mind not being able to support you properly."

"That's the least of it." She sighed. "I don't want to quarrel. I want to love you for the rest of my life."

AFTER LEAVING EDGAR, she did not go directly home. Instead, she went back to her studio, thinking she would take another look at her work, normalize herself by being alone a few minutes. She was surprised to find Lydia sitting there in the dimming light, writing at the table.

"Hello. I was hoping you'd come back."

"Hello yourself. Have you been here long?"

"Quite a while."

"I was with Edgar."

"I thought as much," Lydia said smiling. Her look seemed all-knowing to Mary.

"I've been using the time to write a letter to Aleck. I long so to see him, don't you? I begged him to bring the family over for a visit. Wouldn't it be wonderful to all be together again with all the children? Mother longs for it, too. But—enough of that. How is Edgar?"

"Edgar?" The thought of him sent an unexpected shudder of pleasure through her. "He's fine."

"I suppose you're still busy with your magazine."

"Yes. Edgar showed me Pissarro's work and we talked about the text. We are badly behind schedule and his own plates are not going so well."

"He's too much the perfectionist."

Mary nodded. The mere thought of him aroused her. She turned her thoughts to Lydia, noting the way the afternoon shadows defined her cheeks and chin. There was so much in that face, so much hidden life. "I should like to have you pose for a major work. I want to do something with complex lines, something demanding."

"Why don't you paint me driving the new carriage—or pretending to. I was just telling Aleck about how fine it is. A carriage with all the trappings ought to be complex enough, and there could be big trees in the background."

"Perhaps," Mary said. "Edgar has an adorable little niece he wants me to paint. Maybe I could seat her beside you in the carriage. That would be something different."

"For me as well." Lydia smiled and gathered her things.

IN THE FOLLOWING DAYS Mary worked prodigiously on sketches of Lydia seated in the carriage. It seemed her creative energies ran higher than ever. There was a new ease to her work, and a fresh excitement.

On days when the weather was too inclement to permit Lydia to pose outdoors, Mary finished the pastel portrait of Mary Ellen. Her dark hair was in strong contrast to the bright lights of the theater, and the profile was both delicately beautiful and forcefully regal. However, when the work was finished, Mary still saw possibilities for more loge studies. She wanted to do an elegant middle-aged woman. She asked Clara Barrie, whose hair was darker than Mary Ellen's, to pose. She would be dressed entirely in black for the strongest of contrasts and would be looking through her opera glasses. Instead of light dominating the background as before, this time Mary would show the audience, capturing the mood and excitement of theater intermission.

Each day seemed to be more productive than the last. She saw Edgar almost every day. For appearances sake, Lydia often accompanied them, and the three were a common sight in Montmartre.

Late one morning when they were at Edgar's studio, Lydia said she felt dizzy and asked to lie down. Her face was devoid of color; even her lips were white. "I think it was the turpentine fumes," she said, holding her head and leaning against the wall. "I'm sorry."

"Steady now," Edgar said. "Mary, we've got to get her out of here. Let's take her upstairs."

Mary tried to help, but Lydia fainted. Edgar carried her upstairs, taking her directly to the bedroom where he gently placed her on the bed. Mary bent over Lydia, rubbing her cold hands. After a moment Lydia fluttered her eyelids and moaned.

Mary turned to Edgar, but as she did so, she saw an image, an impression, and she instinctively turned back to look at the wall beside his bed. It was really there: a small picture of a woman undressed to the waist, wearing only a petticoat. If she had been looking in a mirror, it couldn't have been plainer who the woman was. She snatched the picture from the wall. "How could you?" she uttered through clenched teeth.

Edgar glanced at the bed where Lydia lay. Lydia's eyes were closed and she was breathing peacefully.

"I had to have it. I'll put it away." He held his hand out for the picture. She put the picture in his hand and turned back to Lydia, leaning over to whisper in her ear. "Can you hear me, Lydia?"

Lydia opened and shut her eyes and Mary sighed. "Thank goodness."

She put her hand behind Lydia's head, propping her up. "Try to drink a little water," she said.

Lydia took a sip. She opened her eyes and whispered. "I'm weak."

"You'll be better in a minute or two. We'll make some tea and let you rest, and then when you're stronger, we'll send around for the carriage."

"Yes," Lydia said and closed her eyes again. "Tea always helps."

Mary turned to find Edgar. "I'll heat the water," he said.

"Good." Mary followed him out. "Where did you put it?"

"I hid it. No one will ever see it."

"Destroy it, please."

"Cups are there," he said, pointing. He turned and took a box of tea from a drawer. She opened the cupboard and took out the teapot. When she brought it to the light she saw the blue and gold Degas crest.

"I couldn't work on anything else. I tried to finish my plates for the magazine, but I couldn't put that picture out of my head. Don't you see, I had to do it?"

"No, I don't see."

"Really? I'm disappointed. By now you should have experienced at least one compelling image that haunted you until it was painted. Manet speaks of it. Courbet did, too. It's common enough. I had to paint it. It is as simple as that."

Mary turned to go back to Lydia's side, angry at his tone, his insinuation that she must be the lesser artist if she didn't completely understand his doing what he knew she forbade. And she had the right to forbid it. But she couldn't allow herself to become angry now. Lydia needed her. "Tea will be ready in a minute. Do you feel any stronger?"

"A little."

"Your color is better. Perhaps another sip of water?"

Lydia shook her head.

Edgar brought the tea things on a tray and put it on the table. "I'll go for the carriage."

"Thank you, Edgar." Lydia said. Mary nodded as he left. She could not bring herself to speak to him, but began immediately to pour the tea. She put pillows behind Lydia's head and shoulders so she could drink more easily.

"Don't be too angry with him," Lydia said. "It's very special to be painted. I think it's an honor."

"You heard everything."

"Of course."

"I hope you didn't see it."

"Not really."

"It was dreadful."

"May I see it?"

"No one must see it."

"But if I don't see it, I shall always imagine it to be much worse than it probably is."

"I should hate for you to see it."

"Why? Is it sinful?"

"No, it's not that."

"I suspect he hid it under the divan. He paused there, and I heard some shuffling about."

"I'll look," Mary said. "If it's there, I'll show you, and then I'd like to destroy it. But . . ." She hesitated. "Would it be right?"

"I don't know. You're an artist. How would you feel if I destroyed a picture you did of me?"

Mary smiled. "I've destroyed a number of them myself."

"But if a painting was right in your eyes, and I as the model thought it didn't do anything for me and didn't want my friends to see it, would it be all right to destroy it? Is it the model's right or only the artist's?"

"I didn't model for it."

Lydia sipped her tea. Mary continued to sit restlessly on the edge of the bed. Finally she got up and left the room. She went to the divan, moved away a small table that held a lamp, and got down on her hands and knees and looked under the divan. The picture was there.

Perhaps it wasn't so bad, she thought as she examined it. Except for the bare breasts, it was quite beautiful. She did not stop to examine it closely, but took it to the bedroom and put it in Lydia's hands. Lydia looked at it a moment, glanced up at Mary, and smiled. "If it were a painting of me, I would put it back on the wall."

"Anyone who sees it would think—"

"I would think merely that you posed for him. You have posed for him a number of times."

"But not like that."

"I understand, but when have you seen him paint so tenderly?"

Mary examined the painting more closely then. If she ignored the fact that it was a picture of herself disrobed, she could see it was not a sensual painting. If anything, she looked modest and a little frightened. Lydia was right. It was not her prerogative to destroy a work of his genius. This was how he thought of her, and there *was* a tenderness. He remembered the mussed hair, the blue ribbon and lace of the petticoat, and he had painted her eyes as though they were welling with love. Lydia watched as Mary hung it back on the wall.

A little while later Edgar returned. "The carriage is here," he called from the other room. "How is Lydia?"

All of a sudden they heard a thump and a crash. Mary rushed from Lydia's side to the living room. The lamp that had been on the table Mary had moved away from the divan had gone over.

"Damn," he muttered. He rubbed his eyes, then his knee.

She rushed to him. "Are you all right?"

"I didn't notice that damned table. I fell over it. It's hell when a man can't see very well and never forgets to pretend he can."

Mary knew his eyes were sensitive, but surely he wasn't losing his vision. "You didn't notice the table?"

"No, it's usually over there."

"I moved it. I'm sorry."

"You moved it!"

"Yes. I was looking for the picture under the divan. Unfortunately, I think it's quite beautiful now that I have looked again." Their eyes met and after a moment, he laughed.

When they returned to the bedroom, Lydia was sitting up and there was more color in her cheeks. "You look much improved," Edgar said. "Your father is waiting in the carriage. I must warn you he's not happy with any of us for letting this happen."

Before descending, Mary returned to the bedroom to look at his painting of her.

19

It was such a rainy blustery morning, Mary thought she would stay home and work on the portrait of her father she had begun long ago, but never finished.

Mary seated her father so that the light was approximately as it was when she started the work. Her father had never been willing to assume a smiling expression for a painting, but that morning he seemed particularly glum, and the puffy pouches of skin under his eyes were all the more noticeable. "Isn't it nice that Aleck will soon bring the family to Europe?"

"Your mother has quite lost her mind over it. I think it's best to wait until his plans are definite before we anticipate things that may never materialize."

"It's a pleasure to think about, though. The news has given Lydia a reason to get well, she says."

"Yes. Her recovery is taking much too long, though, and your mother wants to run off with her to some spa."

"I know."

"Well, that sort of thing doesn't help. Lord knows we've tried it plenty of times. A summer in the country is what Lydia needs. Sunshine, rest, and country air. Her appetite will improve."

"When the weather warms, surely that will help."

Her father looked up solemnly. "The doctor agrees moving out to the country for the summer will be best."

Mary was suddenly alarmed. "You don't mean the whole household?" Lately she had thought of them as being settled.

"We can lease another apartment when we return from the country. No need to pay rent on two places. A country place would be useful if Aleck and Lois want to leave the children with us while they tour Europe, and this place isn't large enough for guests."

Mary could not find fault with his thinking; surely the country would be good for Lydia and Mother, too. Her father could ride and the children would be freer. But Mary did not want to leave Paris, and didn't want to give up their beautiful apartment and have to find another. "And what of my studio?"

He shook his head. "You certainly won't be needing it in the country. If necessary, when you return to Paris, you can rent another."

"Of course it's necessary." She sighed and painted rapidly. She didn't want to go to the country: she didn't want to leave Edgar.

"I think it would do you good to paint in the country. A change and a fresh look at things never hurt anyone."

"I have my work. I can't leave."

"I'm sure your artist friends go away for the summer."

"Many do, but—"

"But not Edgar. Is that it?"

Mary smiled, though she did not feel like smiling. He had touched home and a smile was often her best defense. "I would certainly miss him."

"You see too much of Edgar. You wasted too much time on that business about a magazine."

He had mumbled and looked down in his lap when he spoke, but she sensed the depth of his agitation. She answered in a low, controlled voice. "I happen to think the magazine is important."

He sighed. "Hang it all, I wish you would meet some other men. Edgar is difficult, to say the least. He's no good for you, and he's keeping you from marriage. Be sensible, Mary. You're approaching mid-life. You're still very pretty and well liked in society. You could . . ."

"Father! I thought you understood I do not want marriage."

"I understand that you wanted to establish your career and you have done that. Your studio pays for itself now. Durand-Ruel is even sending your work to America. Now it's time to think of your future."

"My future is as an artist, not as a woman."

"Your friend, Madame Morisot, has been married for a while now and still paints and exhibits. "

"Yes, she does." Mary had often thought of Berthe's double life and sometimes envied her. But she had married Manet's brother— someone who knew artists and their habits and feelings, and yet he himself was not a serious artist. Berthe was his art, she and their little girl. No, that was not a fair example for a marriage. That was a special case. "If I should ever want to marry—which I won't," Mary said, "but if I ever should, it would be to Edgar." But as soon as she said it, she regretted her words, for her father's eyes grew large and his Adam's apple seemed to protrude. He did not like Edgar and for the life of her, she did not know why.

Mary continued to work on the portrait, but her thoughts were scattered. Robert looked at her apologetically. "Look, I'm sorry," he said, "but Lydia's health is so important. We must all do what we can."

"Of course."

"You have always been good for her. You give her a zest for life your mother and I cannot seem to give." She understood perfectly. Lydia needed the country—away from Paris and Edgar. Where in the country? She was certain her father was serious about it. There was no way to refuse. Three whole long months. Perhaps if they were not too far from Paris, she could journey back once or twice.

"Do you have a location in mind, Father?"

"Not yet."

"Please—not the seacoast. I couldn't bear the sight of it. There are some lovely spots along the Oise valley or perhaps Marly. Manet summers there. I will inquire if you like."

"Yes, yes." His eyes took on more light after her show of enthusiasm.

EARLY the next morning Mary went to Edgar's studio. They were going to meet with Caillebotte and finally make arrangements for having the magazine printed. It would be good to have the first edition done, so they could start fresh on the next.

Edgar was wearing a shirt spotted with ink. His hands were dirty and his hair was uncombed. Mary realized when she saw him that he had been working for a long time. "What are you doing?"

"I started another etching for the magazine. That café scene was impossible. I couldn't let it go. I looked at it again last night and I saw how to do that scene. The angle was too wide."

"I didn't think so. I liked it very much."

"No, it wouldn't do."

"We promised Caillebotte. We said today, and everything was finished."

"I know, but look at this new plate. Here are the sketches for it."

She took the papers he handed her, noticing how his eyes flashed.

"Do you see how this better illustrates the squeezing of space and the use of unusual lighting?"

Mary studied the sketches. "It's very good. It does illustrate that part in the text better than the other one, but you couldn't finish it in time."

He looked down at the plate and sighed. "I've begun. It's coming along."

This meant more delay. There was nothing she could say. Edgar was obviously committed to the plate now.

He sat down and closed his eyes. "I could do with a cup of tea."

"I'll fix it. You rest. Have you slept?"

"Not much."

She made the tea and brought it to him. "Thank you," he said. "You look lovely today."

Before they finished their tea, Caillebotte arrived. Mary greeted him warmly, poured tea for him, and asked after his family. After a few moments he put his cup down and rose.

"I wish I could stay and talk a while, but I must get the materials to the printer's before ten-thirty this morning."

Edgar pointed to a portfolio on the table. "I had it all together there. It's all still there except the last etching, which is coming along very nicely. No need to change the text for it at all."

"What are you saying, Edgar? Surely you don't mean it isn't ready."

Edgar stood up to offer Caillebotte the sketches he had shown to Mary, but Caillebotte pushed them away, refusing to look. His face grew red and his nostrils flared. "You already delayed too long. You promised three times it would be ready and three times I made all the arrangements with the printer. Three times! You didn't keep any of those promises. This time is the last. I can't extend the deadline any more. I've heard too many explanations. The people who wanted to read it no longer care. For a while the delay was a joke they put up with. Now it's a bore. No one cares about your magazine any longer. I can't afford to lose any more money on this. It was a bad venture—and I'm through. I withdraw my support from the magazine. If you want to see it published, you'll have to do it yourself." Caillebotte's eyes were full of anger as he slammed the door.

Mary stared after him, wondering what she should have said. Edgar picked up the copper plate he had been working on, looked at it almost vacantly, then hurled it into the fireplace.

When she heard it crash against the grate, she turned suddenly, looked at him unbelievingly, then knelt down to retrieve it. "We'll publish it ourselves," she said.

"We can't. We have no money."

"All that work, the days and nights we plodded and coaxed words on to paper to explain what we were doing, it couldn't be all for nothing."

He touched her hair, smoothing it. "My dear, my dear, don't think about wasted effort and vain hopes. Don't."

"We could print it ourselves, just a small edition."

"Yes, a small edition, perhaps." He paused, still smoothing her hair. "Would you prefer a stillborn child to no child at all?"

She stood up, exasperated with his way of pushing his hurt away. She looked down at the copper plate in her hand, and after a moment nodded. "Yes, you will finish this and we will have our stillborn edition." She handed him the plate. "Very well," he said.

THAT EVENING when she came home from the studio, Lydia met her with another letter from Aleck full of plans for their crossing. Lydia's cheeks were pink and her eyes sparkled. "We must finish the painting before they come," she said.

Mary laughed. "It will be weeks before they arrive. By the looks of you, we could finish that painting tomorrow or the next day."

The next morning arrangements were made to continue the painting. The horse was hitched to the carriage and Lydia climbed into the driver's seat and took the reins. "I like this pose," she said, "as long as the horse stands still."

The horse behaved well, but the groom stood by. Mary always enjoyed painting outdoors when she was doing it, but it took a lot of preparation, and for portrait work it wasn't very practical. She could understand why Monet preferred it and why Pissarro hardly did anything else. There was a whole spirit to capture. Edgar didn't enjoy it at all. He had tried it for a while with his racecourse pictures, then abandoned it. Sunlight, she suspected, bothered his eyes. He would like what she was doing, she thought. He likes strong lines, and she was handling them with taste, not allowing them to become obvious, but letting them do their work in leading the eye and creating tension and countertension. Edgar would approve of her darkish background. There were times during that bright morning when she was tempted to show the sparkling lights among the trees, but this was not a landscape, this was a double portrait done outside.

When Lydia got down to stretch her legs, the groom jumped up on the back of the carriage and sat facing the backward direction.

How perfect, Mary thought. This image would not detract from her picture, but would give it that interesting contrast that intrigues, if handled carefully. The groom's head would not be done in detail and she would show the back view so there could be no expression to focus upon.

She was creating a new painting from the old one. Everything must work to accommodate the new element. It was the stroke that made the composition unforgettable. She was able to accomplish the change in what seemed like an instant.

The next morning she required very little time to complete her work. In less than an hour she announced to Lydia that the painting was finished.

"Wonderful," Lydia said. "Now let's take this carriage for a ride."

It seemed a fine idea to Mary, for it was a beautiful morning and she was exhilarated by the work. "Where would you like to go?"

"I know of a shop that sells trinkets I'm sure the children would love," Lydia answered, eyes shining with anticipation. "I admire the music boxes myself and I'm sure little Katherine and Elsie would be fascinated. We'll find something for Eddie and Robbie, too."

The shop was in a predominantly Greek market section not far from home. Lydia enjoyed the neighborhood and seemed to know every hidden passage. They bought several handsome music boxes, a ship model for Eddie, a few spinning tops and marionettes. They were walking back to the carriage when Lydia suggested tea.

"I'd love tea," Mary answered. "But is there a respectable place in this neighborhood?"

Lydia laughed. "Around the next corner there's a place with divine teacakes."

Lydia led the way, Mary hurrying to keep up with her. Just as they were passing a secondhand store, a woman dressed in a black coat and shawl came out of the shop. Mary hardly noticed her until the woman exclaimed, "Mary Cassatt! What a surprise."

Mary and Lydia stopped. Mary looked hard at the woman, but didn't recognize her. Instinctively though, she smiled and said, "How are you?"

"I'm wretched. What else? How do I look?"

The voice was more familiar than the face. Suddenly Mary remembered meeting the woman several times at the Barries. Then, however, she had been a beautiful and rich young woman. Mary was aghast at the change. "Emeline, I'm sorry I didn't recognize you at first. This is my sister, Lydia."

Emeline Clay had been one of the most dazzling women in the Barries' circle. Mary had admired her for her grace and handsome bone structure and had once asked her if she would consider posing for a portrait. Nothing had come of it, although Emeline hadn't refused. "How nice to see you again. Won't you join us for a cup of tea?" Mary asked.

"I mustn't be gone too long," Emeline said nervously. Her sunken eyes met Mary's. "I must look a fright."

With their insistence, Emeline agreed to have tea with them. The teahouse Lydia had chosen was respectable enough, lit by candles, and decorated in bright green.

"It's amazing what a difference a few years can make, isn't it?" Emeline said. "You look better than ever, and I congratulate you on your success with the impressionists. I'm sorry I didn't find the time to have you do my portrait back in the days when you had the time and I didn't. It would be something to treasure now."

"What has happened?" Mary asked. "You have changed."

Emeline threw back her head and laughed. The bone structure was still as beautiful as before. But the smile, the dazzle, was gone. "Can't you guess? I married a man I was totally unsuited for, to quote my father. Three years ago I didn't believe it, but now I know he was right."

Mary frowned, not knowing what to say. It was Lydia whose sympathetic voice reached out. "I'm sure your family would want you to come home if your husband makes you unhappy."

"Oh, they would, of course. Turning back would be easy if I were the same. But I'm not. I gave up my old life for love. It was a bargain I made, one thing for another."

Her voice was somber, her eyes deep and eloquent. All at once though, her expression changed. She smiled with something of the gaiety Mary remembered from the past. "I do follow society and the arts. I've heard about you, Mary. You and your friend, Monsieur Degas." Emeline leveled her eyes on Mary, her gaze somewhat teasing, somewhat challenging. "I expect you may soon make a decision that will change your life."

It wasn't exactly a question and Mary only smiled and changed the subject. Lydia carried the conversation back to chatting about people they all knew. Mary's mind, however, was not on the small talk. She remembered Emeline's charm and her strength, and wondered how she could be content with her bargain.

When they parted on the street, Emeline took Mary's hand. "Remember me to the Barries when you see them. And be careful Mary. Love is a double-edged sword."

Mary didn't sleep well that night. The image of Emeline and her echoing words remained. Finally when Mary was able to cast them out of her mind, she longed all the more for Edgar. Maybe a separation would be good for them. She was too much under his influence. It might be good for him, too. He ought to get away from Paris, perhaps visit his sister's family. He often talked about it. She had to admit that the tension between them was sometimes great, and she usually ended it by agreeing with him. She needed to get away to regain her independence of him, but she dreaded it so. She would be lonely without him no matter who else was present. Her days would be barren without Edgar. And she dreaded telling him.

The next morning a letter arrived from Manet.

My dear Miss Cassatt,

It was my pleasure to receive your letter asking about summer homes in Marly. As it turns out, I know of a splendid house near my own. It has six bedrooms, a servant's cottage, a small stable, and a well-kept garden. There is a pond nearby as well as wooded hills. Marly is rich in paintable landscapes and we have always been able to find excellent household help thereabouts. I am enclosing a card with the name of the person who can show you the place. It would be our great pleasure to have you and your family as neighbors this summer.

Mary read the letter after lunch and her father was especially enthusiastic. Ordinarily Mary would have been, too. Well, she was, of course. Manet as a neighbor. How fortunate. But she would have to tell Edgar today, otherwise he would learn of it when he came to dinner the next evening.

20

IT HAD GOTTEN WARM in Edgar's studio and he had opened the window. A soft breeze wafted Mary's hair. "The summer in Marly?" he asked, straightening up and moving away from her.

"Perhaps Marly, somewhere in the country, at any rate. Father has always like the country better than the city. He'll be able to ride more often. Aleck will enjoy that too, and of course, Lydia will get more fresh air. People *do* go to the country in the summer."

"I don't."

"You will come for a visit, won't you?"

"No, I couldn't."

"Why couldn't you?"

"I never cared for the country at all." They were silent for a moment. She waited and he raised his head suddenly. "Damn. Mary, don't go. Stay here." He came to her, his arms hanging lifelessly at his side, his eyes pleading.

"Stay in Paris? You mean have my own place like I did before? I can't do that. Father would never permit it."

"No, I'm sure *he* wouldn't. And he would be quite right to think you would be in danger of being seduced."

"Edgar," she scolded.

"*Quite* right."

She hung her head.

"I won't let you go."

"It's only for the summer."

He paced a few steps, then stopped and turned abruptly. "This is the last time; I shall never ask again. Marry me."

His eyes focused sharply on hers. She felt feverish. She could not look at him. Marry me, he had said. Her lips trembled as she looked down at her hands and imagined a wedding ring. The thought of Berthe flashed across her mind. Marry? She did love him, loved him dearly. He touched her hand. His arms enfolded her, creating a melting warmth. "Don't leave me," he whispered.

She inhaled deeply, shiveringly touched by his pleading. But a voice from within her spoke. "I cannot marry." The words sounded like doom to her own ears. She did not want them to stand in the air, cutting them apart. But before she could say anything to erase them, he drew away from her coolly with only the slightest movement.

"Well then, that's settled," he said. "I do hope you have a jolly summer."

"Edgar, please—I must—"

"Certainly, you must. You deserve a vacation. You've worked hard. Perhaps I shall have one myself. My brother, sister, and cousin have all begged me to come. Perhaps I will. One needs to replenish one's soul. It gets stale in Paris doing the same thing day after day." His voice was icy. There was no way to answer him.

When he went back to his easel, she tried to work on the pastel she had begun, but the silence between them was too dismal to allow her to concentrate. She wanted to talk to him, break the awful silence, change the mood. "Are your paintings framed and ready for the exhibit?" she asked.

She waited, but he did not answer, so she continued. "Have you finished the one of men meeting on the stairs? I did so want to see that one included."

"I am tired of people asking what I have finished. I am never finished."

"I suppose I can wait to find out if it's in the show. I only asked because I get excited about the exhibit. I've thought about it all year."

He was silent. After a moment she put the pastels away, picked up her shawl from her chair, and slowly put it around her shoulders. "I'm leaving. I wish you wouldn't be angry."

"That is not what I am," he said.

"Then you will still come for dinner tomorrow. Good. I shall see you then." She did not wait for an answer but went out the door and closed it.

WHEN THE TIME CAME for dinner she didn't think he would come. He would probably send word any minute. He exasperated her. The more she thought about it, the more she welcomed a separation. He was too difficult.

But he did come to dinner, and brought flowers. He was charming, especially to Lydia and Katherine. After the meal he talked at length with Katherine about music. And when Robert asked him how many paintings he would be showing in the exhibit, he smiled. "Too many for some, and too few for others. My count is never certain until the show is hung. And even then sometimes I change my mind and take one or two away."

"Why is that?" Katherine asked.

"Because you cannot leave a painting on a wall if it doesn't look right there, and walls are not always compatible. Some paintings need space around them, and no shadows or glare."

"You sound French and finicky," Katherine said smiling. "It's quite enviable, of course."

Or he has a monstrous ego? Mary thought, but she didn't really believe anything about Edgar was as simple as it seemed. She was glad he came to dinner though, even if his behavior toward her was distant. He was there, and that must prove something, though she didn't know what.

HOWEVER, she did not see him again for more than a week. He made no attempt to call on her and she could not bring herself to go to his studio, though she desperately wanted to see him. Love was terrible. She was not good at it. She remembered Lorenzo and shuddered. She would probably always be a failure at love. But fortunately she had no time to brood about it, for Aleck and his family were arriving in a week and the 1880 Impressionist Exhibition was under way.

Mary inspected the show before the public opening and met Berthe Morisot doing the same. Berthe looked beautiful, Mary thought. Marriage and a baby did not harm her. They greeted each other warmly, and looked at the show together. Berthe's work was vibrant, painted outdoors with vigor and joy. Mary wanted to spend more time studying it, but Berthe pulled her along. "Look, that's Claude's new work," she said.

They stood and examined a large canvas by Monet. Berthe was ecstatic over it. "He's a master," she said. "When I look at any of his landscapes I know exactly which way to turn my parasol."

"Yes, he captures the moment completely," Mary said.

"I know some day he'll be loved."

"Why must it always be some day? Why not now?"

"I hear you are taking a place in Marly near Edouard."

"That's right."

"You'll love it there. Eugene and I will be there for a couple of weeks, too. You and Edouard and I can all paint together if you like."

"That would be fun." It was the first time she had thought with much pleasure about the summer, but painting with Manet and Berthe was something to look forward to. Her own work was perhaps too precisely drawn. She would welcome the close influence of Manet, whose grand looseness was both his downfall with the Salon and the beginning of impressionism. So much had happened since he took up the gauntlet. If she had come under Manet's influence instead of Degas's she wondered if she would have painted in a different way. Her work showed Edgar's influence just as Berthe's work showed Manet's.

When they stood before Edgar's entries, both became quiet, muttering about a clever line or a sophisticated color arrangement. It was an understated way of talking. What could they say? Genius was the word neither would speak, but how could it be denied. Mary had seen all of this work at one stage or another and some of them after they were finished and framed. Viewing them now in this exhibition hall, as thousands of others would see them, filled her with pride and admiration. She could never lose her awe of his work no matter what he did.

The two artists stopped frequently, assessing a painting, studying, wondering how the public would see it. There was a new streetscape by Pissarro. How could anyone fail to appreciate the freshness of it, Mary wondered.

"Your work is very strong, Mary," Berthe said when they approached it. "Superb, as Edouard would say. You've developed impressively. You must have worked very hard."

"I have worked hard. Can you really see a change?"

"It's unmistakable. Your work has always been competent and had charm, but now there's a strength of style we always talk about and try forever to define. I see it especially in the *Mother About to Wash her Sleepy Child*. It looks so natural, but intelligent lines are there behind all the charm. And the *Woman in Black* has it, too. Who would have thought you could do something so elegant with an ordinary-looking woman with opera glasses at her eyes?"

Mary, pleased at Berthe's assessment, nevertheless wanted to move on. There was something about viewing her own work in an exhibit that chilled her. It was frightening to see it hanging alongside unfamiliar and stimulating things. Her own were so well-known to her, they were beyond judging, and yet it was important to know how they measured up.

After they had seen the show, they went to a nearby café to chat over coffee. Berthe talked about her daughter. Mary wondered what it would be like to have a child. Painting motherhood was not knowing it.

At breakfast, the day after the exhibition opened, Robert sent out for all the newspapers. When the maid returned with all she could find, they went to the drawing room to see what had been printed.

Katherine sat with her jaw set. "I don't see why what those ninnies say should make such a difference. They're only writers. What do they know?"

"They know how not to bore," Lydia said. "If they praised everything, who would bother to read the papers?"

Mary looked through one of the papers while her father did the same. " 'Impressionists—How They Do Persist'," Robert read aloud. " 'The annual exhibit of Salon dissenters is again a wasteland of brightly colored daubs. The daubists this year have outdone themselves, offering even more outrageous slights to the eye than before. These would-be artists seem never to have heard of black, brown, or gray in the tradition of the masters. They did not bother to learn how to mix colors. Like children they prefer the primary colors applied unmixed in little spots or brushstrokes. Often the bare canvas is not even covered at all.' "

Mary listened, knowing all at once their points had been missed again. Hadn't Pissarro and Seurat and Durand-Ruel explained how the eye mixes the colors—three daubs of green, one yellow, and a small bit of red put directly on the canvas is the same green for foliage as could be mixed on the palette; when the eye mixes it, seeing it from a distance, the color vibrates. The effect is more lively than using the convention of mixing on the palette. Were the critics going to forever insist that dark color was better than light?

" 'However,' " Robert's voice rose suddenly, and Mary looked at him as he continued to read. " 'However, to be fair, there are a few artistic treats tucked among the ridiculous. Monsieur Degas's figure studies are not daubs, but rather are rich masterworks by a most competent artist who has refused to be convinced that art is child's play. And Miss Mary Cassatt's paintings of women in loges, women having tea, and a mother and child are worth the time and trouble of ferreting out. They illustrate this artist's meteoric maturing and must be seen.'" Robert let the paper fold in his lap. "Now what do you think of the ninnies?" he asked.

The exhibition was quite well-attended and a few more sales were made than the year before. Gauguin bought Mary's *Young Lady in a Loge Gazing to the Right.* She was gratified, but surprised since it was somewhat delicate, practically the opposite of the sort of thing Gauguin himself did. He would not buy anything that did not touch him deeply. The fact that he had chosen her painting to own, out of all the others, meant more than any reviewer's words.

The only disappointment about the exhibit was her estrangement from Edgar. It had been weeks since she had seen him. She had even gone to his studio one morning, but he was gone. She continued to hope he would come to her, but if he didn't, she would try again to see him. She was not willing to give up his friendship because of her pride.

WHEN ALECK and his family arrived, the excitement in the Cassatt household was heady. Eddie at eleven was the unquestioned leader, cheerful and polite, remarkably like Aleck at the same age. Little Katherine at nine could change from wild teasing to dreaminess in an instant. Robbie at seven fairly burst with exuberence, and the youngest, Elsie, formed an immediate alliance with Imperia. Mary was so caught up in the excitement of having the children actually there squealing with delight over presents and the sights of Paris that she hardly thought of Edgar for a day and a half.

Aleck rented the top floor of an elegant hotel nearby for their stay in Paris. Each day Lois had her hair done by one of Paris's most fashionable hairdressers. She surrounded herself in as much luxury as taste would allow. Mary accompanied her to the top French couturiers where Lois selected the most becoming gowns. Mary enjoyed this shopping and was, even Lois had to admit, excellent at arriving at a good price in a dignified way. "How did you ever learn to do it?" Lois asked. "It would have cost me double, I'm sure. And to insist on that special lining; I wouldn't have dared."

"I learned because I like fine clothes and have limited funds for luxuries."

Those last days in Paris were busy. They went to opera and theater parties in the evenings. There was sightseeing and shopping and people in for tea, and the children to be taken to see the things they might be old enough to enjoy. Aleck and Lois would soon begin a tour of Europe while the children and the rest of the household went off to Marly-le-Roi for the summer, with Aleck and Lois to join them there later.

It had been a busy time, a vacation from painting for Mary, but she wanted to get back to her easel. She had planned dozens of paintings in her mind and was anxious to be settled again and painting.

She did not want to go away without seeing Edgar. Even if she had botched up their love, something could be salvaged. She missed him more than she had believed she could.

One afternoon she declined a luncheon party, saying she felt unwell, and started off to Edgar's studio, afraid to think what she'd do if he wasn't there. They were leaving the next day. It would be wretched if she could not even say good-bye. She was almost prepared to find the doors locked again.

She turned the knob of his studio door. It was unlocked. "Edgar," she said softly as she stepped in. He was at his easel. He turned to look at her. "Edgar, you're here."

"I am, yes."

"May I come in?"

"You are in."

"I wanted to see you before we left for Marly."

"You're going soon?"

"Tomorrow."

He looked down, pressed his lips together.

"It's been such a long time, Edgar. I hoped we could be friends, at least."

"We can be friends if that's what you like."

They were silent a moment. She took a step toward him. "You look well."

He looked at her, but didn't answer.

"You weren't here when I came before."

"I went to Spain."

"To Spain?"

"To visit friends."

"Aleck and the family arrived."

"As planned?"

"Yes. Well. I only wanted to see you and say good-bye and maybe—"

"What?"

"Just—maybe you could write. To say you're all right. A letter now and then?"

He nodded.

"I'll write you too if you'd like."

"If you feel like it, do."

"Of course, I'll feel like it." She felt emotion intruding into her voice. Why couldn't she have more control? "Good-bye, Edgar." She turned quickly to the door. She hurried out and down the street, feeling weak and ashamed and empty and disappointed.

"Mary."

She turned back and saw him running down the street toward her. She stood a moment unable to move. His face told her everything she wanted to know. In another instant she was in his arms.

21

It was with a light heart Mary went to Marly, her anxieties about Edgar put mostly to rest. She could concentrate on Lydia, her parents, and the children. She would miss Edgar and Paris, but perhaps it would be a good summer even so.

The villa at Marly had been so well prepared, there was hardly any settling in required. Robert Cassatt was a marvel at arranging moves. No one could have done it as well. There was soup in the kettle when they arrived and lilacs in a vase on the table. After the meal, Robert took the children for a hike while Mary, Lydia, and Katherine strolled in the garden. The sunlight did seem brighter in the country. There was a quietness broken only by the twitter of birds. They sat on benches and drank it in. Mary wanted to paint Lydia in that sunlight. As she studied Lydia, thinking of how to pose her, it came almost as a shock to see how pale she was. Her forehead and eyes were shaded by her bonnet, but there was a sallowness, a tired greenish shadow about the eyes. Lydia looked up and smiled.

"I know. You want to paint me here in the garden, reading or sewing, wearing a dress that will blend well with the garden blooms."

Mary laughed. "Am I truly that transparent?"

"Yes," Lydia said. "I hope you will paint Elsie. She's such a beautiful child."

"She reminds me of you, Lydia," Katherine said.

"I hope to paint all the children, of course, but I want to give them time to get used to us and Marly and then some morning they won't know quite what to do, and I shall snatch them one by one and paint them."

"Poor little victims," Lydia said.

Mary noticed that Katherine's gaze seemed distant and dreamy. "Do you think you will like it here, Mother?"

"Oh, yes. It's going to be very pleasant. Did you see your father's face? If he's happy, I am happy."

"Really?" Mary frowned. Why should her mother's mood be a reflection of her father's? It seemed all wrong. Even though her mother was a strong-willed person, she experienced life through her family. If Mother was philosophical about caging her own desires and putting all her resources to work for the family, Mary should not be disappointed. It might be the best way for her mother to conduct her life. But Mary had escaped that sort of existence, that wifehood, and she was glad.

SHE SKETCHED and painted Lydia outdoors in many poses, from the front, side, and back, with Imperia on her lap, with trees as background, in full shade, dappled shade, and full sunlight. Lydia seemed to enjoy the endless posing, the conversations they had together and especially the walks they took between sittings. Once Mary persuaded Elsie to sit with Lydia on the grass for a quick watercolor. It became Lydia's favorite picture. She had it framed and hung in her room.

Edouard Manet called the third week they were there. He would have come sooner, he said, but he had been ill. Now that he was recovered, he wanted Mary to paint with him if she could find the time.

When she went to Manet's villa the following morning, they set up their easels in a protected terrace overlooking a pond and a hilly meadow. He sat on a stool while he painted, because his legs ached with rheumatism, he said. He looked rustic in his straw hat, but there were lines about his eyes and a pallor that made the specks of gray in his beard seem to stand out sharply. "It's good of you to come," he said. "Working beside an artist one respects is stimulating; it makes one work a bit harder."

"Indeed it does," she said. "I know I shall be working hard. I seldom do a landscape. I really should get out more." She searched the terrain for a suitable composition.

"Sometimes the pond has a few ducks," he said.

Mary looked at the pond, but saw no ducks. Composing a picture from all of the expanse before her would be difficult. Now, if she could insert a figure somewhere, the picture would practically compose itself. Perhaps if she could think of that scrubby tree as a figure, then at least there would be some focus. She smiled, and the tree became Eddie.

"You seem deep in concentration," Manet said.

"Landscapes are not my forté."

"You must not pay so much attention to Degas that you neglect the study of sunlight."

"I was painting portraits before I met Degas. Though I admit outdoor painting is not *his* favorite subject."

"I should say not," Manet said.

'You and Edgar were once close friends. It's a shame you see so little of each other now."

Manet raised his eyebrows, but continued to paint. "And I must take a good part of the blame. We were close at first. And I had known him well enough that I should have avoided some things— overlooked others. But when Edgar hurls an insult, it hits target."

"Yes, quite true," Mary agreed. "But he greatly admires you."

"He hates me."

"He has a painting of yours hanging in his rooms."

"He does? I thought he got rid of everything when he had his reverses. I did feel tremendous sympathy for him then, but he would have nothing to do with anyone. He secluded himself."

"At that time he could afford to keep only a few things—the most precious—and he kept your painting."

"It's strange he did that." Manet gazed off and spoke softly. "In the beginning when he first came to the Café Guerbois, he was open-minded about everything we discussed. We examined art from all angles and he agreed that his historical paintings were pompous and stereotyped and that it was time for us to cast off aritificiality and paint contemporary life. He did not come to the group as a follower of Courbet. He cared little for realism. He was so steeped in Ingres, and the line. He listened and kept notebooks. I admired his integrity. I thought we would always be friends."

"It was over the Salon that you quarreled, wasn't it?"

"It was my refusal to go against the Salon. I let his insult pass because, damn him, he could not understand. He had wealth and position. He didn't need acceptance; he needed only to rebel. When I didn't join, he looked on me as sniveling and bourgeois. Perhaps I would have felt the same if our situations had been reversed." Manet sighed. "I suppose my work made everyone expect me to be rebellious. I disappointed them, especially Degas. Of course, that was not the end of it. In our discussions of artistic philosophies, we hardened, We gave fewer points—disagreed violently. Degas could always best me in an argument. He was quite literary; I've seen him rather poetic when he drank too much. Half his friends were writers. He not only had the words, Degas had the sneer, the cold eye, the inflection, the conviction that made him absolutely impossible to argue down, no matter how convinced I was. About that time our friendship was worn thin. In retrospect I should have just painted and not talked. But we did talk—so much was happening. One night I was frustrated at not being able to get my point over with him. I went home angry. As soon as I walked inside my house I saw a picture he had done of my wife and me. I went to the wall and gazed at it again. He had *drawn* the arm and shoulder; he had not painted.

His style warred with truth as I saw it. As I looked at that outlined arm, my anger and frustration was so great that I cut away that part of the painting.

"I've never forgiven myself. And neither has he."

Mary was sure Manet was right. "He does admire your work, though," she said.

"And I admire his, more than I like to say."

Mary smiled. "So vanity is not so important, is it?"

"No, but how many times must we learn that in life?"

"My mother learned it only once."

Manet let his brush stray from his canvas. He looked at her with puzzlement.

"What I meant was that for women, vanity is different. Marriage puts them away from their *own* vanities."

"How does it do that?" he asked.

"The husband is the leader and the wife may keep herself pretty in order to please him, but that secondary vanity she indulges in is not very important."

"That seems a harsh look at it. There must be compensations. I can see your pride in your work is as strong as my own. It must cause you pain, my dear."

"Sometimes it does. At the moment, though, it's not going so well. I'm trying to see masses like you do, but I see edges."

"You paint too much with Degas. Seeing is never easy. I've often wished I could have been born blind and regained my sight, and with all of that wonder and innocence, paint exactly what I saw, ignoring all the conventions we've learned."

"I would like to be able to achieve that kind of looseness you did in that portrait of the café singer I saw at Durand-Ruel's. It has a deceiving simplicity."

"Exactly. My advice is, think of the work as a sketch, use broad strokes. Imagine that it's something you have to get down and in ten minutes there will be a downpour and you'll be stopped from going on so you may as well use up all the paint you squeezed out. Put it on like butter."

"Not very academic advice, I must say."

He smiled. "You're getting on. Too bad you put that tree in. It's getting to be a presence, isn't it?"

Mary stood back and looked. Yes, she was drawing the tree with small brushes and the rest she was handling in that lovely loose manner she had admired. Nothing to do but paint out the tree.

They worked for several hours, until she noticed he seemed very tired. She had the groom load the canvas and her paints in the carriage and said good-bye. "Come back Saturday if you can. Renoir will be here for several days and wants to turn out a few canvases. We may want to try a figure seated on the grass."

"Thank you. I will." She smiled and waved as the carriage started away. No, the summer would not be dull.

When she arrived home, a letter from Edgar was lying on the table in the front hall. She picked it up, tucked it into her dress pocket, and hurried to her room to read it.

Dearest Mary,

In my unwanted solitude (I always thought I wanted it), I've reasoned that this long separation is what we needed. How easy it was to depend on your affection and support and believe they would always be. Now I must find my own support, and it is well I am forced to do it while I still remember how. You need solitude to develop your own way. You have been much guided and cherished by your family, and alas me, but within you is a force that needs special nourishment. And you must not deny it. You have strength and courage. There were many easy paths you didn't take. Is that why I love you?

You remind me of the magnificent Christmas ornament I loved looking at when I was small. Once my mother took it off its shelf and showed it to me, a silver angel with glass bells at the hem of its dress and pearls for eyes. I wanted to touch it and make it ring, but of course I could not. It might break. I could touch the other ornaments, but not that one. It was too precious. So naturally that was the only one I cared about. The child never goes away. He gets wrinkled and gray and his sight isn't so good, but he's still such a child.

I am sketching at the opera. The dancers were like flowers in the wind today, but they work hard at it and they sweat while they seek perfection. Everyone on the stage wants the kind of perfection we want when we paint. As long as I can work I shall not complain though the city of Paris is growing dim and fuzzy at the edges. I walk through the streets knowing you're gone and the edges get even more blurred.

I have been seeing my friend Bartheleme. He is encouraging me to work in clay, and I have consented to let him guide me in this. It might be stimulating.

I have taken the liberty of sending you a small reminder of my affection. With all my best to your family,

Edgar

It seemed as though his attitude was changing toward her. She didn't want to be untouchable, only unmarried. She sat on the corner of the bed, thinking of him, clutching the bedpost. Why were her feelings so contrary? She longed to hold him in her arms. That was longing for marriage, wasn't it; or did she long to be his mistress? What a thought! What was she turning into, always wishing for him, thinking of those passionate times? She'd be wise to remember the other times, too.

The next morning Mary intended to work on a study of Lydia sewing in the garden. However, breakfast had long ago passed and Lydia had not come down. Mary went directly to Lydia's room. She knocked twice and walked determinedly inside.

Lydia's head rested on a stack of pillows as she dozed, but it was not a peaceful sight. She was pale and her hair was tangled. The muscles in her face twitched and so did her hand holding the coverlet. Mary touched the quivering hand. Lydia opened her eyes but didn't seem to see. Then she recognized Mary, swallowed and smiled.

"I dreamed of Robbie again. It was so real, Mary. He's content."

"Of course he is." She sat on the bed and held onto Lydia's hand. "How are you feeling?"

"Oh, all right."

"Your color isn't so good."

"I don't sleep very well, even here in the country. I finally took a sleeping powder. That's why I keep dozing off, but I never sleep for long and when I get up I'm nauseated for a while. It goes away."

"I'll send for tea."

"Oh, do, and stay and have a cup with me."

"All right." Mary brushed Lydia's hair while they waited.

"It's strange I keep dreaming of Robbie, isn't it?"

"I don't know. What does he say in your dreams?"

"All sorts of things. He calls me Liddy O. Remember how he used to call me that? I had forgotten until he said it in my dream. His voice has that clear lighthearted ring. Have you ever dreamed of him?"

"Only when I was a child, after he died."

"In my dream he took my hand and we walked through a forest in the mountains. I've never seen anything so beautiful."

The tea tray came. Lydia drank hers eagerly and seemed to feel better.

Lydia sighed. "Do you want to paint me in the garden? It looks like a fine day."

"If you're up to it."

"I feel better now."

"Well, then," Mary said as she walked to Lydia's wardrobe in the corner of the room, "let me see what would look well." She glanced in, took a dress out, then went to the window and held it up, comparing the colors. "No," she said. She went back to the wardrobe and chose a blue silk.

"I like that one," Lydia said. "I didn't really think I'd be wearing it here in the country."

"This should shimmer nicely in the light. And a hat—the white."

"But I look ghastly in that."

"You don't look ghastly. It's a lovely hat with all those soft gauzy ruffles, and a bit of a challenge to paint."

"All right, I'll wear it. After the painting you must keep it for yourself. Wear it when you paint with Renoir and Manet."

After she put on the dress Lydia looked like herself again,

flushed and happy. She had a light breakfast and when she was
ready to pose, Mary had her easel and palette waiting in the garden,
and set to work at once. She was laying in the underpainting when
Mathilde came rushing into the garden. "The delivery post has just
brought a crate for you, Miss Mary," she said.

"Thank you, Mathilde," she said without looking up.

"It's from Monsieur Degas and the crate is making a terrible
noise. It so distressed your mother, she sent me to fetch you."

Mary glanced at Lydia, shrugged, and put down her brush.
Lydia stood up. "What kind of a noise?"

"It sounds like a drunken Englishman."

Lydia and Mary laughed as they started toward the house.
"Leave it to Edgar to send you a drunken Englishman," Lydia said.

The crate had been taken to the porch. Katherine and Robert
stood over it, Robert with tools in his hand.

"Hallo, bloke."

"What's that?" Lydia asked.

Robert bent over the crate. "Hello, bloke. Good-bye."

"It sounds like a—"

"A parrot," Mary shrieked delightedly when she saw its sleek
green feathers.

ALECK AND LOIS arrived at Marly in August, anxious to be with
the children. After a few days Mary asked Aleck if he would sit for a
portrait. It was to be a large, important work, and Aleck seemed
eager, saying it would give them a good chance to visit.

After the first week, however, Lois became impatient, and Mary
suggested she should have her portrait done too, recommending
Renoir. Lois declined, saying she would prefer to have Whistler.
Lois was restless in the country. Perhaps it was difficult to adjust to
such a quiet life after so much travel and stimulation, but Mary grew
tired of hearing her preface every sentence with "when we leave
here," or to Aleck, "if your portrait is *ever* finished." Mary would not
hurry the portrait of Aleck. It was not easy to paint a portrait of
someone she knew so well and cared so deeply for. It was one of the
most difficult studies she had done in a long time.

On one extraordinarily hot afternoon, after an hour's work on the portrait, Mary put away her brushes and they all gathered on the veranda to sip iced lemonade. A soft breeze occasionally touched them with a heavenly relief. Mary looked toward the horizon and wondered with a pang of longing what Edgar was doing.

"On a day like this a person should be on the water," Lois said. Mary felt herself cringe, but said nothing.

"We could be on our way to London, or the Greek isles," Lois went on, "but we've saving Greece for the winter months, aren't we, Aleck? I'm so looking forward to that."

"It won't be long before we are back in Paris," Lydia said. "I'll miss this place."

"So will I," Robert said, "especially now that we have such a fine horse to ride, thanks to Aleck."

Aleck smiled. "We wanted to give you something you'd enjoy for a long time."

Ordinarily Mary would be interested, but on that day, she wanted to get away. Strange images of Edgar plagued her, and Lois was getting on her nerves. "Would you excuse me?" she asked. "I'm feeling tired and could do with a rest."

She managed a wink at Lydia and went inside and up to her room. It was stifling there, though the window was open. She unbuttoned her dress and felt immediate relief. "Hallo, bloke." Startled by the squalking sound, Mary turned and laughed when she saw the parrot shifting himself around in the cage. "Hello," she answered, all of her irritation suddenly gone. She took off her petticoat and stockings and stood a few feet back from the window hoping to catch a breeze, looking outward beyond the horizon. She sighed. It wouldn't be long before she'd be seeing Edgar again. A shiver of excitement went through her at the picture her brain called up and she went to the writing table and took out paper and pen.

My dearest Edgar,

In a few weeks I shall be seeing you again, and I must admit that the thought improves my days. It will be good to be back in Paris, though Marly has been beneficial. Of course, I work every day and some days I am so totally immersed in it, there is no room for anything else. The outside voices cannot penetrate it. Yet there are moments—many of them—like now, when I long to love and be loved, when my thoughts are only of you, my dear Edgar, though such thoughts might make you blush. I hope that when I come back to Paris, you will be as glad to see me as I shall be to see you. Being away like this has made me love you all the more, although I did not expect such longing and desire to take possession of me, and I scarcely know how to live with it. But I am concerned about your feeling. If this separation has affected you, or if you perhaps have developed another friendship, please tell me. There are no bonds to our love so I know I can count on your honesty. Tell me what to expect from you, then I shall expect it.

Then she lay down on the bed, and gazed up at the ceiling. She wished he were by her side. How empty her life would be without Edgar. But of course, she must constantly realize that he could drop out of her life at any moment. There were no bonds. But perhaps there was no harm in thinking of him and hoping he was as anxious for her as she was for him. Her mind conjured the picture of the way he looked, the sound of his voice, the way he held his head, the way he rubbed his eyes. With such thoughts she fell asleep. When she woke later, the curtains were swaying in the warm breeze.

MARY HOPED for a pleasant day when she was to paint with Berthe, Renoir, and Manet, but the weather exceeded all her hopes. Lydia came along too, with the idea that she would pose or just watch.

From Manet's villa the group trekked to a shady hillock near the pond. Lydia sat in the tall grass under a tree with her book of verse. Renoir chose her as his subject immediately, setting his easel close enough to fill his canvas with Lydia and disregard the landscape. Manet moved his easel and stool back to get a more distant view. Berthe and Mary chose the middle ground. In a few minutes they were all silently working.

"This is unbelieveable," Berthe said after a while. "Sunshine, buttercups, no wind, soft shadows, and good companionship. What luck!"

"Impressionists are naturally a lucky group," Renoir said smiling, "and always so full of the milk of human kindness, who could wonder at their good fortune. It's only right that the heavens stay blue."

Berthe smiled. "Impressionists lucky *or* kind! How you do rave. But our situation is improving. I was just telling Edouard how much better things are."

"Those who take impressionists seriously are a very small number still," Mary said.

Renoir smiled at her. "Durand-Ruel says you have done much to help, never failing to put in a good word with people who buy paintings."

"I do get effusive sometimes, and once in a while it helps. It is Durand-Ruel himself who is the sustenance of artists," Mary said. "He never loses faith in us."

"Yes," Berthe said. "I saw him a couple of weeks ago and he talked about sending a group of impressionist paintings to London and perhaps America. It takes forever to make all the arrangements, but he is working on it."

"What other news did Durand-Ruel have?" Mary asked.

Berthe looked thoughtful. "Pissarro was showing a delightful work; Durand-Ruel talked about dazzling London with it. Monet is doing a series on locomotives. It's hard to believe the man's skill. I coughed when I saw the smoke rumbling out of the stack. Degas is being troublesome. You know how he hates to have anything exhibited. When he saw his last painting on display at the gallery, he wanted to take it back to repaint a passage. Durand-Ruel refused to let him and told him to go home and paint another, putting all the improvements in that one. I hear he's doing some small sculptures. What have you heard from him?"

"Nothing lately," Mary admitted. She should have heard from him long ago. She had asked for his honest feelings about her, and had heard nothing. What did it mean? She smiled at Berthe, whose expression had grown concerned. "I've been expecting a letter. I wrote to him weeks ago."

"I can't imagine how you've put up with him so long," Renoir said. "As much as I try, I can't keep from arguing with him."

"That's too bad," Mary said.

"Yes, yes, I know that. He disapproves of me because I exhibited at the Salon."

Mary pressed her lips together. "He is extremely loyal to the group," she said, looking steadfastly at her painting.

"He refuses to listen to reason. I must have patrons in order to live."

"It's difficult, I know."

"He never argues with ladies," Berthe said. "I find him always to be quite gallant."

"The trouble with Degas is he is so easy to hurt," Renoir said. "And he never forgets."

"That's probably right," Mary observed, wondering if she would some day be numbered like Renoir and Manet as one of his close friends that he didn't see anymore.

"He will never forgive me, Renoir said. "At first I tried to ignore his comments, not to let them interfere with friendship, but when he continued to attack me, I wanted to repudiate him. It's a shame I sank so low. I knew what would be the cruellest blow, and I did it."

Mary nodded. "You sold the painting he gave you. If I should ever want to completely repudiate him, I should do the same thing."

"But how I regret it," Renoir said. "It gave me a moment of satisfaction, but now I'm sorry I didn't keep it—for what had gone before."

"Do not regret too much," Berthe said. "Degas will survive and paint masterpieces to compensate."

"My back needs a rest," Lydia announced. Renoir rushed to her at once to help her up. "Are you painting me fat?" she asked him.

"Come and see for yourself." Lydia looked at the painting on his easel and sighed. "I wish I had your eyes."

He kissed her hand and led her to Mary's and Berthe's easels.

"Isn't it wonderful how each of you sees something different? If I could paint, I would do a picture of four artists standing by their easels squinting at me, with such long faces you would think that I had burned the Christmas goose."

EVERY DAY Mary hoped for a letter from Edgar, but nothing came. It had to mean he did not feel the same as she did. As the days went by and there was no letter, she regretted letting him matter so much to her. He was not only her lover; he was the only person who understood exactly her thinking on art. He could put her own thoughts into words and often did, and he would tell her the truth about her work. Moreover, he saw it as she would if she were not so close to it. Sometimes it was like looking in a mirror when she was painting with him. She wondered—would she become as bitter as he? They had both been accused by a critic of having no *joie de vivre*. She told herself at the time it wasn't true. Her family and friends called the remark slander. Maybe there was some truth in it.

Damn him, he could at least write and tell her what he was thinking. She had asked for honesty, and he had never hesitated at saying anything in the name of truth before. He was exasperating. That was why she had to keep her independence. Work can be the only master. She must always remember it. Always.

AFTER LUNCH one day her father asked if she would return to Paris early and see about renting an apartment for them. She agreed to go at once and as they talked about it, she realized how much her father had come to rely on her.

"There will be much to do," Mary said. "Mathilde and I will leave in the morning."

"Remember, we need more bedrooms and a much bigger dining room."

"Yes, yes, I know. I should be able to find something in the quarter."

Mathilde came into the room. "Beg pardon, miss, but a letter came from Paris. There's one for Miss Lydia, too."

Mary's heart leapt. At last, a letter from Edgar. The shivery thrill disappeared when she saw the sprawling handwriting on the envelope. It was not Edgar's. She took the letter. "Thank you, Mathilde." Slowly Mary opened the letter and unfolded the pages. "It's from Louisine."

Robert nodded without much interest. "Well, that's news. She's going to be married, and to an American."

"That's sensible," Robert said.

"She will be in Paris for a few weeks and wants to see me as soon as possible. Well, I shall be busy when I get back to Paris."

"Indeed," her father said.

MARY HAD BEEN IN PARIS only a day. She was dining with Louisine that evening at six. There was still a little time before her engagement, and what was the use of waiting? She had to see him, hear the truth from his own lips. She would be able to tell at a glance whether there was someone else. She took a cab to his studio. She feared losing him so much her hands shook as she knocked on the door. She listened. There was not a sound. Her nervousness turned to irritation, then humiliation. Then she heard something. He was there. She was feverish. Was he alone?

The door opened and his preoccupied face looked out. Suddenly his expression changed. Yes, he seemed glad to see her. After a quick embrace, he opened the door wide and beckoned her inside. She glanced around the room as she entered. There was no one else there. She looked at him fumbling with a book that was lying open on the sofa as he cleared room for her to sit. When she sat down, he stood a moment until she looked up and caught his glance.

"You look well," he said. "Marly has been good for you."

"Yes, I suppose it has."

He sat opposite her, staring at her. There was an awkward silence. "I came back early to find an apartment and a studio."

"When did you get in?"

"Yesterday."

He moved from the chair to the sofa next to her. He took her hand and kissed it. "I've missed you," he said.

"Have you really?"

He smiled. "I never believed I'd survive."

"Then why didn't you answer my letter? Don't be kind. You must tell me the truth, Edgar. We are, above all, friends."

"We are friends," he said, bewildered. "Much more, I thought. What is all this?"

Was he trying to make her feel ridiculous? She stood up. "You didn't answer my letter."

"How can you say that? It is I who wrote last."

"Nonsense."

"Didn't I tell you about the dancer I was sculpting and how exciting it was to work in clay? How I planned to clothe the figure in a tutu of real net? I asked when you'd be coming back, and for days I have expected your answer."

"I received no such letter."

He frowned. "That's absurd. I remember clearly. It was raining. I put the letter in my raincoat as I went off to the café for dinner. I remember how good I felt, anticipating your reply."

"I certainly would have replied if I had seen such a letter."

"Maybe it was lost. So you thought I had not written—"

"When you went out to post the letter, were you wearing that long raincoat you keep here in the studio?"

He nodded. Mary went to the wardrobe. She felt the pockets of the coat and sensed the crinkle of paper. The letter was there. She took it out of the pocket and held it in her trembling hands. Then she threw her arms around his neck.

23

FINDING a more suitable apartment in Paris had not been easy. Mary trudged the streets for days and it seemed there was something wrong with every one she looked at. One had no cupboard in the kitchen. There was another without a bin to store coal. There were places where she could not imagine anyone living, noisy places and some with no garden of any kind. She followed every lead and had begun to despair when she finally did see an apartment that had everything they needed. Almost. There was no elevator and it was necessary to climb four flights of stairs. She would not mind for herself. And her father wouldn't either. But it might be inconvenient and troublesome for her mother and Lydia. However, the owner was not willing to wait for an answer. He had others waiting. Mary weighed the problem a moment. "We'll take it," she said.

With that settled she had only to find a studio, and Edgar

suggested she look at one he had heard about near his own studio. It was on the first floor of a charming building with flower boxes decorating the front. Mary did not hesitate, but rented it at once. That very night she wrote her family and in a few weeks they were established in the new apartment. Aleck, Lois, and the children sailed for London, and the family settled into a comfortable routine.

For Mary the following weeks were a time of intense work as she prepared for the Sixth Impressionist Exhibition. She arrived at the studio at eight each morning and worked until the sunlight failed. Often she would go home and after dinner work on her graphics, since natural lighting was not needed for that. It was as though there were not enough hours in a day for work. Her father insisted she needed fresh air and exercise and must therefore ride with him. She did it for his sake, but all the while she was impatient to get back to work.

She saw Edgar nearly every day for lunch or tea and sometimes the theater. But she was never long away from her work. He chided her for it, but when he saw her painting of *Lydia Crocheting in the Garden at Marly,* he admitted that the excruciating effort had been worth it. Her powers were at a peak. He was no longer the master and she the struggling follower. She was also a master. She still listened to his advice, but they both knew they were talking as equals.

When arrangements for the 1881 show were being planned, Mary and Edgar went together to the meetings. Edgar offered the names of four artists he thought should be invited to exhibit with them. One was accepted by a voice vote of the group but the others were said to be mediocre Salon painters.

"They paint in a style accepted by the public," Edgar said. "I daresay that doesn't make them criminals. They happen to be talented artists who appreciate what we're doing. I see no harm in diluting the show somewhat of the shock of what they call impressionism on the public mind."

"But we don't want them to be won over by Salon painters."

Edgar rose to answer the objection, but Pissarro spoke first. "It will look as though we are backsliding, that we no longer value those principles of light and freedom we have so long sacrificed for."

"Nonsense," Edgar said. "It will show true democracy. We will allow all styles, explore all avenues to achieve art. We do not want to become censors after the fashion of the Salon. Surely we do not think we have the only true religion and will now dictate taste." Edgar was flushed with anger.

Mary stood up. "I think we should avoid quarreling over this. The main points have been made, and we can all think it over quietly and vote when we meet again for the course that will most help the group."

"We ought to settle it now," someone said.

"Miss Cassatt is right," Pissarro said. "We argue too much."

At the next meeting, Edgar's other nominees were all voted down. His mood was black, but Mary convinced him he should not brood about it. He had done what he thought was best, and they must continue. They certainly must not let it cause a rift.

"All right," he said, "but you'll see I was right. You'll see the same mocking criticism as before, when it could have been different."

EDGAR WAS RIGHT about the criticism. They were now even called witless degenerates. However, Mary's portrait of Lydia crocheting was consistently excepted from such criticism and praised for its excellence.

Sitting with Lydia while she cut out the columns to paste in her scrapbook, Mary knew she should be happy at her treatment by the critics, but something bothered her.

"They were generous this time," Lydia said. "Look how many more good reviews I have this year. You're finally getting the recognition you deserve."

"What was it one of them said about using a man's palette?"

"Oh, that one. Here it is. 'Miss Cassatt uses the strong colors of a man's palette, but portrays a delicate understanding of women that only a woman could achieve.' "

"That's it," Mary said. "Why must my sex be important? Either a painting is good and fine or it isn't."

"That wasn't how it was meant," Lydia argued.

"What is a man's palette anyway? Colors are colors. No one has an exclusive right. It makes me angry."

"So I see. I don't know what to make of you. You're the only impressionist praised without qualification and you sit here frowning like a monkey because they call you a woman."

"It's how they do it. They are saying my work is acceptable, but I'm not equal. What they're doing is making a qualification. I don't like it."

"I do. You are a woman and you do capture something about women that others don't. It's the truth and it's probably because you are a woman."

"A 'man's palette' is a stupid idea."

"You're right. The columnist should be challenged to a hair-pulling." Mary laughed and Lydia pasted the column in the book.

THREE DAYS LATER as Mary walked home from the studio she passed a café and happened to glance at the window. There she saw the face of a girl staring intently into the space that Mary had intruded into. The face was separated by the wood framing the panes, which were about five inches square. It struck Mary as a puzzle. She hurried on, as it would have been rude to stare, but the image persisted in her mind. She had been thinking of Lydia's face when she happened to glance in that window, and it was almost as if she were seeing Lydia's face, divided in a way that would allow separate studies of the subject. There was a powerful mood to be captured by uniting different aspects of the same person, especially one such as Lydia. It would be like examining a many-faceted diamond in bright sunlight. The idea took hold of her completely. There were so many sides to Lydia that Mary wanted to show, but it was never possible to capture more than one or two aspects. Painting her through a window made up of separate panes like that opened many possibilities.

When she arrived home, Mary hurried inside, wanting to talk to Lydia about it. She went directly into the sitting room where her sister often sat embroidering or reading. No one was there. "Where is everyone?" she called, and Mathilde appeared.

"They are probably still in Miss Lydia's room," Mathilde said. "She stayed in bed this morning and this afternoon asked for the doctor. He left an hour ago and your mother is staying with her."

Mary bounded up the stairs almost before Mathilde had finished speaking. She hurried to Lydia's room, and as she entered, she found her mother sitting by the bedside. Lydia's eyes were closed; her face looked sallow, almost translucent, and her thin arms lay limply over the bedclothes at her side.

Katherine glanced up at Mary with a strange look, as if, now that Mary was here, things would change for the better. It gave Mary a start. What could she do that had not already been done? She walked up closer and whispered, "Lydia, it's Mary. Are you awake?"

Lydia's eyelids flickered, and a smile played on her lips. "Barely. The doctor has given me a draught. I've slept. Please stay."

"All right." Katherine looked weary. She must have been sitting there for hours. Mary motioned for her to go. Her mother reluctantly left.

"Have you been able to eat?" Mary asked.

"Not much."

"Well, it's important to try to eat. I'll have cook make a special broth."

"What did you work on today?"

"A portrait of a dear little girl," Mary said, trying to seem more cheerful than she felt. "She's the chubby dark-haired girl who lives above the bakery near the studio. I'd often noticed her, and asked if she could pose. Her mother gave me tea and we chatted. The mother could not come along because she had to watch the shop while her husband baked. There was an older brother, though, and he came. First I sketched them both in pastel, and that I gave to the mother. Then I did the girl in oils. She was very good. She laughed at every funny little story I told and never complained once. She even said she would like to come back."

"You do have a way of captivating children."

"I treat them as adults, remembering they've had less experience."

"Did you see Edgar?"

"Yes, but I didn't stay with him long. He was petulant."

"Oh, dear, what was it this time? Poor Edgar."

"His work was not going well. Some days his eyes are very bad. He was doing a pastel and having difficulty. I was not as sympathetic as I might have been, I suppose. I told him to get more sleep, stay away from smoky places, and work in clay until he was better. Then he said I was trying to steer his life for him, so I left him to his misery."

"You were absolutely right. Too much sympathy is not good for Edgar."

"No. I'll save my sympathy for my dear sister who should not be so unlucky as to be sick."

"It was the worst spell I've had. It scared me, Mary. I was so dizzy and nauseated and had a most horrible taste in my mouth. Then there was a sensation of spinning in white light, and I was helpless."

"I shouldn't wonder you'd be frightened."

"The doctor wasn't too upset. He said I just needed rest and medicines."

"And good food."

Lydia looked appalled at the thought.

"I'll see to the broth myself. Food is strength, remember that."

"I'll try," Lydia said, her lids drooping. "It's hard to stay awake."

"Don't. Go to sleep, for heaven's sake. I'll go see about the broth, but Jean will be here. She's waiting outside. I'll send her in."

Lydia didn't answer, but her mouth curled up in a smile as she slept. Mary called Lydia's maid, and when she was satisfied that Lydia was peacefully asleep and Jean was attentively watching, Mary left them, went downstairs, and searched for her mother and father. They were in the library, stony faced and somber.

"What did the doctor say?" Mary asked.

"That it was not unusual in these cases," Robert replied.

Katherine clutched Robert's forearm and spoke hoarsely. "He said people with Bright's disease sometimes get better and go along for a while, but that some day—" Katherine broke off, held her handkerchief over her nose, and closed her eyes to the pain the words brought.

"You don't have to say it, Mother. I know."

LYDIA tried to get well as she always had. Whatever she was told to do, she did. After a few weeks she seemed better and was able to sit in her chair and look out the window as Mary read to her. But she was too weak to leave her room for long. Her eyes bothered her if she tried to read herself. Katherine stayed with her until late at night. And even though there was someone there around the clock, Katherine could not rest.

Time seemed to be a huge unyielding mass of waiting. Mary seldom went to the studio. Lydia needed her. Katherine needed her, and even Robert, who showed no outward weakness, needed her. She would not let them down—now. To relieve the unbearable worry and tension there were times when she simply had to draw. She asked Mathilde to pose for her. Late one night Mary was sketching Mathilde as she sewed by the lamp. The glow of the flame gave striking contrasts Mary could use in her graphics. They had been quiet for several minutes when Mathilde said, "You ought to paint my cousin. She's coming to Paris and doesn't have a position. She'd be fine for posing. She has beautiful skin and a nice body."

"I would love to, but with Lydia sick, well, I don't know when I could."

"But when you paint, it seems like normal and everyone feels better."

"Now, Mathilde."

"It's true."

"I suppose having me walking about looking worried doesn't help the others. I try to look confident, especially with Mother, but she knows me so well."

"That's why she feels better when you paint. Miss Lydia, too. It's good for them."

"I don't know. I want to be available if I'm needed. I can't be too busy."

"Susan is coming tomorrow to see me," Mathilde said. "Would you like to meet her?"

"Certainly, if she's coming."

"I've told the family all about you."

Mary smiled. Mathilde always seemed so sensible. "On a nice day maybe I could paint on the balcony and Lydia could watch from her window or from the library."

Mathilde nodded.

"Is she pretty?"

"Not quite."

"Good. I prefer them not quite pretty."

"I know."

THE NEXT DAY Susan arrived and Mathilde brought tea in the library. Susan was a timid girl, quite young and fresh, but Imperia took to her at once. As soon as Mary saw her, she remembered the white dress she had bought at Redfern because she had wanted to paint it. And a pale pink bonnet. Oh, yes, Susan did have a nice complexion. And she was willing and eager to pose, although she protested that she knew nothing about posing. "I can sit still, though," she said.

"Would you like to meet my sister? She's ill now, but she'll be interested."

Lydia was propped up in her bed, toying with a piece of thread on her bed jacket as Jean read to her. Though her eyes seemed dull, she brightened when she saw Mary.

"This is Susan," Mary said. "She is Mathilde's cousin."

Lydia smiled at Susan.

"Susan has agreed to pose for me. I thought the balcony would be perfect in late morning light with the city buildings off in the background."

"Oh, yes," Lydia said. "In the white dress?"

"And the pink bonnet."

"It will be lovely. I've kept you from your work so long."

"No. I've had a small holiday from it, and now there is Susan and we thought you might feel like coming to the library. We will open the balcony doors and you might find it pleasant to be there."

"It sounds delightful. Do you think we could arrange it? I tire easily, but Jean is very strong and can help me."

"There is the chaise in the library to rest on."

"It would be good to leave here a bit. Do you realize I've hardly been out of my room for months?"

"You seem to be getting quite a bit better now," Mathilde said.

Lydia nodded.

They did not stay long. When they were outside the room, walking down the narrow corridor, Susan mumbled, "She's beautiful." Susan spoke what Mary had been thinking all her life, and it touched her with sadness.

Mary began painting the next day. Lydia was brought to the library. Katherine and Jean sat with her, and Mary had to admit they did seem relieved to have her working. Fortunately, she was able to concentrate on her work. There were no distractions, only Susan in a white dress looking to the left with Imperia on her lap, and the delicate morning light filtering through the gauzy bonnet onto the composed features. The mood of the painting was one of contemplation and rest.

Lydia was able to come to the library for three days, but not the fourth. "Just a little weakness. I don't see very clearly today," she said. "I'll watch from my room here. Please go on with it. You can tell Edgar I sympathize with him completely. When your eyes fail, there is a loneliness that's not like anything else."

If Mary stopped painting now, it would be like she was admitting she was terribly worried, and that wouldn't do. Katherine would read to Lydia. Mary would paint, and it would all go on as though tomorrow would be better. Mary knew that it wouldn't.

The next evening found Lydia worse. The doctor was summoned, but when he completed his examination he was hopeful. It would be all right, he said. She needed rest. The doctor gave her something strong to make her sleep, and he prescribed sleep for Katherine, too. When he had gone, everything became quiet. Lydia slept deeply; Jean poised nearby. Robert retired to write letters and do his accounts. Mary went out, into a soft misty rain. Edgar probably wouldn't be home, she thought. If he went to the café for dinner, he would probably still be there talking. Still, she continued in the direction of his place. If there was no light in the window, she would not stop. Lydia's face was vivid in her mind. The color of her skin, the greenish shadows. The look in her eyes. There was nothing anyone could do. She looked up at the window and saw a faint glow. She went up, knocked softly, and waited.

He opened the door and she went inside. "Lydia is worse," she said, and pressed her face to his chest. She felt his arms soft around her. He smoothed her hair and kissed her brow.

"I shouldn't have come. It's late," she whispered, "but I had to see you."

"I hoped you would come," he said.

"Oh, Edgar, I long for you, too." She felt her sorrow and desolation dissolving as she clung to him.

They did not make love often. She lifted her face to him and their lips met, igniting their passion. Her body trembled as he gently massaged her back. "Come with me," he said, and she put down her jacket and followed him to the bedroom.

Later, she couldn't move, had no will, only a glorious calm. "I wish Lydia had had a lover. I don't think she ever did."

"Men have loved her. She is like a goddess."

Mary smiled sadly. "I must stay close to her now." She clung to him even as she spoke. "She's so sick."

"Is she dying?"

Mary could not answer. Tears came, and he held her while she wept.

24

FOR WEEKS Lydia's health would get a little better, then a little worse. Through it all she managed to stay cheerful, and it was at her insistence that Mary worked. One day Mary had been at the studio working on a portrait and had stayed longer than usual. When she arrived home, she went directly to Lydia's room and, on seeing that Katherine's lined face had taken on a gray pallor, she felt a new fear. Katherine had been stubbornly spending her nights at Lydia's bedside. Katherine said she couldn't sleep, so she sat with Lydia even though Jean or the nurse Robert had engaged was there and promised to call if there was any change. Over the weeks, Katherine's face had become set. She moved as though in a stupor. "Mother, you look as though you need some air. Have a stroll in the garden and then a rest before dinner."

When Katherine left and Mary was alone with Lydia in the quiet of that bedroom, she felt the anguish of the future spread through

244

her. Lydia's vision was almost gone. Sometimes her muscles would twitch frighteningly. She was so weak she had to be fed. She seemed to eat better if Mary fed her, perhaps because Mary talked happily about outside things all the while. That gay chatter was getting harder to perform. She steeled herself as Lydia looked up at her.

"Did you finish the painting?" Lydia asked.

"Yes," Mary smiled. "It turned out well. Jane was dressed in black with a pink bow at the neck. She had grace and style in the way she sat. You should have seen her hat, high on her head and decorated with iridescent blackbird wings and a sheer nose veil."

"Yes, I think I can see it," Lydia said. She sighed. "How many times have you painted me? I've lost count. I counted to thirty-one once."

"If we counted the watercolors and sketches and the drawings, it must be in the hundreds. But finished paintings and pastels—at least thirty. I shall count them if you like."

Lydia shook her head and gazed off. "Thirty-one Lydias hanging on a wall—" she crooned and shut her eyes. Lydia did not wince or grimace, but the pain was there. Mary could feel it in the pit of her own stomach.

"Please," Lydia said, "in my bureau drawer there's an ebony box, and at the bottom of it, there's a letter. It's something I've saved. Will you bring it to me?"

Mary smiled, squeezed Lydia's hand, then went to the bureau.

"I don't think I can made out the words anymore," Lydia said. "Things blur so. The harder I try to see, the worse it seems."

"Would you like me to read it?"

"Please. You're the only person I could let read it. Sit close to me and read it softly. I shall close my eyes and listen."

Mary looked down at the envelope, soft from having been handled. She took out the pages, opened them and glanced at Lydia's expectant face before she read.

Dear Lydia,

I am taking the liberty of writing you because I think you are the only person in the world who would understand. Something happened the first instant when I saw you dressed in

245

your yellow gown—and when you looked at me, you could see the misery that I have lying hidden in my heart. You recognized it and you touched my brow, and changed misery into a force I must use. Your glance and the image of your face has impressed itself on my heart as the image of perfection. I will judge every person, every subject I see by the standards you have inspired. I'll travel over the world, stopping only when I find something of Lydia—your innocence, your perfect trust, your intelligence, uncluttered with bitterness. When I find these qualities I will be able to do my work and express my ideals. I will never forget you. I will always love you.

P.

Lydia's eyes glistened as she held her hand out for the letter. Mary folded it, put it in the envelope, and placed it in Lydia's hand.

"Thank you," Lydia murmured. "Now I won't forget the words." A frightened look crossed her face. "Tear it up so no one will see it. I just want to remember the words when there is pain."

Mary took the envelope from Lydia's hand, looked at it, and hesitated. "Is it someone I know, or would you rather not say?"

Lydia gazed off as though she hadn't heard the question, then she looked at Mary. "It's better I keep it in my mind now. You understand, don't you?"

"I think so," Mary said, remembering the party where Gauguin spent the whole evening talking to Lydia. Could it be?

"At least we met and recognized one another. There were his words. It's enough." Lydia closed her eyes. "I want to sleep now."

Later that same night Lydia's eyes opened and she smiled as though miraculously freed from pain. "I saw Robbie. He's coming for me. I'll never be alone. He's waiting in a garden filled with light." Her eyelids fluttered and shut again. Her skin felt clammy. Mary called the nurse, who felt Lydia's pulse and shook her head.

Hours later Lydia spoke to them again. "You are all so kind and good," she said. Toward morning she spoke again with difficulty. Katherine bent over one side of the bed, Robert the other, and Mary stood near her mother, leaning forward so she could hear. "I cannot bear—to—leave you—but—I—cannot bear—to stay."

"Liddy, Liddy," Robert called out, taking her hand.

She spoke no more. The doctor was summoned. "She is in a coma. It can't be much longer," he told them.

There was nothing more they could do. The hours dragged by unmercifully. A week passed. Then, early on a Sunday morning as they sat quietly with Lydia, the nurse felt her pulse, listening for her breathing. "I think her heart has stopped."

As they looked at each other, the agony that had been held back those last days was released, slowly at first, with a nod, a touch of the hand, a sigh. Robert sent wires to Aleck and Gardner and Mary sent word to Edgar. Robert asked the doctor to give a light sedative to Katherine, as she had not slept more than an hour at a time during the whole ordeal. Katherine did not resist, but dazedly took the sleeping medicine and as soon as the doctor left, she hugged Mary and went off to bed. Mathilde brought tea in the drawing room and Mary sat numbly sipping when Edgar arrived. He paused in the doorway. She put down her teacup and went to him. He put his arms gently around her; tears were wetting his cheeks. He shook his head apologetically for not being able to talk. Mary poured him tea and they sat together on the sofa.

"I'm sorry," he said. "It's just that when I came into this room where I have seen Lydia so many times, and knew—"

She pressed his hand; she could not speak either. After a while, Edgar asked about Katherine.

"Resting. The doctor gave her something."

"That's good. The last time I saw her I was worried."

It was a comfort to have him there, though they lapsed into frequent silences. After one of them, Mary wept. "I'm going to miss her terribly. I already do."

"I know. She was your best friend."

"She was more than that. Lydia gave me so much. She was the first to encourage me to paint, and she never stopped."

"And in return you have immortalized her. Could anyone do more?"

Mary gazed at him, remembering Lydia's words, *thirty-one Lydias hanging on the wall*. "Immortalized?" she said. And he nodded.

25

THE TIME for the 1882 Impressionist Exhibition was drawing near, but Mary had not been able to give much attention to it. She talked to Edgar about it once, and several times considered which paintings she should show, but she did not go with Edgar to the first planning meeting. He promised to stop by the next day and let her know what was decided.

Getting back into her old life after Lydia's death had seemed impossible. At first she could not work at all. Aleck and his family had come to Paris and Gard was planning a trip. Still it all seemed empty. Even the struggle to express in art the world as it really was could not bring her out of her lethargy, although she made an attempt occasionally to sketch. Then one morning she remembered the exhibition. What had happened? Edgar had never come around to tell her about the meeting. She wondered why. The meeting had been days ago. It wasn't like Edgar. He had promised.

The following morning she decided to go to his studio on the way to her own. As she walked she thought it was ominous he hadn't called or sent a note. Perhaps he was not well. He could be sick and alone. Oh, she should have come sooner. She walked faster, and was breathless when she reached his studio. She knocked, thinking she may just as well go straight up to his rooms, when he opened the door. He must have been working, and he did not look in the least ill. "Edgar, I haven't heard from you. Is something wrong? You said you would let me know about the exhibition. It's been almost a week and I've heard nothing."

He adjusted his shirtcuffs as he answered. "I would have been by, but with all the family there, I did not want to ruin anything. Well, it may all blow over anyway. We'll see."

Mary had taken off her gloves and dropped them and her bag on the table with impatience. "Exactly what is it that may blow over?"

His eyes glistened and his jaws flexed. "It's just that they can't abide anything now without drenching sunshine and short broken brushstrokes. Now, I am the first to agree our friends have given much. I own Monets and Pissarros. So do you, and we love them. We have all learned to look at light more carefully. What I am against is elitism. I opposed it in the Salon. I shall always oppose it. They forget the beginnings. The Salon de Refusés. They were so desperate, if they'll only recall, they put their refused work up for the public to judge. Now, twelve years later, it is they who do the shutting out."

Mary heard the bitterness in his voice, the turmoil all over again. "Did you nominate someone again?" she asked.

"I nominated five young artists with talent. Others were nominated too, of course, but the discussion was heavily in favor of excluding anyone who has not imitated Monet. The vote will come tomorrow night."

Mary watched with growing alarm as his face filled with a solemn anger, heightened by being directed not toward his enemies but toward those he called his friends. She felt the pain of it sting her own cheeks. "I shall go tomorrow and vote with you," she said.

He shook his head. "I don't think it will be enough."

The next evening Mary and Edgar arrived at the meeting hall a few minutes early, but the room was already crowded. "There's Rouart," Edgar said. "I'd like to talk to him. I'm sure we can count on him."

Mary spotted Pissarro and excused herself to greet him.

"Camille, how are you?" she asked. "And your family?"

"Fine. We're all well. And you?"

She nodded. "Does it look bad for tonight? Not another fight, I hope."

"Another fight is already underway."

"Oh, dear."

"There is right on both sides as usual, but Edgar antagonizes many. Those he nominates are not vital enough. His vision is failing. Or perhaps his judgment is influenced by young flattery."

Shocked by Pissarro's words, Mary burned. "How could you even suggest that? Not Edgar. He has more integrity than anyone I know."

"Yes, yes. Forgive me. I do not like this warring any better than you, but we cannot accept all the young people nominated. There is never enough room. We are forced to exclude some. Since we are impressionists, we naturally must prefer those who are not also trying for the Salon and using our group as a second-best arena."

"Surely they don't think that about Edgar's nominees. He wants only what is good for the group."

"We all do," Pissarro said. "But what *is* good? That is what must be decided."

"I shall vote with Edgar."

"I have a student of my own I have nominated. We can only vote for six. Theo Van Gogh's brother has also been nominated. I think he has vitality."

"Only six," Mary said. "In that case if only two of Edgar's nominees are selected, it would prove at least that elitism wasn't being practiced."

"Yes, and here is where I agree absolutely with Edgar. We cannot shut out classes and styles. That is wrong. He understands that, but I do not agree with all of his choices."

Mary was full of foreboding as the meeting began. As she looked about, she did not think the vote would go well for Edgar, though Caillebotte and Desboutin were sympathetic. All the young men Edgar had backed were classical in their approach. It was probably true, as Pissarro intimated, that it was Edgar they admired and wanted to be associated with, but Mary would not believe his judgment could be influenced. He was incurably suspicious of flattery, and had never flattered anyone himself, at least not since Mary had known him.

Caillebotte opened the meeting by summarizing the voting rules rather than opening a discussion. When Edgar asked for recognition, Caillebotte said that further discussion would be held after the vote. Edgar was livid. He shouted that it was high-handed, that things should be open and ever man should have his say.

While votes were being counted, Caillebotte continued the meeting. He announced committees and reported on the arrangements already made. The crowd, however, was impatient to hear the result of the vote, and in a short time all the items on the agenda were noted. Then Caillebotte asked that the vote count be read. Those six candidates who received the largest number of votes would be invited to join the group.

The first name announced was Pissarro's student and Mary applauded politely. The next was Van Gogh, who received a bit less applause. Edgar's lips were drawn tight as the next names were announced. The third and fourth were scientific colorists, followers of Seurat and Pissarro. Desboutin, from the chair behind, put his hand on Edgar's shoulder and Edgar clasped it. The fifth name was not one of Edgar's candidates either, and as Mary feared, neither was the sixth. There was no holding Edgar. He stood up. "I want to thank my friends. I have heard principles of equality for all shouted by each of you. I have heard wailing that love of art was the only common denominator in our group. Now I see these principles crushed. Now I shall contribute to the effort in the only way left to me. I shall give you back all the space I would have used if I had chosen to exhibit in the Seventh Impressionist Exhibit. I thank you."

He turned to Mary so that she could walk out before him if she wished. She stood at his side. "I donate my space also," she said. Together they left the crowded hall, walking through the tumult with heads held high, though all eyes were on them.

They rode home in silence, interrupted only by the sound of a horse's hooves hitting the pavement. After a while, Edgar spoke sadly. "Art is the only true friend."

"How can you say that," she snapped.

He shook his head. "You are more than a friend. We've been lucky together. Even though I'd like to be your best friend, I am not. The truest and most constant friend you have is also art."

They were quiet again. Mary admitted to herself he was partially right. They were friends because she was patient and forgave his slights and black moods. She would not abandon him. Her best friend, though, was her art, and he was part of that. Some day they would part, one way or another, but art was constant.

She invited him in for coffee. They needed to talk before they parted for the evening.

"Caillebotte will ask us to reconsider," Edgar said. "He will be charming."

"Of course we can't."

"No."

"I shall send my things directly to Durand-Ruel's," she said. "At least the painting of Susan. He'd be delighted to receive your dancers, too."

"I suppose he would."

"Don't be too depressed, Edgar. You did what you must. They're still your friends. They will always be. Opinions among us have always varied, but the ties last. Art may be your best friend, but the impressionists are still to be counted."

"How can you believe that?" he asked.

"I know them. The next time you meet them at the café, you will see."

26

MARY was too occupied with her work to greatly miss the excitement of the Seventh Impressionist Exhibit. She may have felt a small pang of regret on the day of the opening, but it was soon forgotten when she began the painting she had long waited to do, a portrait of her mother reading the paper. It was a pose Mary had seen every day and now she wanted to capture that look of intelligent concentration.

After several days of intense study of the face and hands, Mary was convinced that her mother's health had not improved the way the family had expected. Her color was seldom good. Her hands trembled if she held the pose for more than a few minutes and she tired easily. Mary wanted Katherine to be thoroughly examined. Robert too was increasingly concerned, and between them, they persuaded Katherine to have the examination.

The doctor said the trouble was with her heart. He prescribed rest and cautioned her against strenuous exertion. As the days passed, however, Mary grew more concerned than ever. A dullness now veiled Katherine's eyes. Even her voice had become monotonous.

It was Katherine herself who supplied an answer. "Paris is all the same," she said. "Such dreariness. These old bones need sun and air."

The remark gave Mary an idea. "Mother, would you like to go to Spain with me for a holiday?"

"To Spain. My goodness. Do you think you need a holiday?"

"We both do."

"Just the two of us?" Katherine's eyes sparkled. That settled it for Mary. She was taking her mother to Spain for a change and a rest.

"YES, FATHER, an absolute rest. I shall take care of her. It's what she really needs, I'm sure of it."

Robert was reluctant to have them go off for an indefinite period, but if it was what Katherine needed, how could he refuse?"

As soon as the arrangements were made, Mary went to Edgar's studio to tell him about her plans. It was not a task she looked forward to, but she hoped he would not act as though it was a personal affront to him. She would tell him in a clear voice and as she spoke, she would look at his necktie rather than his eyes, because when his eyes narrowed a certain way as he listened, her tone would always change and become apologetic. This time that wouldn't do. She must remember not to sound apologetic.

Her brightest smile was already on her face when she knocked on his door.

"Come in," he called. As she opened the door, he looked up from working on a clay model of a dancer. "My dear, I didn't expect you so soon."

She approached the bench where he was working. "You've made splendid progress since I saw it last."

"It's a demanding medium. All the time I am working, the clay is drying so I must press on. There's no going back to change anything drastically."

"That's good. You will benefit by that kind of discipline."

"You sound just like Bartheleme and all the rest."

"I have something to tell you." She paused a moment. "I'm taking Mother away for a holiday. She needs rest. Ever since I began the portrait I've been reminded at every glance how frail she has become. She needs a complete rest, Edgar. I think Spain would do her the most good. There will be sun and change and a slower tempo of life. Don't you think it will help her greatly?"

He put down his tool and wiped his hands. "Indeed."

"We shall be leaving soon."

"How soon?"

"In a few days."

"That soon?" He raised his eyebrows. "Did I tell you I've been planning a a trip, too?"

"No, you didn't."

"Not for a few weeks yet. As you know Bartheleme has been depressed since his wife died, and we talked about setting out in a carriage for the northern coast. He has relatives and I have a few friends along the way. We'll take a fine team of horses and stop along the way often. We want to be close to the country to revitalize ourselves."

"It sounds exciting," Mary said.

"Yes, doesn't it?"

His eyes were lit with pleasure at the plans. It was odd he hadn't said anything about it to her before. But then, she should be grateful that he made no comment at all about her plans. She had worried for nothing.

KATHERINE TOLERATED the long train ride well. When they arrived at the hotel by the sea, the sun was shining. "Oh," Katherine said. "This is perfect. I can't wait to take a little walk."

They took many walks. They sat on the beach. Often Mary

sketched with pastels, and sometimes did a watercolor. There was nothing serious about her work. They had both given themselves up to rest. The closest Mary came to working was when she did a pastel study of two children playing in the sand.

After a few weeks, there was no doubt the change was beneficial to Katherine. As they sat on the beach one morning after breakfast, Katherine held her book in her lap without opening it while she looked over the sea. "I think a person has to get away like this sometimes."

Mary nodded.

"What about you? Are you growing tired of all this? Are you anxious to return to work and to Edgar?"

"I can work wherever I am. That's one advantage of being an artist. I don't miss Edgar too greatly. I think I needed to be away from him too for a while. We were bickering. Withdrawing from the exhibition left us rather defensive with each other. He was very depressed and it affected me because I felt he needed my support, so I stayed and listened to him at times when I would rather have gone away. Edgar isn't easy to be with when he's the least depressed."

Katherine smiled. "No man is. A woman can become obscured in his shadows, a creature of his imagination, performing as he desires. It can be tiresome."

Her mother's words gave Mary a start. "I always thought you were happy."

"Of course I am, but since we've been here, I've let my own imagination take me everywhere. I've watched birds fly and waves break on the shore and I've thought about everything that's happened, and put it in order so I can put it away. Now I feel much better."

"I think I've been doing that, too, especially with my thoughts of Edgar."

"You are too independent for marriage. I was afraid of that."

"It's the way I am."

"You could, perhaps, be the wife of someone not so strong-willed."

"I think I am old for marriage. I have to be free to work."

"What about love?"

"I love you and Father. I loved Lydia, Alex, and Gard. I love Edgar."

"You will miss having children."

"Does that disappoint you?"

"For your sake."

"I would have liked a child of my own. When I paint children I feel almost as though I'm their mother. I'm stroking their arms and tickling their chins as a mother does. I like to paint a child with a mother who always takes care of it herself, not one who has a nurse. There's such a difference in trust. The mother who cares for the child makes a deeper bond. It's clear in the gestures. I hope to do a series of mothers and children."

Katherine smiled. "Thank goodness you have your work."

"Yes, I shall always work. In fact, I saw two old women down on the beach mending sails. They're dressed in dark blue, their hooded heads bent over in a way that makes a composition all in soft curves. I'd like to paint them. A pastel would never do. It wants heavy paint. It's a heavy pattern. If you don't mind I will go down there and draw them to paint later."

"I don't mind. I'll read, and meet you back at the hotel for lunch."

Mary smiled and was off, feeling free. She did need this holiday as much as Katherine did.

Edgar wrote often for the first few weeks, and then as he traveled with Bartheleme, his letters were irregular, but bouyant and sometimes poetic.

Robert also wrote once a week, sometimes twice. He implored them to come back. But Mary was unwilling to return too soon. Katherine was improving every day. Why should they interrupt her progress? No, Mary would not hear of it. She begged her father to look for another apartment with an elevator so Katherine would not have to climb the stairs.

Robert scoffed at the idea. And Mary and Katherine stayed on in Spain. They went to Barcelona and then came back to the seaside. Robert insisted they come home. Mary wrote and asked what progress he had made in finding an apartment.

Edgar sent a sonnet asking if there was someone new. No, she answered at once. There was no one.

And Mary and Katherine watched the birds and walked on the beach. After three months they packed up and boarded the train to Paris, both of them anxious to see the new apartment Robert had rented.

On the train headed for home, they had talked steadily the first hour, but gradually they became quieter, gazing out the window, alone with their own reflections. Mary thought of Edgar and of his sonnets, wondering what it would be like to see him again.

27

MARY INVITED EDGAR to dine on the evening she and her mother returned to Paris. It had been a tiring day, but a bath and a short rest refreshed Mary. Waiting in the drawing room for him, she was filled with nervous energy. She wanted a few minutes alone with him before her mother and father joined them. Impatient with sitting and waiting, she walked to the book cases, then turned her attention to a painting on the wall, a charming study Berthe had given her. She straightened the frame and, satisfied, paused at the mantel, looking at her hair in the mirror. There hadn't been time to have it done properly. Mathilde did the best she could. Where *was* he?

"Monsieur Degas is here," the housekeeper announced. Mary looked up and there was Edgar, the corners of his mouth turned up, a package in his hand. She put the paper aside, rushed to him, and embraced him. How wonderful to touch him again and to smell the scent he used, mingled with the freshness of his shirt. Then she saw how red his eyes were. He stared out of those sore eyes, holding them wide open, careful not to squint. He put the package in her hand.

She untied the ribbon and tore off the paper. It was a painting of roses in a garden, done as only he would do them. She remembered his ranting once about cutting flowers, saying he could not tolerate having them die in his rooms. She had argued that she liked flowers in a room, especially fresh roses. "Thank you. These roses will never die."

They sat together chatting over what happened while she was gone. He had worked on a major painting of dancers rehearsing on the stage and wanted her to see it. He asked to see the sketches she had done in Spain, and she had Mathilde bring some of them in.

After dinner they strolled together to the bridge, stopped at the rail, bent over and watched the reflection of the streetlamp bobbing in the darkness of the river below. He put his arm around her waist and she felt content.

After that they saw each other nearly every day, often working together. He painted her once, sitting forward, with feet spread apart, holding cards in her hand. "I feel like a fat man," she said.

"No, it's charming." She did not agree, but held the pose. After a while he spoke again. "There's an exhibit of work by a young German artist, who I hear paints with great force. Would you like to see it with me tomorrow?"

"I'd like to see it," she said, "but not tomorrow. Susan is sitting for me in the garden."

"Oh," he said, sounding disappointed. "When could you go?"

"Thursday."

"Very well," he said. "If you must."

On Thursday Mary wore a smoky rose-colored dress to the exhibition. It was the latest fashion, with the waist nipped in and the skirt gathered in the back. She and Edgar must certainly have made a handsome couple as they entered the gallery. She could feel eyes following them. Edgar was recognized at once by a pair of students who had also come to look at the show. Mary was presented to them and they all four walked toward the first painting on the left.

"He paints mystery," she said after a moment's contemplation.

"Fear," Edgar said, "but in subtle ways. It has an indefinable character of strangeness."

They studied the painting for a while, then moved to the next canvas. "Would you say it is an evocative blend of Delacroix and Rembrandt?" one of the students asked Edgar.

"Perhaps, and yet there is a strange ambiguity of spaces," Edgar said, pursing his lips and looking critically. "This canvas is more subtle than the first."

Mary too examined it in detail. "The partial impasto is charming here on the tree, but I feel a great hesitation. All it lacks is a sureness of style," she said.

Edgar looked as though he were going to speak, but he paused suddenly and commented smugly. "Are you sure you don't mean prettiness? I admit it does lack that, but what can a woman know about style?"

She looked at him unbelievingly as her head resounded with the sound of his words. "A woman can know *everything* about style," she blurted.

The students slouched a step backward and glanced nervously at one another. Mary glared at Edgar, feeling rage color her face. Her lips twitched for wanting to lash back at him for hurling such an insult at her, but she was too angry to find the words. She turned and stalked away, determined never to speak to him again. She would show the world exactly what a woman could know about style. He would never do that to her again. No one would. No wonder people grew to hate him. No wonder Manet cut his painting. *Style.* She knew precisely the difference between style and prettiness. What was wrong with him?

She did not go directly home or to the studio. Instead she walked, and after a while when the fuming was finished, she began to think. She would paint an austere, almost ugly picture that was *nothing but* style, a stark kind of background, devoid of draperies or china. She would have to find another model. Susan was too pretty. She went over color schemes in her mind. There would be no vibrant color in this new painting. Perhaps whites. They're the most difficult. A plain girl in a white shift in a stark near-white room with the simplest of furnishings. Yes, she thought, and I will show him what style is all about.

Mary went home less in anger than with determination and purpose. As she took off her hat, she called Mathilde and the housekeeper. "In the future I will not be home to Monsieur Degas."

Mathilde looked stunned. "Not at home?"

"Or you may tell him I refuse to see him."

Mathilde followed Mary into the drawing room. "What are you going to do if he comes to your studio to see you?"

Mary paused. "I will lock my door." With a toss of her head, Mary dismissed the subject and she walked to where her mother and father were seated.

"How was the exhibition?" Katherine asked.

"I'm not sure," Mary said. "Edgar became so unbearable I left; I shan't be seeing him again."

"Oh," Katherine said. Robert looked up. "I'm glad to see you finally came to your senses," he said.

Mary smarted at her father's tone. Hurt and angry as she was, she still did not want to hear her father censure him. She changed the subject quickly.

While they were having coffee in the drawing room that evening, Mathilde came to Mary and whispered, "He was here, and I told him you were not in and he said he came to apologize."

"Did you tell him anything else?"

"Only that I was sorry you were not at home."

"Thank you, Mathilde. That was fine."

"He looked truly sorry, Miss."

"I'm sure he was. Why shouldn't he be? Apologies come easily for Edgar."

"The man's a dreadful egotist," Robert threw in.

"All right, all right. Let's forget Edgar for a moment," Mary said and turned to Mathilde. "I need another model, not nearly as pretty as Susan. Do you know where I might find one?"

Mathilde frowned and seemed to be thinking. "Homely?"

"Yes, but not fat."

"Let me think. There are plenty of plain girls. Not fat—"

"No, that's for Renoir."

"I wonder if Henrietta would do. She brings our eggs on Tuesdays. You may have seen her yourself. Her teeth aren't straight. Pretty eyes though, and always neat."

"I'd like to see her. Do you know where she lives?"

"Cook does."

"Good. Find out. We'll go and see her tomorrow."

HENRIETTA had long chestnut hair and good arms. She was ideal, and Mary liked her at once. However, Henrietta was shy and could merely shake her head when Mary asked her if she would pose.

"Come now," Mary pleaded. "It won't be difficult. You can rest whenever you're tired of holding the pose. I'll pay you double the usual modeling fee, and see that you have a good lunch and, of course, tea."

Henrietta's mother cleared her throat. "Certainly she'll do it. She's timid. She's never done anything like that before. That's why she hesitated."

Mary smiled at Henrietta. "Then you'll come?"

"If it pleases you," the girl said and nodded.

"It will please me to begin at once."

Henrietta arrived wearing a plain straw hat and a faded yellow coat. She came to the service door and was greeted by Mathilde, who brought her directly to Mary. Henrietta's voice squeaked. It was clear that she was painfully nervous, and the only cure for that was to begin. "Come along. It's a nice brisk walk to the studio," Mary said.

"First I'll draw lots of quick sketches and study those before I settle on a final pose. I'd like to have you change into this white shift."

Henrietta did as she was instructed, but she was stiff and wooden at first.

"Try looking to the left with your head up. Yes, just like that." Mary sketched hastily. In a few minutes, she moved on to another pose. This time Henrietta reached up as though lighting a lamp. It was a difficult pose, but she held it without showing strain. Then Mary did a series of sketches while Henrietta brushed her hair. It wasn't long until she had completely lost her nervousness. When they stopped for lunch, Mary showed Henrietta the sketches and explained to her what were the good points and bad points of each. Mary chose the one closest to what she wanted and analyzed its spaces, the rhythms, the lines. She thought in color, in the medium of oil paints. After lunch at a quiet café not frequented by the artists in the neighborhood, they strolled back to the studio and went to work again. Mary did two more sketches and when she was satisfied with the composition, she put a fresh linen canvas on the easel and laid on the underpainting. Henrietta had become more and more interested in the painting and at the end of the day when she was allowed to examine it closely, she shook her head and promised to come early the next morning.

That evening when Mary returned home from the studio, Mathilde handed her a letter. Mary recognized the writing as Edgar's. She took the letter to her bedroom, laid it on the bureau and stared at it. She did not want any influences from him now, either good or bad. The painting was all she wanted to think about, and how to make it perfectly right. Edgar's letter would have to wait.

The next day Mary was already in the studio finishing details of the portrait of Susan when Henrietta came.

"That's beautiful," Henrietta said.

"Thank you," Mary said. "A fine painting doesn't have to be beautiful. It only has to be perfect."

Henrietta smiled unsurely, and Mary cleaned the brush she had been using and put the new painting on the easel. As Mary prepared her work place, Henrietta changed into the shift and sat down and brushed her hair. Mary adjusted the pose and they began.

They worked every day for a week and each day the painting progressed steadily toward that perfection Mary sought. Henrietta was fascinated. She looked in the mirror and held her arm the way it was in the painting. "I didn't know I had such pretty arms," she said. "I never noticed."

"Everyone has her own beauty."

"Even someone like me?"

"Of course. The arms are only part of it. Look at your hair and your eyes and the way you hold your head."

"I was afraid the painting was going to be something people might laugh at."

"No, my dear, no. None of us wants to be laughed at."

"No, we don't," Henrietta said, her face serious a moment. Suddenly it brightened. "What are you going to do with all those sketches you made?"

"Most will be discarded. Would you like them?"

Henrietta nodded.

"Good. I'd like for you to have them. Here, I'll put them in an envelope for you. You would probably like something with a bit of color. Sit there a minute," Mary said. She did a small pastel portrait, chosing a becoming pose and using delicate coloring that suited Henrietta. When she presented the drawing to the girl, her eyes welled with tears. "It's beautiful. I can't believe it's me, but it looks like me—I think."

"Here, let me put fixative on it so it won't smudge easily."

That evening Mary remembered Edgar's letter on her bureau. The sight of it reminded her of the insulting words at the museum. Angrily she snatched the letter, ripped it open and read.

> *Dear Mary,*
>
> I should have my tongue cut out. I should be manacled and thrown in a dungeon with rats, bats, and maggots. It would be too good for me. I should be scourged and dumped in dung. And it still wouldn't atone for my inexcusable behavior. Why did I say it? I have a black heart, no doubt. I am mean and jealous. I don't want others to know you like I do. I am selfish and also miserable. I can never forgive myself until you forgive me. I shall continue to remain in the dungeon of my own making until I hear that in your kindness, you could stop despising me and let the sun shine again.
>
> *Your prisoner*

She was not moved by the letter, and definitely not pleased. Words came too easily. He wrote what would ease his conscience to make him comfortable again. He did not say he was wrong or admit that a woman could know anything about style. She tore the letter into small pieces and let them sift through her fingers to the wastebasket.

28

MARY UNWRAPPED six small portraits and put them on the table for Durand-Ruel's inspection. He grinned when he saw them, and picked up one in each hand. "People are buying these," he said. "I think the little girls are the most popular with women, and the young ladies with the men patrons. Now, let's make sure you have signed them all." He examined each of them, clucking his approval. "Yes, all six," he said, beaming at her.

"Now I have something else I want to show you."

"A large painting, is it?"

"Yes. It still needs the perfect frame."

"Let me see," he said.

Mary put the painting of Henrietta on his large easel and removed the paper wrapping. A moment passed before M. Durand-Ruel spoke. "It's exquisite. This is your best work."

"I shall want to show it in the next Impressionist Exhibit."

"Magnificent whites," he said. "You do them as well as Sisley. How did you ever find a model like that to display your genius through? It was clever. It works. My God, how it works."

Mary felt warmth and satisfaction at his words, and was a little ashamed at taking so much pleasure from them. It seemed wrong to her to seek out praise. And yet—hadn't she done just that? She had to know, had to have someone's opinion she could trust. Now she was sure.

He looked thoughtful. "I have a neutral molding with antique gold inset. I wonder how that would do." He showed her a sample of the molding, holding it to the corner of the canvas. She nodded. "That should be fine. You'll take care of framing it?"

"Yes, I will have it done today."

When she left the gallery, she imagined Edgar seeing the painting. A burden had been lifted.

The next day Mary worked on a pastel study of young Emily and her kitten. Emily had shiny dark hair that flowed around her face in a way that Mary found captivating. She was a good little model, but when her mother called for her at three, Mary realized she had worked very hard and was tired. She sat down on the sofa, gazing at the portrait, thinking of simplifying it and using it as the subject of an etching. She thought in patterns of lights and shadows. She closed her eyes to imagine the way it would look. She was brought quickly to her senses when she heard someone at the door.

"I could not stay away," Edgar said.

The unexpected sight of him sent gooseflesh across her arms and blood pulsing at her temples. It was a sudden reaction, quite mysterious: Was she angry or pleased? She wasn't sure. She stood up and went toward him.

"I've seen the painting at Durand-Ruel's and I had to see you," he said. "*That is style.* I had to tell you—you are a genius, Mary. You have put everything about art we both ever knew or hoped to know in that gentle painting. I cannot tell you how it affected me when I saw it. There is everything one can want to know about style."

"Won't you sit down," she said, and sat on the sofa beside him. "It's kind of you to come."

"I couldn't stay away. I must have that painting. Name your price, but take it to the exhibition marked sold. Please. I need it."

"I suppose it should be yours. I painted it with your unkind words in my mind."

"Well then, my life has been worthwhile. I have contributed to the betterment of art. I am justified if my terrible words caused such a miracle."

They laughed together and he took her hand. Their lips met hungrily, and the bitter void she had existed within these past weeks seemed to fill with warmth. Just to feel the pressure of his hand on hers was pleasure enough. They still needed each other. She knew now it was joy she had felt at seeing him a few minutes ago. Joy and something of desire.

After that they pledged to see each other regularly, and the next night they attended the planning meeting for the 1886 Exhibit together.

Again there were the differences of opinion. Some members wanted the show to be held at the same time as the Salon show, while some felt that sales would be better if the show were scheduled sooner. Mary and Edgar thought it should be held at the same time as the Salon's so the public could make comparisons.

Dates seemed to Mary like a minor detail that would be solved easily, but nothing could be solved if neither side would give in and so the argument went on and on until tempers flared again. It had started out smoothly and now they were at each other's throats again, accusing one another of trying to undermine the group and not caring enough about the poor artists who needed sales to survive. Mary was out of patience with all the bickering. It had to stop or the group would collapse. She had consented to invest a sizable amount of money to back the exhibit. She wanted to do it, but it seemed to her that the backers should have the last word about when the show would be held. And she and the other two backers agreed it should be held concurrently with the Salon show. All the wrangling was distressing and tiresome. When several artists threatened to withdraw if their preferences for an earlier showing was not met, Mary stood up and shakingly said she would withdraw her backing if they could not come to an amicable settlement immediately. More shouting ensued and she finally left the hall in disgust. Edgar came along with her, but would have preferred to stay and continue the fight.

Mary could not bring herself to go to the next meeting, and painted instead with all her concentration. She needed peace, and had no patience left for petty, self-serving, self-important posturing. If they had lost sight of the common cause and were unable to pull together then all was lost. Just as she was putting her brushes away and preparing to go home, Pissarro arrived. He looked very old and tired.

"Please sit down, Camille, and I'll fix tea."

"No, don't bother. I'll only stay a moment."

She remembered the bottle of cognac she had on the shelf, and poured some in a glass for him.

"You're very kind," he said, "and that's why I'm here. I know how you dislike all the dissension we are having among ourselves."

"It's unbearable. We should be the best of friends, yet whenever someone says anything, someone else must twist it around to make it sound sinister. Why do they do it, my dear friend? Why can't we help one another?"

"Any reasons they have are covered over by pride and jealousies."

She sighed. "I wish I understood. Then it wouldn't hurt so much."

"These are desperate men," he said. "They have had their hopes crushed in ridicule, but they have held on. They have suffered, and suffering makes you angry."

"Disappointment is not an excuse to turn against your friends."

"I remember," Pissarro began, looking off dreamily. "I had painted for many years and felt I had come so far in my work and conquered so much that recognition had to be near. I painted twelve hours every day and worked another four in the fields so the family might have food. I believed in myself and put each of my paintings carefully away so that when recognition finally came, I would have riches stored up and could buy the things for my family they had always had to do without. It was a beautiful dream to have. Then the Prussians came. They took my house, and my family was forced to disperse. My wife and daughters were taken in by other villagers. My sons and I lived in a cave nearby. We worked in the fields in the daytime. One evening I went to the house and I saw that the Prussians had used my canvases as rags to wipe up their beer or as matches to light their cigarettes. Nearly all my paintings were ruined, over a thousand canvases. All at once my life seemed to wash away. There was no hope. I trudged back to my cave expecting Lucien to have a fire, and when I got there, he was drawing in the dirt with a stick. I snatched the stick from his hand and brought it down on his back, shouting at him to get moving, that he was supposed to be gathering wood for the fire. In my despair I mistreated the boy most dear to my heart. Can you understand why in my hopelessness I did that?

"They feel hopelessness just like I did. They cannot appeal to the public or the Salon or anyone except each other and they react with anger. Yet we must go on. Even when hope is gone."

Mary blinked back tears. "I wanted to help, but they act like I am oppressing them because I am not poor. I am certainly not rich, Camille. The money I proposed to use to finance the exhibition was money I have earned through selling my work. Does that make me some kind of viper?"

"Not a viper, no. You are our only hope."

"Dear Camille, I'd give anything to help you, you must know that."

"Then, I beg you for myself as well as the others, do not withdraw your support. Without it there will be no exhibit, and the exhibit is their only shred of hope."

29

THE FIRST DAY of the Eighth Exhibit was crowded and noisy. Everyone wanted to see what the lunatics were up to now, but interspersed among the curious were a few more serious viewers, writers, and patrons who believed in the impressionist movement. The tone of the critics had softened too. Censure was focused on the little room where Seurat, Signac, and Pissarro were showing their pointillist paintings, executed in dots of scientifically arranged color. Unfortunately, the room was too small to allow the viewer the necessary distance to see the whole picture at once, and by standing too close, composition and color blending were lost in a jumble of dots. The outcry was spontaneous, and by comparison, the rest of the impressionists could be tolerated easily. Edgar's work was highly praised. Mary's earned good notices too. Her *Susan Sewing in the Garden* had to be moved because there was often a knot of viewers standing around it, clogging traffic through the hall.

Although the columnists had been kind to some of them, Mary wished they could have found more to discuss in the works of the others, for there was greatness still being ridiculed or going un-noticed altogether. And the pointillists' color theories were uncere-moniously buried alive.

After the exhibit ended, Mary and Edgar both fell into a mood of searching and experimentation. They worked together, often from the same model. But there were moments when Mary felt a weakening of the bond between them. It had been nearly ten years since he came to her studio and invited her to join the Independents. It was not always easy to be with him, yet no two artists could have worked together as smoothly. For Edgar it was always necessary to go back to line. And Mary was in tune with that discipline, too. For her there was nothing like the copper plate when it all seemed too easy. Printmaking was forever a challenge. They worked in harmo-ny though they each sought their own challenges. It was a time of quiet rapport, and on occasion they acted almost as one. She began to realize how often they would finish a drawing of the posed model at almost the same time. It seemed an odd coincidence the first time, and they smiled over it. The next time they shrugged. After that it frightened Mary a little. She did not want to work so much like anyone—not even Edgar—as to be a parrot or a twin. Though they worked alike, their work was not so similar that Mary's drawing could ever be mistaken for his, or the other way round. There were similarities, and their rhythms seemed matched, but there were enough differences in their work that she did not worry about comparisons. But did he? Once she suspected he deliberately slowed his pace so she would finish first. Perhaps it was time to do some-thing else.

When she put her things away and made ready to go, she casually mentioned that she would be working in her own studio the next day. She smiled, but when their eyes met, she suspected that he guessed why she wanted to stay away. He walked around the table she had been working at. He stood with his head lowered for a moment, then their eyes met again, frightfully, tenderly. They opened their arms to each other and clung together. And although she didn't understand it, she felt her eyes burning. What were they afraid of? What were they losing?

They kissed hungrily, and instantly all her carefully repressed desires sprang to life, choking her in passion. The strength of their mutual need overcame their frequent pledges of virtue, blotting out their impossible standards. Now they cared only for satisfaction. They did not resist the storm that rocked them. Mary went eagerly with him, and they made love. They read each other's moods perfectly. When she was most ready for him, he was prepared. The rhythm was perfect. Nothing could have been improved or more satisfying. "I never want to leave you," he said.

THE NEXT DAY she began work on a mother and child. It was a theme that had a strong appeal for her. She stayed in her own studio for the next two days and when he came to see her on the third day, he seemed genuinely pleased with what she was doing. "I think you have discovered a theme you could make your own. It's something no one else is doing seriously and you do show what it is all about."

"I am an eye, just like you."

"No, your intelligence has put it together. You're an eye and a mind."

"Then I am not a true impressionist."

"No one is. We are all separate. When we quit being ourselves and copy an ideal, we become insipid."

"I know. I do sometimes feel like an eye. I paint realistically, almost photographically. Now that a perfect scientific likeness is possible with the camera, I question myself. What good is the artist?"

"Photography cannot leave anything out. A photograph gives only one expression. It cannot combine what you have seen into one look. Only the artist can do that. Besides, in a photograph there is no color."

"I have seen photographs that have been tinted. After struggling for all these years to learn to paint people, is it possible the value is gone?"

He shook his head. "Some people might be satisfied with photographs. Not most. They are two different things. Enough of that. I didn't come here to worry you, only to ask if you would like to go to the Japanese print exhibition with me?"

"Of course. Let's do go."

They set off immediately and when they arrived at the exhibit hall, they were both struck by the immensity of the show. They had studied Japanese prints for several years and had already experimented with spatial relationships. This exhibit contained many thousands of prints, but through it all, there was a sense of simplicity. There was pattern and the subtle squeezing of space. There was the glorification of line, which Edgar had pursued all his life, and with the perfection of line, the western need of modeling was gone. Mary began to see possibilities for her own printmaking that had not been tried, ways of combining Asian qualities with western practice. They stayed and examined prints until dark. She came back the next day even though Edgar could not, and she stayed all day. That night she wrote down her thoughts and observations and ideas as to what to try in her own work to combine what she knew with what she was learning from the Japanese print. She went back to the show again, once with Berthe and once with her mother.

Soon after the Japanese print exhibition, Louisine and her husband Henry came to Paris for a visit. It was a happy reunion. Henry Havemeyer was a tall man with bright blue eyes and quick smile. Mary liked him at once. She lunched with the Havemeyers at their hotel on the day of their arrival and it wasn't long before Louisine brought the subject around to art. Henry said he admired Mary's work and mentioned that they wanted to begin a collection of impressionist and pre-impressionist paintings.

Mary smiled at Henry. "I have been in correspondence with Louisine as you know, and when I learned you would be looking at art, I watched for opportunities. I have a Courbet set aside for you. I also have some Monets for you to see and I have persuaded Pissarro to leave several of his canvases with me so I could show them to you."

"You're very kind to trouble yourself about us," Henry said.

Henry was enthusiastic and enjoyed being taken to the galleries, and did not hesitate long in his purchasing decisions. If Louisine and Mary agreed a painting was both fine art and worth the price, he bought it. He acquired three Monets, a Courbet, a Pissarro and a Cezanne.

At the end of their visit Mary was nearly as fond of Henry as she was of Louisine. She hated for them to leave Paris, but they promised to return soon. They still wanted a Manet and a Corot. And Henry said they would be interested in a fine Degas if Mary could acquire one for them. Mary promised to do what she could to locate good examples of these artists' work. "But I must warn you," she told them, "that Manets are no longer cheap. He was finally recognized and given the medal. He worked all his life for recognition and lived only a painful two years after it came."

"You must miss him," Louisine said.

"We all do. And his work will never be ignored again."

After Louisine and Henry went back to America, Mary set to work at printmaking. However, her father who had grown frail and cantankerous, was yearning for the country life. Although she did not want to leave Paris and her work, Mary rented a château in the Oise valley for the summer. Both her parents needed a long rest in the country. And she could take a press with her and devote the summer to working on etchings.

"EDGAR, PLEASE. Don't you think I'll hate being separated from you again?" Mary said impatiently. "Don't turn sullen, you know I can't tolerate that."

"Sullen is my nature," Edgar replied, "especially when you tell me you're going away for the entire summer."

"I must."

"I know. It's your father, I suppose."

Mary nodded. "He has been irritable lately. The country will do him a world of good." She looked squarely at Edgar and her gaze hardened. "This time I'll accept no excuses—absolutely none. You are coming out to the château for a visit."

"Oh, I am? I should just drop everything I'm doing and go running out to see the weeds and bugs of the country where I do nothing but sneeze and perspire?"

"Yes—no excuses. You're coming. I am going to devote myself

to printmaking and I will need you to come and wrench me away from my press to see the weeds and bugs. It's your duty."

"Then I shall give it consideration."

"That won't be necessary. You *will* come. *When* is the only decision you will have to make. I am prepared to make that decision, too, should you stall with it."

He smiled and his smile turned to laughter. "What a terrible shrew. What a fishwife you could have been if you had only set your mind to it."

She went to him and put her arms around him. He held her and promised to do what she wished.

THE CHÂTEAU near the Oise river was stately, comfortable and life there was more pleasant than she had anticipated. The country suited them all and was especially soothing to Robert.

Mary set up her press at once and began to work on the prints she had rolling around in her brain in a confusion of Japanese pictorial concepts and western techniques. There were so many possibilities—etching, aquatint, dry point—and she could combine certain techniques and papers. She could work from the light to the dark or the reverse. The extra challenge was that she was alone in the country. There was no one to ask for advice or judgments. She was both artist and printer. Her experiments would be totally her own. She was up at dawn each day and still working until late at night.

Occasionally she asked a few of the neighboring women and children to sit. These pastel studies were useful as printmaking motifs and offered her a pleasant change from bending over the copper plates and printing press. These country people, steeped in the tradition of the land, had the kind of open genuineness she liked best to draw and paint. They were not afflicted with the artificiality of the city, and had a richness that she recognized as timeless and exquisitely human. A few times she dressed a peasant woman in a gown from Redfern or some other Parisian fashion house. It pleased her to see such admirable people in beautiful clothes.

Early one afternoon when she had completed running her fifth print, a dry point, Edgar arrived for his visit. Mathilde called to her when the carriage stopped and Mary ran to greet him. Her first glance of him getting out of the carriage and walking to the château shocked her. He looked so feeble, but it was only because he walked slowly due to the bright sun and his failing eyesight.When she embraced him she saw that his eyes were worse. The eyes of an artist. Why couldn't the condition stop? He must paint. He must see. No wonder he is so tortured, she thought, and so unbearable. How can he accept it, he who has lived through his eyes?

Mary wanted to know what he'd been doing. What were his plans? "I plan to visit Gauguin in Brittany," he said.

"Gauguin?" She was surprised. Both men were volatile, insisting on being right. It was inconceivable that two such difficult persons could be friends for long.

After they had eaten an excellent dinner, Mary wanted to show Edgar the prints she had been working on. As they started toward the studio, Robert stopped him. "She's killing herself with that press, staying up until two or three in the morning. I wish you could talk some sense to her. She still listens to you."

Mary shook her head and hugged him. "Now, Father, I am perfectly fit and healthy and you know it."

"I want you to stay that way," he said, his voice pitched high.

"Nonsense," she muttered as she led Edgar to the studio.

"He worries about you," Edgar said.

"Yes, he's an excellent worrier," she said.

Edgar looked at her sadly. It was a look she did not understand. Did he need someone to worry about *him*? Was that it? She took his hand fondly and showed him the first print. He brought it closer to the light, examined it carefully, running his fingers lightly over the lines. He nodded seriously and looked at another. Mary told him the problems she had with each one, her goals, how she had achieved them. Why didn't he say something? She showed them all to him and when he had seen them, she put them aside. "That's the lot of them."

He nodded. He sat down on the stool and looked at her. "I don't know what to say."

She felt a wave of nausea and apprehension. "Say whatever you think."

"I don't have the words. It's tremendously strong work, and it's really new. I've never seen effects like that."

"I was afraid you hated them. I couldn't tell what you thought."

"You could tell if I hated them."

They laughed together and he took her hands, looked at them. "So frail they look," he said. "A woman's hands, and they have done what no man's hands have done before."

"Are they really good?"

"They're very much more than good," he said.

"I needed to know if you thought so," she said softly. "It's so hard to judge your own work when you are so deeply involved in it."

"Yes, I fear that's what has happened to Pissarro. He is so one hundred percent behind the divisionist theory of Seurat, he is painting pictures that are no longer his. I tried to tell him, but he thinks I am too romantic and afraid to learn new things."

"I think he will gain something from the theories. He will practice it until the formula becomes too much."

"They are calling themselves neo-impressionists," he said with disgust.

"There have been so many names. What do they mean? We paint. We struggle. It's a lonely job, and if a work is good and does what we want, does it matter what they call it?"

"We are really alone. I think we are finished as a group. Some have gone to the Salon. Pissarro and Seurat are showing with Les Vingts. Gauguin will go back to the tropics. Monet, Renoir, Berthe are showing with the internationals. Everyone is going off, each in his own direction. There is no unity. The printmakers are talking about forming another group, excluding the internationals, and so it goes, one against the others. I suppose we can do without each other, but it will not be so good."

"Perhaps it won't just crumble. We've picked ourselves up before. Perhaps you exaggerate."

"Perhaps. I *am* a pessimist. Is that what you think? Well don't. I am very happy tonight."

"You are really very good to come, Edgar. I know you don't like to leave Paris."

"I have grown too comfortable since I have had Zoe to keep house and read to me."

"I shall read to you while you're here if you like," she promised.

"I would prefer if you'd explain what you've done here." He picked up one of the prints, held it close to his face a moment, then pointed to a bit of delicate green shading on a tabletop. "It's extraordinary."

"I'll show you." She brought out the copper plate and set up the press. They worked, oblivious of time, until Robert and Katherine came in.

Robert turned to Edgar. "I see you are of no use at all in talking sense to this midnight printer," he said, his voice more prideful than reproachful.

"The results of all the work have been worth the hours spent," Edgar said.

Robert nodded. "I suspected that. We try to understand."

Katherine smiled. "We thought if you were almost finished, you'd join us for a glass of wine before retiring."

Mary looked at Edgar. "We can finish this tomorrow. I must clean the press before I leave it."

Katherine and Robert went back to the drawing room and Edgar helped Mary. "How inconvenient to have a family," he muttered, "and how wonderful, I suppose."

THE NEXT MORNING, Mary was up early and anxious to continue the work they had begun the night before. However, Edgar did not wake up so early. When he did appear, his expression was glum. He said good morning and then did not speak until he had finished his coffee. Then he only grumbled. "What—eat breakfast? Ridiculous."

"I hope you slept well," Katherine said.

He nodded, but Mary was quite sure he did not sleep well at all. Something was wrong.

"No, nothing is wrong," he said when they were alone. "I am not used to people around me so early in the day."

"I'm sorry."

"Why should you be sorry? You're used to it. You have always had a family around you, and people looking after you, morning, noon, and night." His words stung, and she felt he needed someone besides the elderly Zoe to care for him. She was silent for a moment. "Would you like to finish our print, or would you enjoy a walk first?"

"We'll work first," he said, getting up.

30

MARY STAYED in the country until the first of November. Finally the family packed and readied to leave, promising each other they would be back next year. As always Mary looked forward to coming home to Paris, but for the first time she felt a pang of regret at having to leave the country. She had found peace and strength in its isolation.

One of the first places Mary went after getting settled in Paris was Durand-Ruel's gallery. She wanted to hear about his trip to America. She hoped only for good news of her countrymen.

"Americans are utterly charming and civilized," he said. "Your brothers were especially cordial. They brought quite a few influential people to the exhibition and of course, your friends did the same. All in all it was encouraging, though in America there were the same sort of newspaper articles we have in Paris." He smiled. "Resistance is wearing away, though, and those who embrace the new art do it with enthusiasm."

"Yes, everyone is selling more paintings now. Well, practically everyone. Gauguin is still unaccepted by the public."

He looked off sadly. "I suppose you know about the exhibition the group is planning to have here?"

"No."

"Some of them have reorganized. I had nothing to do with that."

"I have heard nothing about it."

"You were still in the country. Not many of the old group are left."

'When is the show to be? I have done a series of prints I would like to exhibit."

"That's the point. You can't exhibit with them."

"What do you mean, I can't exhibit with them?"

"The new rules prohibit those who are not French. I think it was meant to keep the Belgians out."

"I can't believe they would do it! It's an abominable rule. What about Pissarro? He was born in the West Indies. Did they turn him out too?"

Durand-Ruel nodded.

"What gall!"

"I agree," he said. "I want you and Pissarro both to have an exhibit here, at the same time as their show if you wish. I have mentioned it to him. I can give you each a nice gallery. A one-man show is what you need now. You're ready for it. Your work is mature and vital. Never mind the old group. You can stand alone."

"I have only a few new things, maybe a dozen prints and a few pastels and oils. That's not enough."

"We can get other work on loan if need be. I can arrange it."

"The critics can ruin a person's whole career over a one-man show. It's not like a group."

"There is some risk, naturally."

She hesitated. Was it really happening? "Thank you," she said. "I'll want to think about it."

"Talk to Pissarro. I think you both should do it."

When she left the gallery Mary went directly to the studio and wrote a letter to Camille asking how such an insult could have been thrust at them, and what were his feelings. Should they in fact get an exhibit together to show at Durand-Ruel's gallery? "I'm almost of a mind to do it," she wrote, "but I want to know what you think. You're much wiser than I."

Even after she posted the letter she was angry. Was there no one to prevent such treachery? Where was Edgar? Why didn't he prevent it? Suddenly all her anger was turned toward him. In a frenzy of energy she rushed to his studio to demand an explanation. When she arrived she was breathless and did not bother to knock before opening the door.

There was giggling. Startled, she looked toward the sound. A nude young woman with long red hair was sitting on the model's couch. Edgar stood facing her.

Mary stopped just as the door closed behind her. Edgar and the woman looked up. Startled, he turned toward Mary. The woman laughed. "I'm sorry to disturb your work," Mary said, ignoring the woman, "but did you know I am no longer allowed to exhibit with the impressionists?"

Edgar straightened up, his face becoming serious. He took a deep breath. "The impressionists are scattering. Those who are reorganizing saw a simple need of limiting membership because now that impressionism is only a little bit naughty, there is pressure from all sides to open the gates. They chose to limit their members to native French. I was against it, of course." He walked toward her. "I'm sure they won't enforce it in your case."

"What about Pissarro?"

"That's a different matter. He has been exhibiting with the Belgians. I don't know."

"I see. Well, I'll be leaving," she said, feeling as though she might smother between the strain of Edgar and the amusement of his model. Her hand was on the doorknob when he touched her shoulder. "Don't be in such a hurry. Let me introduce you to Suzanne. We'll all have a cup of tea." He turned his head. "Please get dressed," he said to the woman.

She had a puckish face, with a pretty mouth. Her hair was an unusual dark red color. Her eyes were clear and cold and Mary had the feeling she had seen her before. In a moment Suzanne came out of the corner in a ruffled flowery wrapper.

"I'm Suzanne. You must be Mary Cassatt."

"How do you do," Mary said. "Haven't we met?"

Suzanne's loud laughter rang out in the room. It irritated Mary. What was the matter with this woman? Edgar seemed amused, too. Mary had a sudden urge to slap them both and be off.

"Suzanne probably looks familiar because she has posed for Renoir, Gauguin, and Rafeilli," Edgar said.

"I only pose for impressionists now," Suzanne said.

"I see."

"Suzanne is taking up painting herself now."

"It looked like such fun," she said. "I had to try it."

Mary nodded politely and wished she hadn't come. She certainly was not going to show them how upset she was over being excluded. Perhaps it was good this girl was here. She was too angry with Edgar. He hadn't even told her.

"I hoped you would not find out about it until I could appeal to each of those who wanted to limit membership to the French. I'm sure they will make the exception for you."

"Don't bother," she said. "Monsieur Durand-Ruel has asked me to have a one-man show. He thinks I am ready for it."

"A one-man show?" Suzanne laughed. "That should be even harder for you to qualify for."

With some effort Mary smiled. "A one-woman show, to be more correct."

"Your prints would make an excellent basis for an exhibit," Edgar said seriously.

"Aren't you afraid?" Suzanne asked. "The critics just love jabbing it into artists having one-man shows."

Mary shrugged, though she had to admit the prospect frightened her somewhat. Critics usually compared the artist being shown with all their own favorite artists who worked in similar areas. She was used to being compared to Berthe. They would undoubtedly compare her work with Degas's because in the art world of Paris, she was considered his disciple. She would be compared with Whistler too, another expatriate American enamored of Japanese prints. There would be others the critics would come up with. But there was no way to avoid it if she was ever going to strike out on her own, and now at forty-six she was sure that was what she should do and what she did want. She sipped her tea, becoming more committed to the idea by the minute. She did not want to be the exception made as a concession to Edgar.

"Thank you for the tea," she said at last. "Nice meeting you, Suzanne. I wish you good luck in your painting."

ALL OF MARY'S EFFORTS were now poured into preparations for her one-woman show. She wrote again to Pissarro telling him of her decision and urging him to exhibit too.

M. Durand-Ruel showed her the exhibit room where her show would be hung. She looked at the walls critically. It was a good room, well lit and not too big. She would exhibit the mother and child paintings she had done during the summer and the prints and maybe half a dozen pastels. She must think and select wisely.

Pissarro came to see her as she was choosing the work she would exhibit. Some needed a bit more work. All needed framing.

"I am glad we have decided to do this," he said. "I was so disappointed when I heard what they had done; I thought I would never want to see any of them again. It seemed impossible."

"Yes, I know," she said. "Where were our friends, you wonder."

"Exactly. But to withdraw and live on the hurt will only make us miserable. I have opposed the romantics who refuse to acknowledge the coming of science and analysis. I thought I was attacking ideas only, but there are people behind those ideas and when you oppose a person's ideas, you are putting yourself against him personally. They were uncomfortable with me, and let the hotheads win. In your case they were jealous of your American money. I know it's an exaggerated idea they have. You have talent and influence, and your work has been praised while most of theirs has not. Besides, you are a woman."

"I am *only* a woman. Isn't that what they mean?"

"Some of them may want to think of it like that. Yes. It is not what I think. You are my respected colleague."

She showed him the work she thought she would exhibit. He was particularly impressed with the prints. "My son has been after such an effect as this. He and many others have worked for it, but have never come close to doing this." The old man's eyes shone with pleasure. "The exhibit is coming at the right time for you. You must show these now to a great many people before a few see and copy them and claim the pioneer work for themselves."

"Oh, come now. Copy me?"

"They will. If I were you, I'd keep them under cover until they are hung in the exhibit."

"I have only shown them to Edgar, Durand-Ruel, and you."

"Good, you are safe."

Mary went with him to see the gallery he would be given to exhibit in. His room was bigger than the one she was offered, since his paintings tended to be large. The rooms were arranged so one would pass by them to get to the larger gallery where the new group's exhibit would be hung. They had agreed to exhibit at the same time as the new group would be exhibiting, only Mary's and Camille's show would open a day earlier. Durand-Ruel was pleased at this arrangement. And Mary began to feel a strong surge of excitement and dared to hope the critics would not be too unkind to them.

Pissarro's hopes were strong, too. He confided to Mary that he was abandoning his strict divisionist technique. "Not because I do not think it is valid," he protested. "It is valid and important and I shall continue to support it, but it slows me down so much I cannot create as I go. And this creating is part of my hands and eyes, don't you see? With the divisionist method I'm working against myself."

Mary smiled. How kind he was. He would not abandon Suerat. He had even taken Van Gogh in and helped him learn the new theories of color. "How is Van Gogh?" she asked.

"He is very tense. He has power and he is learning a great deal about color." Pissarro shook his head and frowned. "He will either climb the heights over all of us—or he will go mad."

"His eyes are sometimes so tortured." she said.

"And also his canvases, but not always. You should see how he has adapted the divisionist techniques. At first I was aghast, but after watching him a while I was amazed at the power he produced."

"He told Edgar he was interested in Cezanne's work too."

"Ah, yes, and I wished him well. He seeks in the right directions."

As Mary listened to Pissarro talk, she felt stimulated, glad to be one of his friends. When it was time for him to go back to the country, she took him to the train station in her carriage and they arranged to meet again at the gallery when their shows were hung.

After that, she began to have moments of fear. She hoped the show would be a success. What would happen to her if it wasn't? She was out of the group. She had no other alliances like Pissarro had. Edgar, thankfully, seemed to understand. There was no one else's judgment she trusted so much. Edgar could be unkind, but not dishonest.

"Do not show too much," he cautioned. "Nothing so strong that the prints will be overpowered. No more than three pastels. Perhaps two of your best oils. The prints must dominate."

Durand-Ruel wanted her to include more, but Edgar's plan was so logical and convincing, she could not ignore his advice.

On the day before the opening, she and Pissarro were overseeing the hanging of their shows at the same time. He seemed exuberant, not nervous at all like she was. His show was magnificent. He had a small following now, and he had *Les Vingt* to exhibit with. Her gallery looked almost bare. Maybe Durand-Ruel had been right. She should have shown a few more oils. By midafternoon she developed a rash on her neck, and her head began to throb. She changed and rechanged the placement of a print. She straightened frames when they did not need straightening. She despaired. Then Pissarro was at her side, smiling, apparently in a mood of happy euphoria. She envied him.

"We have been invited to attend the new group's celebration party the night of their opening."

"We have? I haven't received any such invitation."

"That's because when the young man came in here to deliver it, you ordered him to remove the crates from the corner and be quick about it."

Mary's cheeks reddened.

Pissarro smiled and nodded. "He understood how preoccupied you were and he asked me to deliver the invitation. Here it is. They do not want hard feelings, you see. They want to honor *all* the impressionists."

"Pooh. We saw how they honored us." She took the invitation and tossed it into the waste basket.

"My dear Mary, don't let your good heart shrivel. It is their token of good will. We must not turn our backs on them. Let's remember our principles and our goals and stick together."

Seeing the goodness in his face, she closed her stinging eyes and murmured. "I'll think about it."

He took the invitation out of the waste basket, dusted it off, and gave it to her with a wink. "We'll go together if you like."

She shrugged. "All I can think about now is tomorrow."

He smiled reassuringly and patted her shoulder. "Tomorrow everything will be fine."

THE NEXT MORNING Mary looked on as Katherine straightened Robert's red tie before they left for the gallery.

"I don't know how you managed it," Robert said, "I didn't think they'd let anyone in before the gallery opened."

"I just explained to Monsieur Durand-Ruel that you hate crowds of people," Mary said, still nervous that he might be agitated and begin shouting as he so often did nowadays. She had hoped that by going early they could avoid any irritations.

"It's not that I hate people; I haven't the patience anymore. Things grate."

"It's all right, Father. Crowds are trying. I'm too nervous to cope with it myself today. Come along. The carriage is waiting."

They entered the gallery through the private entrance half an hour before the opening. Robert stood at the doorway a moment, then advanced to the middle of the room and turned around. "Not enough pictures in here," he said.

"No, there aren't too many."

"It's fine just the way it is," Katherine said. "I think it shows taste and restraint."

"You ought to have the portrait of your mother here. That's the best painting you've done. No, there aren't enough oil paintings. That's what they want to see, not prints and pastels." He was obviously disappointed and getting irritated. He paced nervously, shaking his head frequently.

The gallery opened then, and a few people walked nearby. Robert was oblivious. "Bring in more paintings," he shouted. "Your mother's portrait here on this wall, and the little girl on the blue chair—what's her name—over here. And a portrait of Lydia. This show needs a portrait of Lydia."

"Robert—please!" Katherine scolded. "Remember where you are. We'll talk later."

"I know where we are. We need more pictures now, not later."

"Father, you may be right, but I don't want you to work youself up about it. You're getting excited and the doctor says you mustn't. Come along; we're going now."

Perhaps it was the tone of her voice or the look in her eyes; Robert allowed himself to be led out of the gallery.

Mary was more upset than she showed. When they were safely home and Robert had gone to his room to rest, she sat in the drawing room with her mother, but was barely able to converse. He was right. This was her chance and she had wasted it by being too timid. Oil paintings *were* what people wanted to see.

"You're not to worry about what your father said. He is not an expert on exhibits. Remember that."

"It's too late to change anything anyway," Mary said. "Now I wish I had included that portrait of you."

Katherine insisted the show was fine exactly as it was, but Mary was not convinced. Her father's voice seemed to be the sound of truth. After tea she went to the studio and tried to work, but accomplished nothing. To calm herself she walked alone through Montmartre, wondering what the critics would say.

The next day, after searching every column of the newspaper, she realized there was no mention of her show anywhere. Maybe it was best. To fail in private at least doesn't ruin future possibilities so much as public condemnation. She tried not to be too disappointed, and in the afternoon she went to the exhibition of the new all-French group.

The show was exciting. There were people crowding about, some laughing and jeering as always, while her exhibit was stark. No laughter or voices came out of her gallery. As she was leaving, thinking of taking another long walk, M. Durand-Ruel stopped her. He was beaming with pleasure.

"Your exhibit has been very well received, as I knew it would."

She stared at him blankly a few seconds. "There was nothing about it in the newspaper."

"Not yet. This evening's issue will say something. All the critics were here." M. Durand-Ruel looked at his pocket watch. "The paper will be out soon. Have coffee with me in my office and we will read the news together. Come along now."

Mary was grateful to be with someone who understood, to sit with him over coffee. She told him what her father had said, and she now thought he was right and wished she'd followed that advice.

"Prints and pastels are just as popular as oils now," he said matter-of-factly. "I trust you are coming to the party tonight."

"Camille expects me to go."

"Yes, he needs your support. I do too."

"You?"

"Yes, me. The whole artist community is in a mood of rebellion, first against the Salon, then the public, and now each other. Monet has turned against me. He blames me for having so many of his paintings in America that he lost sales in Paris."

"That's ridiculous. You have stood by him like a saint."

"He has been through much. I'm aware of that, but his present antagonism is hard to bear. I hope he doesn't take the others away now that we are on the brink of success."

"No, I can't believe he would," she said. "It's strange what a bit of success can do. It's frightening. Maybe he thirsted for it too long, and now he needs time. Renoir has accustomed himself to it and has remained the same."

"Yes, it's probably nothing. We'll all go to the party and be happy together. That will help."

"I hope so," she said, still feeling uneasy.

Finally, the newspapers were delivered. Her hands were moist and her knees felt wobbly. She simply wasn't well-prepared for the embarrassment of being ridiculed, or worse, of being ignored.

M. Durand-Ruel spread the paper out before him and put on his glasses. The room was silent, except for the crackle of the newspaper page turning. She wished it were tomorrow or next week or that she could leave.

"This must be it," he said. " 'Cassatt's Show at Durand-Ruel Galleries Leads the Season.' " He paused a moment and read on. " 'The average viewer will have no trouble appreciating the superiority of the works of this graduate impressionist, and the print connoisseur will be never the same, for Miss Cassatt has enriched the art of printmaking immeasurably by her innovative and impeccably executed prints. She has produced effects so subtle, tasteful, and elegant, the mystery is how a woman of such ability could have waited so long to step out on her own to be counted as one of the finest artists in all of Paris.

" 'Visiting the gallery, the spectator will not be burdened by an overabundance of work, a fault commonly present at most one-artist shows. Miss Cassatt has instead chosen a few tastefully selected samples of her work, but alas, it leaves the spectator hungering for more.' "

Mary was so moved by the words, she could hardly think and felt almost like crying. M. Durand-Ruel turned to the other newspaper.

"Listen to this," he said. " 'Mary Cassatt is the artist to watch. Her prints are revolutionizing the field of printmaking and her portraits are among the most charming of this century.' "

All at once, Mary could not hold back her tears or laughter. M. Durand-Ruel came to her and offered his handkerchief.

"Thank you," she said, taking it. "Thank you."

WHEN MARY left Monsieur Durand-Ruel, she took one more look at her show. It was strange how detached she felt now, how clear it all seemed. Then just as she turned to leave, Edgar appeared, walking quickly toward her. "There you are," he said. "I've been looking for you for hours. Congratulations."

"Edgar," she said, taking his hand. "I was so afraid they'd find me wanting. I thought I'd done everything wrong, and yet they liked it."

"They did indeed. I told you it was a fine show."

They walked out of the gallery together. "You earned four paragraphs in Warren's column."

"I certainly didn't expect such kindness from him."

"Was it he who said that you were much too modest, and you must unveil more?"

She glanced reproachfully at him. "That isn't quite the way it appeared in the column."

Edgar laughed. "Can you stop at my studio a few minutes? I want your opinion. You are a woman and an artist with taste. It's one of my nude series. Desboutin made a comment that bothered me— not even a comment really—an innuendo, hinting that I may have overstepped the bounds of good taste."

"You are a more daring artist than Desboutin."

"There is a line between being unconventional and merely coarse. I cross it freely in my sketching because I must explore, but now I am so saturated with my studies, my sense of good taste is untrustworthy."

"So you seek the opinion of the modest Miss Cassatt?"

"Exactly."

"All right, I'll tell you what I think of it."

When they arrived at his studio, Mary examined the painting for a few minutes and shook her head. "I don't know. It does seem shocking—and yet the shadows are beautiful. The body itself is not. The model's legs are too short to give it much grace. The mouth is what offends, and the eyes. It seems there's a coarse kind of contempt there. I don't know."

"You do know. I think you judged it fairly."

"It's a painting that will bother many people as it does me," she said. "Perhaps it's the combination of nudity and contempt that seem to mock whoever looks at it."

"If the eyes were averted, would it seem less tasteless?" he asked.

Mary glanced at the painting again, squinting, imagining the eyes averted. 'Yes," she said.

"I shall work on them. Let me bring you something. A glass of wine to drink to your success?"

"Tea might be better. I feel a trifle weak."

"Here, sit down. You haven't eaten, have you? My housekeeper has made a most delectable pastry. Excuse me. We'll have tea in a moment."

She did feel famished, but too wrought up to just sit. She supposed she would eventually calm down from all the excitement now that the critics had their say. She paced around the studio, looking at the sketches he had pinned up. There was a sketch on the floor beside the cabinet. She bent over to pick it up, looked at it. Ugly, she thought. What an awful pose. The cabinet door was opened a crack. She supposed the sketch fell off one of the shelves. She opened the door, intending to place the sketch on a shelf, when she saw a portfolio hastily put away. It must have fallen out of that. Mary opened the folio to put the sketch away. The folio was full of sketches. She looked through a few of them. They were all drawings of nudes, some pen and ink drawings, a few gouaches, some charcoal and pastel studies, and they were mostly ugly like the first one. Fat women with short legs and heavy breasts. Two women sitting on a couch together. Thin women shamelessly showing the worst of themselves. A man and a woman. Can love look like this? There was a series of sketches of a nude woman on a chamber pot. Her hands shook as she looked. It's reality taken too far. Much too far. She shuffled through the rest of the sketches. It's depravity, she thought. Shakily she returned the folio to its place on the shelf.

When she stood up and walked back to the sofa, her hands trembled uncontrollably. Nudity didn't have to look like that. He was obsessed with it. What was it he said about it? It's not nudity, it's people stripped of all artifice. She remembered his words, but those drawings were obscene.

She feigned calm when he came back into the studio with the tea tray.

"You look tired," he said. "Here, drink this." He handed her a teacup and she sipped gratefully.

"I hope you will have a good rest before the party."

"Oh yes, the party," she said, grasping at the thought. "Camille and Madame Pissarro are coming on the eight-thirty train. Our groom will meet them at the station and bring them home, then on to the party. Will you come with us? I know they would be pleased."

"I think not," Edgar said. "Madame Pissarro makes me green. These devoted women who have never had a more uplifting thought then how best to patch a sleeve I find very trying after the first thirty seconds."

"That's not fair. She has raised a beautiful family. She has other qualities, though she may not be easy to converse with."

He raised his eyebrows. "To put it mildly." He looked at Mary and his expression changed to worry. "Shall I take you home now so you can rest a bit?"

She realized she did feel extremely tired. It wasn't just that; she was uneasy about Edgar. Knowing about the drawings made her feel ashamed. She was seeing a side of him she hadn't really known and didn't like very well. She stood and put on her gloves. "I do need a rest."

When she got home, she went straight to her room and asked Mathilde to prepare her bath. While she waited, she took off her shoes and stretched out on the bed. She wasn't against nudity in art. Many of his studies of nudes were excellent examples of his genius. No, she was not the prude he sometimes liked to accuse her of being, but she had been disturbed by those drawings. Those women were not models posing for respectable pictures. Those were whores. She wasn't sure how she knew, but she knew. He drew them lounging in disgraceful poses. She sat up and tried to put them out of her mind, but the images returned.

Was some of it her fault? Did he have to seek out that element because she did not satisfy his needs? She knew she had not been the ideal lover for him. She had not given enough. When she was obsessed with her work, she could not give anything. When her family needed her, they came first. She could not be any different than she was. Edgar needed more from a woman.

Mathilde called her softly. The bath was ready. Mary stood up to prepare herself for the party she still did not really want to go to. At least her reviews had been good. She could hold up her head proudly.

ON THE WAY to the party she explained to Madame Pissarro that she still felt hurt at being excluded from the group. "My feelings are not as generous as your husband's."

Madame Pissarro nodded. "Camille's friends are important. There should not be so much enmity."

Mary realized she liked Madame Pissarro very much. Maybe clever conversation wasn't worth as much as her simple values. The three walked inside arm-in-arm as schoolchildren. The noise of the festivities was already at a peak. They were plunged into the light and the laughter. Champagne was being poured and served all around. A group near the entrance broke apart and Desboutin greeted Pissarro with a handshake, and Mary and Madame Pissarro with a kiss on the cheek. Across the room she caught a fleeting glance of Edgar, standing with Rouart and some others. She also saw a bit of sleek red hair somewhere across the room.

Mary would have continued along with the Pissarros, but one of the younger and newest members of the group stepped in front of her, bowed from the waist and smiled. "Ah, Miss Cassatt. I presume you were charitable enough to bring your reviews to share with the unfortunates who may never hear anything but bad jokes about their own work."

"Yes," another said. "She graduates and then comes and rubs our noses in it."

There was laughter and the sound of jeering. Mary's anger flashed. "I did not come here to be insulted once more by so-called friends." She turned to leave. But Berthe and Eugene were suddenly at her elbow. "Please don't be angry at all of us for the rudeness of a few young idiots." She glanced arrows at the offenders, who turned away murmuring.

Mary's logic told her that Berthe could not be blamed. She would never be a party to such shameful behavior, but there would be no peace. If someone compliments your work, grants a bit of recognition, others will insult and jeer. There seemed to be no rest from being tough and independent of all of them. It was not possible to let down the guard. She did not belong. It was not the same— couldn't be again. It was sad, very sad. She took a glass of champagne. "Everyone is a stranger," she murmured, but no one heard and she drank the champagne and looked for Edgar. Where was he? She needed him. There he was, still standing with Henri Rouart. Wasn't that the model she had met at his studio, standing very close to Edgar? Mary walked straight toward them.

"I prefer watercolors," Suzanne was saying, "because with them it's easy to be free. What I really like best is to paint watercolors while I'm in the nude. There's no constraint. Nothing but pure freedom. I use a lot of green, like Diana in the forest."

Henri and Edgar laughed, winked and turned their adoring gaze back to Suzanne. It was clear that Suzanne was a woman who spent her life amusing men when it suited her to do so. When Mary joined them she spoke to her in a different tone. "Whatever happened over there?" she asked.

"I was insulted," Mary said.

"You weren't, surely," Edgar said. His lukewarm solicitude only irritated Mary. She glared at him and felt that her presence was ruining the gay mood they were enjoying before she barged in on them.

"You should have done something," Suzaane reproached Edgar. "I told you something was wrong, but you wouldn't believe me."

"How could I believe such nonsense?"

Mary no longer wanted to talk about it. Why involve Edgar? From this distance he wouldn't have been able to see or hear anything. "Let's try to be cheerful," she said.

"And so you should be," Rouart said. "Your exhibit is something to celebrate."

"Yes," Suzanne said. "Here's to Miss Cassatt and her first one-woman success."

"May there be many more," Edgar said.

Their glasses clicked, but Mary felt it was only a charade. No one really wished her success. They were being polite. She may have done the same thing herself. How alone she felt. How little she really understood Edgar. She could see how he looked at Suzanne, how he must have lusted for her. What would she expect? She drank another glass of champagne and another until the room became a pleasant blur. When several of the men huddled together to light their pipes, Mary asked Suzanne if she wouldn't like to freshen up a bit. Suzanne's face revealed alarm, but she went along.

As they stood at the ornate mirrors, powdering their noses, Suzanne spoke. "I suppose you want to talk about what's yours."

"No, Suzanne, about what isn't. I wanted to ask you how you felt about Edgar. I sense a definite attraction. Do you really like him very much?"

Suzanne stiffened. "He's a recognized genius, and he's charming and rich."

"He's not rich. He has become comfortable again because his work is successful, but he has no wealth other than his collection of art."

"Anyway, Miss Cassatt, if you think I'm trying to squeeze in on your territory, I'm not."

"Call me Mary. I never thought anything of the kind. Edgar is free. I'm sure he likes you very much. If you could only return that—"

Suzanne's eyes widened. She flung back a strand of her red hair. "Edgar is no different than the others when it comes to that."

"I see," Mary said. "He needs someone like you. You are capable of understanding him. His eyes are getting worse, you know. He needs someone to be with him, not let him be alone so much."

"I thought you and he were—well, everybody thinks you are—very close."

"Lovers, don't you mean?"

"That's what everybody thinks."

Mary gazed off. "I've known Edgar a long time. There have been times when we have hardly spoken to one another. We shall always be friends. I just wish there was someone he could lean on in his need. Someone with real compassion for him."

"I'm not sure I know what you mean."

Mary held her head high and looked into Suzanne's eyes. "I wish you would live with him."

"Really? Do you mean it, or is it the champagne?"

"My parents are getting older. My father's heart is not so sound. I cannot give Edgar what he needs. You could if you wanted to."

Suzanne studied Mary's face a minutes. "You're saying you *want* me to move in?"

"Yes, but you must be firm with him. He cannot abide a docile woman."

"You're certainly not a prude."

"Some of me is and some isn't. I'm sure I could never bring myself to paint watercolors in the nude, though the idea intrigues me."

"I'm not as dedicated as you. I love color and design. I paint because I think it's fun, and they say I have a certain flair."

"He will help you."

"No, I wouldn't like that. I hope my son will be an artist some day."

"You have a son?"

Suzanne nodded. "He's very young. He's just gone away to school."

"You do care for Edgar, don't you? More than you cared for the others?"

"He's much deeper than the others, more intellectual. Of course I care for him. I'm not sure he would want me to move in, although I could make him want it easily enough, I suppose."

Mary felt strange. There was an ache deep within her that could not be reached by the champagne.

32

On December 9, 1891, after being sick for nearly a month, Robert died peacefully in his sleep. It seemed the rain would never stop. Aleck and Gard and their families came as soon as they could. By March, when Aleck and Gard returned to America, Katherine seemed a little better, but her health was still fragile and Mary began to think of getting her out to the country.

It was at this time Mary received a letter from Mrs. Palmer, an American woman active in the arts. Mary scanned the letter quickly. Then she blinked and looked more closely. "A mural," Mary muttered.

"What did you say?" Katherine asked.

"Mrs. Palmer wants me to do a mural for the World's Fair in Chicago."

"A mural!"

"Yes. The theme will be the modern woman. Look, Mrs. Palmer enclosed the architect's drawings of the building. It seems quite huge and the mural would be up in the air about forty feet. What do you make of it?"

Katherine took the drawing and put on her glasses. "I would say it's an honor to be asked."

"It surely is. The theme is one I could work with. The figures would have to be painted much larger than life to carry from such a distance."

"You would have to rent a cathedral to paint it in."

Mary laughed. "Or do it in sections."

"Mrs. Palmer—I met her, didn't I? She wore a triple strand of matched pearls and had pearl combs in her hair. And those arched eyebrows."

"That's right."

"Well, you'll do it, of course. It's your chance to show them in America. They have ignored you much too long."

"I don't know. I haven't worked much since Father's illness. I feel almost dried up, and to do this mural I would have to learn an entirely new way of painting. There are problems. It would take many months, maybe a year or more. And if it wasn't good, they'd laugh at me in America."

"Nonsense. Michelangelo hadn't painted ceilings before he did the Sistine Chapel. It's time you got back to work."

"It would be challenging," Mary said, considering it. She had a few ideas. All of a sudden she wanted to talk to Edgar about it. But no, she had decided to stay away from him for a while, let him make his own happiness without her. She hadn't realized how often she would think of him. She would make up her own mind about the mural. After a while she went to the studio and did some sketches. By the next day the idea had taken hold completely.

The following week she wrote to Mrs. Palmer accepting the commission, and began immediately to plan out the design. In her world of modern women, there would be only women, not women in the shadows of men, accepting their minor roles with beauty and grace. There would be education and work and motherhood. She remembered the women Rubens painted. They were larger than life.

As soon as the weather turned warm, Mary, Katherine, and the household moved back to the country, to the Oise valley Mary had come to love. They rented an old place with large rooms. The biggest would serve as her studio. Then she began her studies in oils, using the women and children who lived nearby as her models.

As the days went on she worked from sunup until sundown, with only snippets of time away to visit with her mother over lunch and tea. One day she suggested that her mother come to the studio to watch. A comfortable chair was moved in and Mary relaxed, knowing she was not neglecting her duty to her mother. Katherine became actively interested in the project, even offering suggestions from time to time.

The modern woman was stronger than she thought herself to be, Mary felt, and this humble strength was one of the things she wanted to show. It was not a difficult abstract quality. She saw it in the faces of the country women she painted. They had centuries of resources to draw from. They had the instinct of womanhood, which Mary tried to capture in the pose and the expression on the mother's face as she held her baby while it plucked at an apple on a branch. Mary was stimulated by both the theme and the women she found as neighbors.

Paris was her city, but Oise was the world. She could think universally here. The designs piled up. The studies she had made were completed. The border design was finished. She was ready to begin the mural itself.

She wished she could show her work to Edgar. She was so deeply immersed in the theme and her ideas about it, she was afraid she was losing her objectivity. He would be quick to see flaws in the overall design. She had even written to him once and asked if he wouldn't come and take a look, but she thought again. What if he attacked her conception? He would not share her opinions of modern women. His ideas were different, and he could be devastating when he was in a mood to condemn. She did not mail the letter. A few days later, though, she added a note to an ordinary business letter she wrote to M. Durand-Ruel, asking him to come to the country to visit and look at the work. I need a competent opinion, she wrote, and that letter she did post.

In the meantime, there was the problem of size. The mural would be huge. She could only reach the top of the panels by climbing up a ladder, which made her head light and her stomach queasy. A carpenter who had put a screen on the front door was consulted.

"I could build a scaffold," he said. Mary pictured herself swaying from a scaffold and asked him to think of something else.

"Well, we could take out a couple of boards and put the panel on pulleys and it could be raised and lowered that way." Mary was delighted. "Set to work on that at once." She showed him the boards to remove and left him to work out the details.

In the meantime she went for a long walk. As she started off, the smell of fresh hay was in the air and the outdoors so pleasant she thought she ought to walk far enough to get physically tired, refresh her brain. She had thought of nothing else but the mural for so long, she was drowning in it.

The warm sun and exercise soon made her sticky hot, and to get relief, she walked into a woods near the edge of the property. The shade seemed delightfully mysterious. She found a heavy stick and beat her way through the brush. As she reached the interior of the woods the walking became easier and she felt sheltered. A woodpecker tapped on a hollow tree and the soft thud of her own footsteps echoed. When she came out on the other side of the woods, she discovered a vineyard with a path and a pond. Mary could not resist taking the path, though she knew she was wandering too far and would have to rest. Behind the pond was a hill.

When she reached the top of it, she was out of breath. The view was worth the climb. There was a sight that took her breath away. Nestled in the valley below stood a stately old château, shining in the sun, looking as though it had always been attached to that very spot. The exterior was pale yellow, probably weathered for many centuries. It looked elegant and comfortable at the same time. A rose garden and an ancient stone wall bordered it. She walked lightly down the hill toward it, drawn to it.

As she approached she noticed the narrow windows, the ancient pitch of the roof. It looked like it could be a seventeenth-century building. How familiar it all seemed. It was as though she had painted it in her mind, with stone and chimney, shrubs and green grounds. An old man was in the garden whittling and humming.

"Hello," Mary said. "Could you tell me the name of the owner of this property?"

The white-haired man looked up and stared at Mary a moment. "Oh, you're that artist woman, aren't you?"

Mary said she was. He asked her to come in and sit in the garden. He gave her an orange and showed her his favorite rose, a fragrant yellow blossom.

"I'd like to buy this château," she said, "if the price is reasonable."

"You wouldn't want it. Too old." He shook his head. "I've been caretaker here for twenty-two years."

"You must love the place."

"Hate it sometimes. Needs too much work."

"Could you show me what it's like inside?"

"It's vacant mostly except in August. Come along, I'll show it to you."

They went inside. The rooms were built of heavy board and stone, the walls thick and solid. Everything she touched seemed to need repair. She would do whatever it would take to bring the chateau back to life, if the owner would be foolish enough to part with it.

M. DURAND-RUEL responded to Mary's invitation and journeyed to the country to see her progress on the mural. Mary, overjoyed at seeing him, didn't know what to show him first. The pulley mechanism would be a good place to start since it was both impressive and also close at hand. "Now, I shall send for lemonade and you must tell me what is happening in Paris. How is Edgar?"

M. Durand-Ruel sat down. "He is the same. He won't bring me the paintings he promises and he constantly wants to take back and rework the ones he has brought. He plays with photography now. He is doing mostly nudes and dancers in pastel and some sculpture, I understand, but he refuses to show that."

Mary listened. She wanted to know if Suzanne was caring for him but couldn't bring herself to ask.

"Business is good," M. Durand-Ruel said. "We must be ready to take advantage of it. I want to arrange a large one-woman show. Now is the time for a comprehensive my-life-in-art-up-to-now kind of exhibit."

"I'm up to my neck in my mural and will be for months."

"After the mural?"

"I have nothing planned, but it will take some time to prepare for a comprehensive show like that."

"There is time. You can exhibit the paintings you have decided to keep rather than offer for sale—the portraits of your family for instance—and I can obtain examples of your work as loans from customers. If we could arrange a date for a year from now, I could get to work on it now. I really think it's what you should do to further establish yourself. Other artists are coming along. You must not lose the ground you have gained."

Mary nodded. "I have been so concerned with the mural, I hadn't thought enough about that. I must, I suppose, now that the group is gone and we are on our own."

"Yes, yes. Perhaps you could use some of the studies you have done for the mural in the exhibit."

"That's true. They would be quite suitable, if you like them." Mary got up and went to the cupboard where she kept her oil studies. They were unframed and quite large. "Here's one," she said, showing him the woman in an orchard holding her baby.

"Mmm." he took the painting, placed it in good light and studied it. "This is a powerful work."

"For a mural as large as the one I'm doing, the images have to carry from far up in the air." She paused. "Here's one that turned out to be a family portrait rather than a study for the mural. I couldn't make it work for that. The girl was just the wrong age, ten or eleven, not quite a woman and almost too beautiful to be a child. Hasn't she a lovely profile?"

"It's a striking painting in many ways. The mother, the baby, and the girl. Lovely."

He was openly impressed with all her work. It was fine and strong, he said, and he talked again of her one-woman show and of her place in the art circle of Paris. "As art, everything I've seen is excellent. I like what I see. The design has all the proper elements and isn't too busy or too bare. You should be better known in America."

The next day Mary took Durand-Ruel for a picnic near the pond. She wanted him to see Château Beaufresne the way she had first seen in. She explained how it would be after she rearranged the grounds, that is, if she could only persuade the owner to agree to her price, "which was a fair one," she added. M. Durand-Ruel wished her luck, but it was clear he didn't see what she had seen.

When he left, Mary plunged back into her work with renewed enthusiasm. She still didn't have Edgar's opinion, but Durand-Ruel had understood what she was doing and found no faults. Her approach was classical, but it was impressionistic, too. Detail was simplified. The background was light; the figures, even the flesh, were painted with saturated colors so they would carry.

There were not enough hours in the day and hardly enough light. The nights were becoming very cold, and by November, Katherine wanted to know when they would be returning to Paris.

It would be different leaving this year because of the château. Mary finally agreed to the owner's demands and bought Château Beaufresne as her summer home. It was going to be her castle—*hers*—bought entirely with the proceeds of her work. As soon as the refurbishing was complete, she would move in and become queen of her domain and go on painting the women and children of Oise. If only Lydia could be there to enjoy it.

After being away so long, Mary enjoyed the social business of the season. With her expanding reputation as an artist, she received many invitations and was asked her opinion on a great many things.

It was flattering, and the best part was that she was listened to. She had hardly been aware she had so many opinions and she found herself expressing them tersely, not unlike Edgar.

She had not seen Edgar in the two weeks since she got back, but she thought of him often. Finally she decided to call on him at his studio, though she didn't even know for sure if he was still in Paris.

As she knocked on his studio door, she wondered just what she would say to Suzanne. What would they all talk about? Perhaps it would be best if he wasn't at home.

He was. His beard was grayer, and his face paler, yet those sullen eyes were the same. He seemed to be alone.

"I came to see how you were."

"Mary, my dear, I'm tottering along. Come in."

They embraced as old and dear friends. "Tell me about this mural," he said. "M. Durand-Ruel says it has made your work stronger. Is that so?"

"The mural is a problem that takes strong work to overcome."

"I would never have consented to do it," he said. "Art is wasted on a World's Fair. The crowd is like a pack of animals being hustled along, sucking on their sweets or their cigarettes. They gape at each other, gape at everything. What do they know of art?"

She shrugged. "Some will merely gape, I'm sure."

"But if it's made your work stronger— you can take that as consolation."

"It was stimulating to try something new," she said.

"No, familiar is best. You can never achieve true richness in painting until you're so familiar with the subject it is part of your equipment."

She nodded. They had discussed that, and she didn't disagree with him. What more was there to say?

"How's Suzanne?"

He looked at her strangely. "Suzanne?"

"Yes, Suzanne. How is she? How is it going? Are you happy?"

His voice became brittle. "I'm not designed to be happy. You ought to know that. I am never content, so how can I be happy? Suzanne is a terrible nag."

"Then you have quarreled. I'm sorry."

"A quarrel to you is a normal conversation to us," he said. "She comes and goes as a tyrant."

"You're exaggerating."

"Not at all. Suzanne is a clever tyrant. At first, when I realized what you had done—how you arranged it—I thought it was so generous of you to understand. Suzanne seemed so much like you, or rather, how I sometimes imagined you to be." He looked up at her. "I know what went on between you and Suzanne. You suddenly disappeared, and you left me Suzanne, my fantasy. My dear, you are the only one who ever understood half of what I was. You didn't hate me—for very long periods, at least "

"No one hates you. Why are you feeling sorry for yourself? I had a talk with Suzanne. I didn't force anything. I only wanted you to be happy."

Edgar looked smug. "You mustn't waste your time playing God. Even He would find it impossible to make me happy."

She squirmed. She'd heard enough. She was leaving.

"Now don't be angry. Please, let's have tea."

"No, thank you." Mary paused. "If she's so tyrannical, can't you tell her to go away? If you're not happy, why persist?"

"Why? Why should anyone think he has a right to be happy?"

"Oh, really, Edgar. You're exasperating."

"I always have been. And I'll tell you why I persist. There *is* a reason."

Mary waited for him to go on.

"She has a son, Maurice. I am teaching him to draw. I will flatter her and do any and all of her bidding as long as she brings the boy around."

Mary nodded, realizing she had been right. Suzanne could give him what she could not. "May I see some of Maurice's drawings?"

"Of course," Edgar said. "After we've had our tea."

"Very well," she said.

MARY FOUND how impossible it was to forget an unfinished
work. Even though she was in Paris away from the mural, she was
often nagged by a compulsion to finish.

Fortunately, the prospect of a major one-artist show excited her
almost as much as the mural. M. Durand-Ruel encouraged her to
present a larger volume of her work. His enthusiasm was contagious
and Mary worked very hard; she did not want to disappoint him. She
even wrote to Louisine, since she owned more of Mary's paintings
than anyone else, and asked if she had anything she would like to
lend for the occasion.

Louisine answered in March, saying she would happy to select a
few things from her collection to include in the show. In a long,
chatty letter, Louisine begged Mary to come to the United States for
a visit. She would go in a minute if it weren't for her enemy, the

ocean, and all those days of seasickness. Beside, she didn't have time, with the mural waiting to be finished and her exhibition scheduled right after. She wrote Louisine and promised to visit the next year.

As soon as the weather improved, Mary and her mother moved back to Oise. Her château was not ready, although the workers were busy. The plumbing work was nearly done. The plasterers finished the ground floor and had only to complete the bedrooms upstairs. Broken windowpanes had been replaced and her castle looked welcoming. The American style plumbing and the central heating she was having installed caused something of a scandal among the workers and neighbors, but it was being done in spite of all the warnings. Mary was aware that reports of these exotic improvements had tended to give her a reputation as an eccentric among her neighbors.

Until the château was ready Mary rented the place they had used the summer before. She began at once to work on the mural. It was gratifying to see what she had done before and to pick it up again. After a couple of days it was as though the winter months hadn't even intervened. The mural progressed steadily as she used up rivers of thick, vibrant paint.

In six weeks the château, although still not properly decorated, was ready for tenants. Mary could not wait for the niceties. They moved in the day after the last of the workers left.

Her excitement reached a feverish peak. It was her dream, her home, her contentment. She belonged here. This was where she wanted to finish her mural. She poured the delight she felt at being there into the final stage of the mural.

When the paint dried, she quickly packed the mural and shipped it to America. It was strange having it gone, like sending a child off to war. It might be demolished. She might never see it again.

With the mural gone, Mary turned her attention to her château. It was like creating a living painting, like being a part of one. Curtains, rugs, and chairs; colors, lines, and masses. Even the outdoors could be artistically arranged. Shrubs and trees could be moved and a pool surrounded by rocks could be placed in the garden with benches nearby, and roses and fragrant bushes could be planted wherever it suited the design. She discovered a new dimension in art.

Katherine took almost as much interest in the château as Mary, and though her taste leaned toward the frilly and fussy, Mary often found her mother's choices charming. Ruffled fringes and lace gave warmth and a cosy comfort. The château was so homey that when summer was gone, they both hated to return to Paris. The summer had refreshed her so that it was with tremendous energy and enthusiasm that she opened her studio in Paris.

In a short time she could see that there would be plenty of work ready for her show. She counted fifteen oils, and as many pastels and at least sixty dry points and aquatints.

She was so busy and involved in the new show that when the reviews of her mural arrived from America, she had almost forgotten about the critics there.

The first began with two paragraphs of description. Her mother had nodded, "That's nice."

"I suppose so," Mary said, and glanced over it again. It was a polite review. The only real negative criticism was that there were no men in the mural. It was unnatural, the reviewer said. The reviews seemed to be full of empty words. There had been no real understanding or appreciation. Mary imagined that most people gave it a quick glance as they sucked their sweets and gaped at each other.

"It could have been too high for proper viewing," her mother said.

Mary folded the reviews, put them back in the envelope, and put the envelope in the drawer of her library table, where it stayed.

Later that same day a messenger brought a card from a Mr. James Stillman, saying he urgently wished to call on her at eight P.M. If that was not convenient, would she inform the messenger? Mary had not been there when the card was delivered, and did not like such a high-handed invitation. Still, the messenger had come from the best hotel and the card was engraved and bore a Wall Street, New York, address. She supposed she should see him. He might be a friend of Gard's. She was piqued all the same, and intended to inform her caller that she did not approve of such effrontery.

JAMES STILLMAN arrived precisely at eight in an ornate carriage so highly polished it glinted in the lamplight. He was a tall, slim, gray-haired man in evening clothes. Mary did not keep him waiting. She took a deep breath, smiled politely, and said only that his visit was most unusual.

Style emanated from him. Mary couldn't help noticing how dashingly he moved as he stepped into the entry and doffed his hat.

"Who are you, Mr. Stillman?"

"I am an admirer, a great fan, and a friend of your friends."

"My brother Gard did not send you?"

"Certainly not. No one sends James Stillman. I sent myself. First, I believe you were expecting the contents of a crate I have in the carriage. Allow me." He clapped his hands and two young men appeared from the carriage. At Mr. Stillman's signal, they unloaded a heavy-looking crate and carried it to the entry hall.

"Just there," Mr. Stillman said, pointing to a space on the floor. "Very carefully now." The boys set their burden down gingerly as if it contained something highly explosive.

"What is this?" Mary demanded. "I am not expecting any deliveries."

Mr. Stillman smiled so disarmingly she could not help being somewhat amused.

"Permit me," he said and he held his hand out. The tallest of the crate carriers handed him a tool. With a flourish, he removed the nails from one end of the crate. Then he paused and seemed to be waiting for quiet. Just as Mary felt irritation creeping through her, he smiled broadly and swiftly drew out a framed painting, holding it in front of his chest, presenting it for Mary's view.

She gasped. "Why, I painted that for Louisine."

"Quite right," he said. "I could not bear to trust these irreplaceable treasures to the hands of an impersonal post."

Mary did not know what to say. Should she thank him? His eyes looked as though she already had. "Won't you sit down, Mr. Still-man, and have a glass of brandy."

"With pleasure," he said as they walked into the drawing room.

"How did you get them from Louisine? She didn't write me about this. I didn't expect them for weeks."

"You will receive such a letter eventually," he said. "I took a fast boat. You see, I've known Henry and Louisine a good while. I've looked at their art collection with, I openly admit, some envy. They told me you helped with the selection. You found the Courbet, for example."

Mary nodded.

"I know all about you, and yet I know nothing, of course. I wanted to meet you and see the exhibit of your work and ask your advice."

"My advice?"

"I want a magnificent art collection. I want Goyas and El Grecos and Rubenses and Manets. I want Italians and the work of American impressionist women."

Mary laughed, shook her head and looked at Mr. Stillman with interest. Mathilde brought the brandy, and Mr. Stillman talked for hours, while the young men took tea cakes in the kitchen. James, as he insisted on being called, was going to be in Europe a year—maybe longer—perhaps forever. "Will you help me form my collection?" he asked.

"It would be my pleasure."

Mary saw James for luncheon and shopping that Friday. He bought a large Courbet, one Mary had long admired. It was not a bargain, but James was elated with it and did not concern himself with the price. The next day she took him to see a Corot she knew about at a new gallery. It was a small study of a peasant girl in a red apron, standing at a kitchen door.

"I can see you bring me luck," James said. They looked other paintings in the gallery. Mary realized he had very good instincts. He bought his Corot and took her to dinner.

They had dinner together often after that. One night he took her to the theater and afterward confessed that he wished he had been a couturier. In the next breath he laughed. "Life is but a moment," he said, raising his wineglass to her, "but what a moment we can make it."

Mary found James often on the brink of laughter, always expecting good luck, good times. He brought more joy to her than she had felt in a long time. It seemed so natural. She was as grateful to James as he was to her, and though she saw him often, she worked as much as she ever had. She wished it could have gone on exactly like that.

Then he proposed marriage. It wasn't much of a surprise. She was growing very fond of him and she was not so blind as to miss the looks of adulation she often saw on his face. Although she had tried to let him know in dozens of ways that marriage was not possible, he did ask the question.

She took a deep and painful breath and looked at him with regret, knowing this would change things between them. "James, I cannot," she said quietly, "even though being with you is the pleasantest part of any day. Though I know of no one so congenial as you, I cannot marry. I must be free."

When he saw her determined face, he did not argue. She saw the merry glimmer go out of his eyes, and knew her refusal had stung.

For days he didn't call on her. Eventually they became friends again.

34

EDGAR HAD WRITTEN Mary a letter of congratulations at the time of her show. She was touched. It was a kind letter with comments about many of the paintings, and as she read it, she realized with a mixture of pleasure and melancholy that she had missed him. A few days later she had gone to call on him, but the housekeeper said he was ill with a cold and could not receive visitors. Disappointed, Mary had left a note saying she hoped he felt better soon. She had heard nothing since, although she had made inquiries. One morning, thoughts of him persisted and she sent a note off to James, saying she would not be able to keep their shopping date. She went instead to call on Edgar.

Again the housekeeper said he was not receiving visitors. "I see," Mary said. "Is he ever well enough these days to receive people?"

The housekeeper did not answer for a moment. "Monsieur Degas does not wish to be disturbed. I'm sorry."

"So am I," Mary said, "but he will not get his wish today."

"Miss Cassatt, I have strict orders not to admit anyone. He is unwell."

"Please move aside. I shall only stay a moment." Mary squeezed past the woman and went into the living room. As she stepped inside, her painting of Henrietta came sharply into view. He had hung it in a place of honor on his best lit wall. She paused a moment, remembering. Then she saw him, seated by the window looking out toward the street, his back toward her. "Who was it this time, Zoe?" he asked.

"It was I, Mary, and I will not be told you cannot see me. If I take the trouble to come, you can be kind enough to receive me. Why are you cutting yourself off from your friends?"

He turned around, shaking his head feebly. "Mary, is it really you?"

"Of course it is."

"A man has a right to be left along if he chooses."

"Our friends haven't seen you for months," she said softly. "I have asked after you and no one knows anything."

"There is nothing to know. As long as you're here, you may as well sit down, over here where we can look out the window."

She pulled up a chair next to him. He looked in her direction with eyes that were filmy and unseeing. Everything she had ever felt for him rushed forth suddenly. She bent over and kissed his cheek. He grasped for her hand.

"Oh, Edgar," she said as she sat down next to him. "You're becoming a recluse. What is so interesting on the street that you must sit at your window so much?"

"Nothing. Nothing but light. I can see shadows move, enough to imagine what's going on."

"It has gotten much worse then?"

"Yes."

"Can you work in clay?"

"I do, but I don't trust what I've done. Naturally, my friends will say it's good, when it may be pitiful, but a man must amuse himself in some way."

"A man should allow his friends to come for a visit."

"When I am in the mood to be patronized, I'll do that. Please stop talking about me. If you can't bring me some news about youself, I must ask you to go."

"You are truly wretched, Edgar. But I will humor you. I have been well. I am going to Oise in a few weeks."

"Ah, and what will happen to your rich American, or will he come to the country for a visit?"

"Do you mean Mr. Stillman?" she asked, surprised that Edgar would know about him.

"Who else could I mean?"

"I have been helping him buy paintings. We're good friends."

"Yes," Edgar said. "I know. He also designed a purple cape for you to wear to the theater, and he asked you to marry him."

Mary looked at Edgar in amazement. He couldn't possibly know that. "James did design the cape, as a present. And you know I'll never marry."

"Yes, you decided that long ago."

"How did you hear about Mr. Stillman and the cape?"

"I heard."

"And I, who fritter around Paris a good deal of the time, have heard nothing of you. Where is Suzanne?"

"Gone away. Living with someone else."

"And her son?"

"Gone with her, of course."

"You have just the housekeeper?"

"Yes, it's a quiet existence. Zoe reads to me."

They sank into silence while memories crowded her mind. After a few minutes, Mary helped Zoe fix tea for them. She spent an hour telling him all the gossip she knew. Later, when he was receptive, she persuaded him to show her his sculpture.

He folded his hands in his lap and gazed at her earnestly. "I have been working on a horse. It's a small piece. I do remember horses. Sometimes I can remember the way a dancer curtsies, sometimes the tilt of a head." He called Zoe and asked her to bring the horse.

Zoe put the work down on the window ledge. It was on a wooden base and covered with a damp cloth. It appeared to be under a foot high. Mary braced herself, hoping it would not be pitiful. Slowly Edgar uncovered it.

The joy she felt at seeing such a graceful, powerful sculpture spilled out into laughter. "How could you ever think you could do anything pitiful? You couldn't. What an idea. I must say you frightened me, when I shouldn't have been worried."

"Are you saying the thing is recognizable as a horse?"

"It's recognizable as poetry. It's a horse as graceful as a dancer."

Edgar blotted his glistening eyes with a handkerchief. "You're the only one I would believe."

She touched his hand. "We have many things to talk about, Edgar. I shall come back next Wednesday for tea and the Wednesday after that."

"I suppose you will."

"Will I be welcome?"

"If you're not? If my housekeeper says I am sick, will you go away?"

"I think not."

He shrugged and smiled. "Then I shall see you."

Epilogue

The French government recognized Mary Cassatt's great contribution to art by making her a Chevalier of the Legion of Honor. Later, in America, she was awarded a Gold Medal of Honor by the Pennsylvania Academy of Fine Arts.

Upon Mary Cassatt's advice many Americans acquired fine collections of French and other European art, enriching the store of art in America, one of Mary's dreams.

Mary's friendship with Degas endured to the end. He died in Paris on September 27, 1917. After attending his funeral, Cassatt wrote to a friend: "His death is a deliverance, but I am sad. He was my oldest friend and the last great artist of the nineteenth century. I see no one to replace him."

In her later life, Cassatt underwent surgery to remove cataracts from both eyes. The surgery was only partially successful and with her weakening vision, she worked solely in pastels until even that became impossible. At eighty-two, nearly blind, but still dedicated to art, she died in France at her beloved Château de Beaufresne on June 14, 1926.